Ruler in Hiroona

A West Indian Novel

G. C. H. Thomas

MACMILLAN
CARIBBEAN

Macmillan Education
Between Towns Road, Oxford OX4 3PP
A division of Macmillan Publishers Limited
Companies and representatives throughout the world

www.macmillan-caribbean.com

ISBN 1 4050 02557

Typeset by EXPO Holdings Ltd
Cover design by AC Design
Cover illustration by Josette Norris

Printed and bound in Malaysia

2007 2006 2005 2004 2003
10 9 8 7 6 5 4 3 2 1

CONTENTS

PREFACE

Ruler in Hiroona is an all-time Caribbean Classic. Earlier editions of the work were devoured by readers who clearly recognised, in the imaginary island of Hiroona, their own island homes. Indeed, the beauty and brilliance of *Ruler in Hiroona* lies in its ingenious ability to embody, through its fictional location, the history, society and politics of every country and territory in the Caribbean region. The author, the late G. C. H. Thomas, brings to this infectious tale of Caribbean life his disarming sense of humour, his inimitable writing style, and a bold analysis of the Caribbean political leadership of the 1950s — the period when the region's territories shook off the shackles of colonialism and endeavoured to determine their own destinies.

Set in the 1950s, *Ruler in Hiroona* tells the story of Jerry Mole, an educated but lazy and unmotivated free-wheeler, and his alter ego, Joe Pittance, an uneducated but street-smart stevedore. Both these men are committed in their own ways to the self-determination of their country. Led by Pittance's vision of a locally-governed Hiroona, they start a trade union which gives them their first foothold in politics.

G. C. H. Thomas skilfully and humorously sets out Mole's quest to become the first Chief Minister of Hiroona. In the course of the work, which is written in the form of an autobiography, Mole journeys through complex manoevres fed by egotism and greed, always undaunted in his assurance that 'West Indian masses are very tolerant of the foibles of their political leaders' (p. 66). His efforts are constantly frustrated by the powerful characters of Joe Pittance — politically astute and always one step ahead — and Mole's own wife, Sonia, government minister and would-be conscience, who protests that 'power should carry responsibility rarder [rather] than privilege. It ain't fair fo' me to draw money Ah ain't working for' (p. 213).

In time, and despite recourse to an obeah woman, Mole loses his power and his pilfered fortune and is financially ruined. And so it is that, in order to win a bet of one thousand pounds, he agrees to write the stark truth — the 'naked and unashamed' account (p. 294) — of his ascent and downfall in the autobiographical tale which *Ruler in Hiroona* purports to be.

Pittance's initial challenge to Mole reads: 'Dis is de year 1950, an' Hiroona ain't wake up yet . . . Why don't you do something?' (p. 10). Fifty years on from the story of Jerry Mole's political rise and fall, this is now the decade of the 2000s. Has Hiroona — as reflected in the Caribbean countries — 'wake up yet?' How have politics and political leadership evolved? Have electorates stopped following leaders blindly, on the back of bribery and wild promises? Has corruption in high places disappeared? Have rulers ceased to acquire land and to feather their nests for the unpredictable or inevitable future? Have we done with witchcraft and superstition as a medium for changing fortunes or defeating enemies?

Much progress has been made economically and socially over recent years, although problems such as systemic poverty and illiteracy still plague Island Countries. Mass protests and rallies have in many instances served to wake up an electorate that has become more enlightened, more demanding and more vigilant of the integrity of its leaders. Yet it is fascinating that even now we still hear calls for Caribbean constitutional reform. There are bold declarations of concern that Prime Ministers have too much power. There are demands for greater political democracy, for the strengthening of individual rights and freedoms, and for making government more transparent, honest, accountable and effective.

So Ruler in Hiroona remains as timely and relevant as when it was first published. A benchmark for the 21st century, its pages contain valuable lessons for young and old, for students, for employers and employees, for leaders and the led. Reflections on the confessions of Jerry Mole may yet help bring the region to that place articulated in the St Vincent and the Grenadines 2002 Budget Address: 'First good governance for all the people and second, to build a modern democratic, productive, just, peaceful and caring society to be enjoyed by all its people.' Moreover, *Ruler in Hiroona* is a delightful novel — well worth reading for sheer enjoyment.

Monica Thomas Woodley
February 2002

PART ONE
The Struggle

1

I am committed to tell the stark truth in this autobiography, although this truth is very unflattering to myself. Thus, I am like the vast majority of adult humans who daren't tell the naked truth about themselves without committing character suicide.

In telling this truth, I shall have to relate what may be regarded as some incredible stories about the West Indian islands. But here again, this will be nothing short of authentic history, because I shall be writing about the nineteen-fifties and sixties, and the West Indian islands were incredible places during those times. They still are today in some respects.

There is something cathartic about telling the truth, ridding yourself of the burden of not doing so, freeing yourself of the choke of it in the throat of your conscience. The truth shall make you free in two ways: when you know it, and when you tell it.

But the difficulty of telling the whole truth about one's self is that one usually does not know one's self wholly. The wellsprings of motivation and conduct are often too deep for detection, buried as they are under the compost heap of one's own wishful self, and kept buried by one's refusal or reluctance to probe, and by faint-heartedness to reveal even to one's self what one finds on probing. Thus, the truth a man usually reveals about himself is often conditioned by either ignorance or pusillanimity.

In telling this story of my life, I am under contract to suppress nothing that I know about myself, and to eschew pusillanimity.

And I must begin this story with a detailed reference to Joe Pittance my friend, and enemy; for Joe Pittance is, in a sense, the first cause of this story of my life. Had it not been for Joe, there would be no story worth telling. I am the first cause only because I was born at all — in the West Indian island of Hiroona, with a kink in my character.

If I am to tell the whole truth, I must reveal also that the main reason why I so do is to dare, astound, and thus defeat a certain, wealthy detractor of mine, and deprive him of a large sum of money. This wealthy scion of the planter class of Hiroona will appear in his turn in this history.

And now that the preliminaries are out of the way, let me to the task, to the battle, to the tale and to . . . . . Joe Pittance.

My association with Joe Pittance began in 1950. Joe was then a steve-dore who did waterfront barbering on the side. I was nothing then, apart from a number of ex's — ex-schoolteacher (sacked); ex-police constable (sacked); ex-insurance clerk (sacked); ex-oil refinery worker (sacked). In other words, I was then on the bum; hard-up, unemployed, and by reason of a built-in aversion to constructive, disciplined toil — unemployable.

Joe was a born waterfront man. Any waterfront would have been congenial to him. It happened that the particular waterfront to which he was born was the Kingsland waterfront in Hiroona. But Joe would have been happy in any place that reeked of sun and sea-water and sloops and schooners and tar and sweat, and spilled molasses, and wine casks with broached bungs, and hustling, vociferating porters in near-rags and weird, native grass hats; and shrill hucksters vending fresh fruit and vegetables, muffins, and fried fish. Joe's domain was the bay front and the deepwater wharf area — places cluttered up with heavy crates and cement drums and bags of rice, flour and arrowroot starch, and demijohns, and snake-like water hoses which trip up the unwary; porters' wheelbarrows and trolleys, and heaps of gangling reinforcement iron rods which rattled and shifted underfoot.

Joe was a talkative man. For a stevedore, he did talk a lot of sound sense; but as my knowledge of the man grew, I became convinced that his love for barbering stemmed from the fact that it provided scope for his passion for holding forth. A barber is like a preacher. He has you under him. You can't reply adequately or comment at length or refute heatedly without disturbing or holding up the service.

As a child delights in showing off its best clothes and toys, so Pittance delighted in exhibiting his best knowledge. It was the only thing he had, and he used it to dazzle and impress. Like every garrulous man, Joe seemed inordinately pleased and surprised that he knew so much, and took no chances on your not knowing that he knew so much. To him, a competi-tion in knowledge was forever afoot, and he was head and ears in it.

Tall, lean, flat-bellied, long and delicate of features and limbs, Joe seemed built for a less strenuous occupation than stevedoring. He was listed in the Income Tax Register as a stevedore; but as he grew older, Joe did less and less stevedoring and more and more waterfront barbering, until the time came when he didn't do enough of either to make a steady living. It was during these lean years that Joe used to quarrel bitterly every week, when the shipping agent for whom he occasionally worked as a part-time stevedore deducted a portion of his meagre wages for pay-as-you-earn income tax. 'You rabbing me of a fartune to pay de Government a pittance.' So Joe came to be known as Joe Pittance; and in time everybody, including Joe himself, forgot that he had any other name.

It was in his capacity as a barber that I came to know Joe. I had lost a few jobs, had become a drifter and was invariably hard-up; and as Joe charged no more than twelve cents for a haircut, I became one of his customers.

I was forty-five then. Joe wasn't born on a specific date. His birth occurred vaguely during a series of memorable events.

'It was around de time when dey had dat eruption of Mount Pelée dat wipe out de tung of Sint Pierre. Only one man sovive.'

Klip! Klip! Klip! Then he would stop cutting and resume.

'Dey had a earthquake in Jamaica around dat time too. Kill a lot o'people.'

Klip! Comb! Stop.

'Guadeloupe had eruption, too, at dat time; an' in Sin Vincent de Soufriere volcano got jealous an' let off a big fart as if to show Mount Pelée an' Guadeloupe dat he got muscle too; an' de stench an' de heat kill people in Georgetown an' wipe out a few villages at de foot of de mountain.'

Klip! Klip! Klip! Klip! Stop.

'De Sin Vincen' eruption fling larva ashes as far as Barbados, one hundred miles away.'

He waved his scissors in the direction of Barbados, showed his yellowing teeth in a grin and said, 'De Barbadians didn't know what dis funny ashes was, so dey called it "May Dust".'

Comb! Klip! Klip! Klip! Stop! Comb! Stop.

'Dat was around nineteen nart two. Was a damn good 'ting our volcano here in Hiroona ain't bad-minded'— *Klip! Stop!* — 'else we woulda had a situation like in Sin Vincen' or even like in Sin Pierre.'

Klip! Stop.

'De lava from Mount Pelée surrounded a whole convent an' kill every single nun in it. De convent was like a island surrounded by lava.'

Comb! Stop.

'De Sin Vincen' volcano throw up rocks de size of a house an' drop dem in de sea, miles away. An' when de hot rocks drop in de sea, you coulda heard de sizzling in de island of Bequia, nine miles off.'

And when you thought that this long and terrible recital had driven the pinpointing of his birthdate out of his mind, Joe would surprise you by concluding, 'I was born around dat time.' *Klip! Klip! Comb.*

I was to learn to my cost much later, that that was one of the disconcerting things about Joe Pittance — he never forgot nor missed the main point in an argument, discussion or situation. He was one of these ace-up-his sleeve types of person. This trait in Joe helped me to rise to the political pinnacle in Hiroona and subsequently dashed me back flat on my arse, in the biggest disgrace of my life.

Pittance took one by surprise, not only with the length of his memory, but also with the volume and content of his information. For a man like Joe who could neither read nor write, this was no ordinary achievement. And this possession of knowledge beyond his station gave him power and authority over the other stevedores and wharfside personnel who often expressed their admiration for him by facetiously questioning the accuracy of his information: 'Pittance, man, dat ain't true. Where de hell you get all dis facts from? You learn it when you was sailing, nuh?'

True enough, Joe had worked as a seaman in his younger days, on various sloops and schooners which plied between the West Indian islands.

'Had to start early. Ah had no parents. Me mother died when I was only about two or three years old. So my gran'mother took me over. Dey say me father was a fisherman name Bute; but he only halfheartedly admitted dis when my mother brought him up in the bastardy court for child maintenance. He needed maintenance 'eself, anyway. So Ah worked me way up from captain's mess boy to mate, till rheumatism fling me back on land. Doctor cured me rheumatism a few years ago, but by dat time I had got use to livin' on land. Me sailing days was over, but I had already known every West Indian island under de sun.'

And during that period of his life he had picked up a considerable amount of knowledge about the islands, and had since kept alive the memory of his sailing days and his 'extensive travelling' by walking with a roll, like the mast of a vessel in strong seas, and by holding forth about the past and present histories of the islands. He was forever making canny remarks and comments about their past and contemporary political leaders — information, stories, anecdotes and opinions he had heard bandied about on the several waterfronts with which he was familiar: Trinidad, Grenada, Barbados, Saint Vincent, Dominica, St Lucia, St Kitts, Montserrat and the rest.

It was only when Joe tried to be authoritative about knowledge outside of the local and West Indian region that he made an odd little slip-up or two:

'It ain't Sint Pierre alone dat was wiped out. De town of Pompee-eye in Italy went like dat many years before Sint Pierre, when Mount Vesuvius poop off.'

'The town of what, Joe?' I said. I was standing with my arms folded, awaiting my turn while Joe worked on the head of a forced-ripe teenager who, like many others of his age, did odd jobs around the waterfront for sea captains or for anyone who would hire him. Also waiting were two or three stevedores and two vessel crew men. They were sitting on the edge of part of the concrete structure which framed the deepwater wharf area, their feet dangling over the sea where it broke on the shore in very tiny waves which sighed peacefully as they pushed up and drew back on the black sand, the languid movement seemed to fit in so well with the tranquil Hiroona afternoon and the almost deserted waterfront. I stood a trifle apart from Joe and the other waiting clients to give point to the fact that I was of a better class, and was there only because Joe charged much less for a haircut than any other barber on the island. The teenager under Joe's hand was sitting on an old soap box which the boy himself must have brought. For Joe's barber's chair was usually a stone, bits of planking, or even part of the wharfside juttings — anything that could accommodate a backside.

'The town of what, Joe?'

'Pompee-eye,' said Joe. 'Dey say it was in Italy, near Naples.'

'You mean *Pompayee* — P.O.M.P.E.I.I.?' I spelled out the word loudly in the tones of a pedantic pupil teacher, while Joe's waiting customers turned their heads and looked from Joe to me and back, anticipating an argument. They knew that Joe resented correction, especially in the presence of his colleagues. Correction detracted from his omniscience and undermined his authority. Made him look small — which he was not supposed to look. The situation was now a competition in knowledge, and Joe didn't lose easily. He stared at me and smiled — a weak smile of hurt and embarrassment.

'O' course, Mr Mole,' he said, 'You is a educated man. I prob'ly can't read and write like you, but my gran'mother tole me a very true proverb.' He turned his attention back to the boy's head.

I could see his mind searching for the most suitable, insulting proverb his "grandmother" had told him in order to best and embarrass me. There is always power in a proverb. With a proverb you can slay or subdue a man. A proverb is a morsel of compressed wisdom. It is like a food capsule, unloading a feast while requiring a minimum of effort on the part of the user. It was one of Joe's tools, like his scissors and the dirty, black comb he used when barbering. He tried to pass the comb through the lad's hair. The comb stuck stubbornly.

'Christ, boy,' said Pittance in sudden irritation meant for me but transferred to the lad, 'you does rub yo' head wid glue insteda vaseline, nuh? — Mr Mole, my gran'mother tole me . . . .'

'Chris', boy, dis is de second comb teeth yo' head break fo' de afternoon. Why de hell you youngsters keep so much hair on yo' head, nuh?' He sheared off some hair with his scissors.

'Me gran'mother . . . .' The comb stuck again.

'Look, boy, yo' better try an' comb it yo'self . . . . . Me gran'mother . . . . . Not so to use a comb, boy; you gwine break de damn comb. Give me it back.'

Slowly, pensively, he examined the comb with the two missing teeth. Then he found his grandmother's proverb. He smiled. No weak, embarrassed smile this time. Smile of confidence, of victory, signalling my undoing, my defeat.

'You was a teacher. You got education,' he grinned. 'I ain't got education, but I got *study-ation*. My gran'mother always use to say *study-ation* beat education.'

He had made his point which was beside the point, but he got his applause from the little group. They nodded enthusiastic approval, and laughed with a rush of pleasure far exceeding the issue at stake. Even the lad grinned and looked up admiringly at Pittance. The question at issue — whether the name of the doomed town was pronounced Pompee-eye or Pompayee — was conveniently side-stepped, and the paramountcy of Pittance's general intelligence above my mere book knowledge neatly substituted. And Pittance thus scored a landslide victory. He was the master again; and this triumph not only restored his aplomb, but it also put me back in his usual good graces. He could afford to be pleasant again. He could be my friend now. He had won.

It was on that afternoon that I began to realize that there was something of the politician in Joe Pittance. And it was on that afternoon he invited me to commence action with a view to ultimately taking over Hiroona as the island's first Chief Minister. It soon became clear that the only consideration which prevented Joe from attempting this take over himself was the fact of his illiteracy. He certainly had the desire, the ambition and the waterfront backing to make the attempt, but, as he admitted later, he had held back, restrained by a handicap which, though common enough in Hiroona, was regarded with a kind of shamefaced defiance by the handicapped.

In my case, the idea of taking over anything, least of all a whole government or a whole island, was pure fantasy, on account of my standing — or rather, lack of standing — on the island. Before I met Joe, I had knocked about quite a bit, trying one job after another, lazing, wasting time on the job, becoming cheeky and rebellious when corrected, and getting sacked as the result. I took to blaming other people for my own failures, and when I came to be regarded throughout Hiroona as a lazy, good-for-nothing drifter, I emigrated to the Dutch West Indian

island of Aruba, ostensibly to look for work, but in fact to escape the
unsavoury reputation I had been facing in Hiroona. In fairness to myself,
I must say here and now that the escapist aspect of my emigration to
Aruba was not uppermost in my mind when I left Hiroona. I really
believed that I was going to look for work. I soon realized, however, that
a man looks for work in Aruba with the same mind, the same outlook, the
same character, the same will and the same attitude with which he looks
for work in Hiroona. A man cannot escape from himself by running.

In Aruba, I worked for a few months as a factory hand in the Lago Oil
and Transport Company's Oil refinery which was largely controlled by
Americans. Sure enough, the social, recreational and commissariat
amenities for the employees, and the policy and practice of allocating
jobs were all based on the Jim Crow thing. And, so, a black West Indian,
working on the plant and living alongside the white, segregated Lago
Heights Club atmosphere, had to adjust to a surrealist type of existence in
which he kept feeling that he was not living on a West Indian island, but
in Mississippi or Georgia.

I hated and feared this kind of life; but I was glad about it in a way,
because it gave me justification for doing as little work as possible and
indulging in as much 'protest' as possible. I spent most of my time
begging loudly for dismissal: shooting off my mouth all over the plant
about the need for an NAACP in Aruba; demanding the removal of the
time clock which factory personnel had to punch in order to record their
true time of arrival on the job; asking embarrassing questions like why the
hell should the best part of the beach and the sea be roped off and wired
off to form a swimming pool for the exclusive use of Americans? Even the
unavoidably pungent smell of the oil refining processes came in for
'protest' by me: 'If these damn Americans cared a damn for us sweating
West Indians who have to work close to the unpleasant aspects of the
refinery, they would do something about this smell which fries the
mucous membrane out of a man's nose.'

They sacked me — as I expected and hoped. And on my return to
Hiroona, I cited a number of instances of insulting racial discrimination
as my reason for 'quitting their abominable refinery'. But this excuse did
not improve my reputation at home. After all, everybody knew that racial
discrimination was an ordinary affliction from which some members of
the white race suffered; and if thousands of West Indians then in Aruba
were hardy enough to tolerate making a living with the Lago Oil and
Transport Company, why couldn't I? So I had returned from Aruba to face
a public who regarded me as 'a joke' spending its life getting fired. In a

small community like Hiroona, things get around, and weak and unsavoury aspects of a man's character make popular, joyous town and village talk.

'People say you is a brave man, Mr Mole,' said Joe Pittance, grinning, as I took my turn on the old soap box vacated by the lad who had 'glue' in his hair.

'Brave? What do you mean?'

'Dey say you like to work in de firing line.' The waiting customers laughed loudly.

'Oh!' I said, fighting back resentment. I didn't want a quarrel with Joe Pittance. I still owed him for the previous haircut and I hadn't the twelve cents handy to pay for the present one.

But Joe was more serious than his facetious jibe led us to think. He said, 'But joking aside, Mr Mole, you is a educated man. You bin a teacher. Nowadays all over de West Indies dey looking for educated men to lead de people — de masses. Why don't you form a trade union and go into politics? It don't even need much education for dat dese days. An' you got education.'

'O.K., Pittance. I'll think about it,' I said casually, to get him off my back.

That was some months after my return from Aruba. Hiroona, like other West Indian islands, was fidgeting under British colonial rule. The islands were clamouring for change. The middle and upper classes were content with things as they were. Their sons and daughters went into law, medicine, or the Civil Service, and thus kept a respectable West Indian bourgeoisie flourishing. Among them there was the idol of heavy class ambition, but no social consciousness whatsoever.

There had been, however, a few men with ideas — men like T. Albert Marryshow of Grenada, Captain Arthur Cipriani of Trinidad, Charles Duncan O'Neal of Barbados, George McIntosh of Saint Vincent. For years before 1950, these men had made stirring speeches, organised demonstrations, and written newspaper articles about socialist ideas, the underlying theme being the plight, rights and dignity of the West Indian common man. In Antigua, there was Harold Wilson the pioneer socialist editor of the crusading *Magnet*; and Reginald Stephen the jeweller, who organised the Antigua Trade and Labour Union, and became its first President — to be succeeded by Vere Bird who staged a cane crop year strike (February to August) to force the island's sugar barons to recognize the Union. The ideas propagated by Cipriani, Marryshow, O'Neal, McIntosh, Wilson, Stephen and others were taking root in the islands; and spokesmen for the masses were springing up here and there throughout the British

Caribbean. Pittance knew about all these things because he had 'bin around' the islands as a seaman and had somehow still kept in touch.

I was vaguely aware of all this, but I felt that these events had nothing to do with me. I was not a politically minded person; and up to that afternoon in 1950 when I sat on Kingsland deepwater pier getting a haircut from Joe Pittance, I had seen no job prospect for me in politics. There were no trade unions in Hiroona; I didn't know how such unions were formed or how they worked, and I had never given this matter any thought.

'You ain't sound interested,' said Joe. He passed the comb roughly through my hair, clipping on top of the comb at the same time.

'Politics aren't my line,' I said. 'But I will think about what you've just suggested.'

Joe stuck the comb in my hair, left it there, and came to stand facing me. 'Look here, Mr Mole; when West Indian leaders like Marryshow of Grenada, Manchester and Sebastian of St. Kitts, George McIntosh in St. Vincent and all de other leaders started, politics was not dere line. Love an' compassion fo' de people was dere line. In dose days, it was love an' unselfish feelings in a man dat made 'im interested in his people an' his country. De politics part came after — But maybe you don't like people, Mr Mole. Maybe you ain't love yo' country.'

'Joe, what the hell have people done for me, except to cheat me out of one job after another? What has Hiroona done for me, besides keeping me under?'

'You can get yo' revenge by showing dem you worth something. You can succeed in politics nowadays, if you can't succeed in anyt'ing else. Hiroona badly need a leader fo' de masses like other West Indian islands have leaders already. Dis is de year 1950, an' Hiroona ain't wake up yet. The island is still ruled by planters and by an English Administrata appointed by de Colonial Office widout consulting de people. Why don't you do something?'

'Why don't you wake it up, Joe?'

'If Ah only had de education, Ah woulda certainly take on de responsibility, becarse Ah really like de trade of politics. Dis is your chance, Mr Mole. You will be able to make a fat living in de bargain. I can give you some assistance, if you like.'

I thought I saw through Joe's ruse. *His illiteracy hindered him, so he wanted to use my 'education' and, later demand his share of the 'fat living in de bargain'.* The proposal intrigued me, however. I didn't know at the time that Joe had far loftier ideas and motives than mere greed, and that his assertion about love of country was not mere cant.

Joe knew that I hated work, but he was reminding me that in 1950, a political job in the West Indies was not disciplined and regular work. It was only a method of making a living by exercising a kind of homespun power, after getting people to vote you into the statutory position. Politics were not yet regarded as a profession. It was the easiest of jobs, a sort of junior associate occupation of trade union leadership, requiring no training, no qualifications beyond shrewdness, cunning and persuasiveness in winning votes and manipulating the masses. Devoted and patriotic pioneers like Marryshow, McIntosh, Cipriani and Sebastian had laid the political foundation. They had done all the work then, for no reward save the satisfaction of seeing their socialist ideas take root. Now, in the early fifties, the time had come for shrewd, jobless, ambitious West Indian men to cash in on the work which the political founding fathers had begun, and to raise the art of West Indian politics from amateurish, humanitarian compassion to big, lucrative business.

Pittance had realized this and was trying to make me interested in the business, apparently in the hope of getting a percentage for himself later.

'You will be able to make money in a easy, easy job, Mr Mole.'

'Well, in that case . . . ,' I chuckled, pretending to be joking; but I had begun to listen now.

'You know how to form a union?' said Joe. I shook my head.

Joe spoke to the waiting stevedores:

'This man Mr Mole here, tellin' me he don't know how to form a union. Ben, you an' James an' Henry Stowe here always hear me tell you all about unions in Jamaica an' Trinidad, Sint Lucia, Grenada, Sin Vincent, Babaduz and de other islands. Tell Mr Mole how a union is formed, gentlemen.'

'Well,' said Ben, 'I is only a stevedore. Ah can tell you de right an' de wrong way to handle cargo.'

'James?' said Joe. But James only nodded and looked serious and confused.

'Henry.'

'You tell 'e, Joe.'

'Well,' said Pittance. 'You can start wid de waterfront.' He made a sweeping motion with his dirty black comb, to embrace the bayfront and the deepwater wharf area. 'A lot o' people make dere livin' here; stevedores like myself, porters, lightermen, hucksters. You got enough people for a union. All you got to do is call a meeting. But before you do dat you got to get de people to know you an' trust you. You got to get dem to look to you as somebody who can lead dem. You got to mix wid dem but still keep above dem. Ain't dat so, fellers?'

'Sure,' said Ben Davis. James Carter once again nodded and looked serious and confused.

Henry Stowe's heavy sluggish voice rumbled like shifting gravel: 'Sure. But we don't know Mr Mole. We only see 'im when 'e come here fo' a haircut. He don't mix wid us. He ain't one of us. He one o' dem poor-great --- de sort who always intristed in nobady but heself.' He spat over the side of the wharf into the sea.

'Dat is what Ah was tellin' 'im a while ago,' said Joe. 'You got to love people an' yo' country. You got to realize dat somet'ing is wrong wid yo' country and you got to have de strong feelin' dat only you alone know how to improve de place. An' you got to mix.'

'This union you fellows talking about; suppose the people don't want to join? What then?'

'You coax dem. An' dere's where de mixin' is useful. When Ah was boats'n on de schooner *Baby Face,* carryin cargo from here to Trin'dad -- potato, peanuts, zaboka an' such -- we use to spend two, three days in Port-o'-Spain sometimes, waitin' fo' return cargo. Ah use to see Cipriani come down to de waterfront, mixin' wid de common man, makin' joke wid de female hucksters an' de rough, swearin' men; buyin' goods he don't want and sharin' it out afterwards; sittin' down where he shoulda stand up among dem. But all de time he mixin' you could see he doin' it like a professianal, like someone from higher up, but he doin' it wid love. He mixin' but he ain't wallowin'. Dat is de secret, Mr Mole. An' when you can do dat, you don't need nobody to tell you how to farm a union. De union will farm itself out o' your affectian fo' de people.' He resumed his hair clipping while Ben, James, Henry and the others looked on.

Presently, I got up, brushed hair from the soiled white shirt I was wearing, and said, 'O.K. Pittance. I will think about what you said. But if I go into this business I shall depend upon you four men to help me.'

'You got to mek yo'self known to de people first,' said Henry Stowe.

'Ah will teach you all I know, Mr Mole,' said Joe Pittance smiling, as he began to work on the head of his next customer.

Lying on my sofa bed that night, I made up my mind. I would call a meeting of the waterfront people. I would form a union. But first, I must get to know the crowd and make myself known to it. I must learn to 'mix'. This was going to be difficult. I was not the mixing type. My wife Sonia often flogged me with her tongue for being lazy, bossy, conceited and aloofish. Now I had to try to correct these flaws in my character, because I needed a job, and Joe Pittance had said, 'Maybe you will be able to make a fat living in the bargain.'

So I began to frequent the waterfront. I cultivated a sort of friendship with Pittance, digested his half-amusing stories of the technique of political leaders of other West Indian islands; gradually made friends with vessel captains, crews, stevedores, and waterfront hands. I made myself useful to them in small ways, like filling in forms; saving captains' time by taking their vessels' manifests to the Customs for them; taking sides with them in their frequent disputes with Customs officials; dropping a word here and there in favour of smuggling, and making it clear that whenever there was a dispute between the Government and the waterfront, Government was always wrong. I tirelessly filled out in triplicate the Government-issued shipping forms for illiterate and semi-literate hucksters who brought their bags of fruit and vegetables from the country districts for shipment by sloops and schooners to Trinidad and Barbados.

I frequently lunched, standing, at the bay-front, on a few muffins and saltfish cakes which I bought — and sometimes credited — from a street vendor named Charlotte Cain, a fat jovial woman. Sometimes, the captain of a sloop or schooner in the harbour would let me share a meal with him on board. I dressed approximately like waterfront' workers, taking care to wear a shade cleaner clothes, and of course no necktie. I was one of them, only a shade 'higher' because of my superior education. I mixed with them 'like someone from higher up'. I often talked like them, in a further effort at gap-bridging. All this took several months, but I was learning a lot.

Gradually, they began to trust me. I could recognize the signs: the occasional present of a smuggled wristwatch or a bottle or two of smuggled brandy, which I afterwards sold; confidential gossip about secret happenings on the bayfront; an occasional request to settle little disputes. And Joe Pittance and his colleagues had taken to calling me 'bass'. I still regarded myself as a student in training, however, until the day of the near-tragic accident in the Kingsland harbour.

2

I stood beside Captain Conner on the Kingsland deepwater wharf and looked across the crowded harbour. The three berths of the wharf were occupied by ships unloading miscellany, their cranes dipping long beaks into the ships' holes, then bringing up parcels, boxes, bags or crates borne aloft, like storks delivering babies. Sweating, barebacked stevedores shunted and arranged cargo and luggage on the wharf or delivered them to trolleys which plied busily between the wharf and the adjoining customs warehouses. Khaki uniformed waterfront officials moved about on their duties, pausing occasionally to confer with customs officers in white shirts and black neckties who appeared now and again with small sheafs of paper in their hands. In mid-harbour, wooden oar-propelled barges (lighters) grouped here and there in twos or threes nudged one another on the gently tossing sea, their red-painted hulls reflecting the tropical mid-morning sunlight. Sloops and schooners anchored in the bay dipped and rose and rolled gently from side to side, showing their decks with one motion and hiding them with the other, their nameplates revealing also the island or country of their registration: *SEA HORSE* — Barbados. *BEAUTY QUEEN* — Saint Lucia. *VANGUARD* — Bequia. *PATHFINDER* — Grenada. *SEA OSTRICH* — Saint Vincent. *CARIBEE* — Dominica. *GREYHOUND* — Hiroona. *DUC de MAL* — Martinique. From the galley of some of them cooking smoke issued. Farther out in the harbour two ships waited, while another ship — the *Constructor* — unloaded motor cars on to a lighter manned by four or five stevedores. The lighter rolled slightly and bobbed up and down alongside the big ship.

I had filled out the outward manifest for Captain Connor of the schooner *Lilac Time* hours ago, and he was now waiting with fuming impatience for the customs officer to come and do the routine inspection of his schooner for seaworthiness, check his outward cargo against the manifest and release the vessel for departure to the Dutch West Indian island of Bonaire to which the Captain was most anxious to proceed to collect a cargo of salt. The *Lilac Time* rode in mid-harbour, mains'l halfway up and flapping, Blue Peter signalling readiness to depart. Alongside the wharf the schooner's boy waited in the dinghy, with both oars out. Captain Connor glared at his watch and then looked away across the shipping area towards the line of buildings on Bay Street: shipping offices, department stores, the tourist bureau, the Bay Street Hotel, cook-shops, restaurants and the two-storey structure with the large crown and 'H.M. Customs' on its facade over the door. No customs officer was in sight. The *Lilac Time's* mains'l and Blue Peter must flap some more.

'Christ!' exclaimed Connor, 'these fellers can never understand that a vessel have to sail by wind. I shoulda been off long ago with this favourable noreast breeze. Now the breeze will drop before one of the sons of bitches come to clear my vessel. Mole, you run across there for me and tell the Chief Customs Officer to send somebody to give the vessel clearance.'

I turned to go on the Captain's errand; then my eye caught a motor car dangling from the side of the *Constructor*, dropping slowly, uncertainly towards the lighter beneath. I could see a stevedore standing on the gunwale of the lighter urinating in the little strip of sea between the lighter and the ship, the palm of one hand pressing against the ship.'s hull, and the other hand steadying the spouting penis. It was not the first time I had seen stevedores do this stunt, but I stood and watched the descending motor car as it made a jerky drop then swung erratically. A stevedore in the lighter put his hand out to steady the car. Too late. The car bounced against the peeing stevedore, knocked him off the lighter and against the ship into the sea.

I turned quickly, grabbed Captain Connor's arm and said, 'Did you see that?'

'It's his own damn fault,' grunted Connor. 'Why the hell did he have to stand on the gunwale pissin' without looking to see what comin' down on him? These fellers too careless; and they blame other people when they get injured.'

'I agree with you,' I said; 'but the man is either dead or very badly hurt. He got a hell of a bash from that car and the side of the ship. Better let's rush out there in your dinghy and give them some help.' A man from the lighter jumped overboard, fully clothed. Another man followed. Captain Connor glanced at his watch and looked towards Bay Street. With a mixture of indecision and annoyance, he fingered the collar of his open-neck khaki shirt, looked again towards Bay Street and said, 'All right. Let's go see what happening.' He beckoned the boy in the dinghy to approach the gangway of the wharf. He hurried down the gangway and got aboard.

The boy in the dinghy is sculling rapidly. Captain Connor is sitting in the stern. I am kneeling in the bow of the dinghy, looking back at the Captain occasionally to voice a view of the accident. The captain keeps glancing at his watch and looking back at Bay Street. His khaki cap with the blue celluloid visor is far back on his large round head of thick gray hair, his eyes half shut against the eleven o'clock sun in his jet black leathery face. The wide open khaki shirt front exposes a broad deep chest of white hair gleaming with sweat. Every now and again he angrily hitches his trousers further up his short fat legs as he mutters a waterfront obscenity about the delay of his vessel and the idiotic carelessness of stevedores who get themselves hit by dangling motor cars.

I try to cheer him up by saying, 'I quite agree with you, captain; that man should be sacked for carelessness — if he survives.' The dinghy pushes forward. I have a feeling that I could use this accident to my advantage, and I make my plans as the dinghy streaks towards the ship. The attention of the entire crew of the lighter is centred on what is happening in the water between the lighter and the *Constructor*. People are looking down from the decks of the ship. Two of the ship's crew run down the gangway. The car hangs in mid-air like unfinished business. People on the wharf and on Bay Street seem to sense that something is wrong, and a crowd begins to build up on the wharf. The dinghy reaches alongside as the unconscious half drowned stevedore is being lifted into the lighter. I jump overboard immediately, without removing even my shoes. This is quite an unnecessary gesture, as the rescue operations are practically complete so far. It is a dangerous gesture, too, because I am not a good swimmer. But I am not really interested in the stupid, careless stevedore; I am interested in the accident, and I want to return ashore completely soaked, so that all may see that I have the waterfront workers 'at heart'.

I swim uselessly around the stern of the lighter for a minute or two, shouting, 'This is an outrage. The Government will have to look into this matter and see that compensation is paid to this poor man or his relatives. These poor hard working waterfront men need representation.'

Meanwhile, I am thinking with growing concern about the increasing weight of my shoes, khaki shirt and trousers, in this deep water. I glance at my Panama straw hat as it floats away on the tide. I let it float. The weight of my shoes and clothes drag me down. I gulp sea water. Horrified, I grab the gunwale of the lighter, scramble awkwardly aboard, nearly falling on the prone stevedore to whom one of the ship's crew is administering artificial respiration.

Still saying my piece, I glance across at Captain Connor in the dinghy. He is giving me a nasty look, three vertical lines on his brow; his thick graying eyebrows bristling; his eyes dead on me; his mouth half open and twisted, completing the picture of withering contempt. I look away quickly, and decide to return ashore in the cruising harbour launch that has just drawn up alongside the lighter to collect the half dead stevedore, instead of returning in the dinghy.

Back on the wharf, I resumed my ranting against the Government, the shipping agents and 'British imperialism' for 'indifference to the welfare of the waterfront workers,' as I moved among the crowd in my dripping wet clothes. They laid the stevedore on a small pile of lumber unloaded from one of the berthed ships.

I then took officious control of the situation: 'Stand back! Stand back! Let the poor man get some fresh air. You, Peter there, go tell the Harbour Master to telephone for the ambulance rightaway. These poor hard working waterfront workers need leadership. They need someone to fight for their rights.'

Porters, stevedores, hucksters and 'wharf boys' threw me glances of approval. 'Mole is damn right.' — 'Yo' right, Mr Mole.' — 'We really want somebody to look fo' we rights.'

The ambulance came and took away the stricken stevedore. All work on the wharf stopped, to give the excitement a chance to cool down. I called the stevedores and porters together on the wharf. Before addressing them I took off my wet shirt and ostentatiously wrung it. Then I handed the shirt to the tall lean flat-bellied stevedore who was standing near to me. Joe held the shirt while I held forth, building up my indignation until it looked genuine.

'I have been studying this waterfront for some months now, and I find that you have nobody to talk up for you, nobody to fight your case, nobody to expose the neglect and suffering you have to put up with. Look what happened this morning. That poor man might of die. It coulda been you –– anyone of you. You need somebody to force the Government to bring in a Workmen's Compensation Law so that in cases like what happened dis morning you will get money if you laid up, till you can work again. As it is now, suppose you get kill on the job, your poor wife would be left penniless. This thing must be put right.' I shouted, pounding fist into palm of hand. 'I have made up my mind to help you: to lead you; to fight for your rights. I am prepared to make the sacrifice. Are you ready?' Nods of assent; black sweating faces shine with sudden new hope.

Joe Pittance spoke for the crowd. 'Bass,' he said, 'we wid you to a man. Lead on.'

My political career had begun.

There and then, I announced my intention to form the Waterfront Workers Union that same night. 'On this very spot,' I said, 'this spot near the place where our severely injured comrade was temporarily rested this morning. Come here at eight o'clock tonight and bring your friends. We will hold our meeting right here.'

I knew that the police would not allow anyone to hold a political meeting on the wharf. There was landed merchandise all over the place — stuff which was sure to be stolen during a crowded meeting, and at night besides. I had another place in mind — the market square — which was the usual place at which public meetings were held; but I announced the wharf as venue for the meeting, nevertheless, so that when the police ordered us off the premises, I would be able to point demagogically to their action as conclusive proof that the police and the Government were against waterfront workers. I knew even then that in the curious business which went by the name of politics in some West Indian islands during the 1950's, finding an imaginary or real adversary to blame was of enormous importance. The more influential or powerful the adversary the better. Thus, the Government or the Civil Service was better than the Police, and Colonialism or British Imperialism was better than either.

I dismissed the crowd, then turned to Joe and said, 'How am I doing?'

'Excellent, bass,' he replied. 'You learnin' fast. We arf to a good start. But we got to remember two t'ings. One: if you want to help de waterfront men you got to have a bigger union dan only de waterfront men. Hiroona is a small island. It got only seventy-five thousand people, and de waterfront is small as compare to de waterfront of Jamaica, Trin'dad, Grenada else Babaduz. De Government will listen quicker to a big union instead of a small union of only waterfront people. So you got to bring eeen more people in de union. More workers. De nex' thing you got to remember is dat if you want to bring eeen people into de union, you got to go out into de country districks, in de small towns an' villages to attrack members for de union.'

'You thinking too far too fast, Joe,' I said. 'I need time to work all this out.'

'You don't need no time,' said Joe stubbornly. 'You got to work fast in dis matter.'

'All right. What do you suggest that I do now?'

'You got to change de name of de union.'

'What! Before it is even formed?'

'Yes. Instead of carling it de Waterfront Workers Union, you got to carl it something dat will include all de workers in de whole island — estate workers, labourers, everybady dat is working wid hand. You can do dat tonight. But *now*, today, dis afternoon, you got to go to one of de country districks. We ain't got no time to waste. We got to beat de iron.'

'You're crazy, man,' I said. 'What the hell we going into the country for this afternoon?'

'If you don't go,' Joe said quietly, 'you can include me out of any union you farm. An' if I don't join your union, none o' de others boys will join. If you want to help us, you got to show it.'

Alarm seized me. Here was threatened sabotage, and before my political career had even got off the ground — or off the wharf. Here was the same man who called me boss, now trying to boss me, to push me around. But at this early stage I couldn't risk losing his support.

'All right,' I said, unable to keep the unwillingness out of my voice. 'What part of the country you suggest we go to this afternoon?'

'Mount Horeb village,' said Joe.

'Mount Horeb village? What the hell for?'

'We going to a funeral,' came the surprising reply.

I looked up sharply at Pittance. 'You mad, man. Or you trying to make an ass of me. What's your game? What am I going to a funeral for? And a funeral of somebody I don't know at all? Whose funeral is it?'

'I don't know,' said Joe smiling, 'but I heard dis morning dat somebody dead in Mount Horeb last night, and dat de funeral will be five o'clock dis evenin'. There is a lot o' labourers in Mount Horeb, because dat is de Sugar Cane Belt, and de planters oppressing de people dere, so de people need a leader. All de labourers in de village will be glad to see you at de funeral. They will feel dat if you could take de trouble to come to sympat'ize wid one family, you is de sort o' person who will sympathize wid all families. It is a good way to get dem to jine de union.' He handed back my shirt.

I put my hand under my chin, and looked down thinking for a long time. Then Joe said, in a sort of ultimatum voice, 'You going, or you ain't going?'

'All right,' I said. 'But where will I get a car to go to this blasted funeral? Mount Horeb is twenty-six miles from Kingsland. Who will pay for my transportation?'

'Leave dat to me,' said Joe. 'I will get de other stevedores to stump up, and between us we will pay de taxi fare. I will bring de taxi round to your home at Bottom Town at half pass' t'ree. Dat will give us full time to get to de funeral and back to Kingsland for de meeting tonight.'

I was learning fast. This political career business involved damn hard work — something I was unaccustomed to. It meant submitting yourself to your inferiors — a thing I abhorred. It meant denying yourself — a thing I had never practised. It was true that I had not even quite started on this career, but, paradoxically enough, I had gone too far to turn back. To retreat meant that I would have to resume my rollingstone life, going from job to job, being kicked about and fired, pointed at by Tom, Dick and stevedores as a lazy, shiftless joke.

'All right,' I said reluctantly. 'Bring the taxi, and I will go.' I turned away from Joe.

'Wait a minute.' He touched my arm. I faced him.

'At de funeral,' said Joe without even the ghost of a smile, 'we will have to cry. It is de only way we can show real sympat'y.'

My jaw dropped. I looked at Joe for a long time; then I smiled weakly. 'You making joke, man,' I said, and walked away.

3

THE funeral was a tremendous success. Joe had slipped a large red pocket handkerchief into my hand as we rode in the taxi to Mount Horeb. He made no comment as he did this, but I reflected that as a politically knowledgeable man, he would know that it was then the fashion for West Indian politicians to flaunt large red pocket handkerchiefs and red neckties of the cheap variety. This outfit went well with the politicians' habit of addressing their followers as 'comrades'. Political meetings began and ended with the singing of what was called 'the ode', about 'We'll keep the Red Flag flying high'. So when Joe Pittance handed me a red pocket handkerchief in the taxi, I thought that he was merely investing me with the current badge of the West Indian politician. It was not until we were at the graveside that I fully understood Joe's action.

Our taxi was late in leaving Kingsland, so we arrived at the cemetery just after the minister had said his last prayer and was leaving the graveside. Someone started a hymn which was immediately taken up by the whole assembly. The words of the hymn were intended to convey some sort of hope of an undated 'resurrection morning' when 'soul and body' would meet again'. They sang it *gravissimo*, as befitting a graveside rendition. This gave me ample time to look around. Joe had moved away from me and was standing on an old tombstone. He was looking with mournful pensiveness down into the grave which was being slowly filled with earth by two gravediggers. Several persons were weeping quietly as they sang, so I concluded that the deceased was a very popular woman — or was it a man? Could be. I must find out. I turned to a young girl who was standing near to me, and was about to ask her who the deceased was, when a piercing scream brought me up short. Everybody turned and looked in Joe's direction. A large red handkerchief partly covered Joe's face, his whole body shook with sobs; the veins at the back of his hands holding the handkerchief stood out for all to see, while his wailing voice rose and fell like a tenor banshee in a jumbie choir. It was then that I remembered what Joe had told me about our having to cry at the funeral.

I suddenly remembered, too, a favourite story of his about a political leader in Jamaica who had won a lot of popularity for himself and for his union in its early days by weeping at funerals. I looked at Pittance, then I looked down thoughtfully at the ground. Joe's performance was convincing enough, so convincing that it was highly improbable that anyone had noticed the swift accusing glance he shot at me over the handkerchief when I looked at him. The glance conveyed to me in the clearest, bloodshot, weeping-eyed manner, that I was not doing my part; that I was not playing the game; that I was betraying Joe and the other stevedores and our yet unformed union. The glance conveyed a threat, too: If I didn't cry, I would fail my test as a political leader. *You had damn well better cry,* said Joe's glance, *or go back to your muffin and saltfish cakes and your loafin!* So I was being ordered about by Joe again, I, an educated man being pushed around by a blasted labourer — an illiterate stevedore in food-smudged black trousers, an unpressed white shirt frayed at the dirty collar, and khaki-coloured canvas shoes. *My God, look what I've come to. Look how low I've fallen.*

I felt so sorry for myself, I couldn't keep back genuine tears. Overcome by this wave of self-pity, I grabbed the red handkerchief from my pocket where I had hidden it, and covering my face, I wept. As sobs shook my body, the girl who was standing near to me placed her hand on my shoulder and patted it, comforting me. Then she too began to cry as she said, 'Yo' bin know she, nuh?'

After the funeral, while most of the people still lingered in the cemetery, Joe approached me. 'Bass,' he whispered, 'you was great. When we go back to town I will tell the fellers. Now we will walk around and meet dese people here. They is de kind o' people we need in de union.'

You son of a bitch, my mind said to Joe, as I moved off with him to meet the peasants and shake hands with them.

Without consulting me, Joe said to the crowd, 'De Bass want to say a few words to you.'

I got up on a tombstone and addressed the crowd: 'Something happened in town this morning, and Comrade Pittance and I decided to come up here and tell you about it, at the same time as we attend the fun'ral of our dear departed Comrade.' I told them about the stevedore who was nearly killed alongside the *Constructor.* 'Now in all the other West Indian islands it have what they call Workmen's Compensation by which you get money if you get injured on the job. But in Hiroona we ain't have that yet. So to protect all of you, and to fight for your rights, we have to come together and form a trade union. The Government is not looking after you as it should. You need better wages, better housing, better working conditions. To get all these things, you need a union to talk up for you.'

I paused. For the indignation part of the speech, my voice rose, and my manner became appropriately truculent: 'This island has been too long at the mercy of Government officials who run things in their own way, taking orders from the British Government in England, which is four thousand miles away. We are tired with British imperialism. It is high time for you to have a say in running your own island. You agree? Those who agree, put up your hands . . . . . . Thank you. Fine. Now we going to form a union. We already started in Kingsland. We have all the waterfront people. We going to have a meeting in Kingsland tonight, and I want to be able to tell the people there that all of you are ready to be members of the union. O.K.? Good. That's fine. Now I can't make a long speech, because we got to hurry back to Kingsland for the meeting; but we coming back very shortly to receive your union dues, and take your name for membership. O.K.? Fine. Fine. So goodbye for now, everybody, and may God bless you.'

4

A T the outset of my political career, my aim was simply to enter a field in which I thought I could make an easy living and at the same time win local popularity in the role of leader and spokesman of the stevedores and labourers in the bayfront. After all, I was then a failure, a penniless drifter. The few dollars I had managed to earn in Aruba were already things of the past. I had to eat. So far, I had been living off the minuscule earnings of my wife Sonia who worked as a domestic servant at $10 per month. I must state here, however, that when I married Sonia Haddaway, she was not a domestic servant. She was unemployed living with her mother in a rented room of a tenement house in Swaby village. Her mother worked as a cotton picker and arrowroot factory-hand on the adjoining estate.

Sonia was a young girl with an inviting body, brown skin as smooth as polished cedar. She had a large laughing mouth, full lips, short pretty teeth as white as sea island cotton. She was my height — five feet seven — but whereas I was skinny and the Adam's apple type, Sonia was filled out. I liked to watch her frock cascading smoothly from her small waist over curvaceous hips and buttocks; and I was almost invariably stirred sexually by looking at the back of her thighs when her back was turned to me, and she was busy with some household chore like bending over a pot.

I got Sonia in trouble when she was sixteen. She had just finished elementary school. She had not been a bright pupil, but she was attractive, sexy. I was then a twenty-year old junior teacher, living in the country with my mother and my half sister Myra, and earning a salary of fifteen dollars a month. I didn't want to marry Sonia, but if I hadn't I would have lost my job. So we got married, and Sonia moved with me into my mother's house in the little fishing village with the big, pretty name of Chateaubelair. The child was still-born, and so I felt that Nature had played me a dirty trick.

As I was not a good bread-winner (I was later sacked as a junior teacher, for unpunctuality, laziness and insubordination) Sonia had to go to work to support her mother — now a frail sickly unmarried woman — and me. The strain was too much for the girl; she became irritable; touchy and reluctant in bed; morose, faultfinding. We got on each other's nerves.

After I lost my teaching job, Sonia managed to find a household in Kingsland where she was offered slightly better wages as a domestic servant than she could earn in the country, and she and her mother moved from Swaby village to a miserable little hired shack in Bottom Town, Kingsland. I moved in with them. It was from there I had emigrated to Aruba. It was to there I returned not long afterwards, an unemployed drone. And before I entered politics my life with Sonia was a day to day quarrel.

'Since you come back from Aruba, you do nutt'n but lie down pon de sofa, sleep, sleep, sleep from marnin' till night. You ain't a sick man. Get to hell up and let me sweep under de sofa.' Even in anger, Sonia was still exciting, though a bit weather beaten, old for her age; her hair wild, her face sweaty, her dirty dress unzipped at the side, revealing pink panties.

'Why you choose this time to sweep, just when I am getting a little rest?' I said.

'When de hell else time you expeck me to clean out de house? Today is me only day off in three weeks. You been restin' fo' months now. You should weary rest.' She threw down the broom and went and sat on the single wooden doorstep of the house, her back to me.

I said, 'Since you gave me a little bit of black-water tea this morning, you have not cooked another meal for the day. What do you expect a hungry man to do but rest?'

Sonia jumped up and faced me. She looked ugly now, indignation almost choking utterance. She stood in the yard just by the doorstep and shouted, 'You de most barefaced, lazy an' unreasonable bum Ah ever come across. Where de hell you expeck me to get food to cook? When last you ever give me even a penny fuh buy food? You ain't no man. You is man when man scarce.' I got up from the sofa and came out in the yard, pushing my shirt tail down into my trousers and buttoning up the fly. Sonia's voice had brought out the neighbours. They stood in their yards gaping, laughing, shouting insulting remarks about me; encouraging Sonia. I walked out of the yard, away from Bottom Town. I strolled up Davson Street and made for the waterfront. I could always credit a muffin and saltfish cake from Charlotte Cain.

This sort of thing was almost routine during the nine or ten months after my return from Aruba. My discovery of the waterfront was therefore at first a sort of refuge from the barbs of Sonia and the ridicule of neighbours. Later, Pittance's talent and assistance changed my circumstances for the better.

After the Mount Horeb funeral, Joe and I attended funerals in two other country districts. At these funerals we duly cried. By that time I had become *au fait* with the technique, and so my tears were not of self-pity, as at the Mount Horeb funeral. They were genuine political tears shed for the deceased. After each burial, we followed the established formula: handshaking, introducing ourselves, making speeches about the need for a union to combat colonialism and imperialism. We accepted invitations from some of the villagers to accompany them to their beaten-mud huts where we ate their pelau and drank coconut water in conviviality and the new spirit of comradeship. In those days, the word 'comrade' had not yet become politically archaic. The word had been only recently imported into the West Indies from overseas. It was a new nice-sounding word that had the same effect on certain adults that the gift of cheap candy has on the children of peasants. So, with the indiscriminate use of 'comrade', with tears of bereavement and with extravagant promises, Joe and I were able to add the enrolment of the peasantry of three large country districts to that of the waterfront. Thereafter, we abandoned the tear-shedding approach in favour of drier methods, when recruiting members from the other parts of the island. I appointed a committee of management, drawn from the waterfront members and the villages I had so far conquered. This committee could be revised and extended as membership increased.

We now needed a building which could be used as headquarters of the union; and at this point I ran into my first big difficulty.

'Try old McIver,' Joe advised. 'Patrick McIver. He live in that huge house on Glenmore Estate, an' he own two town houses right here in Kingsland.'

'That's right,' I said. 'One in Fullbank Street and one in Richland Park.'

'He might be willing to rent us de one in Fullbank Street dat he got shut up an' ain't using. But you got to remember dat he is a ole Scotchman. He will want high rent; so you have to prepare fo' strong bargainin' wid him.'

I had never met McIver, and so I was in no position to anticipate his reaction to my request; but I supposed that as a Scotsman he would be interested in any honest deal involving money.

So I drove out to Glenmore Estate, got out of the taxi at the bottom of the driveway and started to walk up to the big house in which McIver lived.

Cultivated vegetable fields, coconut trees, orchards, cotton fields, banana cultivations extended from the walled enclosure of the big house in all directions. From the stretch of raised ground which marked the upper end of the driveway, the big colonial house with its wide veranda on three sides surveyed all things for miles around. In the yard on both sides of the stone steps, crotons, bougainvillea, hibiscus, roses, hydrangea grew in magnificent profusion. The driveway was flanked by well kept lawns. In an arrowroot field in the middle distance from the enclosure on my right, a score of male and female labourers, unmindful of the heat of the ten o'clock sun, energetically wielded their hoes, unearthing the carrot-like arrowroot rhizomes and heaping them into small mounds to be measured 'by basket' at ten cents per big basket. I stood and watched the heat haze which had a kind of mesmeric, soporific effect on me, while it seemed to galvanize the sweating bodies of the labourers into activity at the rate of ten cents per basket. As I watched, my thoughts seemed to blend with the heat haze, rising leisurely, spreading far.

These are the kind of people I have absorbed into my union. Throughout the island, these people outnumber the other people by far. Their numerical preponderance gives me vote-hope. It is going to be a hell of a job leading these barefoot sweaty ignorant people, but their ignorance is my main asset. I have never read a book on leadership. I have never taken a course in politics or government. I have never even seen a book on the damn things, but this is the convenient and encouraging thing about West Indian politics (in the early 50's); *you need no proper schooling to practise it. You just read an occasional newspaper,* I thought, *shake hands, perhaps cry at a funeral or two, make the kind of noises that would ingratiate you with the masses, vilify the Government, the planters, the colonial office in Britain and imperialism. You then start a union of the 'poor downtrodden people'. And you are home on the range. Full literacy is not even necessary; a semblance of literacy, and shrewdness are quite enough. After all, you have the Civil Service to lean on while you play boss to the civil servants, humiliate them, and favour and corrupt those of them who flatter you. You need not even go to your office, except when you feel like it. But your work goes on. You can be absent on sick leave or senility leave for a year or so, provided you send an occasional 'note' to the Government, giving it orders and instructions. You are no longer a layman. You are qualified to make decisions on any subject, scorning the advice of seasoned experts in any field. As leader of the country, you have the last word on any matter you may choose to have the last word on. You are the undisputed dean of experts. You are a Solomon. A glorious profession, this West Indian politics: power without any real responsibility. Your only check and balance is the electoral vote, and you can always get that by the usual spurt at the right time.*

Standing on Patrick McIver's driveway, I suddenly felt very happy about the fact that I had failed in so many other walks of life. *Had I succeeded as a schoolteacher, for instance, I would not now have been on the exciting threshold of the most rewarding career the West Indies have to offer.*

Propelled by these thoughts which inspired me with certainty of success in my present mission to Glenmore Estate, I went up to the open door of the big house and knocked.

5

P ATRICK McIver was a big man; his tall, slightly stooped frame was heavy set. His sparse white hair was brushed back from a forehead made craggy by a prominence on one side. Gray, bushy eyebrows, large hairy ears which gave the impression that the largeness of the lobes was due to McIver's habit of plucking at them. His open-neck blue shirt revealed a red neck full of creases. The armpits of his shirt were dark with sweat, and clusters of burs on the cuffs of his rumpled khaki trousers over heavy dirty boots indicated that he had not long returned from his fields. He came slowly from somewhere inside the house, through the living room, and towered above me on the long wide veranda as he fixed me with his blue watery old eyes. He must have been at lunch, for he was chewing on a mouthful and wiping his mouth with a napkin as he came towards me.

'Mmm,' he said. I slackened my necktie, not only to ease the pressure of my damp shirt collar on my sweating neck, but also because McIver's over-cool manner had unnerved me a bit. I was not used to dealing with these rich white planters, and this one made me feel inferior, uncomfortable.

'My name is Jerry Mole, Sir,' I said.

'Mmm-hhmm,' said McIver, still chewing.

'I have come to ask you whether you would be willing to rent me one of your town houses — the one you're not using, the old one at the corner of Fullbank Street. I notice you have it shut up for some time now, sir. It might be better for the house if you rent it to me. I would be able to look after it, fix the windows, put new boards in, and save it from further deterioration. If you rent it to me I would pay you a good rental for it.'

'What you want to rent my house for?' asked McIver, pulling at the lobe of his ear.

I adjusted my necktie and said, 'Well, we want a place for the head-quarters of our union, and . . . . .'

'Union? Oh, you're the feller I hear going ar-rong from mor-r-n till night, making disrooptive speeches and stirring up workers on the island? Truth, if I had my way I would lock up every good-for-nothing vagabond such as ye. Left to fellers like you, the island woood be a dung heap. Ye have nae brains, nae will, nae skill for wurrk, so ye go from place to place inciting people to prevent them from wurrking.'

'Look here, Mr McIver, I didn't come here to argue with you, or to be insulted. I have come here on business. Will you or will you not rent the house?'

'Bide ye a wee while,' said McIver, as he turned and re-entered the house, pulling at the lobe of his right ear. I watched him as he went through the living room and turned into an adjoining room; then I moved a pace or two down the verandah and stood looking out on the fields which stretched away below the public road and on both sides of the approach to the house.

Presently, I heard McIver's returning footsteps, and when I turned to face him he was pointing a shotgun at me.

'Get out!' he roared. The anger in his voice matched the passion that suffused his face.

As I scrambled down the steps, McIver fired. He must have aimed above my head, because I was too close for him to miss. But as I sprinted down the driveway, McIver fired again, and I could have sworn that something hit me in my back. I fell on my face, scrambled up immediately and continued to bolt. The Scotsman fired again as I fled in panic through the gate to my waiting taxi across the road.

'Drive,' I gasped to the taxi driver, almost before I got into the vehicle.

'He shoot you?' the taximan asked as he roared off.

'I don't know,' I said, my voice shaky, chest heaving, heart pounding. 'I felt something hit me in my back. See if you see any blood.' I showed my back to the driver. He stopped the taxi, looked carefully at my back.

'No blood come through yet,' he said.

You see any holes?'

'No holes there,' said the taxidriver. 'You lucky Mr Mole.'

That man is as crazy as hell, but I will get even with him, so help me God.'

My humiliation at the hands of Patrick McIver only steeled my resolve to continue on the course on which I had embarked. Before this incident, I had only two aims in view in pursuing the career of a politician — bread and power. Now I had a third aim — revenge, to appease my envy. Revenge not only against McIver, but against all like him — all planters, all rich, all who owned something, all those who employed people, all upper crust and all who aspired to the same.

Arriving back in Kingsland, I called a meeting of the waterfront members of the management committee of the union, and briefly told them about my brush with McIver. I played down the incident as much as possible, merely stating that I had asked the Scotsman to rent the old house, and that he had refused, underscoring his refusal with a shotgun. I joked about this; minimizing the humiliation.

Lacking a proper meeting place, I held this committee meeting in the wooden shack I shared with my wife in down-town Kingsland. Down-town Kingsland was the tenement section of the capital. People called it 'Bottom Town', the name having the subtle connotation of dregs. Bottom Town was a community of one-room huts, roofed with rusty galvanize patched with bits of tin, and supported on very short wooden posts. These huts were built years ago by a man called Stewart Cooper, an enterprising negro who had ideas about making money through squalid real estate business. The huts were not built in orderly rows, they were just 'put down' on the plot of land, so that the whole area had the appearance of a jungle of higgledy-piggledy carpentry.

The place swarmed with half naked potbellied children. Women pottered about in the yards. Old men and women sat on the ground in the hot sun, their backs against the sides of the huts, dozing, shooing flies, smoking clay pipes and talking old talk. Four of every five of the younger women were pregnant. In the centre of the community there was a long barrack-like building in an advanced stage of deterioration. This building was formerly used by Stewart Cooper as a warehouse for his building materials, but now it was used by the Bottom Town children for playing 'coop' — the local name for hide-and-seek — during the day. Old men used it as a back rest while they sunned them-selves, smoked, talked, spat and dozed. Young couples used it at night for other purposes which caused the building to be nicknamed 'The Chamber'.

The hut in which my management committee met was a one-room fourteen by twelve thing like the other huts, but a large piece of dark grey cloth on a wooden frame divided the room into a 'bedroom' and a 'living room.' We held the meeting in the living room. The four men — Joe Pittance and three others — sat on the sofa, which was my bed during the day. I sat on a small rough bench, facing them. The only other article of furniture in the room was a small white pine table covered with a table-cloth of red and white squares. A naked light bulb hung from a slight cross beam nearer to the bedroom section, so that the living room in which we sat was almost all shadow.

'Well,' I said, 'Patrick McIver has refused to rent his place, so we are still faced with the problem of finding somewhere we can use as headquarters of the union.'

Ben Davis brandished his fist. Ben was short, thick and jet black. His muscular torso was topped by a large round head of matted hair and a handsome fat-cheek face. The short sleeves of his old polo shirt clung to his bulging biceps. His small feet boasted a pair of reddish brown canvas shoes. He was about 40.

'Bass,' he said, 'if Ah bin there when McIver bring out he shotgun at you, Ah woulda cuff 'im up goo an' proper.'

Joe Pittance turned a stern glance at Ben. 'Stap tarking nansense, Ben,' said Joe. 'We don't want to cuff up nobody. All we want is a place fo' the union headquarters. Let us put our minds to dat. Dis is a urgent matter. Put away your fist, and help us figure out dis t'ing.'

James Carter nodded. James was a nodder. He nodded when he agreed with a remark or a suggestion, and he nodded when he didn't agree. He was medium height, 45, quite bovine. He looked well dressed in a clean dungaree shirt and trousers and no shoes. As he nodded agreement, or disagreement, with Joe's last remark, he looked across encouragingly at Henry Stowe as if he expected Henry to say something. But Henry only grunted, and the beady eyes of his long thin face continued to stare at his bare instep.

Joe Pittance said, "I don't see why we need to have de headquarters of de union here in Kingsland, if we can't get a place to hire here. De headquarters could be in de country, if we can get a place to hire in de country. An' moreover, wherever we have de most members, de headquarters should be dere. How much union members we got in town, Bass?'

'Forty-nine,' I replied, after referring to the rough notes in my copy book.

'An' how much we got in de Sugar Belt?

'About two hundred and sixty-eight.'

'Good,' said Joe. 'How much we got in de Central Windward Districk?'

'A hundred and ninety-four.'

'How much in de Leeward North?'

'Say eighty-five.'

'So we got the lowest number in town so far?'

'Yes.'

'Where we got de most?'

'In the Sugar Belt.'

'Well,' said Joe, 'de headquarters should be in de Sugar Belt.'

James Carter nodded. Henry Stowe regarded his instep. Ben Davis struck his fist on the palm of his hand and said, 'If it didn't hadda been fo' dat frigging Patrick McIver, we woulda had dat house on Fullbank Street. If Ah get me hand on dat son of a bitch, Ah choke de shit outa he.'

'But why we can't have de headquarters in de Sugar Belt where we have de most members?' Joe queried.

'The headquarters of the union *must* be in town, Joe,' I said, 'not in the country. In every island in the West Indies the union headquarters is in the capital, because the headquarters of the Government is in the capital. If we're going to oppose the Government properly, our headquarters *must* be in town too. We can operate *better* in town than in the country.'

Sullen silence. Serious thinking going on.

Joe said, 'Bass, ain't no use we expecting to get a place in town. I have a carpenter friend in de Sugar Belt who might be able to patch up a . . . . .'

'Wait a minute,' I said, placing a hand on Joe's knee. 'I got an idea. What about asking Stewart Cooper to rent us 'the Chamber'? We can fix it up good, and use it till we can afford to build our own place. Stewart Cooper is an old businessman. He will appreciate the commonsense of renting the Chamber instead of leaving it to crumble. I think I'll go and see him. In any case, it would be safer to approach him than it was to approach McIver. Stewart Cooper hasn't got a shotgun. Pittance and I can call on him at his place in Egmont Street. Agreed?'

'Agreed.'

Two days after this meeting, we rented the Chamber. Cooper over-charged us, of course, but we expected that; and I cheerfully paid the first month's rent of fifteen dollars, in advance, from union subscriptions already collected. We replaced most of the rotten boards with new ones. My wife and a few other women scrubbed the floor. We installed a small table and a few second-hand chairs, and I nailed a signboard over the door: 'THE HIROONA WATERFRONT ESTATE AND MANUAL WORKERS UNION.' I felt like a young doctor, architect or senior partner of a law firm, proudly announcing to the public that he was ready to begin professional practice. I stood back and surveyed the sign on my office where I was about to begin the professional practice of politics, 'the art of the possible'.

6

H IROONA'S general election was now only a year and a half away, and I needed every minute of the time to make and consolidate preparations for taking over the island. It was to be Hiroona's first general election under the new Universal Adult Suffrage Act which would put an end to the voting monopoly hitherto enjoyed by the planters and people with incomes. Under the new Act, Tom, Dick and Wilma could vote. No property qualification; no income qualification; no qualification whatsoever. You needn't even be literate. You only had to be born twenty-one or more years ago. The new Act made the franchise a kind of built-in affair. This arrangement would place the island right into my lap. For since the Act made one man's vote as good as another man's, then with my Bottom Town votes alone I should be able to give the Establishment in Kingsland a stiff fight. And the country districts would certainly be mine.

I had no rival party to battle against; for during the pre-adult suffrage years there were no political parties in Hiroona or in the West Indies. There were only trade unions in a few of the islands. The Government was the party, and the planters and wealthy upper class were the Government. The Universal Adult Suffrage Act was the most tremendous thing that came to the West Indies since Columbus; and in Hiroona, I was the first in the new field. Before the Act, there was only Government; now there was going to be some politics — more politics than Government.

I planned a series of visits to the country districts to step up membership in the union; to 'strengthen the brethren' and to make myself more widely known. Then I summoned a meeting of the Management Committee of the entire union. We met in the Chamber on a Sunday afternoon. Thirty-eight of us. Men and women. We sat on old chairs, stools, and short benches borrowed from the Bottom Town community. After we had sung *O God, our help in ages past* — which was not politically true — I handed out bits of paper with the typewritten words of *The Red Flag* — sung to the tune of *My Maryland*. The crowd outside increased. They joined in the singing, crowding the windows and the doors. Partly nude children ran round and round in the yard, playing their noisy games, occasionally shooed, rebuked and silenced by their indignant elders.

After the singing, I said, 'Comrades, we off to a good start. Our union already comprise people from all over the island. We have no Party yet, but we have a strong union — the first union they ever had in this island of Hiroona.' After the long applause, I continued, 'We don't really need a Party. In most of the West Indian islands there is more union-rule and one-man rule than Party rule. But when we go to the polls at the next general election, we got to go as a Party, because that is the custom in the other islands, and in other parts of the world. But our Party will be our union, so that every member of the union will have a voice in the Government when we take over. (Hear-Hear, clapping and stamping.) Now I want a Party-name for the union. Can any comrade help with a name?' I subsided and stood listening to the ensuing heated arguments:

'De *Labour Party of Hiroona!*'

'Naah! Dat name is too common. It got Labour Party all over de West Indies already.'

'Well, what about de *National Party of Hiroona?*'

'Naah! Naah! we ain't no nation yet.'

One of the ladies of the Management Committee stood up. She wore a clean white frock with wrist-long sleeves, and a stiff black straw hat which looked shiny as if it had been coated with varnish and then polished.

I rapped on the table for silence, and shouted, 'Comrade Naomi Sampson wants to say something.'

'Comrades,' said Naomi very slowly, pronouncing her words with exaggerated care, like an old school mistress. 'We have today started a most important work, and we want God to bless it. For it says, Except the Lord build the house, the labour is lost that build it. Except the Lord keep the city, the watchman waketh but in vain. Now we are going to take over this city, this island Hiroona, and we want the Lord to keep the city. We should therefore call our Party by a name that will please the Lord. I therefore suggest that we call our Party the *Party of the Lord.*'

The more irreverent members of the Committee burst out laughing. To keep myself from joining them, I shouted, 'Not a bad suggestion, Comrade Sampson. The *Party of the Lord* — POL. All agree?'

'Naah! Naah!' Uproar broke out again.

A tall, very black man stood up and looked around, glaring. He wore no jacket, but his faded khaki shirt and trousers were clean. It was difficult to tell whether his thick hair was combed or not. His brow was only two deep horizontal lines high.

I rapped on the table. 'We will now hear from Comrade Claude Mason of Dorcas Village,' I said.

'I want to say dis,' said Claude. 'I ain't agree to call de Party de Party of no Lord. My advice is, keep de Lord entirely out o' dis. Dis is serias business.'

I looked at Mason and smiled. Keep the Lord entirely out of politics, he had said, for politics is serias business. Unwittingly, Mason had laid down the guideline I was to follow during the seventeen years of my political career.

Someone outside shouted, 'Call it the Jerry Mole Party. The JMP.'

'You flatter me, comrade,' I shouted back, 'but I don't think we should call the Party by my name. Not yet.'

As I peered outside to see whom I was addressing, three little boys, tired from their play, stood side by side at the back of the yard urinating, each holding his immature bit of equipment as he guided the jet of arching fluid towards the ground. I looked at the three peeing urchins for a moment. Then the idea struck me. I turned my attention back to the Committee.

'Comrades,' I said, 'I think I have a good suggestion. We will call our Party the PPP — the *People's Productive Party*. Carried?'

Everybody was happy now, and free comment and general conversation broke out once more. Naomi Sampson looked so crestfallen over the rejection of her POL, that I hastened to restore her morale. I suggested that she be appointed chaplain of the union. 'Carried?'

'Carried!'

Now I was about to make a very delicate announcement. After all, the Leader of a political party couldn't have a wife working as a domestic servant. My wife Sonia could read easy passages reasonably well, and she could write so-so. Why then, couldn't she be General Secretary of the union, to collect membership dues, keep the books and bank the union funds? Writing down the names of the members would be a little difficult as far as spelling was concerned; but I could help her there. Since the emergence of my political career, which had kept me really busy for the first time in my life, Sonia had softened towards me. Giving her a salary-earning job in my union would soften her up some more, and would convince her of my power. But I had to word the announcement very carefully. The Committee must not be led to think that I was merely providing a job for my wife. It would be unwise to mention the question of salary just then. That could be settled later.

So, looking the Committee over slowly, I said, 'Comrades, we now have a chaplain. We also have a name for our Party. We have branch committees all over the island. We have a Central Committee and we have a

President — me. Now we need a Secretary for the union. Up till now, I have been doing that work; but you don't want your President to be doing secretary work, so I asked my wife if she would help me, and of course she agreed, although it will be a lot of work for her. She can carry the heavy burden with credit, however. All agreed? Carried?'

'Carried!'

Joe Pittance got up and said, 'I think we reach de stage now where we can talk about havin' a rally and a marching, like is done in de other West Indian islands.'

'Naturally, Comrade Pittance,' I said. 'We *must* have a rally and a procession through the town. That will show our solidarity; and the large number of our union members in procession will impress the Government and everybody. But before we hold a rally, we have to do something else. We have to call a strike.'

Everybody looked puzzled. Joe glanced up sharply at me. Ben Davis, the ribald, muscleman stevedore chuckled. 'Goddamit,' he said. 'Dat's fine, Bass. Dat will give ole-man McIver somet'ing to t'ink about.'

General comments buzzed. I rapped on the table for silence.

Joe said, 'Strike? What for? What kind o' strike?'

'Any strike,' I replied. 'The general election is only a little over a year ahead. We have to back up with action our promise to get more wages for our labourers. A strike will bring home to everyone the power of the union in getting higher wages and easier conditions for workers. So they will join the union. When we hold the rally, I want to have thousands instead of hundreds marching through the streets behind me.'

Joe Pittance got up. 'Dis is damn foolishness,' he shouted. 'And I demand now dat dis matter be put to de vote instead o' being decided by any one-man dictator. What de hell you want a strike for? Look how busy dis town is every Saturday when crowds o' labourers come to Kingsland wid their Friday pay-day money. Dey fill up de shops an' stores, an' dey spend money. Plenty money circulatin' on de island now due to de Estates. What you want to strike for? Dis island never had a strike. De labourers ain't complaining.'

I jumped up. 'What *you* call plenty money is only chickenfeed, Comrade Pittance,' I shouted. 'Do you call *ten cents per basket* for digging arrowroot, *plenty money*? In the Sugar Belt, the labourers in the fields get six dollars a ton for cutting cane. In the sugar factory a furnace man gets *sixty cents a day* for burning himself up five days a week. You call that *plenty money*? On Mr Fraser's estate at Long Ground, people toil in the hot sun day in day out for *thirty cents a day*. You call that *plenty money*? Look

here, Comrade, you yourself have driven with me from Kingsland to
several parts of the country. What did we see? Village after village of
lean-to huts with grass roofs; each village a part of an estate plantation,
so that the owner of the estate owns the village too. The villagers *own
nothing,* not even the broken-down pit latrines at the back of their huts.
They have nothing, although they labour day after day on the estates. But
perhaps you travelled with your eyes shut, Comrade. You say that the
labourers are not complaining. Well, the *union must complain* for them.
That is what the union is for — to complain, to call strikes, to raise HELL
where and when necessary.'

My suggestion of a strike was 'carried', but it was my first quarrel with
Joe Pittance. And I had not only won this first battle with Joe, but had also
demonstrated my mastery of protest politics.

7

Penny Farthing was a fifteen-year old mentally retarded labourer who lived in the Sugar Belt and worked as a 'mop' at the Mount Horeb sugar factory.

I got to know about Penny and the details of his accident while I was trying to decide which of the estates would be the best strike target at the time. The strike had to be a popular one, as it would be Hiroona's first strike. I wanted everybody to see the justification for it. A wage-demanding strike would be good, but as there was no popular demand for more wages, I thought that if I could find some other cause, the general effect would be as good. Penny Farthing provided such a cause.

As a 'mop,' Penny's job was to see that no stray bits of bagasse or cane straw were left lying about in the wrong place in the factory yard. To rake up this rubbish, Penny used a forked stick. He would then pile the stuff on to a wheelbarrow, transport it to the rubbish heap just outside the 'mill yard,' dump the stuff on the rubbish heap, and return with the wheelbarrow for more rubbish. Penny enjoyed his job, not only because he was paid the considerable sum of fifteen cents a day for doing it, but also because the fact of his having a job gave him a sense of importance. He was a workingman like everybody else.

Penny took a fierce pride in his job, and everyone praised him for keeping the factory yard as clean as a whistle.

He had a large body for his age, and he was a kind of funny-favourite at the factory, especially for the girls and young women who liked to play teasing games with him. They would pull his shirt out of his trousers, or grab at his 'privates' hilariously making salacious suggestions. In a terrible rage, Penny would chase them with his forked stick. Sometimes, three or four girls would surround him, and while he tried to get his stick to one of them the others would close in as near as they dared, and try to get their hands on his shirt tail or elsewhere. They thought this very funny; but on rare occasions, Penny managed to land an un-funny blow or two while he shouted obscenities at the girls. His tormentors would then scurry off, cursing him good-humouredly and shrieking with ribald laughter. The noise of their teasing often drew the attention of a factory official or some of the elderly labourers who would either stop to watch and enjoy the fun, or shout rebukes at the girls. The game would then end in the usual scamper and laughter, and Penny would return to his raking of rubbish, working off the embarrassing experience with incoherent mutterings and swearings.

However, the day came when this popular pastime ended quite differently.

Penny was busy at his raking. The mingled noises of rushing water, engines crunching sugar cane, turbines activating engines, poured out of the factory and into the yard in a muffled roar. Angie Grell came up from the labourers' outhouse latrine, walked past Penny, went to the standpipe and washed her hands. As she was returning to re-enter the factory to resume her oilwiping job, Angie stole up behind Penny, quickly pulled his shirt out of his trousers and ran.

The unexpectedness of the action must have surprised and frightened Penny. He became all reflex. He couldn't stop chasing Angie, his forked stick held straight out in front of him, his shirt tail flying. They ran round the yard twice, their bare feet pounding. Then Angie bolted into the factory, Penny at her heels. Angie said afterwards that she could hear Penny's breathing, 'going in an' out like he gaspin.' Quite terrified now, Angie rushed down a narrow aisle of the factory between two rows of small cane crushers. Factory hands attending the roaring machines stopped to watch the chase. A man who was supervising the bagging of sugar on an upper gallery in the factory looked down and shouted, 'Hey, you! Stop that' as Angie suddenly turned left and dodged under the rushing belt of one of the crushers. Penny didn't bend low enough; his shoulder struck the belt. His forked stick flew out of his hands as he staggered under the impact, and he put out his hand to steady himself. He shrieked like a wounded wild animal and collapsed on the concrete floor under the belt. Some factory workers hurried over to him, and the man who was supervising the bagging of sugar left the gallery, ran down the metal staircase and joined the little group standing over Penny. Even before they lifted him up they could see that the boy's thumb was flattened like a piece of cardboard and that three of his fingers had been crushed off completely.

I went to see Penny in Kingsland's hospital a few days after the accident, but I could get nothing out of him beyond an inane whimper.

I visited his mother in the Sugar Belt, but even before I entered her yard I knew it would be a difficult task getting anything intelligible out of her. Anything living in a shack like that could hardly be *homo*, and couldn't possibly be *sapiens*. As I approached the yard, I wondered whether it was a kind neighbour or Penny Farthing himself who had placed the two slim greenheart poles against the shack to shore it up on the side on which it was listing so badly. In the place of a window shutter, there was a piece of burlap. The door hung askew on three 'hinges' made of scraps of leather; and where there should have been boards there were strips of wattle sticks which could be seen under thin mud plaster caking off and falling away in places.

She was sitting on a stone at the side of the shack, opposite the listing side. A headkerchief was wound loosely about her head. Her frail body was draped in a very long, dirty frock. The back of her hands which rested in her lap, was a network of large veins under thin black skin. She looked like a human replica of the house in which she lived.

'You Penny's mother?' I asked.

Spaniel-like, she looked up at me, her old eyes sad and watery. A young woman with a naked child in her arms came out of the hut next door and said, 'Yes, she is Penny's mudder. But since Penny got 'e han' crush, she ain't talking; she just sad, sad.'

'I see.' I stood looking down at the old woman and shaking my head. I didn't try to find out how the wretched old thing was being looked after now that Penny was in hospital. I didn't reach into my pocket and hand over one of the ten shillings I had in it. It didn't occur to me to to make an effort to get the old lady into the Pauper's Asylum where she would be properly cared for. I was not concerned about performing charitable acts. I was there on political business, seeking information which I could use against the Management of Mount Horeb sugar factory, with a view to starting a strike which would enhance my political standing and increase the membership of my union. I could not get the information from Penny's mother, so I decided to go and see Angie Grell.

'Angie,' I said, as I stood behind her in her yard. She was bending over a pot. Cooking the evening meal.

She straightened up quickly and turned round. 'Eh-eh,' she exclaimed. 'You frighten me, sah. Ah didn't even hear yo' footsteps behind me.'

'What you cooking, Angie?' I said, peering into the pot.

'Is breadfruit soup, sah.'

'Smell nice,' I said. Angie grinned, and turned away her head with a bashful air.

From where I stood I could see right into the mud hut in which Angie lived. A long, lean young man, stripped to the waist, was lying on his back on a rough wooden bed. Two naked little children sat on his chest, pawing at his face while he playfully tried to fend them off. The three were laughing happily — until they saw me. The man got up and came to the door. He leaned against the door jamb and looked from Angie to me and back, with a question on his face. The two potbellied children sat crossed-legged on the bed, watching. They looked like black little Buddhas.

Angie's trash-covered mud hut was one of a number of similar tenements on a clearing on the estate. The huts formed a village, one beaten-dirt yard merging into another, with nothing separating them. Steam rose from open cooking pots like little Indian smoke signals. The pots rested on three large stones. Some of the villagers turned their attention from their pots, and stood staring across at me. Others drew near to 'hear what happening'. I took out my red handkerchief which had now become my badge of office, and wiped my skin under my soiled open-neck khaki shirt. Then I addressed Angie's young man loudly enough for those who stood around to hear.

'I just come to get some information from Angie. You her boyfriend?'

'Yeah.'

'How many kids you all got?' I asked. He indicated the two Buddhas with a toss of his head.

'You know who I am, of course?'

'Yeah. You Mr Jerry Mole.'

I turned to Angie and said, 'Now Angie, I want you to tell me what really happen' when Penny get his han' crush' at the factory last week.'

Angie gave me a suspicious glance. Then she looked at her boyfriend timidly and said, 'You tell 'e, Fred.'

Fred shouted at her, '*Me* tell 'e? Me ain't been dere when it happen. Me been cuttin' cane at Judy Piece. Ah tired warn yo' don't trouble dat Penny Farthing boy. You garn an' trouble 'im; now yo' warnt me to tell de gentleman. *Me* ain't know nutten. *You* tell 'e.'

Angie hesitated.

'Look here, Angie,' I said quietly, 'I am not the police; you know me quite well. I am a friend to all of you. You have nothing to fear. I am here to help you. Now tell me. What happened?'

Fred blurted out, 'She 'fraid to tell, because Mr Phelps at de factory warn us dat if we give any information to any politician, we go get de sack.'

'I am here to help you all; to save Angie from trouble. Phelps can't do you all a damn thing. Believe me. My union will fight for you all.'

Fred shrugged and said, 'Angie can tark if she like.'

'Tark, Angie! Tark!' The chorus came from the surrounding yards. The village was with me.

'You hear that, Angie? Everybody is advising you to talk. Now tell me what happened with you and Penny last week.'

Angie told. Everyone listened. A crowd gathered. Murmurs broke out now and again.

'Now, Angie, I want to ask you one question. Was there any protection around the cane crushers that crushed Penny's hand? What I mean is, was there any wire or board placed around the crusher so as to prevent anyone from being injured if he fell against the crusher?'

'No,' said Angie. 'No wire nor nothing was dere.' Murmurs and big chorus: 'No wire else board been dere tarl.'

By now, the whole village had gathered around me, flowing over from Angie's yard. Spreading out. Over two hundred of them. Some holding up their young pic'nies. Some munching roasted corn on the cob or enjoying a ripe mango or some such titbit. Some sat on the ground or squatted by the nearest hut.

'Thank you for coming, everybody. And thank you, Angie for giving me all the facts. Now listen to me, all of you. The law say that when you have a factory, all your machines, engines, and crushers must have some sort of protection for the workers in the factory. If anyone get injured by the machines' — I left out the part which says *except through his own carelessness or neglect* — 'the factory boss is responsible, and he have to pay plenty for compensation. I am going now to Mr Phelps and the people who own the factory, to talk up for your rights. None of you is to turn out to work tomorrow until I tell you all that the compensation will be paid. You hear? Good. I will go down to Derricks village and talk to all the truck drivers and cane haulers and cutters and mill hands there. Nobody is to go to work until I give the word. I will see to it that you poor downtrodden and oppressed people get what is yours. You been cheated for too long. You been without rights too long. These are different days. These not like the old days when you didn't have nobody to stand up for your rights. I am here to stand up for your rights. Don't be afraid; Phelps and the factory bosses can't do you a damn thing. They can't sack everybody. If they did that they won't have no factory. We must stick together, and you will get all the protection you need from the union. Hands raise, all those who with me. Good. That is all I want to see. You all leave the rest to me. United we stand; divided we fall. I want to hear everybody repeat that. Now. Everybody say it together. Ready? Now . . . . .'

'United we fall . . .'

'No, no, no. You all got it wrong. Not so it go. Listen carefully while I tell you again. "United we Stand, Divided we fall." Now everybody . . . Fine. You got it right now. Thank you. Now we close the meeting with *The Red Flag*. All ready? Now sing, everybody . . . . . .'

8

Two days after I launched the strike, silence descended like a pall on the Sugar Belt. No activity on the estate; no humming and roaring of the factory; no singing and joking in the cane fields. Everything still, still. In the beaten-dirt villages, the labourers only waited — wondering, watching, lazing in the sun in their yards. When they talked, their voices were low — laden with perplexing questions: 'How long dis gwine last? Who gwine pay us we wages? Mr Phelps gwine sack all o' we. He can't do dat; if he do dat, who will cut de cane and work de factory?' The strike was a new phenomenon on the island; and even I did not like the look of it.

The Management of the factory had scornfully refused to recognize the union or negotiate with me; and there was not as yet on the island any Government Department of Labour through which such negotiation could be initiated.

I spent days going from village to village, trying to cheer up the bewildered labourers. 'You all must have confidence in me, I tell you. Everything will work out all right.'

But I was as frightened and bewildered as they were. I began to regret that I had started this thing, and I cast about in my mind for a way to call it off without losing face.

It was not until the sixth day of the strike that the Management of Mount Horeb factory and their legal adviser granted my request for an interview. I should have liked to take Joe Pittance with me, but there was a coldness between us since the day I suggested the strike, at the committee meeting of the union. So I went alone.

In the Manager's office at the farthest end of the long L formed by the factory buildings, they pointedly omitted to offer me a seat. I stood in front of a large table on which were official papers, four heavy-looking glass paper weights, a large ashtray with a pipe in it, a book with the title side turned down on the table, and a wood carving of the three monkeys seeing no evil, hearing no evil, and doing no evil. The one with the 'do no evil' inscription was covering his genitals with his hands. Some small bottles containing what appeared to be sugar and syrup samples stood in neat groups on one side of the table. Five men sat at the table, facing me as if I were on trial.

The room was a large one. On the wall immediately in front of me was a map of Hiroona. On the opposite wall was a large clock. A number of graphical maps and diagrams covered the other two sides of the room. There were three or four chairs, but these were huddled together (deliberately, I thought) at the far end of the room behind me. The chairs had a 'Do Not Disturb' look.

The small man sitting in the centre of the Big Five said, 'You Jerry Mole?' As if he didn't know.

'I am,' I said.

'I understand from Mr Phelps here that you have been asking to see the Management of Mount Horeb Estate Company. What do you want to see us for?'

As if he didn't know. Fear, and the man's rough, sarcastic, insulting attitude got the better of me.

'Damn you, man,' I shouted. 'Who do you think you are, an idiot or something? You don't know who is Jerry Mole. You don't know what I want to see you about. You don't know that your estate and factory have a strike on their hands. You don't know that a poor labourer on your estate had his fingers crushed off by your factory cane crusher. If you don't know what is happening on your own doorstep, what the hell you doing in the house, then?'

Phelps said, 'Mr Mole, we will not tolerate this type of attitude and language from you. Mr Perkins here, the Vice-President of the Company, asked you a simple, relevant question. There was no need for you to reply in the manner you did.'

'Look, gentlemen, I'm a busy man — a man with a following of six thousand seven hundred and fifty-three out of a total labour force of eleven thousand. I have work to do. I didn't come here to lick boots or wrangle over attitudes. I have a mandate from over six thousand people to come here and ask you whether you wish the strike to continue or whether you are prepared to negotiate with me to end the strike?' That should bring them to their senses.

'What is the reason for the strike?' said Perkins.

'Reasons, Mr Perkins. The reasons are set out in my letter which I addressed to Mr Phelps. First of all, there is the matter of a worker in your factory sustaining serious damage to his hand because there was no protective equipment attached to the machinery which crushed off his fingers. My union wishes to know what compensation you propose to offer.'

The Company's attorney — a lean, astringent Irishman named Sean Dobson — said, 'What was he doing in the factory, anyway? He was employed to work in the yard, raking rubbish.' Dobson then launched into a legal dissertation on carelessness and what it means in law. I moved away from the table and went and stood looking out of a window, my back to the five men. I folded my arms on my chest.

Phelps called to me: 'Mr Mole!'

Without turning round I said, 'When Mr Dobson is through with his law lecture we will resume negotiations.'

Perkins said, 'All right, Dobson, let Mr Mole finish.'

'The second reason for the strike,' I began before turning round and walking slowly back to the table, 'is the workers' demand for a substantial increase in their wages and certain improvement in their working conditions. I am prepared to admit that both the increase and the improvement are likely to hit your investment hard; but you have to admit, gentlemen, that both are long overdue. To increase your financial commitments is the last thing I would wish to do. After all, the factory and estate provide employment for my people and help to support the island's economy. That is the reason why I tried to dissuade my union from making this demand at this time. But . . . . .'

'We appreciate your reasonableness,' said Perkins, 'and the fact that you realize that to go into matters like substantial increase in wages and improvements in working conditions needs careful study and some time. So I suggest that we settle the matter of compensation, and defer the other matters.'

I had got them. That was precisely the kind of reaction I had hoped for when I added the spiel about wages and conditions.

Long discussion followed, with many whispered head-to-head consultations by the five. Phelps left his place to fetch one of the chairs from the back of the room. He placed it close to me. I sat down.

They settled for compensation for Penny Farthing. Ninety-six dollars. I tried to bargain for a hundred pounds — four hundred and eighty dollars — but Sean Dobson shouted down my request: 'What! You crazy, man. A hundred pounds? Over my dead body!'

They finally agreed to pay twenty pounds compensation to Penny. But they took care to force a promise from me that there would be no strike for increased wages and improved conditions. I said that I would endeavour to persuade my union against such a step for at least a year. The twenty pounds compensation for Penny was a sort of *quid pro quo*. But even the twenty pounds was over Dobson's dead body. He came alive, however, to rant at me:

'Mole — or whatever your damn name is — you've got away with murder. Soap-box speechifying and the provisions of the law are two different things. You have disregarded the cardinal provision of the Labour Disputes Act. In the first place, there was no dispute. No application was made by you or anyone else to my client for compensation, before the strike. Next, you started a strike without due notice, and without any lawful reason or justification. This illegal strike has cost this Company thousands of dollars. You should be made to pay for it. Chaps like you should be locked up, or legally prevented from practising your bogus profession on this hitherto peaceful island. If . . . . .' I jumped up.

'Gentlemen,' I began.

'No-no-no,' said Vice-President Perkins, lifting both hands in front of him as if to fend me off. 'For God's sake, no more speeching. Mr Phelps, what is the name of the man to whom compensation is to be paid?'

'They call him Penny Farthing,' said Phelps.

'That's no name,' said Perkins irritably.

'I shall try to find out his correct name, if there is one,' said Phelps.

'All right,' said Perkins. 'Mr Mole, you heard what Mr Phelps said. When he finds out the man's name, a cheque will be made out, payable to the injured man.'

'How long will it take you, Mr Phelps, to find out Penny's correct name?' I asked.

'I don't know,' said Phelps.

'Gentlemen,' I began, rising.

'All right, all right, Mr Mole,' said Perkins, 'the money will be paid to the man by tomorrow noon.'

'I shall inform my union accordingly; and by tomorrow noon all your estate and factory workers will resume work — if I am satisfied that the compensation has been paid to Penny Farthing, or whatever is his correct name. Good day, gentlemen.'

As I hurried out of the room, my whole being light with relief, I heard Sean Dobson say, 'He's a son of a bitch; a swindler. He's got away with . . . . .'

9

JOE Pittance slowly surveyed the crowd in the Chamber. He swivelled his head to take in the whole room as he asked the question: 'You quite sure Penny Farthing really got de compensation money?'

We were at a meeting of the combined central and branch committees of the union. Quite a crowd. I had called the meeting two months after the strike — after my victory over the Directors and Management of Mount Horeb Estate. News of the outcome of the strike had spread throughout the island, increasing union membership and inflating my prestige. The compensation paid to Penny Farthing was a big event. It marked the first time in the history of Hiroona that the workingman received due recognition from Management. The members of the Committee at the meeting were in a mood to rejoice, playing up the victory and praising the victor.

I was thoroughly enjoying the moment, as I sat in the President's chair, head thrown back a bit, chest forward, the smugness in my mind reflecting on my face.

Pittance had remained silent while member after member rose and made congratulatory speeches. Then Joe got up and said, 'What is the object of dis meeting?'

An embarrassed silence followed Pittance's question, as if everybody was trying to remember the reason for the meeting. 'Comrade Pittance,' I said, 'the object of this meeting is to make arrangements for our rally and procession.'

'Well, let us do dat,' said Joe.

Someone said, 'Joe, like yo' vex because we tarking 'bout de strike. You don't feel de Bass did a good job?'

'Good job?' said Joe, 'when hundreds of estate an' factory workers out o' work for a whole week? And without notice or warning to de people in charge. *Who* paid de workers fo' dat week? Dese people live from day to day. Can't save no money fo' next day, because dey don't work for enough. *How* dey live for a whole week *widout* wages? You all ever consider *dat*? I hear 'bout strike in Trin'dad and Grenada an' Jamaica. In these islands, when dey strike, de union pays dem strike wages to live on while de strike is on. *Who* paid de labourers at Mount Horeb while dey been on strike?'

'You tarking nansense, Joe,' said Vera Benn. 'You fo'get dat a poor boy got twenty pounds outa de strike? That is more money than all of us ever see in our lifetime. What more you want? Our Leader even did more than dat: he hire a taxi de same day Penny Farthing was to come out o' de hospital, an' he carry home de poor boy in de taxi. You ever hear people like Penny Farthing riding in taxi before? What more you want?'

'You *quite* sure Penny Farthing *really* got de compensation money?'

I looked up sharply at Pittance; fear gripped my throat like a man's hand. Joe had loaded his question with insinuation that was as clear to me as it was damaging. Where the devil did this illiterate stevedore get his information from? Who told him things? Earlier in our association, he was able to tell me where to find a funeral to cry at. Now, by a loaded question, he was telling me and the crowd that he knew that I had pocketed the ninety-six dollars paid to Penny Farthing as compensation. How did he know this? Barbers are always in a position to pick up news from some of their clients. Was this the source from which Pittance got information? But how could anyone know that I had kept Penny's money, when even the idiot boy himself was not aware of what I had done?

Pittance knew, of course, that I had taken Penny home in a taxi the day he was discharged from the hospital. I wanted everybody to know this, because I did it as a political stunt — openly. But how could Joe Pittance or anyone else know that I had taken the cheque from Penny, franked and cashed it in the boy's name, chucked a crisp dollar note in his hand and kept the balance? How much did Joe Pittance know?

Inwardly seething, and almost trembling with fear, I said, 'Yes, Comrade Pittance, Penny Farthing did get the compensation money. I was at the hospital and witnessed the fact that Mr Phelps gave a cheque for ninety-six dollars to the boy. Are you satisfied, Comrade?'

Joe Pittance showed his long, yellow teeth in a slow nauseating smile.

'How long ago was dat?' he asked.

'Some eight weeks ago,' I said.

'Eight weeks,' said Joe, '*dat* is a long time; but I hear dat Penny Farthing an' his mother *still live in a break-down leaning hut*. Ninety-six dollars could build a house fo' Penny an' his mother and *still* have money left. But I ain't see *no* carpenter, *no* mason, *no* cement, nor *no* lumber go up dere to build *no* house or to repair de one dey live in. Anyhow, we didn't come here to tark about dat; we come here to arrange fo' de rally an' de marchin'. So let us do dat now!'

Joe had made his point, and I didn't like the thoughtful silence with which it was received. For the first time in my life, the resolve to kill a man suddenly crystallized in my mind. My shotgun experience with Patrick McIver had shaken me, yes; but this ruinous betrayal by Joe Pittance was something else.

There should be only one redress — I thought — a traitor's death. Perhaps I could use one of his colleagues to accomplish this. It would be a difficult job, because of Pittance's relationship with the boys. He was much more intelligent than other stevedores, and so he was regarded by them as their spokesman. They trusted him and relied on his judgement. His influence with them was enormous. But I reasoned, my own influence with Ben Davis the brash muscleman was also considerable. Perhaps if I cultivated Ben carefully . . . ? Meanwhile, I thought, I must try by every means to undermine Joe's influence with the stevedores as well as with the union in general.

These thoughts raced through my mind while the committee made plans for the rally, so only a part of my mind followed their discussion.

Joe had planted the suspicion in their minds that I had kept Penny Farthing's compensation money, and I felt that I had to remove that suspicion before the meeting closed. So I interrupted their discussion of the rally to say, 'Comrade Pittance, you said a while ago that you hadn't seen a carpenter, or cement, or lumber for the repairing of Penny Farthing's and his mother's house. Well, let me remind you: I didn't undertake to repair Penny's and his mother's house. All I undertook to do was to obtain compensation for the boy. And I have done that. What Penny does with the money is his business not mine.

There was a sort of stunned silence, as if I had said something in favour of the British Government. I could almost see their feeble minds equating my guilt to the callous untimely statement I had just made.

Joe Pittance grinned. 'Bass,' he said, 'we didn't know you still worrying about dat matter. We discussin' rally business now.'

The damn man's smooth sarcasm was too much. I must put him in his place at once.

Fuming, I got up.

'Look here, Comrade Pittance,' I said, 'I want you and everyone here to understand that I am not worrying about anything. A man who has assumed the tremendous responsibility of lifting labour on this island out of filth and hopeless poverty and ignorance and trash hovels and no-class citizenship, cannot be the worrying type. He got to be tough. A man who has fought planters nose to nose, and faced their shotguns, cannot be the worrying type. We are now preparing to bring the labour force together in a rally. A few minutes ago, I heard the secretary read out the number of our people who will attend the rally — nine thousand eight hundred and seventy-five. The number is so large that Comrade Walker suggested a while ago that we split up and hold the rally in two different districts instead of in Kingsland alone. What an achievement, comrades! What an achievement. A worrying man couldn't achieve all this.'

Now I raised my voice, shouting like an old-time evangelist: 'Comrades, we are on the threshold of great things. The only thing we have to worry about is when we see distrust and suspicion raise their baleful heads in our ranks. I am your leader; you either trust me or choose another leader.' I now proceeded to use the old trick — the shouted question which compulsively calls forth the shouted answer.

'The general election is only a few months ahead. You want to win, or not?'

'We gwine win,' they shouted back.

'You want to take over the Government or not?'

'Yeahse! Yeahse!'

'In a few months from now, some of you will be cabinet ministers in the Government, running the country. You want this to happen?'

'O'course! O'course!'

'You want to choose another leader?'

'Naah! Naah!'

'Do you trust me and give me a vote of complete confidence?'

'Yeahse! Yeahse! Yeahse!'

The catechism finished, I sat down, sweating, but mollified. The Penny Farthing issue had been shoved into the background, forgotten . . . . . or so I thought.

10

THEY say in the West Indies that politics is the art of the incredible. In some of the islands, leaders often get away with political 'stunts' that would make one think that they studied politics under Houdini and Blondin. But politics in the islands can also be the art of the spectacular; and nothing provides greater evidence of this than a West Indian political rally. More preparation sometimes goes into this demonstration of solidarity than into the planning of election campaigns or into the preparation of the Government's Five Year Plans.

There is a lot of letter-writing to be done, too. My wife, Sonia, as General Secretary of the union, was responsible for this part of our rally preparation. Letter to the Kingsland Municipal Board asking for permission to 'use' the city streets for our procession. Letter to the Chief of Police asking for Police protection during the rally procession. Letter to the Administrator, as head of the Government, asking for permission to use the large pavilion in Victoria Park as a refreshment booth. Letter to the Kingsland Sports Association requesting the loan or hire of the Association's microphone.

To every one of these letters, we received the same reply: 'Your letter of March 22, 1952, is hereby acknowledged. Your request . . . is receiving consideration.'

I discussed this disquieting situation with Sonia as we lay in bed one night. Since the rise of my political star, which had brought Sonia the respectable job of the General Secretary of the union, my wife's attitude towards me had changed for the better. Furthermore, I had bought her some dresses and underclothes out of my Penny Farthing compensation money, which appeared to please her greatly. The death of her frail, sickly mother had also removed a cause for worry; and Sonia's wifely ministrations now left nothing to be desired. We had just completed one of these mutual ministrations, and were resting and talking quietly. I asked Sonia whether she had any further replies to her letters.

'No,' she said, 'only de considerations.'

'I should have written those letters myself,' I said, 'but I was too busy organising things. Did you word the letters exactly as I told you?'

'Eh-heh. I write just what yo' say.'

'Did you ask to be favoured with an early reply?'

'Yes.'

'I can't understand it. Nearly a whole month now since you sent those letters, and they still considering them. Our rally is due next public holiday, in three weeks' time. They keeping us back.'

'I know de reason,' said Sonia, 'they still feel dat we an' de union is common people, beneat' dere notice.'

'Well, I'll show them. I am going to see the Administrator tomorrow, and I'll raise hell.'

I had to wait three days before I saw the Administrator. Every time I went to the Administration Building, some clerk or secretary — all natives — would pop out of one of the innumerable offices in the building, or confront me in one of the corridors with the question, 'Have you an appointment with His Honour? Their attitude was as snobbish as Patrick McIver's shotgun.

'Well — er — not exactly,' I would stammer, 'but I've been coming here for the last few days, trying to make an appointment. Could you arrange an appointment for me, please?'

'You would have to see His Honour's secretary.'

'How do I see him? Where is he?'

'He is in his office, I believe, but he is very busy. You had better come back this afternoon or tomorrow morning. With luck you might catch him.'

So I decided to telephone; but even that was a big problem. People like myself and my followers did not have access to telephones. In Hiroona, up to the late forties and early fifties, a telephone was a brown oak box fastened to a wall, above the reach of certain people. However, I had a friend at Stan Myers' filling station in the centre of town, and I went there and asked my friend Soapy to call up the Administrator's secretary for me. When Soapy handed me the ear-piece after calling up the secretary, I shouted into the mouth-funnel.

'Who is that, the Secretary?'

'This is the Administrator's secretary, yes,' said a cultured native male voice.

'Well, I want to make an appointment to see the Administrator,' I said.

'Who are you?'

'Oh, excuse me. Jerry Mole speaking. Mister Jerry Mole.'

'What do you want to see His Honour about?'

'Well, the Secretary of the Hiroona Trades and Manual Workers Union wrote a letter to the Administrator a month ago, asking permission to use the Victoria Park Pavilion just for our rally day. We got acknowledgement of the letter, but no reply; so I wanted to see the Administrator about a reply. We are willing to pay for the use of the pavilion if we can't have it free.'

'His Honour is very busy at present, Mr Mole; but I shall see to it that you get a reply shortly.'

'Thank you. But the matter is urgent. We have to plan ahead, and time is running out on us. Could I see you, then, at your office?'

'That won't be necessary, Mr Mole. You will receive a reply as soon as possible.'

So I called an emergency meeting of the Management Committee of the union and told them of the difficulties in the usual political way.

'There is an insidious conspiracy in this island to undermine and over-throw all that I have built up by sweat, grit and intelligence,' I shouted. 'The Administrator, the Chief of Police, the Kingsland Municipal Board, the Sports Association, have all refused to even reply to letters we wrote them in connection with our rally. When I try to see the Administrator, a whole army of clerks and secretaries bar my passage in what appears to be the sacred corridors of the Administration Building. These clerks and secretaries are black people like us, but they enjoy the role of stooges to the white-man boss. I tell you, I *promise* you that when we take over this island, a lot of these white-man *stooges* will be swept out like chaff.'

When the cheers and stamping died down, Joe Pittance got up before I could continue.

'What exactly is de problem?' he said. He deliberately pitched his voice low, soft, cool, reasonable as if to rebuke my loudmouthed hysteria.

'The problem? Not problem. *Problems.* These conspirators in high places; these stooges . . . . . .'

'I hear you say you want to see de Administrata, Bass. Right?'

'Yes, Comrade Pittance,' I said.

'But Bass,' said Joe, 'seeing de Administrata is de easiest t'ing on earth. If you did tell me yo' wanted to see de Administrata, you woulda see him already.'

'What you mean by that?' I said into the deep silence of the Chamber.

'Well,' said Joe, 'it is a simple matter. You got to know how de Administration Building is run. All de clerks and secretaries go off to lunch twelve o'clock, but Mr Forbes de Administrata stays back in de office till half past twelve, doing overtime, because he seldom come back to de office after lunch till four or five o'clack. So all yo' got to do is go see de Administrata between twelve and half past twelve.'

'Yes, Comrade Pittance,' I laughed harshly, 'you seem to know every-thing; but you don't know that a policeman is always posted at the door of the Administrator's office, standing guard. He lets no one pass.'

'I know dat, Bass,' said Joe. 'Everybody know dat. Ain't no secret. But de policeman who does duty by de door between twelve an' half past twelve is P.C. 43 Cunningham. Cunningham is a secret friend of de union. If you let me go wid you tomorrow between twelve an' half past twelve, we will get in to see de Administrata.'

Where in hell does this man, this barefoot stevedore, get his information from? I thought. The eyes of all in the room were on me now, wordlessly urging me to follow Joe's lead in this matter. Everyone seemed to be saying to me, *You got to hand it to Joe; he knows much more about it than you.*

'All right, Pittance,' I chuckled to ease my embarrassment, 'we go to see the Administrator tomorrow at twelve. Meet me at the Administration Building.'

Joe was at the building on time. We went up the stairs. Sure enough, the young stocky policeman at the door of the Administrator's office sported the figures 43 on both sides of the neck of his black tunic. Joe went up to him and said, very quietly,

'Cunny, de Bass here and we want to see Forbes about de business I explain to you yesterday. You got a toilet nearby?'

The policeman nodded and pointed down the corridor. 'Straight ahead, Joe,' he said, smiling.

'Not *me* want de toilet, Cunny. *You* want it. To ease yo' bowels while me an' de Bass go in to see Forbes. Remember?'

Grinning, Cunningham turned off, soft-footed quickly down the corri-dor, straight ahead. When we heard the toilet door click, Joe Pittance knocked on the door of the Administrator's office.

'Come in.'

Administrator Forbes looked up from an open file he had before him on his desk. His eyes popped; his jaw dropped.

'How the devil did you get in here?' he said agitatedly to me and Joe.

'We rapped on the door, sir,' I calmly replied, 'and you told us to come in.'

Forbes jumped up, his monocle swung like a frightened pendulum in front of his sea island cotton shirt, then came to rest above his belt. I looked at the neat blue bow tie with the white polka dots, below his long, veiny, loose-fleshed neck, and I felt a little surprised that the bow tie re-mained steady, unmoved.

Mr Forbes went to the office door, yanked it open. He looked up and down the corridor, 'Cunningham! I say, Cunningham! Where the devil is this constable?' He went down the corridor in search of the constable. Probably to order the policeman to eject the two intruders.

I stepped quickly to the desk, and leaning my head over, read from the open file which Forbes was studying when Pittance and I came in:

Dear Mr Administrata,

We going to have a rally next publick haliday and we the members of the Hiroona Trades and Manual Workers Labour Union asking you to let us use the Pavilion at Victoria Park for refreshment boots thanking you in antecepshian.

I am,
Yours sincerely
Sonia Mole
Secretary Union of Trades and Labour Manual Union!

O God!

I flipped over the page, and read rapidly:

Your Honour,

The foregoing letter from the so-called Trades and Manual Workers Union reflects the mentality of the . . . .

I flipped back the page, did a quick jump back to my place near Joe, and suddenly became absorbed in a painting of the Royal Family on the wall just behind the Administrator's desk. Mr Forbes stamped into the room. He stood, hands akimbo, and looked us up and down like a cook wondering how two cockroaches managed to get into her callaloo soup.

'Have you an appointment?'

'No, sir,' I said.

'Well, you had better arrange one with my secretary. I can't see you now. I am busy.' He glanced dismissingly at the door. Joe Pittance quietly lowered himself to one of the two chairs in the office. His dirty canvas shoes and denim overalls looked incongruous there.

'Look here, sah,' Joe spoke softly to the Administrator, 'I suppose you know dat dere was a riot here on dis island on de twenty-first of Actober nineteen t'irty-six. Dat was before your time. England call' home de Administrata after dat riat. You want annudder riat?'

Mr Forbes pulled in his neck. His hands dropped from akimbo. The back of his hands had little whitish-brown spots. I couldn't tell whether the sweat on the two bald areas below his receding hair was due to his recent exertions up and down the corridor, or whether it was due to Joe's mentioning riots. He glanced beyond the open door, this time obviously looking for P.C. 43 Cunningham. I went to the door and shut it; then I returned and sat on the other chair.

Forbes went to the telephone on the wall, turned the handle and said into the funnel, 'Give me the Chief of Police's desk at Police Headquarters.' He stood, waiting, the black wooden earpiece jammed against his ear.

Joe Pittance chuckled and said, as if to himself, 'De Chief of Police always go to lunch at ten past twelve, and de Deputy, Comrade Robbins, take over.'

Forbes hung up the earpiece, turned, and stared at Joe.

'What did you say just now?'

'I say,' said Joe, 'dat dere was a riat on dis island on de twenty-first of Actober, nineteen . . . .'

'What do both of you want, anyway?'

I took over from there.

'Mr Forbes,' I said, 'Comrade Pittance and I represent the Hiroona Waterfront Estate and Manual Workers Union. As Comrade Pittance has remarked, I don't think you want another riot . . . .'

'The devil take you and your riot. You are wasting my time. What do both of you want, I say?'

'We want a favourable reply to our letter of nearly a month ago, asking for your permission to use the pavilion in Victoria Park for a refreshment booth on the first Monday in May next, the date of our rally.'

Mr Forbes went around the side of his desk and sat down. The open file with Sonia's letter was before him. He looked down on the file, and remained still for a long time, appearing to be reading the letter. He turned over the page, and appeared to read the adverse comments of his secretary on Sonia's letter. Then he looked up at me and said,

'I take it that you are Mr Mole, the man who organizes strikes on the island.'

'No,' I said, 'the man who represents ten thousand hardworking inhabitants of this island. Ten thousand people by whose labour this island is maintained. Ten thousand people who plough and hoe and plant and dig and reap, in order that the planters may sell, export and grow rich; and in order that this island may earn money to pay you and keep you in Government House, free of rent.'

Mr Forbes made an impatient gesture with his hand. He said, 'My secretary will send you a reply tomorrow.'

'Not so, sah,' said Joe. 'Your Highness can write, just like yo' secretary can write. We want de reply now, please. De rally is just around de carner. Ain't no time to waste. Please write de reply, an done wid it.'

'That would be your quickest way of getting rid of us,' I added.

The Administrator cogitated for a long moment, then he took a piece of paper from a drawer in his desk and began to write.

A few minutes after, when Joe and I got up, I said to Mr Forbes, as I pushed his written reply in my jacket pocket, 'You are the supreme chief of this island. You are a man of Peace; you don't want any more strikes or riots on this island. So please instruct your white Chief of Police to send us a reasonable reply to our letter in which we asked permission to use our own streets which we are paying taxes for, to do our rally procession, on the first Monday next month.'

Joe and I moved to the door. The Administrator kept his seat. He was still glaring at us when Joe opened the door and I gave a parting glance over my shoulder. P.C. 43 Cunningham was standing at attention just outside the door. We exchanged winks and grins. As Joe and I walked down the corridor, Mr Forbes came out of his office.

'Where the devil have you been?' he said to Cunningham.

Joe and I were out of earshot when Cunningham replied; but Joe said, 'Bass, you will have to give Cunny a good job when you take over de Gover'ment. Forbes an' de Chief of Police will sack him because he help us today.'

'They can't sack him,' I said, and dropped the subject.

'By the way,' I said after a while, 'in the Administrator's office just now you referred to Inspector Robbins the Deputy Chief of Police as 'Comrade' Robbins. Is he a secret member of the union?'

'Could be,' said Joe evasively.

11

ONLY a few months now stood between me and complete victory; and during those months, I worked as I never worked before. First came the rally, then the general election. The rally was a sort of debut of the union. And what a debut!

I had hired seventeen trucks. Ten of them rushed back and forth, bringing union members from the Central and Windward districts to their meeting place at Merry Vale Pasture, one mile from Kingsland. The other seven trucks brought members from the Leeward districts to Victoria Park in Kingsland. In Victoria Park, the Leeward districts sorted themselves out in area Branches — the Belvedere village branch, the Vermont Branch, the Moorne district branch and so on. These were joined by the Kingsland Branch. The crowd, some five thousand, then formed up, procession style, four abreast, and prepared to march through Kingsland to Merry Vale pasture to join the Central and Windward branches.

The sun was at the eight o'clock point in a flawless Caribbean sky.

I rushed about the park, fixing this, adjusting that, shouting orders: 'Hold that banner up higher . . . Comrade Farrel, let your group move back a bit, their banners are crowding the Sandy Point group's banners too much . . . Comrade Southwall, you're in charge of the four steel band orchestras. Get them into place while I go and test the microphone on the pavilion gallery . . . Now where in Hell is Comrade Fatylin Adams — O yes, there he is. Hey, Comrade Adams, go back to your group and stay with it; they having a little disorder down there . . . Now, let me see . . . Oh, Comrade Young! Tell the Management Committee members to go to the head of the procession. I am coming to give the order to march in a few minutes . . . They making too much noise in that corner down there . . . Go tell them keep quiet; we nearly ready to march . . . '

I looked around for my wife Sonia who, like other members of the Committee, was busily moving up and down, helping to get things in order. Not seeing her, I shouted across a section of the park,

'Comrade Mole! Where is she at all? Com . . . '

'Look me here, Comrade Mole,' Sonia called back as she quickly emerged from a tangle of banners and placards.

'Get all members of the Committee together in front of the procession, and tell them to remain there till I come. And keep that section across there quiet, for God's sake . . . Tell that man with the placard, 'WE WANT A NEW DEAL' to hold it up higher.'

I turned, trot-walked to the pavilion, ran up the steps to the gallery and grabbed the microphone.

'Comrades,' I boomed, 'you ready to march?'

'Yeahse! Yeahse!'

The park was all sound and colour — khaki, cheap cotton frocks; red, blue, green, white banners; placards; 'AWAKE HIROONA!'; 'DOWN WITH THE ADMINISTRATOR'; 'WE TIRED WITH MUD HUTS'; 'FORBES MUST GO!'; 'WE SPIT ON IMPERIALISM'; 'OUR GOAL IS MOLE' — and so on and so forth. Steel bands tentatively ping-ponged like orchestras tuning up, their metallic notes co-mingling with the lively babel.

'Comrades! Comrades! Too much noise! Please! Comrade Marksman, your group sagging out of line . . . . Now . . . . quiet please! . . . . That's better. Now, listen carefully. We marching from here, straight up Kingsland Main Street, right through town, straight up Happy Hill. Then over the hill, down Merry Vale Hill, through Merry Vale village straight on to Merry Vale pasture. There we will join our comrades from the Central and Windward districts. We will then rest a while, have a little jump-up dance and some light refreshment provided for you on the pasture. Then the Central and Windward districts will march back with us right back here in this park. Then I and a few comrades will address you from this gallery here. Then we will have our feast. You understand?'

'Yeahse! Yeahse!' *Ping-pong. Ping-pong. Boom. Bong!* said the steel bands.

'Comrade Southwall, please quiet those steelbands . . . . Fine. Now one last word, comrades: I notice that some of you seem to be having trouble with your shoes. If you don't feel comfortable in shoes, take them off now, so you can march at ease.

My words had a similar effect to that of a spitting machinegun trained on a crowd of people. Almost the entire assembly dropped to the ground and began to fumble with their footwear. When they got up again, some had their shoes strung across their forearms; some tied the laces together and hung the shoes around their necks. Some of the men had their shoes sticking awkwardly out of the side or hip pockets of their trousers. Even some of the members of the Committees of Management took advantage of this opportunity, to revert to type.

'O.K., comrades,' I said at last. 'Now we ready. You know the words of the song we going to march with. The steel bands will play the tune and the chorus right through first. While they doing this I will hurry down from this gallery here and get in front of the procession. And when you see me raise this sword I have in my hand here, then you start to sing and we march off. You understand?'

'Yeahse! Yeahse!'

As I ran down the steps of the pavilion to take my place at the head of the throng, I felt my heart strangely warmed. My entire being thrilled to the scene in front of me. *Could it be that I, Jerry Mole, son of an unknown — or at least uncertain — father; Jerry Mole, sacked from job after job for laziness, insubordination and incompetence; Jerry Mole the drifter, the bum — could it be that this same Jerry Mole was now striding down the fairway of political power?* I thought of my mother. *I knew who she was. She was not, like my father, the unknown quantity X. She was Christine Mole, the obscure, peasant woman who had given me her surname because she had no other surname to give me.* I didn't have to think about her *in vacuo,* as I thought of my 'father'. She was an identifiable person living in Chateaubelair, a remote fishing village, in a tidy little two-room cottage; broken in health at sixty-nine; kept alive by the regular remittances from her daughter Myra Mole who was married and working somewhere in the Dutch island, Curacao.

About my father I could only speculate. Of one thing about him I was fairly certain, however, he could not possibly be a jet black negro like my mother. If he had been, I would not have had this fairish skin, straightish hair and thin nose with retroussé nostrils.

I shall have more to say about my mother and my half sister Myra later in this narrative; but now, I am moving rapidly down through Victoria Park; down the long lines of streamers and banners and placards and enthusiastic unionists eager to begin their confrontation of the Hiroona *status quo.*

Policemen saunter in front of the crowd of onlookers. Steel bands are playing the rousing tune of the song we are to march with, and several people in the lines begin to sing before they should. I put up my hand, signalling them to hold their singing until I get to the head of the lines.

I am wearing a khaki cork hat, a red necktie, khaki bush jacket, shirt and khaki shorts, blue puttees above new shiny boots. A broad ribbon of red cotton cloth is draped diagonally on my torso like a Sam Browne. A long wooden sword dangles at my side; when I forget to control it with my right hand it gets in my way. My red pocket handkerchief is in constant use, drying my sweating face and neck.

I arrive at the head of the lines. I unbutton my sword, tie my red handkerchief to the point of it, raise the sword above my head and shout,

'FOR . . . WUD!' I lower my sword and point it smartly forward. We move off. The steel bands hit *fortissimo,* and five thousand voices take up the road song . . . .

> See the mighty hosts advancing
> Jerry leading on —
> Hold the fort, for I am coming,
> Jerry signals still.
> Wave the answer back, Hiroona,
> By Mole's help we will.

We had to change some of the original words of this 'ode' a bit, to suit our purpose. The changes resulted in bad theology but good politics — which is usually the case, anyway.

Commenting on this, the *Hiroona Weekly* (the only newspaper on the island), said:

> The pathetic adaptation of the words of a well-known Sankey hymn became in the hands of Mr Mole and his followers, a compost of inadvertently apt personification, blasphemy and confusion. In the first verse, 'Jerry' is substituted for 'Satan'. In the refrain, 'Jerry' is substituted for 'Jesus'. The resultant confusion — like the absurd costume of Mole himself — is a reflection of the policies and politics of Mole Company — — — Limited!

The *Weekly's* only comment on the other aspects of the rally was,

> Shoes around necks. Shoes sticking out of hip and side pockets, or carried in hands! Good God! And these are the would-be rulers of this country! God help us!

Of course, all this left me unmoved. The *Hiroona Weekly* always thought and wrote in terms of exclamation marks. The *Weekly* was easily astonished; the only 'ideas' it could express were astonishment and indignation. What wasn't astonishing was not worth reporting. So it did not report that the rally was the most significant event in the political history of Hiroona, up to that time. It did not realize that the rally was the first outward and visible sign that the upper and middle classes were being seriously challenged. The *Weekly* didn't see history in the rally, it saw only impudence.

Its Editor, Paul Darcy, six foot three, was long of body, short of nous. But what he lacked in intellect he made up in opinions. Like many an Englishman before him, Darcy had come from England to Hiroona with a 'sense of mission'. The local planters could not find a Hiroonian who was Tory enough to run their little Merton Street newspaper in a manner acceptable to Establishment ideas. So they had sent for Darcy who, judging from the quality of his journalistic output in the planters' *Hiroona Weekly*, must have been a Fleet Street dropout. Nevertheless, Paul had done fairly well during the five or six years he had lived on the island. With his editorial ploy, he had combined — with the planters' cooperation — efforts at a little planting himself, leasing lands and cultivating cotton or arrowroot. Success and his good standing with the planters and the Government had not only increased his confidence as a self-styled pundit, but had also revealed a tendency in him to think that he knew more about what was good for Hiroona than the most locally knowledgeable native of the island. As one walked past his one-door printery on Merton Street, one frequently saw him pouring points of view into the ears of people who either went to him on business or just dropped around for a chat.

Darcy usually held court on the pavement, just outside his printery door. In one hand he always grasped a sheet of paper and a pencil; and, probably as a further distinguishing mark of his profession, he invariably kept another pencil stuck behind his ear. His favourite speaking gesture was palms up, shoulders slightly hunched. A thin growth of white hair skirted the sides and back of his head, the remaining dome-like infertile area looked polished. His eye-brows were thick, bushy, graying. His spectacles were the rimless square-lens type, on a straight, largish nose.

I was passing by his place one morning, about two weeks after the rally when a member of his small audience hailed me: 'Hey, Mole; a word with you.'

I stood and looked across the street. Two men were standing with Darcy on the pavement, just outside Darcy's printery. The three of them were dressed in lounge suits. Two shiny Hillman cars were parked close to the pavement.

I crossed the street and stood on the pavement, on the edge of the group. Through the open door, I could see the wooden partition which partly separated Darcy's printery from his office. Two or three boys in the printery were standing before what looked like large slanting trays with small, square pigeon holes. The boys were distributing type into the squares. The wooden partition was decorated with posters, bits of printed paper, and what appeared to be cards made and printed in the printery.

'Yes, Mr Seton,' I said. 'You called me, didn't you?'

'That's right,' Seton replied. 'You put on a hell of a show the other day. I mean your rally. How the hell you manage to get all those people together?'

'I just pressed a button,' I replied.

'You'd better control your button-pressing, or you'll run into serious trouble.' Darcy muttered this, tight-lipped, without looking at me.

Seton turned to me, smiled and said, 'Myself, Darcy, and Mr Johnson here were just discussing your rally when we saw you passing. Tell me, Mr Mole, what do you and this — erm — union hope to achieve?'

'Well, you never know,' I said.

Darcy spread his hands, palms up, hunched his shoulders and said, 'What can a bunch of ignorant rowdies with their boots in their pockets hope to achieve, except confusion, trouble?'

'So far, we've made no trouble, Mr Darcy,' I said.

'No trouble?' Darcy exclaimed. 'What do you call that strike you all caused in the Sugar Belt a few months ago?'

'We don't boast about our victories, Mr Darcy,' I said.

Darcy stared at me fiercely. His eyes were pinpoints behind his rimless glasses.

'Victory!' he spat, 'My God!'

Seton said, 'Mole, you're too damn cool. I am not against you and your people, but you'd better watch out. You making a hell of a lot of trouble. And you're offending too many people.'

'I wasn't aware that I was causing any trouble, Mr Seton. At least, that is not my intention.'

Darcy took me up: 'You weren't aware that you are causing trouble? What about the new, irresponsible doctrines you and the leaders of your union are preaching?'

I looked at my three assailants, and I knew from what they had said, and how they said it, that they were frightened men. I could see that my efforts so far had jolted them out of the good old complacency. Here were three high priests of Hiroona plutocracy. Powerful men in the island's scheme of things. One of them — Seton — a wealthy attorney, representing the interests of Hiroona big business. Another — Peter Johnson — the owner of the Annadale, Palmyra, and Barrymore estates and the adjoining village settlements. The third man was their tool, yes, but a member of the *status quo*, nevertheless. And they were scared. A year ago, these men would not have even deigned to notice me, never mind talk to me. My work was having a telling effect. I was succeeding.

'You refer to *leaders* of my union,' I said. 'There is only *one* leader of the union — Jerry Mole. And the doctrines I preach may be new, but not irresponsible.' I grinned, and this seemed to make Darcy more angry.

'You're a barefaced liar,' he said. 'Everybody throughout the length and breadth of this island knows that you have been planting disruptive ideas in your people's minds. Thousands of people listened to your demagogic speech at the close of your rally on Victoria Park. One of my reporters was there. Your address was nothing but a rehash of your habitual fierce condemnation of people who own anything; and a Hitlerish shrieking of wild ideas: more wages for less work; maids must be rude to their mistresses if they don't like the orders their mistresses issue to them; down with this, down with that; to hell with the British Government whose money supports the island; the Administrator must go; the rabble must rule the country. Doctrines like these were never thought of on this peaceful island before.'

'Peaceful, Mr Darcy? Hiroona was never peaceful; she was only sleeping. It is time she wake up, for the morning has come. My union is the morning.'

'Big-shot words and arrant nonsense, Mole,' growled Seton. 'You talk like the old Bible prophet. You should go around wearing a long beard. But let me tell you this: you're misleading your people; you'll soon force the estates to fire the workers right and left for rudeness and laziness. With your doctrines, production on the island must fall heavily while the cost of production rises high.'

'Do you appreciate what such a situation would mean to the cost of living on the island?' interjected Johnson in his slow, rumbling drawl. 'Have you ever studied economics, Mr Mole?'

'Studied hell!' exclaimed Darcy. 'These self-styled politicians only study tricks. They make a living by deceiving people and lining their own pockets. I have proof of that. And they soon prove to be liabilities rather than assets to their country.'

'You sound like a superannuated homespun editor I once read about somewhere, Mr Darcy,' I said, and burst out laughing.

Pleased at having had the last laugh, I was moving off. Darcy stopped me.

Shaking his index finger at me, he spluttered, 'I hope you do bear in mind what Mr Seton just told you — you're offending too many people.'

'Good God, Mr Darcy, you're back on that again?'

He ignored my question and continued, 'I want you to bear something else in mind, too: my family is one of the victims of your new, disruptive doctrines. We had a maid. A sweet little girl. This girl had been working with us for five years. Since this union business started, the girl suddenly got cheeky and bumptious. A week ago, my wife threw a party, entertaining a few friends. She told the girl that she would have to remain to serve, and to wash up after the party. This was a thing she had done willingly during the five years she was with us. To our astonishment, the girl told my wife she wasn't working after seven o'clock. My wife paid her off and sent her packing. We have not engaged a servant since. I demeaned myself by going to the girl begging her — almost on my knees — to come back, because she was good. But she refused. Several families are complaining about the sudden change in the attitude of domestic servants. You have disrupted my family, and people don't forget things like that.'

Darcy's story was a confession as well as a complaint. I felt certain that he had lost more than a maid.

I couldn't suppress a broad, happy smile as I said: 'You say I disrupted your family when your maid left you. Was the maid your family, Mr Darcy? You said that you begged her to return, because she was good. Good at what, Mr Darcy?'

Seton burst out laughing. Johnson smiled. Darcy reddened like a boiled lobster.

I continued to look at Darcy as if expecting an answer. The happy grin on my face was just about to explode into a laugh when Darcy hissed:

'You filthy-minded vagabond of a nigger. Mark my word, your confounded impertinence will be short-lived. I am a newspaper editor. I get reports. I know things. And I know that months ago you drew a large sum of money — ninety-six dollars, to be exact — from the Mount Horeb Factory Management, which was due an idiot boy called Penny Farthing, as compensation for the loss of his fingers. I know that this money was paid by cheque. I know that up to now, that boy has received only one single dollar out of it! And you are supposed to be the champion of the 'poor and down-trodden'. A damn good-for-nothing hypocrite. That's what you are. A thief, robbing your own people. Robbing even idiots. But bear this in mind, the whole story is in my Newspaper's files, waiting. And you know what is waiting there, too? — the story of how, at one of your meetings, your own second-in-command, a man called Pittance, accused you of stealing the idiot's money. And your only defence was a resort to your usual cover — bluster. Yes, Mr Champion Mole, the whole story is there' — he jabbed a finger towards the door of his printery — 'in there waiting. Now put that in your filthy political pipe, and smoke it.'

He turned and stepped into his office. Seton and Johnson got into their cars and drove off. I walked away slowly, pensively, without glancing at the small crowd that stood in the street nearby, listening.

12

I T was not fear of Darcy's threatened *exposé* that made my head fuzzy and my feet heavy, as I walked away. In the West Indies of the fifties and early sixties, a politician had little to fear from an *exposé*. He took these in his stride. The vast majority of his supporters was the masses whom he not only led but also manipulated. And West Indian masses are very tolerant of the foibles of their political leaders. A misdemeanour that would bring the career of an English politician crashing about his ears would only win for his West Indian counterpart the *cliché* compliment 'shrewd', or the tolerant, salacious remark, 'he good fo' heself'.

Knowing all this, I was not perturbed over Darcy's threat to expose my foul play with Penny Farthing's money, which I had no intention of handing over, anyway. Hadn't I worked for it? What disturbed me was the sudden realization that delicate union business had somehow leaked out to my enemies, and that my humiliating rebuke by Joe Pittance was also known to outsiders. Pittance must pay for this. He was an obvious threat to my leadership, to my political career. That was more than sufficient reason for having him 'removed'.

I had already decided that Ben Davis would be my hatchetman when the time came to remove Pittance, but I realized that this project would require long and very careful preparation. With Darcy's revelation in mind, I decided that the time had now come for me to seriously begin cultivating Ben for this job.

First of all I had to try to detach Ben from Pittance and the other stevedores; to win him completely over to myself, and make sure that he remained with me. I had little doubt that this could be done, with a bit of flattery and the bestowal of some big favour which would pleasantly surprise Ben and deepen his loyalty to me, through a sense of indebtedness. There was no other suitable person I could trust for this job, and misplaced confidence in a matter like this would be embarrassing.

I had all this in mind as I talked with Ben on the wharf one day during his lunch hour. It was a week after my encounter with Darcy.

There were two ships in the harbour, and the stevedores had been loading and unloading cargo since six o'clock that morning. It was now noon, and the men had knocked off for lunch. Some of them ate at

Haddaway's Eatery on Bay Street, where they paid fifty-two cents for an enamel plate of rice, vegetables and stew-meat or salt fish. Some ate on the wharf, sitting on cargo in assorted spots, while their women who had cooked and brought the lunch sat or stood near to them, talking quietly.

Traffic on the wharf had stopped. There were only the few stevedores and their women; and even these were not very much in evidence, as they were hidden or partly hidden behind stacks of galvanize sheets, packing cases, bags of flour, heaps of reinforcement steel, lumber, bags of arrowroot starch, crates of things, and other items of cargo.

The two ships lay steady alongside the wharf, some of their passengers sunning themselves on their decks. A few sloops and a schooner lay in the harbour, dozing quietly.

Ben Davis was sitting on the wharf, his back supported by a pile of lumber which also gave him shade from the noonday sun. A basket covered with a white cloth was close beside him. His concubine had brought his lunch, left it with him and had gone to the Bay Street fish market 'To look fo' fish fo' supper'.

'Hello, Ben,' I said.

'Good day, Bass. You lookin' fo' Pittance, I suppose.'

'No, no, Ben, I am not looking for Pittance. I know that he wouldn't be here now. He eats at Haddaway's Eatery, doesn't he?' I carefully stepped over some spools of barbed wire, jumped over a few sacks of flour and sat down near to Ben. I took off my felt hat, unbuttoned my khaki shirt and fanned myself with my hat. Ben removed a plate of food from the basket. He put the plate on the ground, then he took from the basket a large mug of 'William'. I watched the bits of ice floating on the black mixture of syrup, water and lime, and I wondered why West Indians drank beer, when 'William' was such a thirst-quencher and strengthener. Ben took a swig from the mug, placed the mug on the ground, took up his plate and began to eat.

'Excuse me, Bass.'

'O.K. Ben. Go ahead. It's a bit hot today, eh?'

'Yes, Bass, but it cool near dis pile o' lumber.'

He scooped a spoonful of rice, dasheen, jackfish and gravy from his plate, chewed energetically, rested the spoon on the side of the plate, pulled a few jackfish bones from his mouth, flung them away, wiped his fingers on the front of his dungaree shirt and dipped up another spoonful.

'How the election campaign goin', Bass?'

'Damn good. We held a meeting at Greggs last night. On the cricket ground. You couldn't stick a pin, for the crowd.'

'Sarry Ah couldn't come, Bass. We work late last night. Lot o' cargo. But Ah heard 'bout de meetin' dis marnin'. Some fellers bin' tarking 'bout it. Dey say it was wanderful. Ah hear dat de crowd lift you up on dere shoulder after de meetin'. Dey say you tark like fire.'

I chuckled. 'We've got Hiroona in the bag, Ben, come the election. You know, Ben, I been thinking. Suppose when we take over the Government, I were to offer you a job as a cabinet minister in the Government, how would you feel about that?'

Ben stretched out his legs before him, pressed his back against the pile of lumber and laughed. He took a long draught of 'William' from the mug, wiped his mouth on his sleeve and said, 'Bass, t'ings like dat ain't fo' me. I is a workin' man, makin' a honest living. I ain't high. I ain't smart. If you want a man fo' a Government minister, Pittance is de man. He smart. He bright. And Bass,' he lowered his voice to a confidential rumble, 'for a job like dat you want a man dat can read and write. Me can't read. Me can't write.' He laughed, embarrassed.

'Ben,' I said, 'forget the question of reading and writing. There is nothing in the law to prevent a down-right illiterate person from voting, or from running for election, or from being appointed a cabinet minister if he is elected. All you need be able to do is scratch something that looks like a name; and any illiterate adult can do that with a few hours' practice, if he really want to.'

'Is dat de trute, Bass, so help yo' God?'

'So help me God. Look, not one of the statutory qualifications for the Adult Suffrage or for a ministerial appointment specifies any measure of literacy. Read the law for yourself. There is nothing to prevent us putting up a candidate as dumb as hell; and he can win, and then there is no law to prevent us appointing him or her to a ministry, and making him responsible for a portfolio which he can't even read the first word of.'

'But, Bass, when a man like dat get up to tark in de high Council of Government, how de hell he gwine to manage?'

'Let me tell you something. In Trinidad, many years ago, they had two Honourable Members of the Government who couldn't read and write. One was a rich man, and one was a wrestler. In one of the Windward islands, they have a woman who is a cabinet minister. They say she can't even read three-letter words. In fact, in every one of the West Indian islands, Ben — except Barbados — popular government or universal adult suffrage as they call it, brought people into the government with *your* level of literacy, or a level not far from yours. Of course, things will im-prove. As the West Indies grow up politically, even the masses will become more discriminating in choosing their leaders and representatives. But until that time comes, this is our chance. The wonderful thing about present West Indian democracy is that it is government by Tom, Dick and Jerry.'

Ben and I laughed, and Ben took another swig of 'William' to wash down a mouthful of rice. Then he said, 'Bass, Ah see yo' point, but Ah ain't keen.'

'Look here, Ben. Let me tell you something between us. In a country with a high percentage of illiteracy or semi-literacy, the democratic idea of one vote for one man is bull shit; but for people like you and me it is good shit, because it gives us the kind of opportunity which no other kind of shit can give us. It gives us power over people who used to consider themselves better than you and me. It rectifies in our favour the old system which worked in favour of the upper-better-richer class who formerly monopolised the franchise and used it against us. We can now use it against them. It puts us in the way of good money, and a steady job in which you can order the civil servants to do all the reading and writing for you. So forget about your not being able to read and write. You understand?'

'Me and de rest boys prefer you to choose Pittance fo' de job, Bass. He got de goods, and all de stevedores an' de Committee members like and respeck Pittance. Try Pittance, Bass; not me.'

'Oh, damn Pittance!' I shouted out before I could control my tongue. Ben looked sharply at me, astonishment and disapproval in his glance. I changed my pitch quickly.

'Pittance is all right,' I said, 'but he can't read and write either.'

'I know dat, Bass; but you said dat doesn't matter.'

'Look here, Ben; I am offering you the biggest chance you ever had or will ever have in this world — the chance of being a cabinet minister in my Government, when I take over the island. Wait. Don't interrupt me. Give me a break. You say you want to be able to read and write.'

'I didn't say so, Bass. All Ah say is Ah ain't want de jab.'

'Don't be modest man. I have a surprise for you. Listen. All the writing you need to do is to sign your name — or something that looks like a name. And all the reading you need is the short little oath just before you take office as a minister. Now I can arrange for somebody to teach you to sign your name; and teach you the oath, word for word, so you can learn it and recite it; so the Administrator and the crowd of people in the Legislative Council Chamber will think you can read. I know somebody who would be willing to teach you these two simple things — signing your name and memorising the oath. O.K.?'

'Who is this somebody, Bass?'

'Comrade Naomi Sampson. She used to be a pupil teacher in the old days. She will teach you good and willingly. O.K.?'

'As you say, Bass; but it ain't look right to me.'

'Ben, man, you needn't look so troubled. I am offering you the biggest chance in your whole life. The kind o' luck some people only dream about. And you have me to lean on and back you up. Have no fear, Ben man. You will do fine, and surprise everybody. Believe me. I will go and see Comrade Sampson tonight, and arrange everything. Depend on me.'

He nodded. I got up, and brushed the seat of my pants, preparing to leave.

'Now just one thing more, Ben. This is very important. Do not breathe a word to a single soul about this. You understand.'

He nodded, 'O.K. Bass.'

13

As I walked away from Ben, I looked back and waved to him, but he was not looking towards me. He was gazing into the mug of his unfinished 'William', his hand under his massive jaw.

I walked off the wharf and up Bay Street. It was nearly one o'clock, and the street traffic was building up again — government officials, business men, shop clerks, returning from lunch to their work. On the mountains and hills round about Kingsland, dark gray clouds slowly piled up. Pedestrians glanced up at the blackening mass, and quickened their steps to reach cover before the shower, which would cool the heat and soften the day, descended.

It began to rain. It started up in the hills and came striding down to town. One could see the rain actually walking, like a grey giant curtain, high like the heavens, broad like the world, hurrying from the hills as if to keep an appointment in Kingsland. It struck the streets, at first like heavy footfalls of huge drops, then as a deluge. Parasols went up here and there; windscreen wipers began their metronomic arc dance; the smell of asphalt and steam rose from the street.

Cars and rain now monopolised the street. Pedestrians walked or stood sheltering on the covered pavement immediately in front of the line of shops, restaurants, business offices, warehouses facing the street and the open bayfront. The pedestrians shared the pavement with vociferating refreshment vendors who sat on low boxes in front of their stalls plying their trade.

I hurried to the pavement for shelter, and stood there waiting for the rain to stop. People passed up and down the pavement, some stepping into the shops; some continued on their way, only to stop sooner or later, and wait, while the rain poured.

As I glanced up and down the pavement, quietly surveying the scene, my roving eyes came to rest on a young man whom I recognized as P.C. 43 Cunningham, the police constable who had made it possible for me and Joe Pittance to enter Administrator Forbes' office and force permission from him to use the pavilion on Victoria Park as a refreshment booth during our rally. Cunningham was standing a few yards away from where I was. He was in mufti — gray flannel trousers and white open-neck shirt. He seemed to be looking for someone. I hoped not me. The man was Joe Pittance's friend, and I did not want to see Pittance or any friend of his.

I turned and walked down the pavement, increasing the distance between me and Cunningham, and stood behind a group of people who were chatting as they sheltered from the rain. But when I glanced again in Cunningham's direction, he was walking briskly towards me. Escape was no longer possible. Cunningham greeted me:

'Hello, Mr Mole; I've caught you at last. Been trying to contact you for the past few days.' His perfect teeth flashed in a bright smile. He looked clean. His handsome black face and large eyes were evidently glad to see me. He obviously regarded me as a comrade, or perhaps as a sort of accomplice.

'I expect you know that the election is only a few months away,' I said, 'I've been very busy. Sometimes I go out to the country districts in the morning, and I don't get back to town till late at night. I have no time for private conversations.'

My coldness must have surprised and shocked him. He could hardly have expected this aloofness from a person to whom he had done a favour so big as to be unforgettable. The smile left his face. He gazed thoughtfully down on the pavement, and stroked the back of his head with his hand.

'Oh, I see,' he said. 'I see.'

After a short embarrassing silence, I said, 'Well, what did you want to contact me about?'

He looked down at me for a long moment; then he said, 'Sorry. It's nothing.' He walked away.

I felt no compunction over my unkind treatment of Cunningham. He was Pittance's friend, and therefore my enemy. That settled it. Or so I thought.

I turned my mind to speculating on how Naomi Sampson would react to my request that she teach Ben Davis to sign his name and recite the oath. I smiled as I tried to imagine Ben holding a pen, for the first time in his life, while Naomi, like an old, rectifying school marm, peered anxiously over his broad, thick shoulders, making hortatory noises. *Relax, Comrade Davis. Don't hold the pen so tight; you are squeezing it too much. A fountain pen is not a toothpaste tube; you can't squeeze out the ink, Comrade . . . . . No, no, Comrade Davis; you have pressed* too *hard on the paper that's why you punctured it. Oh dear . . . . . Oh dear . . . . . . My, My, your hand is so heavy! And do not hunch up your shoulders like that; you are not heaving cargo, Comrade. You are only writing. Re . . lax . . . Now try again . . . . . That's better — 'B' — that's the first letter. Then you do a loop for the 'e' — like this . . . . . . Pity you have such a long name — Benjamin. You will need a few weeks to be able to write, but it can be done. Others have done it, so why can't you? Now, pen in hand again . . . . So . . . .*

It was still raining, but the sun was trying to come out again. Street traffic had dwindled to an occasional taxi in search of fares. Two little boys, wearing only torn khaki shorts, pranced-marched down the street, bathing in the rain and tunelessly singing at the top of their voices,

Rain are come
Sun are shine
Devil an' his wife are fight
Fo' piece o' ham bone.

Everybody on the pavement looked at them, and some smiled, envying them. Further down the street, the two urchins suddenly changed their game. They chased each other, round and round, then streaked off across the street, on to the beach and sloshed into the sea where they continued to romp like two black dolphins.

Way down along the bay, the two ships alongside the wharf looked small, their outlines blurred behind a curtain of rain.

I went over in my mind some of the work I had to do during the months that lay ahead. The general election was three months off. I had already held crowded political meetings throughout the eleven constituencies into which the island was divided. Of course, I intended to contest the eleven seats, but I had not yet openly chosen any candidates, although I had made up my mind as to who they were going to be. It was now only a matter of announcing their names at a meeting of the Management Committee, and this meeting had already been arranged.

The rain diminished. Separate drops on roofs and on the asphalt became audible, and the gutters on the sides of the street gargled loudly with muddy water mixed with pebbles.

People moved off the pavement, leaving it to the vendors of black pudding, peanuts, muffins and fried fish, potato pudding wrapped in banana leaves.

I was about to step off the pavement and onto the street, when someone called my name. Even before I turned round I knew it was Charlotte. Everybody in Kingsland knew Charlotte Cain and her voice.

Charlotte never spoke. She shrieked. Her voice was superbly suited to her occupation.

'Comrade Mole!' Her voice stopped me in my tracks. I turned and walked down the pavement, and stood in front of her tray. The low stool or bench on which she was sitting was completely hidden by her large wide body and voluminous skirt. Her tray rested on a trestle table with castors.

'Charlotte, why the hell you so damn noisy?' I laughed.

'Noise is me line, Comrade Mole. God give me voice to make a livin' by.' And as if to give me a further unnecessary demonstration of her God-given voice, she lifted it another unconscionable decibel, 'Get yo' fresh muffins and salt fish cakes, everybody! Only a few left! Come an' get it! Come an' get aaate!'

I jammed my fingers in my ears, and this delighted Charlotte. Her lovely teeth flashed in a broad grin which lit up her fat round face.

'You ain't buy no muffin an' salt fish cake from me fo' months now, Comrade Mole. What happenin', you eatin' home dese days?'

'Well, you see, I bin very busy looking after union matters in the country, and campaigning for the elections.'

'Yes, Ah know. Ah only pullin' you leg. Ah hear things goin' good fo' de union an' de PPP. Very glad. Is time we take over de country an' run it.'

A little man further down the pavement looked up from his black-pudding stall. Wiping his hands on his apron, he called out, 'You right, Charlotte. Time we control t'ings in dis island. We got de men to do it. Right in Kingsland here we got Misser Mole, an' we got Pittance, nat to mention de men we got in de country districks.' He left his stall and came up to Charlotte's. 'Ah heard you knockin' de daylights outa de planters an' de Government,' he said to me conspiratorially, smiling and winking at Charlotte.

'Dat is true, Johnny,' said Charlotte to the entire pavement and street. 'We never had a greater speaker like Jerry Mole in dis island. He an' Joe Pittance open de people eyes since de union started. Dat man Joe Pittance is great. He ten foot tall.'

I suddenly felt sick. Why should everyone consider this man Joe Pittance such a wonder? Why all this support for Joe Pittance? Is he secretly working to become my rival? Are people beginning to regard him as my equal?

'Look here, Charlotte,' I said, 'You must excuse me. I got to run off. Plenty still to be done before elections.'

'Don't go yet,' shrieked Charlotte. 'Ah want to tell you dis: you owe me two dollars fo' muffin an' salt fish cake you truss from me long time, but Ah so please wid you, dat Ah decide to write off de whole debt. You don't owe me a cent. Hear?' She made a wide gesture with her fat arms. 'De whole o' Kingsland an' Johnny Baynes here witness — you don't owe me a cent. An' moreover, dis is yours.' She picked up two muffins and three fish cakes from her tray, dropped them in a small paper bag and handed the bag to me. I took it.

Johnny Baynes grinned at me. 'We is wid you, Misser Mole,' he said. 'All de way, to de end; we wid you an' Joe Pittance.'

'O.K., O.K., comrades,' I said, and hurried off.

14

'**Y**ou should rest tonight,' Sonia said, as she transferred a boiled jackfish from a steaming bowl to my plate of rice, cabbage, sweet potato and chunks of dasheen. Of late, she had been showing much solicitude about my health, worrying over the fact that I was neglecting my meals somewhat, and helping me at table when we ate together. I loved her all the more for her new attitude.

'Rest?' I said.

'Sure, rest. Every day fo' de last month, you out in de country, or you up an' down in Kingsland, fixin' election business. Every night you out till late. An' you ain't eatin' as you should.'

I laughed. 'Wonders never cease,' I said. 'Who would have thought it possible? — Jerry Mole working, and too hard! Aren't you pleased?'

'Yes, but you should rest sometimes.'

'You used to tell me that I should work sometimes. Nowadays, you tell me I should rest sometimes. Women are a puzzle.'

We laughed together.

'You stayin' in tonight?'

'Not tonight. Got to go out.'

'Where to?'

'To see Naomi Sampson.'

'Fo' what?'

'That reminds me,' I said. I got up from the table, went to my jacket which was hanging on a nail near the door, and took from one of the pockets the paper bag with the muffins and salt fish cakes.

'Charlotte gave me these today,' I said, as I emptied the paper bag on the table near my plate. 'We may as well eat them now before they get stale.'

'What you goin' to see Naomi Sampson about?'

'I want to see her about Ben.'

'Who Ben? You mean Ben Davis?'

'Yes.'

'What wrong wid Ben?' Briefly, I told Sonia about my plans, omitting, of course any reference to Joe Pittance.

'But why you want to make Ben cabinet minister for?' asked Sonia. 'Ah can understand you choosin' one of de waterfront men fo' dat jab; but not Ben.'

'Why not Ben?'

'Well, Ben ain't de type. He can't even read an' write. People will laugh at us.'

'If not Ben, who then?' I asked.

'Joe Pittance better than Ben.' She popped a salt fish cake in her mouth.

'Pittance can't read and write, either. I don't trust him, anyway. He is a Judas. You remember how he tried to expose me about the Penny Farthing money? I don't trust that man at all. Ben is my man. Naomi Sampson will teach him to sign his name and recite the short oath. That's all he needs.'

'You always sayin' you don't trust Pittance. Ah know he did try to expose you, but you over-ruled him, an' everybody done fo'get about de matter. Pittance fo'get about it, too. So why hold dat against him? He help you from de start of de union an' de Party. You yourself used to praise him before de strike an' de Penny Farthing matter. Now dat you nearly reach de top, you can't fling Pittance aside fo' Ben. It ain't right. Everybody will say you ungrateful.'

I stopped chewing, put down my spoon and gave Sonia a long, savage *et tu Brute* look. It hurt like hell to hear her supporting Joe Pittance against me. She had allied herself with Charlotte Cain and Johnny Baynes and all the waterfront crowd against me her husband, who should also be her hero, considering all the good I had done for her. The fact that her attitude was correct and her argument just, only exacerbated my resentment. Pittance had entered even my own house and stolen support.

Fuming, I stared at Sonia, but she was not paying much attention to me. She was wiping, with a piece of muffin, the remains of food and gravy from the plate. She put the bit of muffin in her mouth and said, chewing:

'Ben is only a rough man. He ain't suit cabinet minister. — — — An' dat policeman, P. C. 43 Cunningham, who did help you and Pittance to get into Mr Forbes office, they sack him because he help de union. People who help us, we got to consider dem.'

So that was what Cunningham wanted to tell me when he approached me on the pavement this morning — that he had been fired from the police force. Pittance had predicted it: 'Bass,' he had said, 'you will have to give Cunny a good job when you take over the Government. Forbes and the Chief of Police going to sack him because he help us today.'

Pittance always knew, always planned ahead of me. But this time he'll see who is the faster thinker; and when the time comes for me to announce my choice of ministers, *I shall confound him and Sonia,* I thought, *and all his other supporters with the unanswerable argument: Ben can sign his name and read the oath. Pittance can do neither. I am not having anybody on my cabinet who cannot even sign his name and read a simple oath. If Pittance were able to write his name and read the oath, he would have been the first man to be chosen as one of the ministers of Government.*

With this ace up my sleeve, I said to Sonia, almost pleasantly, 'O.K. We'll see how things work out.'

As she collected the used plates, dish and spoons to take them outside in the yard for washing up, Sonia asked, 'When you goin to hold de meeting of de committee to give dem de names of de candidates you intend to put forward?'

'Oh there is plenty of time for that. The election is three months away. At present we are holding meetings and doing house to house campaigning for the support of the Party generally. I am not naming any candidates until two months before Nomination Day.' *That, I said to myself, should give Ben sufficient time to learn to scratch the scrawls and pot hooks which would have to pass for his signature on the Nomination Form; and later, under the oath.*

I got up from the table, took my jacket off the nail, draped it over my arm, and left for Naomi Sampson's place.

15

KINGSLAND is a crescent, the horns of which enclose the wide Kingsland harbour. If you stood on the deck of a ship in the centre of the harbour, facing the town, you would have on your far right a low promontory — — — Lord Nelson's Point. Away on your left would be Fort George, rising six hundred and fifty feet above sea level. The Fort was named for the English King, George the Third who ruled the British Empire during his intermittent periods of sanity, from 1760 to 1820. From your ship's deck, you would not be able to see the big guns hiding behind the parapet of the fort; but they are there; their black, yawning muzzles still lurk behind the embrasures from which they roared and spat discomfiture on French, Spanish and Dutch naval vessels, in the days when great nations of the earth fought bloody battles over West Indian sugar, tobacco, spices and dirt. Between Lord Nelson's Point on your right and Fort George on your left, the town of Kingsland arcs, the tower of its big Georgian Anglican cathedral rising somewhere about the centre of the arc. The three main streets run parallel; rows of houses, shops, offices on both sides, except in the case of Bay Street with its wide pavement, its line of shops, hotels, restaurants and cheap 'eateries', facing the open harbour.

Just behind the town, St. Andrew mountain range stretches, the upper slopes of its four thousand feet covered with lush forest; the middle slopes with terraced cultivations. Below these, at the base of St. Andrew, is the district called Ottley's. Here, villas, suburban cottages and a few better-class peasant houses dot the scene. Naomi Sampson lived in one of these peasant houses — half an hour's walk or ten minutes' drive from Bottom Town, where I lived. Naomi lived alone. Many years ago, when she was very young, she had aspired to the teaching profession and had written the First and Second Years Statutory pupil teachers' examinations. But she failed twice at Second Year, and so was dropped in accordance with the Board of Education's 'Code of Regulations'. She had subsequently taken to seamstressing, and was making a modest but adequate living in this field, although she still thought and behaved like a schoolmarm.

I spent the ten minutes in the taxi gloating over the surprise I was preparing for Pittance and his supporters, and wondering how long Ben Davis would take to learn to sign his name.

As the taxi drew up in Naomi's yard, I saw her come to the window of her cottage. She stood looking at the taxi, and when I got out, Naomi cried, clapping her hands softly, 'My, My, who should it be, but Comrade Mole. Come in, comrade.'

'Hello, Comrade Sampson,' I called cheerfully, as I turned and paid the taximan his fifty-cent fare. The taxi drove away, and I entered Naomi's cottage.

I halted suddenly on the threshold, my jacket thrown over my shoulder, one hand holding on to the neck of the jacket, the other hand supporting my dropped jaw.

Joe Pittance had risen from a chair which was drawn up close to a small table in the centre of the tidy little room. An open exercise book and a fountain pen lay on the table, and from where I stood I could see that a page of the exercise book was covered, line after line, with blocks of crude characters reminiscent of a child's efforts to improve, through repetitive trial-and-error, his ability to write his name.

'Hello, Bass,' Pittance greeted me, smiling.

Naomi Sampson prattled as she patted the cushion of an upright chair: 'Sit here, comrade. You have walked right in on our little secret.'

She straightened up. Resting one hand on the back of the chair, she continued to explain, smiling brightly:

'For three weeks now, Comrade Pittance and I been trying a little experiment to give you a pleasant little surprise which we know will please you greatly.'

She reached for the exercise book on the table, stepped up close to me, and proudly exhibited page after page of the experiment.

'Now tell me,' she enthused, 'as one teacher to another. You were a teacher and so was I. Now tell me, am I not doing a fine job with Comrade Pittance, here? Now see here.' She flipped the leaves of the exercise book until she came to the first page. 'Here is where we began. I even wrote down the date. See it here. Second of August. Only three weeks ago; and yet, look at the great progress!'

I just stared at the page as Naomi gushed on.

'See here. These were his first scrawls. Look at that first "J" for Joseph, like a nervous drunken man, trying to draw a straight line.' She flipped pages. 'But look at the same Joseph here, just one week later, as firm as a rock. You can make it out easier than you can make out the signature of most of the office men in Kingsland. Now let us look at his surname. "B" for Bute. Did you know his name was Joseph Bute?'

I shook my head weakly, staring at the page. Said nothing.

'Everybody knows him as Joe Pittance, and I thought that was his name. Luckily, Bute is a short name, easy to write, but a capital "B" is a difficult letter to form. But see here, how manfully he struggled with it.'

I daren't look at Pittance, but I knew he was standing there, smiling at me with pride, and waiting for me to congratulate him. I didn't even touch the exercise book and after a time I ceased to hear what Naomi was saying. As I stared and nodded at the page of scrawls and scrapes and scratches, my mind kept spitting at Pittance. *You son of a bitch, you. You scheming son of a bitch.*

Aloud, I said to Naomi, 'But why would he want to take all this trouble to come here every night, as you said, just to practise writing "Joseph Bute" over and over, in an exercise book?'

'It is trouble well worth taking,' said Naomi, 'and Comrade Pittance — Oh, excuse me — Comrade Bute will gladly explain his reason to you. He said it would please you very much, but he didn't want to tell you too soon, because he wished to give you a very pleasant surprise.' She turned to Pittance and said, 'You want to explain your reasons to Comrade Mole now?'

'Well, is like dis, Bass: to be a member of de Government, when we take over, you got to be able to . . . .'

I cut him short. 'Look, we'd better go into this some other time. I just came up here to do some house-to-house campaigning in the district, and I dropped in to discuss a little matter with Comrade Sampson concerning the last rally. But I'd better you to go on with your experiment. It is getting late.' I turned to leave. Naomi Sampson said, as she rested the palm of one hand on a treadle sewing machine close by, as if for support:

'Oh, just a minute, Comrade. I suppose you heard that they sacked the young policeman Cunningham who helped us in our efforts to see Mr Forbes the Administrator.'

'No, I hadn't heard,' I flung over my shoulder and stepped into the yard.

As I stood in the lightless yard before moving slowly and thoughtfully away, I heard Naomi say, 'He seems very strange tonight. He is not at all himself. Must be these lots of meetings and electioneering getting him down. My God, he was sour!'

16

I headed back for Kingsland. Defeat, bafflement, jealousy and frustration had taken such possession of me, that anger couldn't shine through. My thoughts kept going round and round in a small circle, like a caged animal confused.

I sat on the bulging root of a mango tree by the side of the road, and tried to organise my thoughts while I waited for transport back to town.

What was to be done now? With every step I took, I found that Joe Pittance was one step ahead. With every person I approached, or who approached me, I was made to realise that Pittance was, wittingly or unwittingly, my rival for pride of place in the esteem of the electorate.

The man was disturbingly knowledgeable, damnably resourceful and influential. True, it was precisely these qualities in him that had paved the way of my present political success. And before he betrayed me in the Penny Farthing compensation issue, I believed that he was just an illiterate but faithful, loyal follower and an unambitious adviser of mine. His habit of addressing me as 'Boss' confirmed this belief. But now, it was abundantly clear that the man had a mind of his own. This was disquieting. I did not like working with people who had minds of their own.

Perhaps much of Pittance's popularity stemmed from the fact that I frequently permitted him to speak at my political meetings. He was always well received, and I thought that I could use his platform popularity to increase my party support and build up my own standing. But my visit to Naomi Sampson's had brought me the unsettling revelation that Pittance was ambitious. I decided to stop him making political speeches. This would have to be done tactfully.

As to my plan to build up Ben Davis, through the bestowal of a cabinet post, for the job of ridding me of Pittance permanently, a bit of revision was clearly necessary. Since Pittance had got to Naomi Sampson before me, I was no longer inclined to ask Naomi to teach Ben. She would most likely refuse if I asked her. And it would appear that I was copying Pittance's idea.

Furthermore, Ben was far from being enthusiastic about the post of a cabinet minister or about learning to read and write. And the fact that Ben liked and respected Pittance would certainly make matters more difficult for me. I must find some one else for the job of removing Pittance. But who?

As I sat by the side of the road, thinking things out while waiting for a bus or something to take me back to Kingsland, I decided that no matter if Joe Pittance learned to sign his own name with the facility of a Fellow, he would never be one of my candidates for the elections, much less a member of my cabinet.

Headlights appeared in the distance up the road. A bus, car or truck was coming towards me. The bus stop sign was a few feet down from the mango tree where I was sitting. The streets in that district were poorly lighted — even when there was not one of the frequent sudden failures of the Kingsland electricity plant — but I could see the short wooden pole with BUS STOP written on a piece of tin near the top of it.

I didn't move to the bus stop to catch the approaching bus — if it was a bus. I stayed where I was, on the mango root. After all, I had already paid a taxi fifty cents to drop me at Naomi Sampson's place — on a fool's errand. To pay a bus ten cents to take me back to town would be compounding folly with extravagance. I had been waiting for a bus 'or something'. The bus would cost me ten cents; the 'or something' — a truck or a car — would probably drop me in town free, except it was being driven by an estate owner or an upper middle or middle class person. So I waited under the mango tree as I watched the vehicle approach.

It happened to be an old dump truck, belonging to a young businessman in Kingsland. The driver was speeding. The contraption sounded as if it had every bolt, nut and screw loose. I moved a cautious distance towards the middle of the road and waved my jacket. The truck stopped; the driver looked down at me. A man in dirty working clothes was sitting close to the driver.

'Can you give me a lift to town?' I asked.

'Dis truck is nat fo' carryin' people,' said the driver. 'Mister Veira charge me not to give nobody no lift, but as is you Mister Mole, you can get in — but it ain't got no room in de front seat, as is two of us here already.'

'Oh, it's all right,' I said, heaving myself up into the front seat, 'I am quite happy to squeeze in. After all, it's only a short distance to town.'

'Move up more, Fred,' said the driver.

The other man now had to crowd the driver so much that driving became difficult and dangerous. The only dubious improvement on the previous situation was that the breakneck speed had to be drastically cut down.

'Just coming from Ottley's doing house to house,' I said, trying to make conversation. 'I hope you fellers will vote PPP when the election come round.'

'Ain't no other party to vote for,' replied the driver. 'De only other people runnin' for gover'ment is de planters, but dey ain't got no party. Each man runnin' fo' himself. De PPP is de first black-people-poor-man party we ever had in dis island.'

We talked about the 'wickedness' of the planters, the 'neglect' by the Government, the 'ignorance' of the Colonial Office in England about local conditions, and the 'great blessing' the PPP was to the island. It was obvious that these two chaps had been attending my political meetings.

I was enjoying the ride and the conversation until Fred said, 'But apart from you, Misser Mole, de greatest man we got in Hiroona today is Pittance. O Gord, Joe Pittance is a giant.'

'You damn right, Fred,' said the driver. 'We proud o' Pittance. Man, Pittance can talk all right — — — like fire. And to see, he just a ordinary stevedore; but dat man know stuff. An' everybody say he is a honest man — which you can't say fo' every politician. Pittance is *great*.'

'If you don't mind, gentlemen, I would like you to drop me off right here at Mr. Potter's place. I want to have a word with Potter.'

The truck rattled to a halt in front of Potter's. I didn't want to see Potter. I hardly knew the man. I had never met him, never been into his place; but I couldn't stomach any more laudatory opinions about Pittance. I had been listening to this kind of thing all day, and I was sick to the pit of my stomach of it. It did not matter that I, too, was getting my share of recognition. What mattered was, that in giving so much praise to Pittance, people were making him equal to me.

I got off the dump truck and stood under the lighted sign, POTTER'S BAR ETCET'RA, and watched the truck move away. I did not intend to go into Potter's to drink. I was not very fond of alcoholic stuff. I didn't smoke. Apart from my wife Sonia, I was not interested in women. As a matter of fact, I used to pride myself on being 'free from the vices'. So I intended, that evening, to stand at the door of Potter's place, to give the dump truck time to drive out of sight; then I would walk the short distance from Potter's to my house at Bottom Town.

It started to drizzle. In one of the rows of houses across the street, someone was rendering a one-finger, hunt-and-hit, do-it-yourself version of *Smoke Gets in Your Eyes* on a tinny piano. It sounded lonely, fitting into my present mood.

I was on the point of moving off to go home, when George Reid hailed me from across the street. At his 'Mr Mole!' I turned and watched him as he came towards me, his stride long and firm. Reid was white, but he was known throughout Hiroona as a liberal racially, and had demonstrated his freedom from colour prejudice by getting a number of black girls pregnant. He was a bachelor, but it was said that he supported all his children well, even paying the cost of the education of some of them at the Hiroona Grammar School and the Girls High School. On account of his freedom with 'native' women, Reid was regarded as an outcast by people of his own race. And the upper and middle class coloured people saw in him a loose liver whose contempt for the coloured race was demonstrated by his 'liking' for the female members of it.

Reid was one of the directors of a firm with supermarket shops in various parts of Hiroona. He was about thirty-eight or forty years old. He was wearing neither hat nor jacket, and his white shirt was open at the neck.

Tall; smooth; pink skin; his jet black hair seemed to have a sheen not derived from pomade. And although I was not in a sociable mood when he hailed me that evening, I couldn't help thinking, as I watched him approach, that it was Nature's fault, not his, that he was so successfully wild.

'Delighted I caught you, Mr Mole,' he said, 'I see you're just about leaving.'

'Not *leaving*,' I replied, my attitude unfriendly, 'because I didn't go in, and I have no intention of going in. My taxi dropped me here, and I am on the point of walking home, for the exercise.'

'People with agile brains like yours,' said Reid, 'do need some physical exercise sometimes, as most of your exercising is done above the neck.'

The observation surprised and pleased me, and I smiled, as Reid laughed at his own pleasantry.

'You know,' he continued, 'for some weeks now I've been hoping for an opportunity to have a little chat with you. I don't know anything about present-day West Indian politics, but I am very interested in the study of the art of Government. I have a few books on the subject and I read them sometimes. Of course, there were no politics in Hiroona before you came on the scene. You have introduced something new to the island — something new and dynamic — and I want to see where it will lead.'

His attitude was warm, friendly; and his inclination to praise my work lifted my spirits.

'But I am getting a lot of opposition from your people,' I said.

'*My* people? I have no people, Mr Mole. I am a member of the human race, I hope. *All* humanity is my people. I was born in Hiroona, and *all* Hiroonians are my countrymen, my people.'

'You surprise me.'

'And as for your experiencing opposition from the planters and white people on the island, why, you should expect that. You are a pioneer socialist in Hiroona, your Labour Movement, as you call it, is a movement towards history, and there are people — black as well as white — who resent movement and hate 'Movers'. However, you may take comfort in the fact that you are the first Hiroonian to begin to give the island a history in which the people themselves have a hand.'

I wanted to embrace George Reid. He had said things to me that no one had said to me before. He had summed up the situation on the island with a penetration of which I would not have believed that he or anyone of his class was capable; and he had attached to my work an assessment, a significance, which far exceeded even my own estimate of it.

I had entered politics in Hiroona because I couldn't enter anything else. I was not inspired or prompted by any humanitarian considerations, or by a desire to make history. I entered politics to better myself, because I saw political leadership as a job which offered security, status and power. But now, George Reid had put words and ideas into mind that were never there before — words and ideas that would make excellent platform material. Reid's mind was operating on a political plane that was different from the usual. No stupid talk about Penny Farthing's compensation money; no unsympathetic reference to my 'disruptive political speeches'; no foolish talk about my 'offending too many people'; nothing about P. C. 43 Cunningham being sacked, and — thank God — no opinion about the excellencies of Joe Pittance.

It was as if I had listened to sensible talk for the first time in all my years. Reid was a breath of fresh air; he was new wine, lifting my spirits.

'Thank you, Mr Reid,' I said. 'You are the only person on this island who seems to have a full appreciation of the nature of my work.'

'That gives you at least one white supporter,' said Reid, smiling. 'But why do we stand here talking? We would be more comfortable inside, sitting and exchanging ideas over a few drinks.'

'Lead the way,' I said, as I turned to follow him, my heart light, my confidence quickened, a new spring in my step.

17

'What will you have?' asked Reid.

'A little whiskey, I think,' I replied.

Reid called to the boy behind the counter, 'Scotch. Two.' The boy stopped wiping the counter with his bar rag, and said,

'With soda as usual, sir?'

'As usual,' said Reid.

The large bar-room was well provided with plastic-top tables on spindly iron legs. Groups of individuals sat at the tables drinking, smoking, chatting, arguing. Some men and women were having their drinks standing at the counter. Waiters were fetching drinks and empty glasses to and from the counter.

Placing his hand under my elbow, Reid steered me towards a door which, he said, led to an inner saloon. As we threaded our way between the tables, towards the inner saloon, several members of the crowd greeted us or waved to us. Arriving at the door of the saloon, Reid turned, and shouted to the boy behind the counter, 'Hey Gerald, where is Mr Potter?'.

'He just run upstairs,' Gerald shouted back; 'he will be back just now.'

'When he comes down, tell him to join us for a few minutes in here. Tell him I have Mr Mole with me.'

'Right, Sir.'

This inner room was not as large or brightly lighted as the bar-room, but the furniture was more expensive and more comfortable. There were only three medium size, low, round tables in the room. These were placed at discreet distances apart so that conversation at one table need not be heard at another. Three stuffed morris chairs were drawn up around each table. The room was obviously designed for *tête-à-têtes* or small private parties. It was a cosy place, dimly lighted.

I draped my jacket over the back of one of the morris chairs before I sat in the chair and faced Reid across the low, round mahogany table with a large ash tray on it. The ash tray advertised 'Younger's Stout' and I secretly wondered whether I should not have chosen a glass of stout instead of whiskey which might prove too strong.

'Nice place Potter's got here,' said Reid, stretching out his long legs, leaning back in his chair and surveying the room.

'Mmm,' I said, appreciatively, as I looked around at the light blue stucco walls and the two bulbs which hung from the ceiling, in shades of native wicker work. Some homespun artist had prettied up (or disfigured?) the walls with cartoonlike paintings depicting local themes: a steel band on one wall; native women with large baskets of fruit on their heads, on another wall; and, just behind where I sat, a coconut tree under which two lean black men lazed, their faces partially hidden under large straw hats like Mexican peasants dozing by the roadside.

'You come here often?' I asked.

'Often enough,' said Reid. 'I like the relaxed, low-voice atmosphere of this room. Potter designed this place with some sense. The noisy outer room we have just passed through is where you carouse. In this room here you take it easy with a friend or two, discussing private affairs, business, or just gossiping over a few quiet drinks. Under dim lights like this, you don't feel like raising your voice above *tête-à-tête*. Now, you see that heavy curtain over yonder, to the left of that couple sitting in the far corner? Well, that curtain hides a door which is always closed.' He chuckled. 'The lights behind that door are even dimmer than these here, and there you don't raise your voice above an involuntary grunt or a discreet ecstatic squeak, the squeak being very expensive.'

'I see.'

I was not interested in Potter's arrangements for the wine-and-women convenience of his wealthier customers. My mind was on other things; but as Reid described the layout of the joint, I became anxious to meet the owner of it.

A girl brought in our drinks, placed them on the table and withdrew. We touched glasses, and sipped.

'Now, tell me about the state of the union and the party,' Reid said, 'one hears so many rumours. Some say you're sweeping the country.'

'True,' I said happily.

'Some say you're having a bit of difficulty in the Sugar Belt on account of unpaid compensation money to some labourer or other who lost some of his fingers in the factory.'

'False.'

'There is even the rumour that you had a pavement brawl or quarrel with Paul Darcy.'

'True,' I admitted.

'I hear, too, that the planters and the professional group and some businessmen — George Duncan, Sammie Ballantyne and others — have approached Sean Dobson the Irishman attorney for the Mount Horeb Company, and pledged him their support if he run against you in the Sugar Belt constituency. I hear they are begging him to run, and I understand that he is likely to.'

I had not forgotten my brush with Dobson during my contention with the Mount Horeb Company directors at the factory. The Irishman was a tough customer, but I did not fear him as an election opponent, so long as his candidature did not have popular support. I said to Reid:

'You say *they* are begging him to run. *They* who — the people of the constituency, or the men in this upper crust group?'

'The group,' Reid replied.

'That's all right, then. So long as they remain a group, they are harmless. The group used to control matters in the past, but now that adult suffrage has come to Hiroona, and the West Indies, groups are no longer significant.'

'Granted, but don't forget Mr Mole, that pressure groups can exert tremendous influence on the politics of a country; and every West Indian island has such a group, Barbados has its Laurie Piles, its Reeces and its H. B. G. Austins. Grenada has its Hughes, its Knights and Neckles. Trinidad has its Ambards, De Verteuils. Montserrat has its Howes and Griffins. Jamaica its Asheneims *et cetera*. St. Vincent has its Frasers and Punnetts. The Bahamas has its "Bay Street Boys" — and so on all through.'

'With adult suffrage, groups of the kind you mentioned will become hopelessly out of date throughout the West Indies. You just wait and see,' I asserted confidently.

Reid looked up, smiling, as Potter entered the room.

'Hi, Dave, come and join us. You know Mr Mole?'

'Who doesn't?' replied Potter, extending his hand to me. His handshake was the soft, loose variety, but his manner was genial, approaching heartiness; and when he smiled, you immediately remembered the tooth paste advertisement you saw in *Ebony*.

Potter was in his middle thirties, but he tended to paunchiness, and when he sat down and drew up his short legs, a small pout of abdominal fat circled his middle, overhanging his belt.

The girl who had served our drinks returned and stood waiting.

'Repeat three,' said Reid. The girl left.

I looked at my glass and was surprised that it was empty. I had got through my first scotch and soda before I knew it.

Dave Potter turned to me and said, 'I hear you will be contesting the eleven seats, and it looks like you going to win by a landside. Congrats.'

'Don't congratulate me yet, man,' I said.

'Impossible for you to lose,' said Potter. 'At least fifty percent of the lower middle class and one hundred percent of the peasants are with you, judging from the talk I hear all over the place. Of course, you have my vote and all my staff's. George, what about you?'

'He will certainly have mine,' said Reid. 'I am a student of all that is new, and politics is new here. But my staff runs to about ninety people. I can't talk for all of them.'

The girl returned with the drinks. She placed one before each of us, removed the two empty glasses, and went out.

Potter lifted his glass and said, 'To victory and the PPP.' We drank.

I never felt better in my life. I was having a foretaste of the improved living and higher level of association I would enjoy when I took over the government of the island. I lay back in my chair and looked around. The couple who were sitting at the table in the far corner when Reid and I came in, had left. I asked Potter how it was that they did not pass us on their way out. We were sitting near to the door. Potter smiled, and Reid explained:

'This room, and beyond, are private, Mr Mole. You can come in and go out by back entrances, without anyone out there seeing you.'

'Perfectly simple,' said Potter. 'And I want you to feel free to use my place any time you're in the mood.'

As I said, 'Thank you, Dave,' I couldn't help reflecting that two years ago, Dave Potter would not have said a thing like that to me. You don't offer the freedom of your place to a resident of Bottom Town slums. Reid had said, 'It is expensive,' which meant that it was a success place, for successful people.

Dave himself was an example of 'successful people.' It was well known throughout Hiroona that, as a teenager just out of elementary school, Potter had started in business by renting an ancient broken-down Hillman motor car from old man Charley Farrell, fastened up the sagging accessories with wire and string and arranged with some of the big dry-goods and grocery merchants in Kingsland to fill up the Hillman with goods which Dave took to all the practically inaccessible country districts and sold for a commission. Later he had bought a small one-door all-purpose shop on part of the site which he now occupied. The man had prospered and was soon able to own, expand and develop the whole site into the present 'POTTER'S BAR ETCET'RA'.

'I knew him since his old Hillman days,' Reid had said to me earlier that evening, 'and I like him for his business acumen and for the fact that prosperity doesn't go to his head.'

Now Dave was offering me membership in the club of the successful; and although my own success had so far been only nascent, and as nothing compared to Potter's or Reid's, I had a feeling that it had even then begun to go to my head.

In the days when I had to swim in Kingsland's harbour, and lose my new hat; when I had to cry at funerals; when I knocked about the bayfront seeking odd jobs, filling in export licence forms for hucksters; when I was content to be led and shoved around by Joe Pittance; when, as we say in the West Indies, I was 'catching me arse' — in those days I couldn't even afford the outer public room of Potter's place, and would certainly not have been considered for entry to the inner private rooms. Dave's offer made me realise that I had come a long way since those days which now seemed so far behind me. The thought filled me with a new elation. A new life was opening up for me. Soon Hiroona would be my oyster. I was not yet in the saddle, the election was still ahead; and yet, I was being offered the freedom of Potter's place. Who knows, I may one day be offered the freedom of a city: Bridgetown, Port-of-Spain, Georgetown, Ottawa, Montreal, Toronto, or even London.

I took a deep draught of my scotch and soda, replaced my glass daintily on the table and lay back in my chair, savouring the moment — and the liquor.

We talked politics and local gossip far into the night. The girl returned to the room every now and again to execute the order from Dave or George Reid, 'Repeat three.'

Then Dave Potter came to the point. He said, 'We have plans to extend the service here. Make the place better. At present, a fellow can have his drinks in the bar room. Special people can come in here, have their drinks and go further in and have their privacy. Now, we want to add some slot machines to the service, so that our customers could have some additional amusement, and win a few shillings at the same time.'

'Slot machines!' I exclaimed. 'You mean those things that people call "man eaters"?'

Potter nodded.

'But the law is against slot machines here, man,' I said. 'The Government is dead against them. The Customs suppose to confiscate any "man eater" imported into the island, and the importer pays a hell of a fine for the first offence, prison for the second offence. "Man eaters" too hot to handle, Dave.'

'We know the law,' said Reid, 'but the laws of Hiroona are not the laws of the Medes and Persians which altereth not.' He laughed as he mouthed this biblical *cliché*.

The girl appeared again. She seemed to have had some occult means of knowing when we needed service.

'Repeat three,' said Potter.

When the girl left, I said, 'The law can be changed, yes, but you and Dave can't change the law, and import "man eaters".'

'Dave and I can't change the law,' said Reid, 'but *you* will be able to change any law you want to change. So long as the change does no damage to the people's rights.'

'I? Meee? How can I change the law?'

The girl brought fresh drinks, placed them in front of us and went out.

'Look, Jerry,' Potter said, 'we all know the elections is only a few months off, and we know you can't lose.'

The scotch and sodas had already begun to have their way with me. On the only two previous occasions, years ago, when I got drunk, I went through the usual five stages — the jocose, the bellicose, the lachrymose, the regurgitose and the comatose — before I recovered. Now I was operating on bellicose.

Reid started to say something. I put up my hand and shouted, 'Wait! Wait!! Wait!!! Let me speak.' I lifted my glass and drained it. Some of the liquid spilled on my shirt. I felt the wet coldness on my skin in a negligent sort of way. I put down the glass a bit too heavily on the table, and ignored the exchange of glances between Reid and Potter. I said ——

'"Man eaters" were banned on this island because they presented too great a tempthation — er-to — er — my people, the labouring classeth, to lose money they ain't had. You will remember, gen'l'men, that the police reported a lot of cases of — er — thefth — I mean stealing — by youngsters who had developed an addiction to these machines. They were ruining the morals. Ruining the morals. Ruining.'

I glared at my empty glass, then at Reid and Potter, and demanded, 'Now where in hell is that girl? Whath's her name again? Oh yes, I know — Repeat Three. That's the name. Repeat Three.' I struggled up from my chair, weaved towards the door and shouted, 'Where the hell are you, Miss Three? Ah'm thirsty. Need a drink, Ah'm . . . .'

It was Potter who told me all that happened then, and filled me in on developments, when he brought my jacket to my shack at Bottom Town next day. He came in his new Bentley.

'Christ, man, you live it up last night,' he said laughing. He remained in the car, my jacket on the seat beside him. I had come out of the house when he blew his car horn. I stood beside the car, wearing a sheepish grin as we talked. I was still in my street clothes. Had slept in them. Sonia was too vexed to undress me. I passed my parched tongue over my dry lips and said,

'Lived it up? What did I do? Tell me gently.'

'You didn't do anything. You just passed out, calling on "Miss Three" for a drink.'

'Miss Who?'

Potter laughed again. 'Reid grabbed you before you fell; then we carried you through the back door, put you in this car and drove you home. All this time you fast asleep. When I went back I saw your jacket hanging on the chair.'

'I didn't cuss, or anything like that?'

'Naah, man. You were all right. Just a little loud. But that little matter about the slot machines; you gave us a hell of a sermon about ruining morals.'

'I musta been damn drunk fo' true.'

Potter and I laughed loudly at this. Then Potter said, 'Reid and I depending on you to help us, you know. You won't regret it.'

'That will be O.K.,' I said. 'No problem.'

'Good. So when you dropping in again?' He handed me my jacket.

'Soon, Dave. As soon as I can make the time. Still I got a lot of campaigning to do, and there's this meeting of the party officials to select my candidates.'

'You going to be busy, yes. Anyway, drop in again as soon as you can.'

Potter drove away, and I went back into the house, prepared to face Sonia's wrath. It turned out to be only mild chiding, however. And when she said, 'Two men bring you home drunk last night. You have to be careful now, Jerry. You ain't a ordinary man no more. You aimin' for a high position, and yo' have to respeck yo'self,' I felt very contrite. So I fondled her, guided her to the bed behind the thin cotton cloth blind, and after a wordless exchange of views, we fell contentedly asleep.

18

BEFORE the introduction of universal adult suffrage in the West Indies, there was an aura of privacy about general elections. The vote was a sort of reward for material success; the franchise was the privilege of only those people who had the requisite income and property qualification. As such people were comparatively few, a candidate could win public elections at his club or at a cocktail party or two. Public elections took place behind the public's back. Words and expressions like 'politics,' 'political campaign,' 'majority' were unknown outside of a dictionary. The only party was the cocktail party, and the 'masses' had not yet put in its appearance as a political force. This was the situation in Hiroona up to the early fifties.

Universal adult suffrage was not granted to all the West Indian islands at the same time. Jamaica got it on the 20 November 1944. It was introduced into Trinidad in April 1946. Barbados got it on 20 February 1951. St. Vincent on 5 May 1951. Grenada, 16 June 1951. Dominica, 16 July 1951. St. Lucia, 1951. St. Kitts-Nevis-Anguilla, 10 May 1952. Montserrat, 30 January 1952. Antigua, 1 December 1951.

Out of this milieu of constitutional advancement, a new type of society and a new type of leader emerged — a leader with a sort of Moses complex, who appeared to regard the local masses as oppressed Israelites, the local Government and the Colonial Office in England being the bad-minded Pharaohs.

This 'let-my-people-go' approach to politics provided the political leader with an indispensable reservoir of profitable emotionalism, and it encouraged the masses to put vague, charismatic considerations above intelligence, solid achievement and even integrity, in estimating the worth of some of their political leaders. This was one reason why I was able to achieve such a rapid rise in Hiroona by simply advocating down with this, that and the other, and by preaching the idea of taking over the Government. Demagoguery was the key which opened the door to political leadership. The more or less widely known fact that I had stolen money from a poor boy and his sick, indigent mother was no setback to my political stature. The charisma of a Moses placed him above censure for petty moral lapses.

I was complacently aware of the general recognition of this built-in immunity, and I exploited it. I was to learn, however, that immunity, like privilege, cannot be pushed too far without being challenged.

The time had come for my meeting with the branch committees of the union, to choose the Party's candidates for the general election. The list of names was in my pocket, to be produced in due course for formal approval by the committees.

We met in The Chamber at Bottom Town on Sunday afternoon. The meeting did not go according to my plan, however.

After *O God our Help in Ages Past,* and *We'll keep the red flag flying high* and a prayer by the Chaplain Naomi Sampson, Comrade Claude Mason rose on a point of order to ask whether I knew how many candidates the planters were putting up.

'So far as I know they're putting up eight candidates,' I said, 'including Sean Dobson who is supposed to be opposing me in the Sugar Belt.'

'I hear they are making all sorts of sweet promises at their political mass meetings,' added Naomi Sampson.

'Which reminds me, Bass,' said Joe Pittance, 'we shoulda had a manifesto, an' we ain't got one.'

'A *what*?' I snapped.

'Manifesto,' said Joe.

'Now what de hell is a manifesto?' said Comrade Jessop, while all eyes sought an answer from Pittance.

It was the first time I had heard about the word. My ignorance of the word and its meaning was an instance of the strange credibility gaps that sometimes occur in people's education. So I said, 'I am the party's manifesto. We have no need of any other manifesto. Does this satisfy you, Comrade Pittance?'

Heads turned to look at Joe, as if expecting him to make a decision. Joe grinned broadly, shook his head several times and sat down.

'Now, comrades,' I said, 'let us proceed.'

Consulting my list, I announced, 'I have here the list of candidates who will represent the party at the polls: I will take care of the Sugar Belt constituency, which includes Mount Horeb and the nine villages as set out in the election boundaries legislation. Comrade Claude Mason will run for the North Leeward constituency. He lives in that constituency, and I think he has a great deal of influence there. Comrade Sonia Mole, General Secretary of the union and party, will represent the Central Leeward constituency. That constituency adjoins the district in which Comrade Mole was born and grew up, before we got married and moved to Kingsland. She knows Central Leeward well, and is well known there. I have decided to assign the South Leeward constituency to Comrade James Carter, one of the foundation members of the union . . .'

After the recital, I sat down and said, 'Now, that covers the eleven constituencies. I hope you are satisfied with the selections.'

Naomi Sampson took over from there. Tall, slim, schoolmarmish; graying hair; white bodice with wrist-length sleeves; the hem of her neat, black, pleated skirt touching her ankles; stiff, shiny black scalloped straw hat kept in place by long hat pin. Diction meticulous; class-room voice commanding respect.

'We are not satisfied at all,' said Naomi primly.

'How so?' I questioned.

'Well, you have selected Comrade Carter who, as you remarked is a foundation member of the union; but you have left out the most useful foundation member of us all. Why have you done that?'

'Which foundation member you talking about?' I asked, knowing very well who she was talking about.

'I am thinking about Comrade Joseph Pittance — I mean Joseph Bute. Why have you left him out?'

Before I could reply, two members of the committee got up simultaneously and began to speak.

'All right, comrades,' I said. 'One at a time. We will hear Comrade Jessop first. You will come next, Comrade Francis. Go ahead, Comrade Jessop.'

'As Ah was saying,' Jessop continued, 'I agree with Comrade Sampson. We can't afford to leave out a man like Joe Pittance.' He struck his meaty fist in his palm. 'We ain't leavin' him out. Pittance been wid this union an' de party even before it start. He help us out from de beginnin', goin' up an' down de country wid you, Comrade Mole, leavin' his jab dat he gettin' his livin' by at de waterfront. When we wanted to see de Administrata to get de pavilion fo' de rally, it was Pittance who tell us how to do it. It was Pittance who help arganize de waterfront. It was Pittance who . . .'

'All right, all right, Comrade Jessop. I do not wish to hear any more. Pittance cannot be a member of the Legislative or Executive Council of the Government, because he cannot read or write. I am not saying this against him. I am only stating a fact.'

Naomi Sampson jumped up. She strode to the table on the platform. 'Lend me that pen,' she said to Sonia at the table. 'And that piece of paper there.' Sonia handed the pen and paper to her.

'Come here, Comrade Bute,' ordered Naomi. Joe Pittance got up and approached the platform. His large canvas shoes made a soft, wettish sound on the floor as he walked.

'Here. Take this.' Naomi pushed the pen and paper into Joe's hand.

'Sit at the table and write your name,' said Naomi. Sonia got up, and Joe lowered his lanky frame to the chair, bent over the piece of paper for a few seconds, then straightened up, gazing at what he had written. Naomi took up the piece of paper, and handed it to me. 'What do you think of *this*, Comrade Mole?'

'That's all right,' I said, 'but a member of the Councils must be able to write and read other things besides his name.'

'Very well,' said Naomi. 'Comrade Pittance, please write this sentence, as I dictate it.' She dictated the sentence, calling two words at a time, repeating them slowly while Joe wrote. Then she said to Joe, 'Now, pass the paper to Comrade Mole and let him see what you have written.'

I took the paper from Joe and read, *My ant gave me a dog.*

Slowly, I looked from the paper to Joe, then to Naomi; and instead of admiring them I hated them; for in Joe's performance I did not see solid achievement. I only saw conspiracy — conspiracy against me.

But they were not even finished with me yet. They had another surprise in store for me. Leaving the platform, Naomi quickly returned to her seat, where she had left her handbag. She snapped it open and pulled out a sheet of paper. Holding it up, she said to the Committee, 'On this sheet of paper is typed the oath that each member of the Government Council has to read aloud in the Legislative Council Chamber in the presence of the large crowd that comes to witness the swearing in of the members of the Government.'

She handed the sheet of paper to Joe. 'Stand up and read this,' she commanded, her clear, high-pitched voice dominating the room.

Joe took the paper and read, 'I, Joseph Bute, do swear that I will be faithful and bear true allegiance to Her Majesty Queen Elizabeth the Second, Her Heirs and Successors according to law. So help me God.'

He read it too well; and his facility with the big, unfamiliar words was a clear hint that rote had been sedulously brought to bear. But he had read it. And in the silence that followed, the thoughts of my heart were dark.

Naomi quietly returned to her seat. Joe left the platform, padded down the aisle between the rows of benches and resumed his place among the other stevedores.

Leslie Francis then took his turn. 'Where we gwine from here, Bass?' he said.

'Ask Naomi Sampson,' I replied testily. 'She seems to be in charge.'

Naomi ignored my sarcasm. She said, 'There is only one thing to do; put Comrade Bute in place of one of the candidates.'

I said nothing. Percy Lett, the candidate for South Windward got up and said, 'Put Pittance in my place, Bass. I have a acre of land dat Ah renting from Mr Richards at Petit Poie Estate. If Mr Richards hear dat Ah runnin' fo' Government, he will take away de acre fram me. I prefer to cultivate me little acre of land than to be in de Govern'ment. Put Pittance in my place, Bass. I will willingly resign from a candidate here an' now, to give Pittance my place.'

Claude Mason suggested, 'Move Smallmilk from Kingsland and put Pittance there. Kingsland need a stronger man than Smallmilk. He goin' be runnin' against dat powerful lawyer Hugh Haywood, I hear. A situation like dat call for a man like Pittance. We could put Smallmilk at South Windward in place of Comrade Lett.'

'Who is Smallmilk?' I said petulantly, although I knew damn well who was Smallmilk. 'You mean, Comrade Leon Samuel?'

'Well we all know him by the name of Smallmilk.'

'Comrade Samuel will remain for Kingsland,' I said with finality. I was determined to be firm. I would have none of Pittance. I put my foot down.

Stalemate. Uneasy silence. Then one candidate after another got up and announced that he would not accept candidacy unless Joe Pittance was assigned to a constituency. I was beaten. I was embarrassed and a bit confused, too, by the charge of ingratitude which I knew was in the minds of everyone present.

'All right, comrades,' I said, rising. 'I have no objection at all to including Comrade Pittance in our list of candidates. The reason why I hesitated to nominate him was that I had other plans for him. As you know, Comrade Sonia Mole will be running for Central Leeward. If she win, the union would need a good General Secretary, because Comrade Mole would not be able to perform, the secretarial duties of the union and those of a cabinet minister at the same time. So I had planned to make Comrade Pittance General Secretary of the union. But since you prefer him to be a candidate for the elections, it's quite O.K. with me. He will take Comrade Lett's place.'

'Excuse me, Comrade Mole,' said Naomi Sampson, getting up. 'How could you have planned to appoint Comrade Bute General Secretary of the union, when you knew he couldn't read or write?'

'I intended to ask you to teach him.'

Naomi gave a snort of disgust and sat down. Pittance took the floor.

'It was good of you, Bass, to consider me for de jab of General Secretary of de union. And since you say dat de jab will need someone to carry it on when your wife become a minister of de Government, I want to put a suggestion to de Committee. It is dis; a certain young man did de union a great, great favour when nobody else would help us. If dis young man didn't help us when he did, our rally woulda suffer a big inconvenience. Dey sack him from de Police Force because he help us. Now he ain't got no jab to support his family, on account o' helpin' us. I am askin' you please to consider him fo' de jab of General Secretary of de union if an' when Mrs Mole give it up. You all know de young man I am talking about — Vincent Cunningham. He was P.C. 43.'

As Pittance spoke, I kept remembering a story I read at school, about an English King who was so repeatedly thwarted by an archbishop called Thomas Becket, that on one infuriating occasion the king cried out, 'Can't someone kill the son of a bitch?' or words to that effect. I looked steadily at Ben Davis, the man who, I secretly hoped, would rid me of Joe Pittance in due course. But Ben could not read my mind, and from him I received no answering glance. In fact, I had long concluded that if Ben could divine my intentions for Pittance, he would recoil from me in horror.

I had not the slightest intention of removing Sonia from the secretary-ship of the union. Indeed, I had calculated and discussed with her the lucrative and politically strategic benefits which her being the holder of the posts of General Secretary of the union and a cabinet minister would bring us. My telling the Committee that I had planned to appoint Pittance when Sonia vacated the secretaryship was a lie which Naomi Sampson had immediately detected. Joe Pittance, too, had undoubtedly, seen the lie; but with his usual cleverness, he promptly decided to use it against me by taking me up on it, impaling me on it, and then sitting down to watch me wriggle.

How in God's name could I appoint a man like Cunningham to a key post in the union? Cunningham was young, apparently intelligent and, judging by the way he had walked away from me because I snubbed him when he tried to talk with me on the Bay Street pavement that rainy afternoon, he certainly had pride. Therefore, he was not the kind of person I cared to work with. I preferred my subordinates to be unambitious, elderly, tractable, semi-literate or illiterate. So far, these types comprised my entire following, and I was even now having serious trouble with them. To bring in young Cunningham would be to beg for more trouble.

However, the present mood of the Committee made it unwise for me to reject out of hand Joe Pittance's proposal for Cunningham. In the eyes of the Committee, I was ungrateful to Pittance in the first place. If I openly refused to accept Cunningham, I would lay myself open to a further charge of ingratitude.

So I said, 'Comrade Pittance, I congratulate you. You have put up a good case for Mr Cunningham. I will bear it in mind, and when the time comes, I shall certainly see what can be done for your man. After all, the elections are eight weeks away, and we don't know whether Comrade Sonia Mole will win or lose. So we cannot decide now to appoint Cunningham to a position which, after all, might not fall vacant.'

'Bass, I am asking de Committee to promise *now*, dat if Mrs Mole win de seat fo' de Central Leeward districk, then Cunningham would get de jab of General Secretary of de union.'

'There will be plenty of time to decide a matter like this, Comrade.'

'Bass, I would like it *write down* in the minutes *now*, so dat when de time come we won't have to go over de matter again. De promise will be in de minutes already.'

'We will have to wait, Comrade. Cunningham is not even a card carrying member of the union. We cannot appoint a non-member to an office in the union. The members would take offence. I am sure that a good many of our comrades would prefer Comrade Sampson, who is a member of long standing, and a well educated lady, to be General Secretary of . . . .'

'I do not want any post, Comrade Mole,' Naomi interrupted almost shouting. 'I am a well employed person. I am a seamstress, as everybody knows. And I am not ungrateful.'

'Well, in that case, comrades, all that Mr Cunningham has to do is to become a member of the union. He would then be in a position for consideration when the time comes.'

'Cunningham is already a member of de union, Bass,' said Joe, a mocking half smile on his lean face.

'He is not,' I barked.

'He is, Bass,' said Joe quietly.

I looked at Sonia, a question on my face. Sonia nodded twice and said, 'He is a member. He pay up, and have his card already.'

'Why was I not told about this?' I said.

'Are you supposed to be told about every single member who joins the union?' Naomi asked me.

'No, but in a case like this — well — anyway, let's get back to the real business of this meeting. There are a few announcements. I . . . .'

'On a p'int of order,' said Pittance, rising. 'De question of a promise to appoint Comrade Vincent Cunningham Secretary if an' when de jab becomes vacant is not settle yet, Bass. I am now asking your permission to put de question to de vote, so dat it would be recorded in de minutes.'

'We will come to that later, Comrade Pittance. Just let me make the announcements. As you all know, each candidate for the elections must deposit a hundred dollars on Nomination Day when he goes to register as a candidate. Now the party is putting forward eleven candidates. I will pay the one hundred dollars for each candidate from union funds. You won't have to pay a cent. I will take care of this. Of course, if you don't lose your deposit, it will be paid back to the union.'

I paused to make way for the applause, giving it time to smother the Vincent Cunningham issue. When it died down, I said, 'Well, comrades, I think we had a good meeting. There's only two things we have to do between now and election day: campaign like hell and win by a landslide. You already have the schedule of nightly mass meetings in all the districts. I shall be present at every one to assist you. Remember, you have to look out for Nomination Day, the date will be published a few days before Election Day. I will come around to each candidate, of course, and go with him to give in his name. And I will take care of the deposit. It is getting late now, and we are all tired, but happy. So those who have union dues to pay to the secretary will do so after the meeting. Now stand and let us sing our closing ode: *Abide with me*!

As the Committee rose to begin to sing, Pittance put up his hand and said, 'But Bass . . . .'

'O.K., comrade,' I said quickly. 'We will talk after the meeting. Now, everybody — *Aaabide wid mee . . .*'

A few minutes after the singing of the 'ode', I left the Chamber, feeling tense, spent. I hurried off, making straight for Dave Potter's place. I could do with some refreshing conversation — and some refreshments.

19

THE boy at the bar said, 'Mr Potter ain't dere, Mr Mole. He garn up at Mr George Reid. He leave a message fo' you. He say in case you call, I must tell you to let Bryan bring you up in de Bentley.'

'Where is Bryan?' I asked.

'He someway in de back. Ah goin' fetch 'im fo' you.'

When Bryan came, he said, 'This way, please, sirrr.' Bryan was a Barbadian. He was good at the letter 'r'. He didn't roll all his 'r's. If an 'r' came before a vowel, it had an easy time from Bryan. It came out soft. But God help any unlucky 'r' which came after a vowel — Bryan simply worrrked it to death. He rattled it. He made it sound like the way a Maxim gun pronounces it. Sitting beside him in the car, I said, 'You're from Barbados, aren't you, Bryan?'

'And proud of the fact,' he replied, smiling. Bryan was about twenty-four, medium height, stocky, black, handsome. A small tuft of well kept moustache decorated the centre of his upper lip. He wore a T-shirt, the short sleeves of which were filled to bursting by his biceps.

'How long you been in Hiroona?'

'About a yearrr and a half. I help Mr Potter run the business; do odd jobs for him; service his car; general handyman — that sorrrt of thing.'

'You like it here?'

'Well, so-so. Of course, I prefer Ba-biadus. Therrr's no place like home — if. you can make a living therrre.'

'Tell me about your country. What is it like?'

'Well, it's the oldest British colony in the West Indies, barring St. Kitts. Sirrr Thomas Warrnerr settled St. Kitts in 1623, and the *Olive Blossom* brought settlerrrs to Ba-biadus in 1625. But while St. Kitts is two yearrrs olderrr than Ba-biadus, Ba-biadus is two worrrlds ahead of St. Kitts.'

'And how many worlds ahead of Hiroona?'

'Well, since you starrted to operate herrre, Hiroona has woken up. But of course you only started in 1950 — two years ago. Charles Duncan O'Neal laid the foundations of progressive socialism in Ba-biadus since the 1920s — twenty-five yearrrs ago; and Grantley Adams was in operation in Ba-biadus since 1934 — eighteen years ago, when all the otherrr small islands and Trinidad were asleep. Of course, therrr's nothing surrprising about this.

Ba-biadus is the most educated island in the West Indies — perrrhaps in the worrrld. Long before any of the otherrr islands had any institution of higherrr learrrning, Ba-biadus had Codrington College, Harrison College, Comberrmere School, Lodge School, and schools upon schools of flying fish.'

We laughed.

'I must visit your wonderful island one of these days,' I said. 'What do you suggest that I make a special effort to see, when I go?'

'Well, you should go to the House of Assembly for a demonstration in parliamentary quarrelling and procedure. Then you should travil all overrr the island and see things you won't see in any otherrr parrt of the worrrld.'

'Things like what so?'

'Well, in the first place, if you go to Christ Church cemetery, you will see the vault wherre the duppies — or jumbies, as you call them in Hiroona — used to fight one another.'

'You don't say.'

'Yes, it's true. So help me God. This was a family vault; and every time they opened the vault to put in the body of anotherrr member of the family, they would find the coffins they put in previously, in a hell of a disarray. Some of the coffins crouching in a farr corrnerr of the vault, some standing on tiptoe, and a lot of funny business — some even upside down! The surviving relatives would fix the coffins back in decent orrderr, laying them side by side, but when they open the vault again they would find that the coffins simply refused to federate. Each one wanted its own way, each one jostling and shoving the otherr. They all fighting among themselves. So the Government had to step in and take out all the coffins from the vault and bury them in separate graves, and leave each to fend for itself, to go it alone and fight with itself. So each coffin got its independence, and Government sealed up the vault. You must go and see the vault and the graves. They'rrr tourist arrtractions nowadays.'

'O God, Bryan, man; that's a hellish story,' I said.

'But it's true,' said Bryan, as he swung the Bentley into the short driveway leading to George Reid's house. George and Dave were sitting on the lighted patio which formed part of the front of the house.

As the car entered the yard, Reid got up, came and stood at the door of the house, which was the large bungalow type.

'Hi, fellers,' I said, getting out of the car.

'Hello, man,' said Reid. 'How did the meeting go?'

'How do you know I had a meeting?' We shook hands.

'Hiroona has no secrets,' Reid replied. 'You should know that.'

I followed Reid onto the patio, and dropped into an aluminium, canvas deck-chair.

'God, I could do with a drink.'

'Take off your jacket first, man,' said Potter. 'We informal.'

'What's your drink, Jerry?' Reid said. 'You could have a couple of Martha's lovely sandwiches, too.'

'I think I'll try a whiskey with soda.'

'O God, again?' said Dave Potter, laughing.

'I'll make it weak this time,' said Reid, joining in the fun. He left the patio and went into the house.

'Want a drink, Bryan?' Potter asked.

'No, thank you, Misterrr Potterrr. Got to hurry back to worrk. Only one bar boy on duty tonight, as you know.'

Bryan turned to leave. 'Good night, Mr Mole,' he said. 'And don't forget to visit Ba-biadus after the elections.'

'O.K., Bryan, I'll do that; and I will go and see the place where the jumbies used to fight one another. What's the name of the place again?'

'Christ Churrrch cemetery.'

'What the hell you two talking about?' Dave asked. I turned and waved to Bryan as he drove away. George Reid brought drinks, handed them around, lowered himself in his chair, sipped his scotch, rested his glass on the floor beside his chair and said, 'I hear you were to choose your candidates this afternoon. Got through all right?' I took a swig and put down my glass on the floor.

'Mmm hmm,' I replied.

'Who're the candidates?' Dave and George asked simultaneously. I told them.

'They sound like a pack of dumb bitches — except your wife, of course,' said Dave, 'and possibly that smart Alec, Joe Pittance, that everybody is talking about. The rest are just sheep. But that's good: They give less trouble.'

Reid chuckled as he said, 'Well, it is said that a flock of sheep led by a lion can accomplish more than a pride of lions led by a sheep. I hope you're a lion, Jerry; but you got to remember that sheep can be troublesome at times.'

'I discovered that this afternoon,' I grumbled.

'They can't stop you putting the island on a good footing, anyway,' said Dave.

'Naah,' I said, realising that for Dave Potter, putting the island on a good footing meant granting him a special permit to import 'man eaters'.

'Well, here's to a better Hiroona,' Dave raised his glass. We drank up.

Then George Reid said, 'What is this you and Bryan were talking about a while ago — jumbies fighting in a Barbadian cemetery?'

'He was telling me about a family vault in which the inmates used to play at some sort of mayhem, using their coffins as weapons.'

'O yes, I know,' said George. 'You can read about it in almost every travel book about Barbados.' He related the story.

'Balls,' said Dave. 'When a man dead he clean done. All this talk about soul and spirit and religion is church talk, nothing but balls. If Man had soul, why the hell we can't see it all these years?' He took another draught of his rum and replaced the glass on the floor.

George pointed to the glass and said, 'Dave, how the hell that diphtheria germ got on the rim of your glass?'

Dave took up his glass and looked at it, scrutinising the rim. Then, re-covering himself, he said, 'George, man, you playing the ass. People can't see germs with the naked eye.'

'Why not?'

'Well, we just ain't made that way. Germs too small for people to see without microscope or something like that. The human eye by itself is not sufficient. Nothing strange in that.'

'And suppose I say that the human eye by itself is not sufficient to see soul? Anything strange in that? Does that prove that soul doesn't exist?' George linked his fingers behind his head and lay back in his chair, smiling at Dave.

'Balls again,' said Dave. 'Soul and germs is two different things. Furthermore, you can see germs if you look at them through a microscope. But you can look through all the microscope in the world, you never see soul. Why?'

'Because soul and germs are two different things,' said Reid. 'Besides, even with the assistance of the most powerful microscope known, you can only see certain types of germs. Before the invention of the microscope, people didn't know of — and few people believed in — the existence of germs. A lot of people in the world today will never believe that Man has a soul, until somebody invents a psychoscope.'

'What the hell is a psychoscope?' said Dave.

'Something you look through to see soul. Microscope is something you look through to see microbes. Psychoscope to see psyche. Soul.' He smiled broadly, challengingly, at Dave.

'Balls!'

I sipped my drink in uncomfortable silence. My pet dislike, as far as conversation is concerned, is any subject relating to non-material things.

As soon as you begin to talk about soul or death or after-life survival or religion, I lose interest. I either walk away or shut up in sullen, impatient indifference or become disrespectfully flippant or irritable. Childish, pointless talk! I had come up to George Reid's house to talk politics; to gossip about happenings in Hiroona; to relax under the beguiling influence of good, interesting conversation about my labour union and party; about what I was going to do when I took over the government; about West Indian political personalities; about imperialism and the Colonial Office; and about corruption here and there. I was in no mood — I was never in the mood — to listen to idle, speculative nonsense about non-existent rubbish like soul and after-life. I got up, and turning my back on Dave and George, and on the discussion, I stood admiring the view of Kingsland and the harbour.

Reid's house was perched on the plateau which juts out into the sea, and ends, like an enormous index finger, in Nelson's point. The patio commanded a panoramic view of the multicoloured houses on the lower slopes of the plateau — of the harbour, stretching across to Fort George at the opposite end — and of Kingsland, with its back to the mountain, its face to the sea. This was my element, my world. It didn't require 'proof,' like soul and other world and after-life did. It was there for all to see. *See.* *You* didn't have to torment your brains with baseless, useless, nonsensical speculations about it.

My eyes swept the view — the lights of town-cars moving on streets hidden by the night and the distance — the greater lights of three steamships in the harbour, embarrassing the lesser lights of small yachts, schooners and sloops — the revolving light of the beacon of Fort George, doing its warning beat like a robot policeman.

'Wonderful view you got here, Reid,' I said, without turning round.

'It is,' said George. 'Magnificent at night and you should see it in the afternoon when life seems to move with a kind of cool, dreamy slowness, and you can watch the goings-on below as from a box seat in an opera house.'

Reid came and stood beside me.

'Lovely, isn't it?' He indicated the view with his chin.

'It sure is,' I said.

'Ever been up here before?'

'Never.'

'Not even for house-to-house campaigning?'

'No. The people who live in this area are the wealthy, respectable, upper-middle class type — the type that would bring out their shotguns, like Patrick McIver did, if I even entered their yard. I promise you I'll get even with old McIver, though.'

Reid laughed. 'That must have been excellent Gilbert and Sullivan,' he said.

'You hear that, Jerry,' said Dave, laughing, as he got up and joined us, his empty glass in his hand. 'Gilbert and Sullivan. What the hell is that? I always tell George that for a planter's son and a cocksman, he has some strange beliefs — and he talks like a book: human survival after death, soul and psychoscope. A while ago he was talking about box seat in opera house. Now it is Gilbert an' Sullivan. Christ, George, man. Why you don't talk like a planter and a cocksman?'

Reid threw a playful cuff at Dave's head and said, 'This king of ignoramuses has the stupid, old-fashioned idea that as I am a playboy (as he calls me when I am not a cocksman), I should believe in women, but not in the God who made them in the very first place. This, to me, is as illogical and ungrateful as hell.' We laughed. Reid sipped his drink. 'And the way some people talk, you would think that the old planters had no interest in books and the finer things of life; that their only interests were crops, labourers, land, high living and oppression. Come, fellers — let me show you evidence to the contrary.'

That was how I came to see Reid's library, and to get my first glimpse of the issue of the *Hiroona Weekly* in which Paul Darcy had made good his threat to expose my fingering of Penny Farthing's money.

20

R EID led us through the sitting room into an adjoining room — a fairly large room, with shelves neatly stacked with books. Some were large books of the tome variety. Most of them were old books in good condition, but some were so old that they were kept from falling apart by bands of blue tape. The shelves were labelled in sections: History, Fiction, Religion, Government, Art, Biography and so on. There was even a section given to a few books on 'The Psychic'.

'These were left to me by my old people,' said Reid. 'You can see for yourselves that this library has been in use for a hell of a long time, and that the books were not mere ornament. I've only added a few — mainly those paperbacks you see over there — from time to time.'

'Snob,' said Dave, as he bit into a sandwich and washed it down with rum.

'You've made your point, anyway, George,' I said. I had never been into a private library before. I was not even aware that people, much less planters, kept all these books in the house. Since leaving school, my own reading was limited to an occasional newspaper.

Looking around Reid's library, I pointed to two large gilt-framed portraits on the wall. One was of a white woman of about forty, but still strikingly attractive. The other was of a trifle younger-looking, handsome man in military clothes.

'Daddy and Mother,' explained Reid, 'Dad enlisted in the West Indian Regiment in the 1914–18 thing. Killed in France. Same chap whose name you see second from top on the war memorial in the Market Square — "Lt Herman Adolphus Reid, V. C." Mother sold the estates after he died. We didn't much like the feudalism involved in running an old West Indian plantation.'

'As planters, you and your parents were eccentrics, then,' said Dave and dodged a clout from Reid.

On an old untidy desk in a corner of the room were some papers and a large dictionary. Among the papers I saw a copy of the *Hiroona Weekly*. I had not read the latest issue, so I decided to borrow Reid's copy after our tour of his library. Before appropriating the newspaper, however, I took up the dictionary to look up the word 'manifesto'. Reid removed the newspaper, folded it and shoved it in the pocket of his slacks. He made the action look casual. 'Martha forgot to tidy this desk before taking her day off,' he said, and began to arrange the papers and things on the desk. Dave broke in with a remark which sparked another argumentative discussion between him and Reid. I was drawn into the argument, and by the time I had found my word, and put down the dictionary, the *Weekly* had dropped out of my mind.

It was nearly midnight when George and Dave brought me back in George's car to Bottom Town. George drove the car. Dave sat in the back seat, dozing, his head askew. George and I chatted quietly about the forthcoming election and about Hiroonian matters in general. Dave woke up every now and again, said 'Balls,' and went back to sleep.

George was driving very slowly, and as he and I talked I got the impression that he wanted to tell me something which he found difficult and embarrassing to express. And when he suddenly said, 'By the way, what type of political ruler you planning to be?' I knew that my impression was correct.

'What type? How you mean?' I said, puzzled.

'Well, you know for instance the "Papa-Uncle" type. These try to encourage a sort of Father Christmas image of themselves to offset their indiscretions, arrogance, injustices, and even despotism. This type does not flourish in sophisticated communities like Britain, the United States or Canada. But you've heard about them plenty in the West Indies and elsewhere. They always "do a lot for the people", but very little for the country. Some of them begin with very good intentions, but soon succumb to power. Power is at once their highest ambition and their deadliest enemy. They kill, impound and suppress people who disagree with their policies. They are the President for-life type; ukase-minded men, with an affinity to Greats like Tiberius Claudius Nero of Rome, Czar Paul the First of Russia, Hitler of Germany, Stalin of Russia, Batista of Cuba, Jiminez of Venezuela, Trujillo of Santo Domingo and Magloire of Haiti. They are either murdered in bed, or they murder themselves, or they're killed by their own disgusted, disillusioned supporters, or they're forced to flee their country with loot which they spent their time salting away, or which they snatched from the public treasury just before their flight. Now, you could be that type of political leader. On the other hand, you could use your position to make your island prosperous, energetic, corruption-free, while you, as leader of your country, play the political game with all your heart, intellect and skill, bowing out gracefully when the rules of the game so require. Which of those two types you going to be? I am interested, because the economics of a country and its volume of trade depend to some extent on the politics of the country, and I earn my living in business. Besides, I like politics, but abhor oppression in any form.'

'I don't agree,' I said, ignoring his question. 'The ruler of a country must rule it. If in ruling it you have to be a bit ruthless at times, well, so be it, you just have to be ruthless. You got to maintain your position at all cost. If you can succeed by only using strong-arm methods, why not use them? What sort of leader would allow people to keep opposing him, obstructing his government, impeding progress? What sort of leader would just stand by while another man or another political party snatch the country from him, right under his nose? Mustn't he put up a fight to maintain law and order? In such a struggle you can hardly avoid bitterness, ruthlessness. But that is politics.'

'I see,' said George Reid thoughtfully. 'In other words, you won't mind imposing a worse kind of imperialism on your own people than the kind of imperialism we now accuse Britain of imposing on the islands — if you "have to"?'

'That is beside the point. A strong-arm leader usually does more for a country than a weak and stupid one can ever do for it. Take Hitler. Hitler did more for the West Indies than some people realize. If Hitler had not taunted Britain about the bad conditions in the British Colonies, the British Government would not have sent out the Moyne Commission to the West Indies in 1940 to investigate these conditions. It was from that time that the islands began to receive consideration for Colonial Development and Welfare aid.'

'I see,' said Reid. 'In other words, Hitler did more for the West Indies than he did for his own country?'

'Why you say that?' I said.

'Well,' replied Reid, 'Hitler took over a Germany that was united since Bismarck, and he left it cut up — fragmented. Part of it in the hands of foreigners. At the same time, according to your view, he did a wonderful job for the West Indies — he provoked Colonial Development and Welfare aid. Man alive!'

'Have it your way. One thing is certain, though: it is all over with old Adolf. What he has done he has done. He hasn't got to worry about it now, because he, too, is done.'

Reid laughed. 'That's snugly put, Jerry. But if you are planning to model your government, as a ruler in Hiroona, on strong-arm principles — or rather on strong-arm *lack* of principles — in the belief that you escape accountability through death, good luck to you. I happen to be one of those simple-minded people who hold to the superstition that crimes against humanity are crimes against Nature, against God if you like. For tyranny is blasphemy, and death is not a pardoner or an absolver of such guilt. That is not death's function — to pardon or absolve. Death is a receiver of wrecks — wrecked bodies. Not souls. So the superstition makes damn good sense in its declaration that, "after death, the judgement, the accounting".'

'Stop it, Reid, man. Christ! A ghost story like that can frighten hell out of a feller. You make me nervous. You got a drink anywhere in the car? I could do with one right now. Even tomato juice will do.'

Then Reid gave me the crowning surprise of the night. He stopped the car, turned in his seat and gently shook Dave, trying to arouse him. Dave only groaned, shifted his position and continued in half-drunken sleep. Reid gave up. He returned to his driving. We were quite near to Bottom Town now. Reid said, 'You know, Jerry, I wanted Dave to hear what I am about to tell you. It is this: You remember that Dave and I asked you some time ago to amend the law of Hiroona to enable us to import slot machines when you take over the Government of this island? Well, I want you to forget it, so far as I am concerned. Dave may continue to pursue the matter with you, if he wants to, but I am no longer interested.'

21

S ONIA turned over and made a peevish little sound as I entered the bedroom and accidentally stumbled against the bed. I switched on the single naked light bulb which hung over the thin cloth screen that separated the bedroom from the other room. Sonia slept on. She was one of those people who sleep with all their might. To arouse Sonia from sleep, you had to use strong words like, 'Lazarus, come forth,' or some such infallible incantation.

I did not want to awaken her on this particular occasion, however. There was my supper on the table; Sonia had covered it with a bath towel to keep it warm, and she had gone to sleep, expecting me to awaken her as usual, when I came home. She would then come and sit at the table, and we would discuss the day's news and happenings while I ate. But my visit with George and Dave had gone well past bedtime, and Sonia couldn't wait up. I decided to let her sleep. After that long session at George's bungalow, and my strange argument with him in the car, I didn't want to talk with anyone, not even with Sonia. I would undress, then eat alone. I wanted to think.

I was still trying to arrive at a probable reason for Reid's preachment to me about tyranny and accountability. It was hardly a tactful 'lecture' to throw at a friend who was on the verge of taking over the control of a country.

I was wrestling with this thought as I sat down to my late, cold supper. I removed the towel with which Sonia had covered the dishes. Cockroaches scurried in every direction. Three of the huge brown beasts had managed to get their mouths under the saucer which covered the rice. They remained perfectly still. Perhaps they were so intent upon their feast that they didn't realise that the cloth was removed; or they simply froze in fright when I uncovered them.

I looked around for the flit gun, and found instead a copy of the *Hiroona Weekly*. Sonia must have placed it on the sofa and it had fallen to the floor, between the sofa and the table. By the time I straightened up from under the table, the three cockroaches had come to their senses and fled.

I sat down, placed the newspaper near to me on the table, removed the saucers which covered the food in the one or two plates, and was about to take over from where the cockroaches left off, when glancing at the newspaper, I saw the enormous headline on the front page. I froze like the three cockroaches, staring at the newspaper.

It was a typical Paul Darcy headline. It said so much that it was hardly necessary to read the comments under it. The huge, heavy, black words were spread out on the top of the page like a flag, no, like a banner, waving in the breeze from the top of a pole:

MOLE RETAINS COMPENSATION MONEY

POOR BOY AND DESTITUTE MOTHER CHEATED

I sprang up from the table and rushed into the bedroom to awaken Sonia, but I must have succeeded in waking up the neighbours instead. At last, after I had shaken her somewhat like a dog shakes a rag doll, and pushed her and shouted, 'Sonia! Wake up! Sonia! Git up! Git up!' several times, she sat up, mumbling, 'Mm? Mm? Who dat? Jerry?'

'Yes, Sonia. Wake up! It's me.' I shook her some more. She opened her eyes, looked up at me and said, 'Oh, is you? Way you bin all dis time? Ah couldn't sleep at all till you come in.'

'Sonia, you saw this?' I shoved the newspaper in front of her as if she were responsible for the article.

'Wha' dat?'

'The *Hiroona Weekly* newspaper. Have you read it?'

'No. But Ah heard it had something about you, so Ah borrow it from Job Sayer's wife Laura, and put it on de sofa so you could see it when you come in.'

'But you mean to tell me you heard that this paper was saying bad things about me, and you didn't read it? You're a hell of a woman, girl.'

'Well, Ah did start to read it, but Ah doze off, so Ah say to meself that Ah better leave it till you come, so you could read it to me.'

'Okay. Come let's go sit to the table.'

She slid from the bed, and used the chamber pot briefly before joining me at the table. I opened the door to let some fresh air into the poky, stuffy shack. Then I sat down, cleared a place on the table and rested the newspaper in front of me.

'Sonia,' I said, 'this is a hell of a thing. Listen.'

I read the headline slowly, and then said, 'Now listen to what he says underneath:

Some two years ago, the orderly and peaceful ways of this island were assaulted by the appearance of a movement informed by inflammatory ideas borrowed in part from neighbouring West Indian islands and in part from certain communist countries. The badge of identification with this movement is the word 'comrade', and the aim of the movement is to assault existing institutions and gainsay accepted principles of government and conduct. Inspired by this movement, so-called trades unions and sub-unions have broken out all over Hiroona like a pus-producing rash, a putrid eczema, on the fair skin of our island. The leader of this affront is an ex-bum who calls himself Jerry Mole. This man Mole has attracted a large following drawn from his own class — the rabble. To bolster his own standing and to increase membership of his unions, Mole organized a strike — the first on the island — in the Sugar Belt nearly two years ago. Mole gave it out that the strike was a protest on behalf of a mentally defective boy known as Penny Farthing, whose fingers were crushed by one of the factory's grinding machines, and to whom the Management of the factory had paid no compensation for this injury. To settle the matter, the Management paid the boy by cheque a very large sum of money — ninety-six dollars. The cheque was cashed by the boy in Mole's presence at the Barclays Bank. Mole then took the boy home to the Sugar Belt by taxi. Two reporters from this Newspaper made contact with Penny immediately after Mole drove away from the miserable hovel (photograph at left) in which the boy and his sick indigent Mother live. The reporters asked Penny how much money he received. Penny proudly showed the reporters a new one-dollar note — serial number D2 638891 — which, he told the reporters, was given to him by 'Papa Jerry'.

'Is that all the money you got?' one of the reporters asked. 'Yes,' Penny replied, 'all I get.' 'Aren't you going to spend your dollar?' 'No,' replied Penny. 'I no spend nice pretty money. I keep.' Up to yesterday, Penny was still hugging his dollar, which is all that he has received so far, from the ninety-six dollars paid in compensation for the loss of his fingers. The sum of money paid by the Management of the factory could well have built the boy and his Mother a decent little home, with a sizeable balance. We understand that at a meeting of Mole's union, one Joseph Bute, alias Joe Pittance, accused Mole to his face of appropriating Penny Farthing's compensation money. *Mole did not deny this accusation of theft.* Mole's retention of the boy's money is proof positive that Mole lied when he gave it out that the strike was a protest in Penny Farthing's interest. It is now beyond doubt that the strike was in Mole's own interest, and that the people in the Sugar Belt, who took part in the strike, were duped by Mole who is now seeking votes for himself from those same people whom he has so ruthlessly deceived. This same man, Mole, is now — to use his own words — 'preparing to take over the Government after the forthcoming elections'. God help this island if it falls into the hands of a man without conscience — a despot, a man without scruples. Let the people of Hiroona take warning and careful thought while there is still time.'

The interesting thing about my reaction to Darcy's recital of this scandal was that I began to read it with mounting fear, but before I got to the end of it my attitude changed to daring, defiance. The thing was all out now, anyway. Published. Even George Reid believed it. That's why he had tactfully hidden the newspaper from me, and then lectured me about tyranny and Papa-Uncle Somebody or other, and about accountability in his blasted imaginary Eternity. His bringing in this business of accounting in Eternity was his way of telling me that he believed that I would get away with it in Hiroona, but that they would catch up with me in Valhalla. Ha! Well, I shall deal with Eternity or Valhalla when it comes or when I go to it.

Perhaps Dave Potter, too, knew about the newspaper article, but he would take a less squeamish view of the matter, anyway.

Reid had opted out of the 'man eaters' deal because his sensitivity was outraged. After listening to my points of view in the car, he was now certain that I was dangerous company — unworthy of a cultured cocksman with a private library and a conscience.

Well, the only sensible thing for me to do now was to fight this scandal with brazen-facedness. Meet the challenge with a sort of hubristic head-on. There were only a few minor points I wanted cleared up. Sonia might help.

'Does Pittance know about this newspaper article?' I asked. 'Ah don't know,' replied Sonia. 'But Pittance always does know things, so prab'ly he heard 'bout it already.'

'Does Naomi Sampson know about it?'

'Well, you know how Naomi outspoken. If she did know 'bout it she woulda surely bring it up at de last meetin'. But she must be hear about it by now.'

Damn it. I pounded the table. The saucers and the plate rattled.

'Look here, I intend to fight this,' I said, striking the newspaper violently several times with the back of my hand. 'I am going to see a lawyer tomorrow.'

'Don't do dat, Jerry.'

'How you mean? Let this libel go unchallenged? Paul Darcy will have to *prove* that I took Penny Farthing's money. He can't prove it. I am not leaving it so.'

'Jerry, even if Mr Darcy can't prove dat we took de money, we did take it. A lot of things dat is true can't be proved. It is a fact dat we did take de money. You even said to me when Ah told you dat you shouldn't take all, you said we need de money more than Penny Farthing need it. If you go to court, you will only make de matter more public, an' people will laugh at you an' shake their head and say Pittance is a more honest man than you; and people ain't gwine vote fo' you, and it will be your own fault.'

'Pittance more honest than me, eh? Pittance, Pittance, I am fed up to the gills with Pittance.'

Suddenly, I hit her. Hard on the mouth. I just couldn't sit there and look truth in the face. I had to hit it. To shut it up. To smother it. I wanted to hit Pittance, but as he wasn't there, I hit Sonia.

'After all I've done for you,' I hissed. 'You ungrateful bitch.'

Sonia gazed at me in wild surprise for a moment. A little blood seeped out of her lower lip. Suddenly, she swung. An explosive cuff. It jarred my temple, pressed numbness against the side of my head and dashed me on the sofa on my right. Tiny, tuneless music sang inside my head like a chorus of little fireflies. The girl had half arisen and leaned over a bit before delivering the blow, so that her whole weight was behind it.

Before I could right myself and rise from the sofa, Sonia leapt on me like a panther. I pushed her away with both my hands. She smashed against the table. A plate and a saucer clattered to the floor before the table righted itself. The din woke up the night. Sonia's body ricochetted from the table and bounced against the chair on which I had been sitting a while ago. She and the chair crashed to the floor. I sprang at her, but she was surprisingly nimble for a medium-sized woman. Before I could reach her to pin her on the floor she was up. Her thin nightgown was torn in front, exposing her breasts. We grappled, hitting in the clinch. Her nightgown now had a rent right down the front exposing her completely. My violence suddenly changed into passion; my fist-punching merged into fingering. But the attempt was stillborn. Sonia disengaged herself and pushed me with a mighty shove against the table. Table, dishes, plates, newspaper and I went down.

Our neighbour, old Job Sayers and his wife Laura appeared at our door. Laura gave one startled look and began shrieking. 'O Gord! Murdar! Murdar! Police! O God! Murdaar! Murdaar!' Job rushed into the house and held Sonia just as she was about to spring at me. The commotion in the house and Laura's shrieks brought out almost the whole Bottom Town community. People filled the yard, some jostling to get near enough to the door for a look in. Some stood, eagerly asking questions and making remarks. They were all in their bed clothes which were, in most cases, their working clothes slackened up. A few of the more malicious ones, lovers of excitement, took up Laura's cry and began to shout 'Murder! Murdoor! Murdaar!' just for the hell of it. The din in the house was now replaced by hubbub in the yard.

Panting I went to the door. I tried to make my voice sound as even and controlled as I could. 'Comrades,' I shouted, 'no murder here. That's laughable nonsense.' I emitted a funny sound which I hoped would be regarded as a laugh. 'Sonia and I just having a little rough play. Man and wife bedroom fight. You know. It's around election time, so we got to blow off steam a little bit. But I will still vote fo' she, and she fo' me; and Ah hope all o' you will vote fo' we.'

Everybody laughed, and a little cheering went around.

'Good night, Comrades,' I shouted, concealing the big rent in the front of my pyjama pants with one hand, and waving gaily and shutting the door with the other.

'Good night, Comrade,' they shouted back, as they went away, laughing.

Sonia had wriggled free from Job Sayers' restraining hands, and, without saying a word, had returned to the bedroom and to bed, not even bothering to change her torn night gown. I tried to clean up the mess in the room. I raked up the bits of broken ware and shovelled the food into the only lucky plate left. I set the chairs and the table upright, picked up the copy of the *Hiroona Weekly*, shoved it in the pocket of my jacket which was hanging on the nail near the door, and went and lay down on the bed. Sonia was lying on her side, her back to me. Presently, I heard her slow, even breathing. She was fast asleep. I just lay there, unable to think clearly, unable to sleep.

I got up to leave the room. As I walked past the foot of the bed I paused, and looked at Sonia. Even in her sleep she was seductive. Her generous mouth was slightly open, like a woman in heat; her two full young breasts reached out from her torn nightgown with provocative insouciance; her rippling brown thighs and smooth bulges were subtly revealed under the diaphanous material that barely concealed them. I fought back another sudden thrust of sexual desire. Sonia's reaction to any amorous approach on my part at this time would very probably bring out the Bottom Town community again.

I switched off the light, went out into the other room and lay down on the sofa listening to the lusty crowing of cocks, and the dogs calling to one another.

I watched the dawn as it invaded the room on hesitant tiptoe.

22

I got up, hitched up my pyjama pants, and was about to go out to the lean-to kitchen in the yard to wash my face with water from the bucket which Sonia kept on the beaten-dirt floor in a corner of the kitchen, when I noticed that the big rent in the front of my pyjama pants was exposing my sex. I went into the bedroom, took off my pyjamas and put on trousers. Sonia was still lying on the bed with her eyes closed, but I knew she was not sleeping. I didn't disturb her.

I went out into the kitchen in my trousers and vest, dipped a calabash of water from the bucket, 'shook out my mouth' and washed my face. Then I made the usual 'camp' fire on the kitchen floor, put a pan of water on the fire, dropped a piece of cocoa and a few bay leaves in the pan, added a pinch of salt and a dash of essence of vanilla. The bay leaves were to season the 'cocoa tea', the salt gave it 'body' and the vanilla gave it flavour.

Leaving the chocolate to boil, I went into Davson Street to buy two penny loaves of bread. I passed the Reliance Bakery with its fresh bread, cakes and pastries displayed in its glass windows and its glass-fronted counter. The Reliance Bakery was owned and run by upper middle class coloured people — enemies of my party, and therefore retarders of progress on the island. So I walked on to Barney Marksman's pokey little one-door shop where I usually bought my bread. Barney retailed liquor there, too. The liquor section was divided off from the grocery section by a rough wooden partition. The shabbiness of the place didn't matter to me, because Barney was a supporter of the PPP.

As I entered Barney's shop, I heard a man behind the partition say, 'It's true. I did hear 'bout de story before, but Ah didn't believe it till Ah hear some fellers talking 'bout it under Popular Traders' gallery yesterday morning. One feller was reading it from Parl Darcy newspaper, de *Hiroona Weekly*. Ah never thought Mole woulda done a thing like dat. He is a son of a bitch. Only a ass will vote fo' a man like dat.'

'What yo' quarrelling about?' said another voice. 'If Mole t'ief, that ain't anything. Everybody does t'ief. So what?'

A third man cut in: 'But Christ, man! Fancy a man who call 'eself a leader, t'iefing from a poor little bwoy like Penny Farthing! O' course, I ain't surprise. I always look on Mole as a trickster lookin' for a easy job wid money an' position. I always tell you fellers so. Mole an' his union can go to hell for my part. He is a blarsted rabber. Give me anudder rum, Barney. Chalk it up.'

Standing alone in the grocery part of the shop, I heard Barney measure and pour the drink. He said at the same time, 'I have to agree wid you, Joey — such a man ain't got no conscience, no honesty, if he do a nasty thing like dat. But he does mix wid de poor man, and he does give de white man hell. So he is a good man. An' if we don't vote fo' him and his party, who else we got? Dat is de big question. Who else we got?' He turned, picked up a piece of chalk and briefly surveyed a list of creditors which was written in white chalk on the wall of the shop behind the counter on the liquor side. Under the name 'Joey' he jotted down 'Rum–8 cents'. He put the piece of chalk back in its place, turned back to his liquor customers and said, 'A country is in a hell of a mess when you can't trust your leaders. An' you in a hell of a fix when you only got one leader an' you can't trust 'im. I agree dat ————' He glanced towards the grocery part of the shop, and saw me.

'Eh-eh! Comrade Mole? Didn' hear you come in. What can I do fo' you, sir?'

'Oh, I just dropped in to get some bread.' My smile was weak, embarrassed.

'We was just talking about you here — about a nasty rumour goin' round sayin' you t'ief money from a poor bwoy in de country name Penny Farthing.'

'It is not true, Barney. So help me God, I swear it is not true.'

Three men emerged from behind the partition. One said, 'How yo' sayin' it ain't true, an' Ah heard some fellers readin' it wid me own ears yesterday marning from de newspaper under Popular Traders' gallery?'

'Listen Comrades, the thing you heard about in the newspapers is nothing strange. I expected Paul Darcy to tell lies on me. He hates me because I am trying to open the eyes of the people.'

'But how can a man write a nasty thing like dat about you when it ain't true?' said Barney.

'Comrades, you forget how wicked an' evil Paul Darcy an' dese white people is? Ah can't stay now, but I will come back an' explain everything to you. O.K.?'

'How much bread you want to buy, Comrade?' said Barney.

'Two penny loaves, and a half pound of sugar, Comrade.'

I shoved a loaf in each of the two sides pockets of my trousers, took up the sugar, paid Barney and said, 'O.K., Comrades. See you tomorrow night.' As I walked out of the shop and up Davson Street, back to Bottom Town, I could feel the cold, heavy silence of doubt at my back like a pistol pressing against me.

In a daze of apprehension, I re-entered my kitchen, took the pan of boiling chocolate off the fire, carried it into the house, poured out an enamel cup of the hot liquid and sugared it. Sonia was still lying in bed — which was unusual for her at that late morning hour. She appeared to be brooding heavily, seriously. I said nothing to her. I had trouble enough on my mind.

As I sat at the table breakfasting off my cocoa-tea and a loaf of bread, my mind raced all over Darcy's *exposé* and the awkward situation to which it had given rise. Sean Dobson and his supporters must have had a field day with it in the Sugar Belt over the weekend.

Suddenly, I remembered the word 'manifesto'. Joe Pittance had stumped me with it at the committee meeting yesterday afternoon. Later, I had looked up the word in George Reid's dictionary, in his library: 'Public declaration by sovereign, state or body of individuals, making known past actions and motives of actions announced as forthcoming.'

Leaving half my breakfast, I raced out of the house and down to the Chamber — the union headquarters. I shoved the door open, rushed up to the table on the platform and pulled out the little drawer at the side of the table. Yes, the exercise book in which Sonia made semi-literate jottings at meetings was there all right. And the pen.

I opened the exercise book in the middle, and wrote across the top of the two blank pages, in large capitals, 'MANIFESTO'. I filled the rest of the two pages with a series of squares. In each square I wrote the name of a villager of the village in which Penny Farthing lived, so that the whole layout of squares represented an exact ground plan of the entire village, and each square was the position of a villager's shack. In the square containing Penny's name I wrote in red ink, '$96 already deposited', and underlined it twice. Then I wrote a longish letter, purportedly addressed to Mr Forbes the Administrator. I back-dated the letter by eighteen months. Then I carefully removed the two middle pages of the exercise book, so that the pages came away together, thus keeping intact the entire layout of the ground plan of the Sugar Belt village. Under the 'plan' I wrote down the same date I had written on the 'letter to the Administrator'.

I folded the three pages from the exercise book, pushed them into my hip pocket, replaced the exercise book in the drawer, closed the drawer and left the Chamber. I was now quite ready to deal with Paul Darcy, Sean Dobson and company.

I hurried back to my shack, dressed quickly — khaki shirt and trousers. No tie. No jacket. I gulped the balance of my cocoa tea which was now cold and heavy, swallowed the remaining half loaf and rushed out to find a taxi to take me to the Sugar Belt.

I had four agents in the Sugar Belt. They kept me informed of happenings there, and looked after my general political interests in the area. I tried to contact them as soon as the taxi dropped me in the district. I could not get in touch with three of them immediately, however. I had to wait until the twelve o'clock factory whistle blew the lunch break which would release Gertie Small from the factory and Sonny Benn and Beamish Ashton from the cane fields for one hour.

My fourth henchman was not a labourer. He was Vance Dennie, the headteacher of Saint Petrus elementary school. St. Petrus was the largest village in the Sugar Belt. The elementary school there served the other villages as well. Vance Dennie was about thirty-five and as black as kettle bottom. He was short and thin, with small, piercing eyes in a longish head with hair as thick and matted as an African bushman's.

He was not the tractable type of henchman. He was bumptious and temperamental, but he was one of my strongest supports. His knowledge of the people of the villages was quite remarkable, and I had often drawn upon this knowledge.

The trouble about Vance was that he was a kind of political eccentric. He had read extracts of *Das Kapital* and things like that, and he went around talking and behaving like *Das Kapital*. He had cut out the morning and evening prayers and grace before and after meals, from the time table of his school; and when the Education Authority threatened to dismiss him for these omissions, he had stubbornly substituted prayers of his own making, which were worse than the omissions. He referred to himself as 'the spokesman of revolution', and boasted that he was 'the leading and only exponent of socialism on the island'. Vance was always in trouble with the Education Authority.

What made me hesitate to call on Dennie as soon as I arrived in the Sugar Belt on that Monday morning was my uncertainty as to what his reactions were to Darcy's damning newspaper article, which he would certainly have read during the weekend. I therefore considered it prudent to consult Gertie Small, Beamish Ashton and Sonny Benn before calling on Dennie. And while I waited for the factory's twelve o'clock whistle, I decided to visit a few of the villagers who were not working that morning and ask them a pointed question or two.

I went up to Penny Farthing's hovel, first of all, but the wretched place was closed up, and there was no one in the yard. I wondered where Penny and his mother were. I wanted to be seen visiting them. It would show interest. I looked across to the next hut, in search of the friendly woman who had spoken to me when I visited Penny's mother on the first occasion I called there. I saw the woman all right, but she wasn't friendly this time. She came out of her house humming a tune. She was carrying a naked child on one arm and held a calabash in the other hand. She was coming in my direction when she looked up and saw me. She halted, scowled, turned back and re-entered her shack.

Hurt and perturbed, I went across to her yard and called, 'Eudora, what's the matter? Why yo' shun me so all of a sudden?'

'What yo' say, sah?'

'Why yo' so cold dis marnin'?' I asked.

'Ah ain't gat no time fo' tark, sah. Ah looking after Herman lunch. It naily twelve o'clock.'

I wanted to ask her where Penny and his mother were, but I didn't. This rudeness from a Sugar Belt villager was new and strange and disturbing. Sean Dobson and his supporters had been at work here.

'I see. O.K., Eudora. Thank you. How is the baby?'

'It well.'

I left the yard.

As most of the villagers were at work in the factory or the fields, the village was very quiet at that time of day. A semi-deserted atmosphere pervaded the place. Only grandmothers were at home, for the most part, looking after the children and cooking lunch for their sons and daughters who were working on the estate. Here and there a few indolent oldsters sat in the shade of a hut, smoking dreamily on stumpy clay pipes, popping smoke from toothless mouths and shooting spit far and wide. A few young women — concubines of male workers — who had too many children to look after and had no grandmother with whom to leave them, fussed over pots in dark lean-to kitchens or in their yards, preparing the midday meal for their men. The sing-song drone of school children saying their lessons at the St. Petrus elementary school a quarter of a mile away could be faintly heard every now and again, as the wind changed direction.

Having failed with Eudora, I decided to try another of the young women — Clarissa.

Clarissa was an incorrigibly cheerful woman. Her heartiness reminded me of Charlotte Cain, my muffin and saltfish vendor in Kingsland. Clarissa was young, about thirty, but she looked really shop soiled. She had fourteen children, for nearly as many fathers. Fortunately, she had started to 'bring children' at the early age of fourteen, so now she had three strapping men of fourteen, fifteen and sixteen years old working on the estate, to support her and the other children. And so she had not a single worry in the world.

She was in her lean-to kitchen when I walked into her yard. Some of her children were playing in the yard nearby; naked, happy.

'How yo' do, Clarissa?' I said, peeping into her kitchen.

'Eh-eh. Is you, comrade?' said Clarissa, turning round quickly from a boiling pot. 'You will live till dey sun yo'. Ah was just dis minute callin' yo' name in me mind, t'inkin' 'bout yo'.' She covered the pot and placed the tasting-spoon on the cover.

I asked, 'Something in the pot made you think of me?'

'No. Not in de pot. In de village.' Clarissa's smile seemed to flatten her nose some more. Her missing front teeth somehow made her look younger. She wiped her hands on her soiled frock.

'What's happening in the village?' I questioned.

'T'ings happenin'.'

'What things?'

'Mis'er Dabson an' dem.'

'What Mr Dobson and them doing?'

'Nutten. Dey only saying dat you is a t'ief an' a liar. Dey go fram village to village, fram house to house all night Saturday night an' all day yesterday Sundee an' all night. Mek you wonder if dey does sleep at all. Dey readin' fram a big paper — newspaper — sayin' you t'ief Penny Farthing money an' a lot o' big words. Ah said to meself dat de big words must be mean dat you is a big t'ief, comrade.' Clarissa grinned happily. She sifted her frock from her petticoat, bent her head, lifted the frock a bit and wiped sweat from her face.

'So you believe that I am a thief and a liar, Clarissa?'

'Yes, comrade.'

'So you will give Dobson your vote?'

'No. Ah will still vote fo' you. After all, you is our people. You does tark nice to us. You does mix wid us like one of us. Mis'er Dabson always use to pass us pon de road in 'e car, not even sayin' "good morning". Only now, because he want us to vote fo' him, he does smile an' pucker up 'e long face full o' false friendliness. He t'ink he smart, but he can't fool me. Ah know what he after.'

'You are a very sensible woman, Clarissa. Ah wish everybody in de Sugar Belt was sensible like you. Now, tell me; who and Dobson was working on de people during de week end?'

'He an' Mis'er Phelps and Mis'er Creese an' some high mens fram Kingslan'. Mis'er Dabson use influence an' get de Gover'ment to take Penny Farthing mother to de poor house in Kingslan', an' Penny get back de jab as map at de factory yard.'

'Christ! De bitches work fast, eh Clarissa? But of course you know why. How come they suddenly get so interested in de people?'

'Sure, Ah know why. All dey doin' now is only tryin' to fool people an' get us to vote fo' Mis'er Dabson. But dey can't fool me. No sah. Dey ain't foolin' Clarissa. Ah know who Ah votin' for, an' dat is you, comrade.'

'Thank you, Clarissa. I always know where I stand wid you. I think I will hold a meeting in de Belt tonight. You coming?'

'Sure, comrade.'

I stepped into Clarissa's kitchen, took the spoon from off the pot cover and uncovered the pot. I dipped a little hot liquid out of the pot, with the spoon, cooled the liquid with my breath and tasted it. Clarissa beamed.

'Mmm,' I enthused. 'Damn good food, Clarissa.' She burst out laughing.

'It is poor people food, comrade — not good enough fo' you.'

'This food is good enough for anybody. You can cook real good. So help me God, Ah will give you a good job as a cook at de Kingsland Hospital when Ah take over de Gover'ment.'

'You mean dat, comrade?'

'Cross me heart an' hope to die. So help me God. You wait and see.'

'T'ank you, comrade. Ah really need a jab to help me wid all dese chil'ren. T'ank you, comrade.'

I handed the spoon to Clarissa, patted her bottom and walked out of the kitchen. Clarissa turned back to her pot with a happy coquettish laugh. As I left the yard, I quietly spat the raw, fishy, offending tang of the liquid out of my mouth and wiped my lips with my handkerchief.

23

The factory's twelve o'clock whistle was a huge, long shriek which penetrated to the fields and villages for miles around. It shattered the silence in the villages. It broke up the lively gossipings of the sweating labourers in the cane, cotton and arrowroot fields. Women threw down their hoes, and men stuck their cutlasses in the earth or on the nearest tree, to return to them an hour later. Factory workers poured out of Mount Horeb to begin the short walk to the village shops to lunch or to their huts for their simple fare. The children at St. Petrus elementary school put away their books and slates, stood up in their classes and prepared to go home for lunch. At a command from Vance Dennie the Headteacher, the children raised their clasped hands to the side of their faces and recited Dennie's controversial grace before meals: 'For what we are about to receive, only the Lord could possibly make us truly thankful. Amen.'

I went to the village shop where I knew I would find Beamish Ashton and Sonny Benn. The shop was crowded with labourers, buying or crediting their lunch: a small tin of sardines, a loaf of bread and a soft drink. Some stood around eating; others, especially the women, took their purchases to their homes where they could sit on their doorsteps or in their yards and lunch quietly. Some of the men washed down their lunch with a tot of rum. There was a lot of talking, and a little argument here and there. The place was noisy, lively, as it usually was at lunchtime. Joey Caines the shopkeeper interrupted his busy trade every now and again to write down misshapen figures with chalk against a list of names chalked up on the wall of the shop, where he did his book-keeping.

The greeting I received when I entered the shop lacked the usual heartiness and hero worship. There were still the outward signs of respect, but too much of this. The crowd even parted to let me pass, instead of propelling me through with the usual backslapping, hand-shaking and 'Hello, Bass'. And I didn't like the silence which fell on the place when I entered it. Beamish did come forward and say 'Hello, Bass', but his manner had an element of defiance in it, as though he was demonstrating to the crowd that he still trusted me and didn't give a damn about what the crowd thought. Sonny Benn remained where he was, in a corner, pre-occupied with a glass of rum and water.

The atmosphere of the place upset me — frightened me. I decided to use my 'manifesto' and my 'letter to the Administrator' immediately.

Putting on an air of acute indignation, like someone unjustly accused, I held up my hand and said, 'Comrades, I don't want to interrupt your lunch time, but I had to come here to see you and clear up the most wicked and evil scandal I have ever heard about in my life. One of my greatest supporters in the Sugar Belt sent an urgent message to me this morning, asking me to hurry and come up here, because Sean Dobson and his stooges were going around with a newspaper in which they had printed a damaging, lying article about me, saying that I stole money from Penny Farthing. Now before I expose this damnable lie, I want to ask you one question, comrades: Do you think that a man like me who has been fighting for you and for all the poor, downtrodden people of this island, would be so heartless, so wicked, so evil, as to steal money or anything else from a poor comrade like Penny Farthing? Now, let me show you proof that Sean Dobson and his henchman — those emissaries of the devil who hate your guts and mine, and who only trying to fool you now because they want your vote — let me show you proof that they only wanted to start a scandal so as to prevent me from fighting for you all. Those filthy liars. Those hypocrites.'

I was really mad, now, and I was compelling myself to believe every word I was uttering. I dragged the two 'documents' from my pocket and dashed the 'letter to the Administrator' down on the counter in front of Caines the shopkeeper.

'Comrade Caines, I want you to read this letter aloud so everybody can hear what I wrote to the Administrator months ago. Read it!' I shouted. 'You can read. Read it out aloud!'

Caines read:

Dear Mr Administrator,

    As I may be taking over the Government after the elections, I want to put a certain matter to you early, because this matter is very urgent. I notice that in other West Indian islands like St. Vincent, St. Kitts, Grenada, Antigua, and St. Lucia, they have what is called a Self Help Housing Scheme for the poorer people. In those islands the Government acquire some of the estates' lands and other lands, too, and build decent and comfortable cottage homes for the poor people. The people deposit a small amount of money, and help with the labour, while the Government provides the bulk of the labour and builds the cottages for the people. The people then occupy the houses and pay a very, very small amount of money every month until they pay for the houses. Now I want a Housing Scheme like that for the people of Hiroona, beginning with the people of the Sugar Belt. In the Belt villages, the poor hardworking people live in little wattle-and-mud huts with only one room. In some cases, the bedroom is not even separated from the other room, so that there is no privacy, and the children are always exposed to the private actions of the adults at night. This is bad. Now my people in the Sugar Belt are ready for a Housing Scheme to help them get their own house lot and a nice house. I have already drawn the ground plan of one of the villages; and one of the villagers — a poor boy called Penny Farthing — has already deposited ninety six dollars to get his house and lot, as the hut he and his poor destitute mother live in is not even fit for keeping pigs, and they need a good house at once. Penny Farthing has given me his deposit, and I have put it in the union funds to keep it safe for him until the Self Help Housing Scheme starts in the village. I would be grateful for a very early reply to this letter, so that I would be able to tell my people in the village about the Scheme.

I have enclosed a copy of the ground plan. You will see from the plan that I have acknowledged in red ink $96 deposited by Penny Farthing.

Yours sincerely,
Jerry Mole,
President of the Waterfront, Estate
and Manual Workers Union of Hiroona.

Caines handed back the letter to me. Nodding several times in perfect understanding, he looked around at the crowd and said, 'Comrades, you see how Mr Dobson an' his helpers been accusing our leader falsely. Dey even get me an' nearly everybody in de villages to believe dat Comrade Mole t'ief that poor bwoy money. All the time, the truth is that Comrade Mole is trying his best to help de bwoy and to get good house for all of us. It's a damn shame, de way dese people like Dobson is spreading false rumours an' writing lies in de newspapers, just to damage a good man and prevent him from helpin' us. Comrade Mole, sir, we now quite see de light. You have explain to us de trute of de matter. We see from de letter you wrote de Administrator why you couldn't tell us about de Housing Scheme before now — you had to wait for a reply from de Administrator. Dobson and his supporters is wicked people. Evil!'

During the general murmurs of enlightenment, contrition and satisfaction, I said, 'All of you come and gather round me here, and see for yourselves.' I opened the MANIFESTO and spread it on the counter. They all gathered around.

'You see this word here — "Manifesto"? It means a plan you propose to carry out. And you see these squares here? Examine them for yourselves, and you will see your own name written on a square. There is where I have planned your house and lot to be. And you see Penny Farthing's name here in this square? Good. Now tell me what you notice about it. Ain't you see the words "$96 already deposited" underlined twice in red ink for the

Administrator to see? Now tell me, as sensible people, all of you; if I intended to steal that poor boy's money, would I have acknowledged openly that he deposited it for a Housing Scheme — and underlined it in red ink, mind you? Twice!? Twice!! Good God!'

Loud talking broke out. Everyone wanted to go and tear Dobson and his supporters to pieces. One woman said, 'You get a reply fram de Administrata yet, comrade?'

'No,' I said. 'Look at the date on the letter, and look at this date here on the manifesto. Over a year and a half ago. And the only reply I received is the usual little piece of paper saying "the matter is receiving consideration". I was so damn annoyed I tore up the piece of paper. Since then, everytime I ask the Administrator about it, I get the same answer — "the matter is receiving consideration". That is how the Administrator treats us. It was the same thing when we wrote him asking for the pavilion in Kingsland for our rally. He refused to reply for months. I had to go myself and force him to reply.'

'He might even want to say now dat he didn't get yo' letter 'bout de housin' scream,' one discerning female comrade shouted.

'You damn right, comrade,' I quickly replied. 'Now I will explain to you all, the reason for Dobson's big lie: the Administrator must have called Dobson and shown him my letter and my manifesto. So he, Dobson, found out that I was trying to get Government to acquire some of the estate land for your house lots. A thing like that would frighten and annoy Dobson, Phelps and Company, because they hate you, and they hate to see you own anything. So they twisted the whole thing, to get you against me, so that you may vote for them — against yourself, against your own party.'

'Christ! What wickedness!' exclaimed Caines. 'What evil in dis country. Look here, comrade, I think you should call a meetin' at once. Now. To hell wid de half day. I will shut me shop now, and I and all of us here will go round to the other villages and bring everybody here to you, so you could explain to everybody and expose dis damnable scandal dese wicked people trying to cook up. What you say, comrades, you want to go back to work now or you want de meetin' now?'

'We want de meetin'. We can go back to work tomorrow, but we want de meetin' now. Come. We go round up de villages.'

'No, comrades,' I interposed. 'Go back to work, but spread the news around; and send round word to the villages that I will hold a meeting here this afternoon as soon as you break off at five o'clock. Tell all our people to come. Meanwhile, I will do a little house-to-house in the villages, chat with the old people till five. Comrade Caines, you better let me have a soft drink and a bread for lunch.'

I stood among them, talking with them and listening to their condemnation of Dobson and his fellows while I ate my lunch. Caines refused to accept payment for the bread and aerated drink. 'De pleasure is mine, Bass,' he said smiling.

I shook hands all round, and left. 'See you at five this afternoon, comrades.'

The feeling of their backslapping and the echo of their adulation remained with me for weeks after. There was something self congratulatory, too, in the episode: I was undoubtedly a shrewd politician. The thought that the Administrator would most certainly deny — perhaps publicly — having received any letter or village plan from me when he heard the news, did not worry me in the least. I would simply tell 'my people' that he was lying. And they would believe me.

24

I was in excellent spirits when I returned to town that evening, after the five o'clock meeting. I was hungry and tired, yes, but I felt supremely triumphant. Sonia was stirring about in the bed-room when I entered the house. She had cooked supper and placed mine on the table and had covered it with the bath towel as usual, to keep it warm.

I went straight to the table and began to eat. Of course, I noticed that Sonia had not waited to eat with me, and talk shop. This was unusual, as it was quite early in the evening. She could certainly have waited, as she always did. However, elated as I was over the day's victory, I was in no mood to worry over a small matter like eating alone. I had not forgotten the violent affray of the previous night between myself and Sonia; but the events of the day — the masterful way in which I had handled the news-paper article crisis, the tremendous success of the five o'clock meeting, and the fact that I had bested Sean Dobson and his supporters in political encounter — had pushed my fight with Sonia to the background of my mind and had shorn it of significance. Furthermore, I was eager to tell the story of my victory to someone — to whom if not to Sonia? So while I wolfed curried rice, jackfish, dasheen, yam, bits of onion boiled in the fish water seasoned with green pepper, I said, 'I spent the day in the Sugar Belt. Girl, it was a day of days.'

I paused. An opening like that always made Sonia wild-eyed with curiosity. It never failed to bring a spate of questions out of her. On this occasion, however, she remained in the bedroom and didn't even say 'Boo'.

'You listening?' I called.

'Yes.'

The tone of her 'yes' was unusually formal. As a matter of fact, 'yes' was the wrong reply. Sonia's reply should have been 'mm-hmm' or 'Eh-heh' or 'yeah, man', or some such friendly, homespun vocable. Not 'yes'. 'Yes' was when you vex, or when replying to a stranger. However, I pressed on regardless.

'It was a damn good thing I went early; for when I reached the Belt, I heard that Sean Dobson and his supporters been working on the people day and night during the weekend. They been using that Paul Darcy newspaper article against me, and practically all the people in the villages had turned me down flat. I had to think fast. Ha! Ha! Ha! I called a meeting in Joey Caines' shop immediately after the twelve o'clock whistle. Girl, they wanted to lynch me. I talked as I never talked before. You shoulda heard me. When I was finished with them, they wanted to lift me up. You listening?'

'Yes.'

'*Christ!* They were so mad with Dobson and Phelps for using Darcy's article against me, that they didn't want to go back to work. I begged them to go back to work, because I didn't want it to look like I was staging another strike. So I fixed a meeting for five o'clock this afternoon.'

Sonia continued to move about in the bedroom. I thought that she was busy cleaning out the room while she listened to me; so I went on, telling her the wonderful story:

'While I waited for five o'clock, I went to see that communist funstick Vance Dennie. Wow! As soon as I entered the yard of the headteacher's quarters where he lives, he flew at me: I was a disgrace to the Cause and a disappointment to the people. How was I going to defend myself against Paul Darcy's accusations in the *Hiroona Weekly*? He could not continue to give me his political support unless I returned the money I had stolen from that poor boy. I had made Karl Marx turn in his grave. What would Harry Pollitt say about conduct like mine? What would Castro say? How could the people trust me? I should read *Das Kapital*. I should read Harold Laski. I should acquaint myself with the ideas and ideals of the Fabian Society. I should read Strachey. I should read Trotsky. I should read . . . . Oh! he let me have it, all right.

'When he ran out of breath and reading matter, I very calmly said to him, "Vance, every story has two sides. You have heard Paul Darcy's side. Come to the public meeting at Parsons Village at five o'clock this afternoon, and you will hear my side." He came to the meeting, all right. I could see him at the edge of the huge crowd — small, cocky, long head with hair thick like bush; khaki open-neck shirt, white trousers, both hands pushed down in his trousers pockets, shoulders hunched to make height and show scholarship. He stood listening as I spoke, after Caines had read some correspondence I had with me. Girl, after the meeting, when the men who had lifted me on their shoulders put me down, Vance Dennie was among those who came and shook my hand. I wished you were there. Dobson hasn't got the chance of a snowball in Hell against me. He is now a political has-been, even before the elections. So you see, Sonia, in spite of all your fears and your tantrum of last night, I have beaten our enemies to the punch. I ———.'

Job Sayers and his wife Laura entered the house. Job was carrying a large, old valise. It appeared to be heavy. I seemed to recognise the valise as one which Sonia kept under our bed.

Completely ignoring me, Job and Laura stepped to the 'door' end of the thin cloth blind on the flimsy wooden frame which divided the house into bedroom and sitting room. Laura called softly, 'Sonia?' Sonia came to the bedroom 'door'.

'Hello,' she greeted Laura, smiling a little.

Laura said, 'We bring back your clothes. We been thinkin' t'ings over an' we feel it ain't right for you to leave your husban' now. It will look bad. People will say that if you and your husban' can't keep togedder, how can you all expeck to keep de Gover'ment togedder when you all take over de Gover'ment. So we bring back your clothes.'

Sonia broke down. Between sobs, she said, 'Ah ain't want to stop in dis house fo' no man to beat me up. An' Ah don't intend to take no blows from no man. Ah'm nat Jerry Mole childe fo' him to walk hand 'pon me as he like. Ah ain't stannin' for it.'

Laura gently placed her hand around Sonia's shoulder, comforting her. Job put down the valise at Sonia's feet as gently as if it were full of eggs. 'Take it easy, Sonia,' he said; 'take it easy; fo' de Gover'ment sake.'

'Yes, me dear chile,' said Laura. 'Fo' de sake of de Gover'ment.'

They stood there for a few moments while Sonia appeared to think things over. Job, long, lean, neck scraggy, large round head completely grey; shirt and trousers baggy, soiled; his black old face puckered with near-tearful sympathy. Laura, short, plump, younger; her cotton print frock clean, her round face stern as she spoke soothingly to Sonia.

Presently, Sonia said, 'O.K., Laura, Job. Thank you.' She took up her valise and disappeared behind the blind with it.

Without even a glance in my direction, Laura and Job left the house, Job screwing up his face as if he had a pain; Laura's head held unnaturally high, her lips pushed out long like a gar fish.

For a long time I was too stunned to speak. When I found tongue, I said, 'But what is this at all? Sonia, come out here and let me ask you something.'

She came out of the bedroom. She had changed into a clean, pretty frock and had combed her hair, as if she were going out.

'What is this about Job and Laura bringing back your clothes and talking about you clearing out?'

'Ah may as well tell you dis now,' said Sonia. 'We bin livin' together, man an' wife fo' over twenty years now, but you ain't seem to know me yet.'

'What you mean, Sonia?'

'Ah mean dat I is not de kind o' woman who is so carried away by yo' greatness dat Ah will take any an' everyt'ing from you, especially blows. An' Ah ain't de kinda wife who will see you do wrong things an' tell you dat you right. Because Ah tell you you was wrong to take Penny Farthing money, you ups an' box me. Ah say to hell wid dat!' *My God, she's attractive!* I thought.

'But you boxed me back, so we even,' I said, as I smiled at her winningly. She ignored that.

'An let me tell you dis from de start: if dis politics means dishonestness an' shrewd an' foolin' people an' tricks an' newspaper writin', Ah want no part wid it. T'ings like dat frighten me.'

'O, come now, Sonia. You're just being childish. Where did you propose to go and live when you tried to walk out on me just now?'

'Ah was going straight up to Chateaubelair, so help me God. Your Ma and me lived together before. She will be glad to have me back. She is a poor woman, but she honest and she clean. Like Job an' Laura, de only two decent people in de whole Bottom Town. They ole, they poor, but they clean.'

'But Christ, Sonia; try to understand, nuh. In politics, if you always study to be clean you won't last long as a politician. In politics, clean means stupid.'

'Well, if dat is so, Ah don't want no job as Minister. I prefer to be just Secretary to de Union.'

O God! I was really frightened now. I got up from the table and went to her. 'Please, Sonia,' I said. 'Please let us go out for a little walk round the block. The house is too stuffy. We can talk better in the fresh air, strolling. Please.'

She hesitated, looked at me suspiciously, then gave in.

We returned after an hour or so, arm in arm, which was damn good advertisement of political solidarity. And after our passionate exchanges before falling asleep that night, I tenderly stroked her naked, wonderful body and said, 'I knew you would understand.'

She sighed, yawned, turned on her side and slept.

25

DURING the weeks that followed, time roared by with the speed of light. There was so much to be done; mass meetings in the afternoons and nights; house-to-house in between; keeping a watchful eye and listening ear for sharp practices on the part of the opposing candidates; planning and executing sharp practices of our own; reading up carefully the rules published by Government from time to time under the Constitution and Elections Ordinance; filling in the necessary forms for illiterates to ensure that their names were included in the electors' list; ingratiating yourself generally with people you won't notice after election.

I frequently dropped in at Dave Potter's place after a late night meeting, for refreshment and talk with him and his man, Bryan, the Barbadian raconteur.

Then there was the big candle light procession to be organised. The candle light parade is one of those West Indian political extravaganzas which are associated with all important events in which the masses and their leaders are the actors. These extravaganzas are conducted in a sort of carnival spirit, the props or equipment varying according to the creative ingenuity of the political leader and the 'cause' that is being demonstrated for or against. When, for instance, the political leaders in St. Kitts wanted to demonstrate against the Colonial Office appointment of Sir Kenneth Blackburne to the governorship of that island and the other Leeward Islands some years ago, they armed their union members with old chamber pots and sticks, and led them up and down the island, making a hell of a din, beating the old po's with the sticks and chanting 'Down wid de Colonial Affice. To hell wid Blackburne.' And when, five years later, they wanted to demonstrate their *regret* at the Colonial Office's transfer of Sir Kenneth from the governorship of St. Kitts/Leeward Islands, they organised the biggest cocktail party ever staged on the island for a Governor, and inundated Sir Kenneth with laudatory speeches and wishes for his speedy return for another tour of duty.

I had borrowed the candle light parade idea from St. Vincent and Grenada, leaving out the part where a Grenadian leader rounded off his procession by leading the crowd down to the beach, getting into a boat, pushing out a few yards into the sea and 'preaching' to the crowd on the beach from the boat, like Jesus the Messiah.

The candle light parade always occurs about one or two nights before Election Day — a time when party officials and candidates are busy and tired. Organising this demonstration is therefore taxing business, even if the 'Messiah' part of it is omitted. It is a good vote-getter, however, like the rally.

Pittance and I held different views as to how the demonstration should be organised. We put forward our views at the Candle Light Committee meeting which was held at the Chamber two weeks before the parade.

'Bass, we been telling de people in every constituency that de message behind de candle light procession is dat de party intend to bright light to de whole island, to dispel de darkness of de present Government. Therefore, de procession should not be held in Kingsland alone. Every constituency should have its own procession.'

'No. We will bring the people into town from the country by trucks and buses, as we did for the rally, and have one big parade in town. That would be much more impressive than having separate little parades in each district. I must be able to supervise the whole affair myself. I can't do this if the demonstration is scattered all over the island. I can't be in so many places at once. Carried? Carried. The comrades will provide their own candles, as we cannot afford to supply them from union funds. We have already paid a hundred dollars for each of our eleven candidates' Nomination Deposit, and so we are now short of funds. Carried? Carried.'

Some ten thousand union and party members from all over the island marched with lighted candles through Kingsland on the night before Election Day, singing, 'See the mighty host advancing, Jerry leading on'. As I strutted in front of them, my wooden sword held high, I glanced up occasionally at the spectators who crowded the windows of the houses on both sides of the streets, and I knew that they were awed and impressed by this new, spectacular and compelling sight of barefoot democracy on the march. I knew, too, from the gaiety and the encouraging remarks that were being shouted by the crowds that followed the parade along the pavements, that I had defeated Paul Darcy and his people, not only in the Sugar Belt, but also in Kingsland and in the uttermost parts of the island.

I lifted my feet higher . . . . *Tomorrow, Hiroona will be mine.*

PART TWO
The Prize

I spent Election Day going from district to district, assisting my candidates in collecting the maimed, the lame, the feeble, the blind and the reluctant, and transporting them by hired taxis to the polling stations to cast their votes. In the secrecy of the polling booths, they laboriously marked their 'X' near to the fowl cock or the spoon or the bicycle — symbols by which the illiterates identified the names of the candidates on the ballots.

To supplement the party's hired taxis and trucks for transporting these voters, and to enable me to move from place to place on the island, my friend Dave Potter had put his big Bentley, and Bryan, at my disposal for the day.

At five o'clock when the voting stopped and the ballot boxes closed, Bryan and I returned to Kingsland. We drove straight to Bottom Town, intending to ask Sonia to come with me to Dave's place to listen to the election results over Dave's radio. Sonia was not at home, however. Probably she had remained in her constituency, Central Leeward, to listen there. Bryan and I left for Dave Potter's place.

Bottom Town seemed deserted; most of the people there had gone uptown to mingle with the crowds in front of the Court House or on the streets, under the windows, to listen to the radio announcements of the results.

Policemen sauntered among the crowds, their training in professional self control showing. In the houses which lined Grenville Street on both sides, loud mouthed radios were playing calypsoes while waiting to relay the elections figures to the groups of people who clustered on the pavement under windows.

Dave's bar-room was crowded now, and business was brisk. Dave had brought his big Phillips radio downstairs. It stood on one of the tables in the centre of the room. A male voice from the small local radio station began to comment on the orderliness with which everyone behaved throughout the elections — Hiroona's first, under adult suffrage. The bar-room became quiet. The crowd tense, listening.

'In a few minutes,' said the radio voice, 'the count, which will forecast the political destiny of our island over the next five years, will be relayed

to you over this station.' A Sparrow calypso took over, and the room broke
out in chatter.

'Hi, Chief. How you feel?'

'Don't know yet, man.'

Smiling, I shook a few hands and patted a few shoulders as Bryan and I
pushed through the crowd in the room. Dave greeted us at the bar: 'You
fellers look like you had a hard day. Better have a pick-me-up now, before
you drop dead or something. What fo' you, Jerry?'

'Nothing yet, Dave.' I lifted the front of my sweaty khaki shirt and
shook it to fan air over my hot, wet skin.

'Scotch an' soda. Double,' said Bryan. Dave turned to pour the drinks —
one for Bryan, one for himself.

'Hi, Chief. How yo' feelin'?'

'Better have a rum on me, Chief.'

The radio broke into *Lord, what a night, what a night, what a Sateday
night*. The crowd was really noisy now; some of the people began to cut
capers to the rhythm of the Jamaican calypso. Comment was loud and
free:

'Turn down de radio little bit, man. It too loud.'

'Naah, man. It ain't too loud.'

'Yo' want to bet me, Smallmilk beat Hugh Haywood?'

'Haywood goin' win, yes. All dem stupid civil servants an' dem
Kingsland white people will vote fo' Haywood.'

'It got more workin' people than white people an' civil servants in
Kingsland. So Smallmilk gwine win Haywood. Ah bet you two dallars.'

'Done! Show me yo' two dallars. Look my two dallars here. We will give
de bar boy de four dallars to hold.'

'Eric, yo' got two dallars yo' can len' me let me tek dis bet?'

'Sorry, Ah low in change. Ain't got enough to len'. Ah goin' do some
betting meself.'

'Christ, man! Anybady here can len' me two dallars?'

Bryan handed over two dollars to the Smallmilk supporter, as we left
the bar and followed Dave to the private room. I dropped in the chair —
the same in which I had sat on that first night I visited Potter's Place with
George Reid. Dave and Bryan, holding their drinks, stood expectantly at
the door, looking at the radio . . . .

Carry me ackee down Lindstead Market,
Not a quatee don't sell.
Lord, what a night, what a night, what a
Sateday night —

The radio fell suddenly silent. The male voice came back:

'And now, ladies and gentlemen, we have just received the results of polling station number one in the North Leeward constituency. Here are the figures: Claude Mason of the People's Productive Party — the PPP — five hundred and fourteen votes. Felix Holmes — independent candidate — thirty-three votes. I repeat . . .'

The bar-room came noisily alive again, and the radio augmented the din with *Gimme back me shilling wid de lion pon um.* Dave and Bryan moved away from the door and joined me in the private room.

'Shape of things to come,' stated Bryan elatedly.

The calypso stopped suddenly.

'Ssh! Ssh! All yo' shut up, nuh. More figures comin'. Ssh!'

Bryan and Dave jumped up and went back to the door.

'We now bring you the figures from the three polling stations comprising the Kingsland constituency.' The silence in the bar-room deepened while the announcer told the story briefly in figures: Leon Samuel alias Smallmilk had beaten Hugh Haywood in the Kingsland constituency.

The bar-room went crazy. Hats were flung up into the air. People hugged one another. Men grabbed women and executed frenzied dance steps. Some rushed out of the room to go in search of Smallmilk to lift him on their shoulders. Some rushed into the private room to give me handshakes.

'Chief, we bag two. De rest will come.'

'Smallmilk lick Haywood by six horse lengths an' a donkey.'

'Way de bar boy? Ah win de bet. De bar boy holdin' de stakes. Ah want me four dallars.'

Gimme back me shilling wid de lion pon um, lion pon um, lion pon um . . .

'Ah did know Smallmilk woulda beat Haywood, but Ah didn't t'ink he woulds beat 'im so bad. Christ, t'ings lookin' up.'

. . . . *lion pon um. Gimme back me* . . . .

'Way de hell dis blasted bar boy gone? Ah want me money.'

'Ssh! Too much nise. Hush! Dey comin' wid some more figgers.'

Dead silence. Bryan and Dave go back to the door. I join them. I am still tense. The voice comes through the radio, but it gets smothered in a welter of grating noises like someone was operating a pneumatic drill in it. Dave leaps across the room to the radio, quickly adjusts knobs. The grating noises cease, and the voice comes over clear and smooth:

'. . of the South Windward constituency. Here are the figures . . . .' The static occurred again, drowning out the voice, and filling the room with grating irritation.

Dave Potter emitted an obscenity and bent once more to the radio. He hurredly twisted knobs this way and that, making the grating noise worse.

Three men and a woman rushed noisily into the bar-room, waving their arms, dancing. Presently they paused, surprised that the bar-room was so quiet, except for the screeching of the radio. One of them said, 'Eh-eh, wha' happenin'? All yo' ain't hear what just come over?'

'No! Just as de announcer goin' to give out de figgers fo' South Winward, de blarsted radio start up a flippin' nise. Wha' happen?'

'Joe Pittance beat Ed Turpin by over one thousand votes. Ed lost e depasit.'

I turned away from the door, went back into the private room and sat down. The pandemonium and half the crowd swarmed into the private room.

'Chief! Chief! O Christ, we pon top.' Some of them rushed out again, shouting, jumping up. I shook hands, slapped people on the back, got my back slapped in turn. Someone handed me a drink.

'Drink dis rum, Chief. You look tense. Rum will quiet yo' nerves.'

I gulped the liquor, unmindful of my aversion to rum. I handed back the glass to the donor. He took the glass, lifted both hands high in the air as he did a 'bump-and-grind' out of the room. The words of the ribald calypso he was shouting as he went were drowned by the din in the bar-room and private room.

The rum had pressed a button in my stomach and sent a stunning voltage of electricity to my brain. The impact was only a second or two in duration, but it left effects. It changed my mood. It unlocked the tenseness which had held me in its grip all day, up to that time.

The radio continued to alternate between lively calypsoes and the relaying of elections results. The crowd in the bar-room kept up its spirited carousel, becoming suddenly silent at intervals, then resuming the shouting, cheering, throwing hats in the air and jostling to and from the bar counter.

When the radio announcer relayed the figures which placed Sonia far ahead of the competing candidate for the Central Leeward constituency, I shouted into Dave Potter's ear, 'I think we must fire one on that, Dave. Mine's a whisky and water. Double it. Plenty ice.'

It was not until near midnight that the last of the results came: the PPP had swept the country. Every candidate of the party was returned.

The crowd surged around me. Two men lifted me on their combined shoulders. I clapped my hands and shouted, 'Silence! Silence! Caesar speaks. Now, I am going to make a speech, but not here. We're going down to the Chamber where the whole thing started two years ago. Come to the Chamber and be the guests of the union; all of you — everybody.'

'To the Chamber! To the Chamber!' they shouted as they moved to the exit with me still perched on the men's shoulders. They carried me through the streets. Lights were still on in almost every house. Crowds walked up and down the streets, singing noisily, commenting, shouting. Most of them joined my crowd, and 'To the Chamber!' became a chant accompanied with foot stamping.

As the crowd moved down Merton Street, approaching Paul Darcy's printery, I noticed that the lights were on in the printery. A large radio stood on a table just inside the window of Darcy's office. The window sill was only three or four feet above the pavement. Darcy must have set up the radio there to enable himself and his staff to receive the election results, set them in type at once and so get them ready for publication in next day's issue of the *Hiroona Weekly*. The radio was silent now. It had, no doubt, done its 'dirty work', having relayed to Darcy the worst bit of information he had received since the day his maid informed him that she was not coming back.

When the crowd reached opposite the printery, I saw Darcy and three of his friends standing on the pavement in front of the printery, looking like mourners at the funeral of a dear friend.

'Stop a minute, comrades,' I shouted to the crowd. From my perch on the men's shoulders I called to Darcy and his friends: 'Gentlemen, you've kept a rather late vigil. Anything to report?'

Darcy swung round and started to spout. As he spoke, I got the impression that he was quoting to me and the crowd the text of the editorial he had written for the coming *Weekly*:

'Now hear this, all you people. This is a time for facing facts and taking warning from the facts we face. All of you are illiterate; semiliterates at best. You, like your leader, have been servants or worse, throughout your sorry history. You have had no experience in the art and responsibilities of government, and yet you now have these responsibilities thrust upon you by an over-optimistic British Parliament. Now, I am not what you would call a religious man, but the present circumstances are such that I cannot resist warning you from the *Bible* — The Book of Proverbs, chapter thirty, names four things that always cause trouble: and the first of these four things is "a servant when he reigneth". You have, on this fateful day, chosen a member of your class to exercise rule and authority in this island. Now go and sit back and watch what happens to this island, to you, to all of us — and to the servant, when he ruleth.'

'Boo him, comrades,' I shouted.

'Boo! Boo!' They resumed the march to the Chamber, their feet thudding to the rhythm of Boo. Lower down the street I shouted an order to change the theme, and the rhythm once more became, 'To . . The . . Cham-ber.'

As we approached Bottom Town, I could hear sounds of merry-making coming from the direction of the Chamber; and as we drew nearer, I saw that all the windows of the building were open, and that the two naked bulbs hanging from the rough rafters were alight. The wooden shutters were hanging askew as usual, due to the fact that some of the bits of leather on which they were hinged had cut away.

People swarmed all over the place, arguing, gesticulating, slapping backs, while they drank beer from bottles, or rum from paper cups. The community rang with laughter and prattle. Four trucks were parked in the yard. They had brought in people from the country districts.

As the crowd that was bearing me to the Chamber approached the place, it was met by some of the people who ran down from the yard of the Chamber to join in the foot-stamping 'jump-up'.

The crowd rushed into the Chamber which was already full of people. They carried me up to the little platform. I climbed down from the men's shoulders and stood on a chair. I was a little unsteady from the half glass of rum and the double whisky of a few hours ago; and as I clapped my hands for silence, my palms missed each other a few times.

Among the crowd, at the back of the room, Sonia, Naomi Sampson, Joe Pittance, Smallmilk, Ben Davis, Claude Mason, Joey Caines and other party officials were busy handing out bottles of beer and soft drinks and pouring and distributing rum in paper cups. I felt like hugging and kissing them all, including Joe Pittance. We had worked hard towards this wonderful hour, and I felt a comradeship with them that I had never felt before.

When the room became reasonably silent, I made a short speech: '. . . and so, Hiroona is now in good hands — in your hands and mine.'

During the applause and the drinking up, I carefully got down from the chair and the platform and pushed my way through the crowd, to the back of the room, shaking hands and having my back slapped all the way. Ben Davis brought out a bottle of whisky from behind some cartons of beer. 'We save dis bottle o' Scatch fo' you an' us, Chief.' Candidates, union and party officials grouped around. Sonia brought out paper cups. With tipsy solemnity, I poured whiskey from the bottle into the paper cups and handed a drink to each member of the group. Naomi and Sonia spurned the liquor and chose a bottle of soft drink each. We toasted one another. We drank to the union and to the party. Then Pittance proposed a toast to 'the new Hiroona'. We drank.

It was the last occasion on which there was real comradeship and goodwill between myself and the officials of my party.

2

I was still in my pyjamas. I sat by the table, my elbows resting on it, my hands supporting my head, and just under my chin was an untasted cup of coffee.

'What's the time?' I said to Sonia.

'Ah don't know. Must be long after nine.'

'You been to the shop to buy the alka seltzer yet?'

'Mm-hm.' Sonia poured water into a glass from an earthen goblet on the table, dropped the alka seltzer discs into the glass, and handed me the mixture.

'Christ!' I said; and groaned. 'If I didn't have to go and see this damn man Forbes this morning, I would not have got outa bed.'

'What you have to see Mr Forbes for?'

'To be invited to form a Government.'

'Form de Gover'ment?'

'Christ, Sonia, I explained this to you already sometime ago. You mean you forget?'

'I have no head fo' dese t'ings.'

'Listen again, then. Christ! The day after every general election, the leader of the successful party has to call on the Administrator — The Queen's Representative — "at ten o'clock in the forenoon", and present the names of the party's candidates who will be Ministers in the Government — the Cabinet.'

'Drink some coffee, nuh. You got to try and rouse yo'self. All de Comrades for de Committee meeting waitin' in de Chamber for you since morning.'

'Let them wait.'

'Ah went down an' told dem you still sleepin'. Too much celebration last night.'

'Let them wait.' I sipped the coffee slowly. I knew that there would be trouble with the Committee again over Pittance. This thought did not improve my mood which was already soured by my morning-after feeling.

I was still under the weather when I went down to the Chamber, some two hours late for the meeting; but as I entered the Chamber and saw Naomi Sampson earnestly conferring with a group of party officials standing at the back of the room, suspicion perked me up. I was suddenly quite alert.

They had cleaned up the room, but there were still empty bottles — some broken — and used paper cups in corners. There was a strong smell of earthy dust in the Chamber, and the yard was littered with evidence of the night before.

I opened the meeting with a brief reference to the results of the elections. Then I said, 'That victory is now behind us. Where do we go from here? In a few minutes I shall be reporting to Mr Forbes, the Administrator, who will ask me to form a Government. This means that this island will be having its first experience of the *ministerial system* of government. Now I am to choose from among the eleven successful candidates at the elections. I have given this matter some careful thought during the past months. There are to be four Ministers, listed by the Colonial Office, on the ground that this island cannot afford more than four: Finance, Works and Communications, Education and Social Services, Labour and Lands. I am taking over two ministries — Finance and Labour and Lands. I shall let you know who will be the two other Ministers after I have had my discussion with the Administrator. There will also be a Minister without Portfolio. As to the question of how much salary will be paid to Ministers, I shall have to discuss this, too, with Mr Forbes before I finally decide on a figure. Now . . ?'

'Wait a minute.' Naomi arose as she spoke. 'Why can't you tell us now who will be the three other ministers? You said you gave the matter careful thought during the past months. Don't you think we're entitled to know what you thought?'

'I must discuss the matter with Mr Forbes first.'

'So we who helped win the elections, and we who will form part of the Government — we must have no voice in the Government we forming part of?'

Rising, Pittance said, 'Comrade Sampson made a good p'int, Chief. You should tell us now who you have in mind to be Ministers. After all, you might go and mention names to de Administrata an' then when you come back an' tell us, one or even two of the people you name might not want to be Ministers. Then you would have to go back to de Administrata wid different names. Dat would look like you don't know yo' own mind — like yo' don't know what yo' doin'. Take me for instance, I don't want any ministry. So if you mention my name to Mr Forbes you would have to go back an' tell him I refuse. Dat will look bad on your side. So if you tell us de names now, you will know where you stand, and we will know where we stand.'

The fellow sounded frank and reasonable. I was relieved by his decision to refuse a ministry. I did not intend to include him, anyway; but as I was quite certain that excluding him would cause trouble for me at the meeting, I had decided to keep the three names secret until the appointments were actually made by the Administrator on my recommendation. It would then be too late for protest by the party or the union. But as Pittance had spoken his mind on the matter, I felt it would now be safe to announce the names.

'Very well. If that is the feeling of the Chamber,' I said, 'I shall now announce the names of the two candidates who will be Ministers, and the name of the Minister without Portfolio.'

I named Sonia and two men, and immediately realized that I should have known better. The two men got up and declined. 'We all feel dat de party would have a better chance of success in de Government if Comrade Pittance get a chance to help wid de Gover'ment as a Minister.'

'But you just heard Pittance say he does not want a ministry.'

Dead silence.

'Very well. Since you have declined, I shall have to think of two others. But I must remind you that there will be a big salary attached to the post of a minister. If you refuse a ministry, you refuse the salary also.'

'We are all working people, Comrade Mole,' said Naomi. 'We didn't join the union just hoping to get money or a job. We joined because we wanted to see the island improve. We want better working conditions and better wages for everybody, not big salaries for ourselves. We are not like some West Indian political leaders who entered politics because they failed in everything else they tried to do. To such politicians, only money and position and power really matter; and they think that politics is the easiest and best means of getting these things. So don't dangle big salary in front of us. The . . .'

'Look here, Comrade Sampson, we haven't come here to listen to any lecture of pious political moralising from you. The issue before the Chamber is . . .'

'Excuse me, Comrade Mole. I was not finished speaking. As I was saying when you interrupted me, the two men you named have told you that they are not interested in being Ministers. Perhaps they don't feel up to it. None of the eleven candidates here know half as much about political matters as Comrade Bute — Comrade Pittance, as we call him. None of them know how to get things done in Government. Comrade Bute has shown over and over that he knows. If we are thinking of the party and the island, and not of ourselves, we would think seriously before deciding to start the Government without Comrade Bute in it. And we all feel that he should be in it as a Minister. Not for the salary, but for the good of the island and the union. The Union, the Party and the Island being the same thing to us.'

'Am I to force Pittance to accept a ministry if he doesn't want one?'

'You have not offered him one,' said Naomi.

I ignored that. I named two other candidates. They declined. Then two others declined. I was beginning to look foolish. I launched into an angry speech about the undermining of acknowledged leadership; about 'subversion in our ranks'; about 'the good work I've done for this island and for you all, at great sacrifice to myself'.

'We have succeeded in uniting our people, so that today they are the only true power on the island. Let us not spoil the excellent work we have done so far. Let us not have our enemies say that we united others but can't unite ourselves . . . .'

Another two candidates declined. The sons of bitches! The problem I was facing was that nobody in that room, apart from myself, was ambitious. Nobody wanted to get anything for himself out of my position as leader, nor out of his own position as supporter. To a tyrant, indifference on the part of people to the lure of derived power, and reasonable disregard for the spoils of office, are dangerous impediments. If he can't find people who are willing to fall for these two glittering temptations, he would lack the necessary hatchetmen, favourites and lackeys — the props of the dictator. Without these props, he may still be able to govern, but not as a despot. Other people's fear, greed and ambition are the sustenance of the dictator. This is why when a dictator falls he drags a retinue down with him.

'Comrades, how in God's name can you expect me to lead if you're not prepared to follow?'

'Maybe we don't like what you leadin' us into, Chief,' said Claude Mason.

'What do you want me to do, Comrade Mason?'

'Suppose you ask Comrade Pittance to change his mind?'

'He has already said that if he were offered a ministry, he would refuse it. Do you want me to go crawling to Pittance, begging him to change his mind?'

'We will change our mind if he change his.'

'I never crawl. If Comrade Pittance wants to change his mind, let him say so,' I said angrily.

Naomi Sampson got up and said, 'Let me do the crawling then. Comrade Pittance would you accept a ministry if it is offered to you?'

'Well,' said Pittance, rising slowly, 'I can see that de Chief will not be able to form a Gover'ment if I refuse; and it would look bad for de Chief if he had to go and confess to de Administrata that he can't form a gover'ment. So I will accept a ministry if de Chief offer it to me.'

'It is up to you now, Comrade Mole, ' said Naomi, and sat down.

Pittance was in.

3

I left the Chamber soon after, but I did not report to the Administrator at once. I was too worn out by anger and frustration to face what I believed would be another unpleasant meeting. I went to Dave Potter's place instead. It was from a private room at Dave's business place that I telephoned Mr Forbes at two o'clock.

This particular private room was a special place that Dave had fixed up for me as an election victory surprise for a 'hideout'. It contained all the necessary conveniences: divan, desk, liquor cabinet, telephone and a small fridge.

By the time I telephoned Administrator Forbes, I had eaten — a sandwich and soft-drink — in my new private room, and felt refreshed. Forbes was not at his office when I phoned, so I asked the girl at the telephone exchange to connect me to Government House.

'But Mr Mole, you were supposed to report at my office at ten o'clock this morning. I waited there until twelve thirty.'

'I am sorry, Mr Forbes. I was detained at an important meeting. When can I see you?'

'I shall be returning to my office at four this afternoon.' He hung up while I was saying that I would be there at four.

A policeman was at the door of the office when I arrived. I remembered the time when, as an ordinary man, I could enter only with the connivance of the policeman – P. C. 43 Cunningham. This time I was entering as the elected Head of the Government.

Forbes did not stand and extend his hand when I entered his office. He sat at his large desk in his dark lounge suit and polka dot bowtie. A file was on his desk in front of him. His secretary, a stocky native similarly dressed, except for a dark blue necktie, got up and moved a chair forward, inviting me to sit down; then he resumed his seat at the side of Forbes' desk.

'I take it that you are the acknowledged leader of the party that won the elections,' said Mr Forbes.

'Yes.'

'Then it is my duty to ask you to submit the names of your colleagues whom you wish to recommend as elected members of the Government of this island for the next five years. But before I do this, I shall read to you the despatch from the Secretary of State for the Colonies, setting forth the structure of the Government and matters pertaining to the conduct of the same.'

'I have already read the despatch. You will remember that it was published in the Government Gazette and the local press — the *Hiroona Weekly* — a few weeks before the elections. I have a copy here.' I produced a copy of the four-page document from my pocket. 'It would save time if we just discussed it rather than you reading it through.'

'Very well. But I shall have to give you a stamped copy, for which you will sign as having received.' He handed me the copy, and his Secretary presented a large, thick, red book of what appeared to be a number of similar documents stuck together. The coat of arms of Hiroona was embossed on the cover of the book. The secretary indicated the place I was to sign in the book. I signed, and he shut the book, holding the covers tightly together as if to prevent my signature from escaping.

Forbes said, 'You say you have read the despatch, so you must be aware that there are to be four ministries, each headed by a Minister; and there is to be a Minister without Portfolio.'

'I've got the names of the Ministers here,' I said, 'with the ministries assigned to them.' I handed a paper to Forbes. He read it, grunted, and passed it to his secretary.

'According to the provisions of the Constitution,' Forbes said, 'there should also be two Nominated Members, who will not sit in the upper "House" — the Executive Council. They will be members of the lower "House" — the Legislative Council. This, as I suppose you know, is the present form of Government in the Windward and Leeward Islands and other parts of the colonial empire.'

'I know all that, Mr Forbes. I used to teach it at school. I also know that under the old arrangement, the two Nominated Members — so called because they are not elected by the people — were appointed to the Legislative Council by the Administrator; but under the new constitution, the Chief Minister — me —' I touched my chest with my thumb, 'submits the name of one Nominated Member who *must* be appointed by the Administrator without question. You, the Administrator, are to name the other Nominated Member, but he can only be appointed after consultation with me. Now, here is the name of the man I want appointed.' I handed him a paper. Forbes read the name, turned to his secretary and said, 'Do you know this man David Potter?'

'Yes, sir; he is the proprietor of a bar and entertainment business in Oakley Street.'

'Is his education of sufficient standard to enable him to serve on the Legislative Council?' Forbes looked at me, requesting my answer.

'That used to be *your* business, but now it is *my* business. I want David Potter appointed to the Legislative Council as a Nominated Member. Education or no education. Now, who is your candidate for the second Nominated Member?'

'I am suggesting Mr Hugh Haywood, one of the most prominent and useful members of this community.'

'You can't have him. Haywood was a candidate at the elections. In spite of his prominence he was defeated by Smallmilk — sorry, I mean Mr Leon Samuel. In other words, Haywood has already been rejected by the people. It would therefore be unseemly now to make him a member of the people's Legislative Council. You can't have him.'

'Mr Mole, I do not agree that a Government should be deprived of the services of the sterling qualities and proven usefulness of Mr Haywood, simply because . . . . . .'

'I don't care whether you agree or whether you don't. If you appoint Mr Haywood over my objection, I will protest in the strongest terms to the Secretary of State.'

'Very well, Mr Mole. I shall consult with the Attorney General this evening, and inform you tomorrow morning of my decision. The constitution requires that in this particular matter I must consult with you, but it does not say that I am compelled to accept your advice.'

'All right. You appoint Haywood, and then there'll be hell to pay. You will be made to realize that colonialism has entered its twilight.'

Forbes appeared to ignore the threat. He turned to his secretary and said, 'Is there anything else to be discussed?'

'Yes, sir.' The secretary turned over some sheets of paper which lay before him on the desk. 'The island's budget; the present position of the public revenue and expenditure; the grant-in-aid from Britain; salaries of the Ministers; the buildings to be allocated to them for offices; the . . . . .'

'I suppose,' Forbes cut in, 'Mr Mole would wish to discuss the question of salaries before the other matters.'

I ignored the insult. Said nothing. Forbes continued. 'On the question of salaries, Mr Mole, I invite you to look at paragraph forty-two of the Secretary of State's despatch. I trust you will appreciate the Secretary of State's contention that one cannot expect equality of salaries of Ministers throughout the West Indian islands, as the revenue of the several islands varies, and so do their budgets. Hiroona's revenue is small, and the British Treasury does not intend to increase its grant-in-aid to this island to meet any demand for enormous salaries to Ministers. Before the introduction of universal adult suffrage, the elected members of the Government served without salary.'

'That was because the Government was run by civil servants. The elected members served for privilege and status. They didn't have to neglect their private business and occupations. They were not Ministers and they didn't serve full time. They merely attended meetings and made laws and arrangements to suit themselves. They did not plan or work for the good of the people or for the general improvement of the island. These are different days, Mr Forbes.'

'I've noticed that,' said Forbes drily. 'What figure are you thinking of as salary?'

'What do the other islands pay their Ministers?'

Forbes relayed my question to his secretary. The Secretary read out from a list the salaries of ministers in Antigua, Barbados, Dominica, Grenada, Montserrat, St. Vincent, St. Kitts and St. Lucia. 'These figures,' he continued, 'do not include internal Transport Allowance, which ranges from one hundred and forty dollars per month, flat. Nor do they include Entertainment Allowance, which ranges from a hundred to two hundred and fifty dollars a month, flat, whether the Minister entertains or not. There is also a large provision under a General Entertainment vote on which the Chief Ministers may draw at will. Over and above all these there is provision for travelling and subsistence when Ministers go abroad on official business. And of course the Chief Ministers are entitled to a free, furnished and suitable house, free telephone etcetera. The figures I have quoted may be a little more or a little less in some islands, but that is the general pattern.'

I was goose fleshing with excitement. *Christ, what a bonanza!* I found it difficult to focus my mind on Forbes and public business. I kept comparing the Secretary's figures with my Bottom Town life and living; with my jetsam days when I was thrown out of one form of employment after another; with the long period of flotsam when I drifted about the waterfront seeking odd jobs. When my circumstances began to change with my entry into politics, I had often discussed our rosy prospects with Sonia. Now all I wanted to do was to hurry from Mr Forbes' office and run home to my wife with the news that the half was not told.

With simulated indifference, I said to Mr Forbes, 'I shall need a little time to digest all these statistics before I can make up my mind on the question of salaries for my ministers. I've had an exacting time, what with elections yesterday and a hard night last night. I suggest we meet again tomorrow morning to discuss this and the other matters.' 'What time tomorrow morning will suit you?' Mr Forbes consulted his secretary by look.

'Your Honour has two appointments tomorrow,' the secretary said. 'One at nine-thirty and the other one at three in the afternoon.'

'When can we see Mr Mole?'

'Shall we say ten forty-five, sir?'

'Ten forty-five, Mr Mole.'

'Thank you, Mr Forbes.' I left.

Sonia was not impressed. She lifted her nightgown and fanned herself vigorously with the lower part of it as she lay on her back on the bed. I lay beside her in my pyjama pants only. There were only two windows, and when the house was shut up on a hot night it became a veritable furnace.

Between spurts of fanning, Sonia spoke her mind.

'All dat lot o' money and salary an' so on maybe all right; and I admit Ah will be glad to move into a better house than dis one. But Ah must tell you straight, Jerry, Ah don't half like de way you does try to browbeat de members of de union and party committee. When you don't get your own way, you goes on like you crazy. You should have enough sense to see by now that you ain't smarter than Pittance an' Naomi. You have more power than dey have, becarse you is head of de Union an' de Government. But if you have power and you ain't got no commonsense, you in a bad way. You lack. Sometimes a man shows more power when he submit to people, dan when he try to browbeat dem. You ain't got all de sense an' learnin' in de world. Other people got some, too. If you fo'get dat, de Union an' de Government will go to nothing, because intelligent people who have good, clean, strong minds will refuse to work wid you. You should realize dis from what happen today at de caucus meetin' when you was trying to choose your Ministers. Ain't you notice that all of dem gang up against yo' and compel yo' to choose Pittance even though you didn't want to?'

'Then why the hell didn't you get up and support me? You only sat there as dumb as hell.'

'If I did open me mouth Ah woulda told you in public what Ah telling you now in private. Ah supported you by keeping me mouth shut.'

I got up, went into the other room and lay down on the sofa. *It's no use*, I thought, *Sonia and I will never see eye to eye when it comes to the consideration of important matters.* Before we entered politics, our life together was trivial, and we had nothing to discuss but trivia. In fact we seldom discussed anything at all, although we quarrelled often about my aversion to work and my inability to hold a decent job. I was fairly certain that success and my achievement of big things would draw Sonia closer to me. I even expected a little apotheosising from her. But I realized now, that this was not to be. Sonia's mind was that of a peasant. She was utterly devoid of ambition, and was unable to appreciate the dynamics of the uncompromising struggle for political power.

As I lay on the sofa that night, I decided to have no more arguments or discussions with Sonia. My discussion with the Administrator and his secretary had strengthened my conviction that in Sonia's future earnings and mine I had a guarantee of ease for the rest of my life. Nevertheless, Sonia's cool attitude towards our new financial prospects, her lack of loyalty to me in my struggle against Naomi and Pittance and her failure or refusal to show me warm and open acknowledgement of my shrewdness as a political operator deprived me of a sympathetic sharer of the joy of my success so far. In short I had no one to turn to. True enough, there was Dave Potter, my hero worshipper. I greatly appreciated Dave's friendship, encouragement and admiration: but this kind of recognition, if it came from a man's wife — especially if he loves her, and I did love Sonia — would inspire him with a confidence which cannot come from any other source, in the same measure. Furthermore, certain secrets and intimate domestic matters which I could discuss with Sonia, I could hardly discuss with anybody else — except, perhaps, my mother.

4

M Y mother. Christine Mole, sixty-nine, going on seventy. Every time
I thought of her I indulged in flashbacks, mentally reviewing my
childhood, my unknown paternal origin, my earlier days, my still-born
careers.

Ma was a real black beauty when she was young. She came of good,
negro stock, too. Perhaps that was the reason why she never told me
about my father until I forced the revelation out of her. The story was too
sordid for her sensitive mind. She did not like to dwell on it or even reveal
it. She was never married, but she had two children — Myra and me.
Myra's father was a sweetheart of Ma's youth, who, after Myra was born,
emigrated to Curacao with the intention of 'bettering himself' before
returning to marry Ma. But the marriage never did come off, because of an
unfortunate incident which Ma revealed to me on the day I visited her to
bring her news of my great victory.

She used to speak about her parents, especially her father, as one would
speak of a revered king and queen. Her father was a small peasant farmer
— 'a hard working, God-fearing man. He had only five acres of land he
rented from the Government, on the slopes of Welches Mountain; but he
cultivated fruits and vegetables so well, he was able to marry and support
my mother and me in this little cottage I now live in — this house he had
built with his own hands.' Her parents had given her a good elementary
school education — 'like my mother had. She used to help me with my
sums and read to me from the Bible and from a book called *Basket of
Flowers and Other Tales.* And she could write copperplate and upright
Jackson. You young generation children don't know anything about
copperplate and upright Jackson; that's why the modern generation's
handwriting is so poor.'

Her father could neither read nor write, but he didn't have to; his wife
did all the reading and writing required in the family.

It was cholera that robbed Ma of her "king and queen". The epidemic
had already hit Barbados and Montserrat as it had struck St. Vincent in
1854. Hiroona's turn came in 1908, and Ma lost her comparatively
young, energetic and ambitious parents. Ma, then a young girl, went into
service with the Cricketts family, and was so employed even after

retirement age. She retired, however, when the Cricketts sold the estate, arranged a small pension for her and left the island for England. Later, arthritis further incapacitated Ma.

Before arthritis had slowed her up Ma used to visit me and Sonia in Kingsland occasionally. That was during the bad old days when I lived like a drone. Ma used to come all the way from Chateaubelair by bus — a journey of twenty odd miles over hilly country and rugged roads. She usually came down to Kingsland on Saturday morning, bringing with her a basket of fruit: mangoes, sapodillas, *zabbocas* (avocado pears), tangerines, sugar apples, mammy apples, Bequia plums. And vegetables: tannias, dasheens, sweet potatoes, yams, eddoes. She brought us fresh fish, too, wrapped in an old paper bag and tied with a string to form a handle for the little parcel, which she held in her hand. I liked the - fruity-ripe smell that came from the basket, and I was always the first to open it and sample its contents while Sonia and Ma talked about the hard times, and gossiped about news of town and country. Ma and Sonia got on well together, and the old lady always said a good, affectionate word for me when Sonia complained to her about my laziness and my shamelessly living off the pittance she worked for as a domestic servant.

'Ah really can't understan' him,' Sonia would whine. 'Jerry going' on like he ain't got no mind, no canscience; an' sometimes he does carry on like he crazy.' And Ma would shake her head sadly, smile and say, 'Maybe he can't help. Poor feller.'

Ma invariably excused my lapses and excesses with this strange expression — 'Maybe he can't help.' Even as a little child, growing up in the fishing village of Chateaubelair, looked after during the day by Myra, my half sister, who is three years older than I, while Ma did housework for the Cricketts at their big house on Shapiro Estate, I was used to hearing Ma explain to Myra, 'Maybe he can't help', when Ma came home at night and Myra related to her the story of some outlandish prank or tantrum perpetrated by me during the day.

On only one of the several occasions when Ma had to whip me, did she do so in anger and with the necessary force. She usually flogged me at what Myra scornfully described as 'half volley kept low', the slender blacksage rod merely tickling my calves. But when on one memorable morning, I nearly caused the drowning of a little boy, Ma's approach to my anatomy was more general and definite.

The incident occurred in the sea, on the Chateaubelair beach, at the place where we children bathed every morning before going to school.

There were some twenty or thirty of us, all naked, swimming near the shore and romping noisily in the sea, as usual. I was about twelve years old, small for my age, but cocky and aggressive. Most of us (boys and girls) could swim well. The non-swimmers kept to the water mark or waded in to safe standing distance. Higher up on the beach, fishing nets were spread out. Fishermen sat on the black sand, the broken sections of the nets resting on their laps, their long, broad, wooden needles moving in and out as they mended the broken meshes. The fishermen seemed oblivious to the shrill hubbub the children kept up as we splashed and swam about in the sea, or chased one another along the shore. They were used to this daily hubbub.

One little non-swimmer — Janey Tucker's six year old boy — sat where the little waves occasionally washed up on the sand. As each wave came up, he dipped water with his hands and splashed himself. I crawled up from the sea to the little boy, pulled him in and tried to hold him under water. The boy put up a terrific struggle. Some of the children shouted to me to let him go, but I refused to release him. Releasing him would be admitting that I was bullied by the orders from the children into doing what I didn't want to do. Then the children shouted, 'Help! Help! Jerry drownin' Milton. O God! Help!' One of the fishermen rushed down to the sea, jumped in and pulled the child away from me. Artificial respiration brought Milton to, and then they took him to the little casualty hospital and left him in the care of the district nurse.

The incident was a scandal in the village.

When Ma came home that evening, Myra told her what I had done to Milton. Ma was reaching in the corner for the little blacksage rod when Janey Tucker and some of the neighbours came to our house. They were still fuming.

'You should do somet'ing 'bout dat bwoy of yours, Christine. Dat bwoy is de devil 'imself. When he' ain't fightin' de other children, else choppin' dem, else stonin' dem, he drownin' dem. Only last week de police been here at yo' door, complainin' 'bout Jerry an' Adriana James' bwoy suspected of t'iefin' cake out o' Miss Dublin Bakery. Dis bwoy Jerry will get you into serious trouble, Christine. Or somebody bigger dan he will break his ass fo' him.'

Ma went to the little bush at the back of the house and broke off a thick blacksage rod. Then she stripped me naked.

It was one of the very neighbours who, minutes after, hauled me away from Ma. 'Dat's enough, Christine. Christ, dat's enough! You gwine kill de bwoy an' get yo'self in trouble.'

Later, Ma washed off the little blood cakes from my shoulders, my back and my bottom. She smeared the welts with vaseline. And when Myra, looking on, said, 'He got it good that time, but he deserves it,' Ma spun round on her and said, 'Shut up. You just shut up. Maybe he can't help.' Then Ma started to cry. Myra moved away. I could see she was puzzled and upset. And from that night she never again reported to Ma any wrong I did during Ma's absence. I must admit, however, that the near-tragedy of little Milton, the indignation of the entire village and the result to my own hide sobered me a bit thereafter.

At school Myra and I were bright. Myra was an all-rounder, good in all the school subjects, while I only shone in English Grammar, English Language and British History. In those days, the language emphasis was on grammar; and the two great and indispensable authorities were Nesfield and West. In Arithmetic and elementary Mathematics, you had to work through A. R. Layng's and Workman's textbooks if you wished to be an elementary school teacher. My performance in arithmetic and elementary maths ranged from modest to poor, but I knew Nesfield's Grammar and West's *Revised English Grammar* almost by heart.

I had the gift of a wonderful memory. I could mentally recall, literally, pages and pages of any literature or history textbook I read. And as for analysis and parsing, which were fashionable in those days, these were my scholastic meat and drink. The more intricate the passage to be analysed and parsed, the more I enjoyed the exercise. The local Educational Authorities were in the habit of including in the examination papers for Pupil Teachers chunks of Shakespeare to be analysed and parsed, and I can never forget the thrill I experienced when in 1925, I sat down to write the Third Year Pupil Teachers' Examination, and saw in the English Grammar paper, the question: 'Analyse in tabular form, and then parse the nouns, pronouns and verbs in the following passage':

'For when the noble Caesar saw him stab,
Ingratitude, more strong than traitors' arms,
Quite vanquished him: then burst his mighty heart;
And, in his mantle muffling up his face,
Even at the base of Pompey's statue,
Which all the while ran blood, great Caesar fell.'

This sort of exercise was supposed to bring home to the adolescent child the fact that the functions of words and phrases can be technically analysed and examined, and. that the more one knew about this kind of analysis, the better one appreciated the niceties, the delicate sensitivity of language.

The headteacher of the primary school in which I was brought up was a man of words. He was very fond of quoting to us, young pupil teachers, passages from the English classics. He often quoted a little piece from Milton:

'What in me is dark,
Illumine. What is low, raise and support.'

He uttered these two lines, not as if he were quoting them but as if he were addressing them on his own behalf to some distant Deity, as a kind of prayer. As I recall and write this now, it occurs to me that if, like my old schoolmaster, I had the insight, the faith, to address these two lines meaningfully to the same Deity at the outset of my political career and during its turbulent days, my career would not have come to the squalid end it came to, and maybe I would not have lost my Government in the way I did. But, perhaps, politics and what people call Godliness are not bedfellows.

I successfully wrote all the Pupil Teachers' Examinations. Myra did not remain at school after she had got the ordinary seventh-grade Primary School Leaving Certificate. She emigrated to Curacao and got married there. She was sixteen then.

All the tuition I received as a pupil teacher was from the Headteacher of the school. He was obligated by law to teach all his pupil teachers in the afternoon after school hours. In those days, there was no other arrangement in most of the small West Indian islands for the training of teachers.

In Barbados, there was the Rawle Training Institute. In Jamaica, there was the Mico Training College for teachers. Trinidad had its Government Training College, and later, Antigua opened Springfield Teachers' College. Gradually, the smaller islands took to sending student teachers to Barbados, Antigua or Trinidad. But in Hiroona there was no such opportunity for a long time, and so training was entirely in-service, and the Headteachers received a bonus of seven dollars and twenty cents from the Government for each of their pupil teachers who were successful in the local statutory examinations. Seven dollars and twenty cents was a lot of money in those days. The maximum salary of a primary school Headteacher was then forty-eight dollars a month.

It was just after my Fourth-Year pupil teacher-ship that I met, mated and married Sonia, and brought her to live with me in Ma's little cottage at Chateaubelair.

Ma continued to work for the Cricketts in the Great House on Shapiro Estate. She came home every night as usual. She liked Sonia, who seemed to have taken Myra's place in the house.

Soon after Sonia lost our child, I lost my teaching job. It wasn't my education that was at fault. It was my character. I could analyse and parse better than almost everybody else. I could quote large pieces from notable English authors. I even memorised one or two Latin words and stock phrases which I used in my school essays. But I was lazy, and I didn't like discipline. I was often late for school; and when my Headteacher reprimanded me for my lapses and neglect, I became sullen, cocky, insubordinate, unreasonable. In spite of my 'superior' education, what in me was dark remained dark; what was low, low. My view was that having a good education was an end in itself.

Ma was not as cross with me as Sonia was, because of the loss of my job. 'Maybe he can't help,' said Ma. Sonia took a different view of the matter.

She sought and obtained a household job in Kingsland, left me and went to live in Bottom Town, taking her ailing mother with her. I missed her, longed for her. I had frequent wet dreams and intolerable dry ones about her. I just couldn't live without the girl's body.

After a month or two, I moved in with her. I adjusted without effort to a drone's life with Sonia and her mother in the miserable little shack at Bottom Town. But Sonia's recriminations and repeated insults drove me to seek a job in the police force. I lost that job before I had completed eighteen months in it: absence without leave, and insubordination. Ma sent us a basket of fruit and vegetables, and a soothing scribbled note. Sonia took the note out of the basket, read it, flung it at me and said, 'Ma say maybe you can't help.'

'I didn't like the police force, anyway,' I said to Sonia. 'So I have arranged with old Ormsby Forde to go and work with him as a clerk in his insurance agency. It's a more decent job than polishing the boots of N.C.O.s in the police force. And the pay is better. After all, you must remember that I was a teacher, and some of these N.C.O.s can barely read and write. Why should I be their lackey?'

My days with Ormsby Forde were numbered. I discovered quite early that the man was a stickler for time. There was always work to be done 'on schedule'. If I was a few minutes late for work in the morning or after lunch, old Forde demanded an explanation, as if I were some little school-boy. If I made a few mistakes in the book-keeping, he would carry on as if I had broken a bank. I mustn't do this and I mustn't do that. I mustn't doze on my desk, even though the temperature was ninety-eight in the shade. I mustn't use his office stationery for my private correspondence, although the only person to whom I wrote occasionally was my sister, Myra, asking her about job prospects in Curacao. I mustn't argue with him about insurance business, he knew more about it than I — I who was intelligent enough to have achieved a teacher's post and could quote stray bits from Omar Khayyam and Milton and Shakespeare.

The man was simply impossible to get on with. I left the job. Later, with a few dollars I borrowed from Sonia and a few from Ma, I emigrated to the Dutch island of Aruba and worked for six months in the oil refinery there. Then they sacked me, and I returned to Hiroona and to Sonia.

Now as I lay on the sofa thinking back on my past, I felt that I had come a long way. I had done exceptionally well. I had organised the labour force of my country and made it the instrument of my present good fortune. In a few hours from now, I should formally assume the highest position of political power on the island as its Chief Minister. *I shall be the ruler in Hiroona.* If my wife was not impressed by my achievements, my mother would be. If, in Sonia, I had no one to turn to, there was Ma, whose affection for me was unwavering. True, she was twenty-five rugged miles away in Chateaubelair, but that problem would soon be solved when I moved into my official residence. I would bring her to Kingsland and install her in my new house. Sonia would hardly object to this, as she was used to living with Ma, and they liked each other. Furthermore, Ma would be able to supervise the servants and look after the house while Sonia and I worked.

I turned over on my side on the sofa and dozed off, after deciding to pay Ma a visit at Chateaubelair next day, as soon as I had concluded my second interview with Mr Forbes the Administrator.

5

L IKE most villages in Hiroona, Chateaubelair is a settlement adjoining
a plantation or estate — a settlement originally established to provide
ready-to-hand labour for the estate. In time, these settlements expand,
and as the population increases and schooling becomes available in the
village, the youths with brains and ambition eschew the hoe and cutlass
of the estate labourer, and enter other fields: the building trades, shop-
keeping, dressmaking. Some of these young people become teachers,
nurses, student pharmacists, policemen. Some leave the village for
Kingsland and become shop clerks, civil servants. Some rent and cultivate
a few acres of land and earn their living as peasant farmers. And some, like
my sister Myra, emigrate.

There are, in Hiroona, several villages of this kind — villages which
seem to develop and foster more ambition and enterprise than other
villages on the island. The results are a cleaner, brighter community, one
or two good dirt-surfaced streets and tidy houses in orderly arrangement
along the streets, instead of wattle-and-mud lean-to hovels set down
higgedly-piggedly on a clearing near the estate.

Chateaubelair village is part of Shapiro Estate, but it is one of the better
kind of villages. Small wonder it produced me!

The village slopes from the base of a little hill right down to a wide
beach of black sand. Fishing boats stand here and there along the beach,
or bob up and down at anchor on the calm, clear water in the harbour.
Fishing nets lie drying on the sand or coiled in large mounds in the stern
end of two-bow fishing canoes, ready to go out to sea. Wooden cottages
with galvanize or shingle roofs fringe the upper parts of the beach. Ma
lived in one of these cottages. She had ceased to work at Shapiro Great
House years ago, when the Cricketts sold the estate and returned to
England.

She came out of the little kitchen, wiping her hands on her apron, as
my taxi eased into the yard. A grin, full of wrinkles, suddenly spread over
her face, and her old eyes lit up when she saw me. We had not seen each
other for over a year, and now I was surprised to see how much she had
aged. She used to be tall, yes, but not as angular as she now looked. And
even as she wiped her hands on her apron with a sort of pushing

movement from waist down, I could see the ravages of arthritis in the large nodular joints of her slightly swollen fingers and wrist. Her black, lean face still retained just a vestige of its past beauty if not its smoothness. Her hair was no longer black.

'Lunch will be ready in a few minutes,' said Ma, as if continuing a conversation from where we left off a year ago. I got out of the taxi. The taximan backed the vehicle out of the yard and departed to hang around the village until I summoned him for the return journey to Kingsland.

'Come and tell me about the Government. They say you own it now,' said Ma, as she led the way into the house.

'I think it's the other way round, Ma: the Government owns me now.'

Ma laughed. She laughed in Edwardian English, rather than in the West Indian dialect of laughter. This was a habit she had cultivated during her long years of hearing and imitating the way Mrs Crickett laughed — a sort of dry, dehydrated, sophisticated snort, which played down the joke, while at the same time giving the impression that she thoroughly enjoyed it.

Ma eased herself down on her old rocking chair by the window. I sat on a straight-back chair opposite her.

'Maybe you're right,' she said. 'When we possess things, they possess us, too, in a way. Sometimes they possess us so completely we can't shake them off.' Ma talked like her old mistress, too, so that her accent sounded a bit 'English'.

'Who would want to shake off power, Ma?'

'Power?'

'Yes, power. As Chief Minister or Premier of Hiroona or any other West Indian island, you're the most powerful man in the country.'

'That's what you are now? Chief Minister or Premier?'

'Yes, Chief Minister. That's the title of all the political leaders in the smaller islands of the West Indies who carry their party to victory in the general election, as I did two days ago. I made arrangements this morning to take over the Government, and then I came straight here to see you. Maybe later, when Hiroona gets a more advanced constitution, I shall be Premier; and later still, when the island achieves independence, I shall be Prime Minister. With each constitutional advance, my power increases.'

'So now you're Chief Minister.'

'Yes.'

'You ever been Chief Minister before?'

'Ma, what are you saying?' I laughed. 'How could I have been Chief Minister before? It's a new thing. I became the first Chief Minister of

Hiroona today. Appointed by the Queen of England through Her Representative, the Administrator of Hiroona, Mr Forbes.'

'That is grand, Jerry. Really grand. You're lucky, too, because you've never been to any college or high school to study to be Chief Minister, like you would have to go to college to study to become a doctor or a lawyer or a member of any other profession. Is Chief Minister a profession?'

'It begins by being just a job, then if you're lucky it becomes a profession. You pick up the technique as you go along.'

'You get paid for doing this job profession?'

'Oh yes. I practically fixed my own salary and the salaries of the other ministers in the Government, this morning.'

'Wonders never cease,' said Ma, smiling, as she gazed at the floor, nodding her head slowly and thoughtfully meanwhile. Presently, she looked up at me. Her broad, wrinkled grin made her face as merry as an old pixie's. 'But, Jerry, this is wonderful. Of course, as you said, this is a new thing, so you must be very careful. All new things must be handled with care until you get used to handling them. What are you going to do when you get back to Kingsland?'

'I'm going to rule the island, Ma.'

'We must eat first.'

She got up. I rose, too, and followed her outside into the kitchen. A coal pot stood on a waist high stand. The contents of the pot simmered over a slow fire. Ma opened the pot, releasing the appetising aroma of excellent West Indian cuisine.

'Ah! *Callaloo* soup,' I said. 'Only you can make minced dasheen leaves, chopped onion, okras, shallots, bits of corned pork, black pepper, thyme, small flour dumplings and water smell like this and taste like it smells. Have you got crayfish in it?'

'Of course. It wouldn't be callaloo without shrimps or crayfish.'

'Boy, oh boy! I can't wait.'

Ma laughed her dry snort as she stirred the soup. Then she ladled out two platefuls. I carried the plates with the steaming concoction into the house and placed them on the table. Ma joined me at the table.

'You know, Ma,' I said as I attacked the delicious meal, 'I was thinking that now that I've got this good secure job, it would be a fine thing if you came to live with me and Sonia in Kingsland. How about it?'

'Your house is too small, Jerry, and besides, I couldn't live in that filthy place, Bottom Town.'

'Ma, I'm surprised at you. How could you expect the Chief Minister of Hiroona to live in Bottom Town? The Government is fixing up a lovely five-bedroom house for me in Fairfield — that quiet, residential area on the outskirts of Kingsland. Fairfield House is to be my official residence. Only this morning I settled the matter with Mr Forbes. I move into Fairfield House as soon as the Public Works Department put in suitable furniture. This will be in a matter of days. So?'

Ma chuckled. She smoothed the white tablecloth unnecessarily with the palm of her hand as she said, 'Son, you are amusing. You are so keen on every new job you get, then later you find fault with it, and then you lose it. Then you go on to a new one, only to lose that, too. But maybe you can't help. You have something of your father in you.'

'My father? I didn't know I had one. You never told me about him, Ma.'

Ma smoothed the tablecloth pensively. 'You never asked me,' she said.

'Isn't he Myra's father, too?'

'No. I was in love with Myra's father. He had emigrated to Curacao. We were to be married when he returned.'

'Who is my father, then? Is he alive?'

'No.'

'Well, who was he, Ma? What was he like?'

'He was Mr Crickett's younger brother. His name was Charles. He had come from England to help his brother run Shapiro. But the arrangement didn't work, because Charles didn't work. He started out all right. He was very good at starting out, Mrs Crickett used to say. His job was to keep the estate's books. He did this all right for quite a few months. Then he took to hanging about the house instead of going out to his work in the estate office. I never liked Charles Crickett. I was suspicious of him from the outset. He was a smallish man. The thing I remember most about him is his nose. It was big and beaky, and his eyes always seemed to stare like two black shiny beads close to his nose bridge. Mrs Crickett didn't care much for him either. She often told me he was unstable. She meant that he had spells, I suppose.'

'Spells? You mean fits, like epilepsy?'

'Is epilepsy a sickness?'

'Yes. They say it puts you out of the running for short periods.'

'Charles Crickett was not sick in that sense. He was a very strong man. During the eighteen months or so he worked at Shapiro, he was never confined to bed for a single day. It was his mind that was sick. He and Mr Crickett used to have some terrible rows. Then Charles would shut himself up in his room, and we could sometimes hear him smashing things or throwing them about in his room, during his tantrums. One day Mrs Crickett went to Kingsland. Charles was supposed to be way out at Benders, getting some figures from the stockman there. Before Mr Crickett left the house to attend to some business on the estate, he told me to clean up some mess that Charles had made in his room a few days before. None of the maids liked the idea of going near Charles' room, but one of us had to go every now and again to tidy up the room. Before going, we always made sure that Charles was nowhere around the place. I was just coming out of the room, with some smashed crockery, when Charles came up to the door. He pushed me back into the room. I threw the pieces of teacup and saucer in his face. I was young and strong. I wasn't afraid of him. But he was stronger, and he got mad — I mean mad, Jerry — when I threw the broken china in his face. He grabbed me, coiled his leg behind mine, threw me and held me down, his hand over my mouth, his feet jammed against the bottom of the door of a clothes closet to add to his weight and to give him purchase. With his free hand he ripped my underclothes off. When he let me up a few minutes after, I bolted out of the room, feeling unclean and ashamed. I am telling you all this, son, so that you may know your origin and keep a watch on yourself, now that you have this big responsible job. Your father was a violent man, lazy and headstrong and without self-control. I said nothing to Mr Cricket, but as soon as Mrs Crickett came home I told her what happened. She was so angry that she told Mr Crickett to get Charles out of the house at once. I had never seen Mrs Crickett so angry before or since. Mr Crickett told his brother to move out and go into one of the vacant overseer's houses in the back yard. Charles refused, and Mr Crickett had to send for the two policemen at Chateaubelair police station to help him remove his brother out of the house. But Charles was so violent that the policemen had to overpower him, handcuff him and take him down to a cell in the police station to let him cool off. He never did quiet down, though; and when they got a doctor to him, the doctor advised Mr Crickett to send him to England. They had to give him injections so they could take him to Kingsland and put him on a ship. Mrs Crickett told me afterwards that Charles was certified by the doctor as a person of unsound mind. He didn't last long, poor man, after he got back to England. But, lucky for me and you and Myra, nobody except Mr and Mrs Crickett knows who your father was. Not even Myra knows.'

'God, Ma, what a nasty experience!' I rubbed the back of her arthritic hand gently.

'I feel unclean ever since, whenever I think about it. So much so, I have never let a man touch me, from that time. Myra's father wanted to marry me after he came back from Curacao, although I had birthed you by then, but I put him off. He couldn't understand why, and of course I never told him.'

I got up, took a few turns round the room, and stood by the window which faced the table at which Ma sat, apparently deep in thought. From the window I looked at the black sand beach, then lower down where the smooth, calm sea occasionally broke in tiny and almost noiseless waves and receded behind a long, serrated stretch of foam. A little further out, my eyes and my mind came to rest on the spot where, years ago, I had held Janey Tucker's boy, Milton, underwater, and nearly caused his drowning. And Ma said maybe I couldn't help. Although she loved me, she had doubted whether I could rise higher in my conduct than Charles Crickett, my 'origin'. It was the same in the days when I lost one job after another; Ma had felt and said that maybe I couldn't help. Charles Crickett was unstable, and so Ma believed that his offspring had to be unstable. Even now, when my recent achievements should have dispelled her doubts, she still regarded such proof of my superiority to Charles Crickett as inconclusive. She hesitated to accept my offer of a better life in my official mansion in Kingsland, because she doubted whether I would hold my new job longer than I could help. I was conceived in accursed circumstances, and so, Ma felt, I was blighted forever.

My birth, my very existence as a human being, was the direct result of violence and injustice. A man's filthiness had given me life. I, Jerry Mole, Chief Minister, was the result of an unfortunate and sordid accident. In that sense, I myself was an accident.

I did not shudder at the thought. I smiled instead, as I wondered how much good or evil had been done and was being done all over the world by accidents like myself. Not necessarily 'accidents' which were the result of rape, but 'accidents' which were the result of chance meetings, chance circumstances, chance love, chance affection, chance courtship, chance marriage. To this extent, the existence of every single human being is conditioned by an 'if', a circumstance or a set of circumstances. *If* Charles Crickett had not come to Hiroona, I, Jerry Mole, would not have been born. *If* Charles Crickett *had* come to Hiroona, but was a chaste, clean-minded man of integrity, I would not have been born. *If* well, I was like every other human being — there was an 'if' about me, about my existence. So why worry? I was here already. In existence. Like everybody else — with me — little 'ifs'. But I wanted my mother to believe in me now. I wanted to make her realize that what was done was done, and that from now on, it was up to me to justify my existence and my 'ifs'.

'Ma.'

'Mmm?' She looked up with a start.

'I'm glad in a way that you've told me about this man Charles Crickett. One's origin is always of interest to one. But I want you to forget the past. What is done is done. I want you to believe that I have no intention of going through life with Charles Crickett hanging around my neck. You should realize by now, Ma, that I have shaken him off. What I have achieved, I have achieved by real hard and sustained effort — something of which Charles Crickett did not appear to be capable. This should convince you that I have left Crickett behind, I intend to keep him behind. By God, I intend to hold on to what I have now. It's my biggest prize yet. It is not a mere job, not merely a profession. It is both and much more than both. I cannot afford to lose it, Ma, because I cannot afford a come-down. If I lose it, I have nothing else to hold on to — to live by. I have no qualification for any other decent, lucrative employment, and I cannot step down from my present exalted position and go job-seeking in an island in which I once exercised pre-eminent authority. And I cannot go back to poverty, to joblessness, to being a nobody. This, too, I cannot afford. This I don't intend. This I will resist with every weapon or means my wits can devise and Hiroona can provide. I swear to you, Ma, that after crossing the stream which separates Bottom Town from Fairfield House, I burned my boat.'

'But Jerry, you speak beautifully, and with power. I am proud of you, son. You, should have been a schoolmaster instead of an ordinary — what you call it — chief minister?'

I burst out laughing. 'Ma,' I said, 'you are as quite contrary as Mary, Mary. You haven't understood a single thing I've been trying to tell you.'

'Of course I understand, Jerry. What you take me for, an old dunderhead? Of course I understand. You are Chief Minister now. You will be Premier and Prime Minister later on. You're leaving Bottom Town to live in Fairfield House, and you burned a boat. Oh yes — I haven't forgotten your job carries a big salary which you practically fixed yourself. See? I've got it all.'

'O.K., Ma. Now Sonia and I really want you to come and live with us in Fairfield House. You will be very happy there. All your needs will be supplied. Ma, you would make me and Sonia very happy if you come with us. What do you say? You promise to come to Kingsland as soon as our house is made ready, eh?'

'I will come to visit you and Sonia, son, if you send a taxi for me. I can't ride in the bus as I used to do. The jolting over the bad roads is not good for old bones. But I have lived in Chateaubelair and in this house too long to be able to live anywhere else now, at my age. Old people have a way of wanting to stay in one place — the place they are used to. They don't like moving around too much. I really believe that you will make good in your present job. I can see that you seriously intend to hold on to it, and I am proud of you, Jerry. I have no doubts about you now, my son. But life in Kingsland is not for me. I am used to getting up at mornings and seeing the sea almost at my door. I listen to it burping at night when it is rough, and I like the sound. I like to see the fishermen hauling the seines ashore, and the fish jumping up in the nets. I like to go down to the beach, with the crowds from the village, and buy my own fish. I am used to all these things. I was born in them and I grew up in them. I can't change now, at my age. I even like to hear the fishermen swear, although I pretend to re-buke them sometimes. I have lived here all my life. I intend to die here. You must go back to Kingsland, my son, take up your new job and be a great man. I will remain here, praying for you, feeling proud of you. My son.'

It was no use trying to persuade her. No use arguing.

6

M R Forbes the Administrator did not accept with grace the political changes ushered in by the new constitution. Perhaps he could be forgiven for this. Come to think of it, the changes were revolutionary, and they demanded a great deal of psychological adjustment on the part of the old Administrators and Governors. For whereas in the past these high officials, representatives of the Sovereign, were the dominant executives in the Governments of the territories, now they had to share authority, and share it in some cases with individuals who, like myself, were hitherto considered unqualified or unsuitable for the role of men of state. By training and experience, these top ranking executives were used to Government by civil service rules and principles. Now, they had to accept government by political expediency, the euphemism for which being 'the will of the people' — which 'will' must always prevail. The transition from civil service supremacy to supremacy of the people's representatives was a trying time for both sides. Forbes and I realized this at the outset.

I had instructed my Permanent Secretary to submit two memoranda to the Executive Council. The Council met to consider these as well as other business on a long agenda.

'Mr Mole,' — (Forbes never addressed me by my official title, 'Mr Chief Minister', even at meetings of the Executive Council) — 'Mr Mole, you have been only ten months in Government. You still have a lot to learn. Government is not Government unless it is responsible government. You've shown scant sense of responsibility, in these two memoranda you have submitted to this Council for its considerations.'

'I did not come here for a lecture from you, Mr Forbes. And I am not interested in your opinion about my sense of responsibility.'

He picked up one from the small pile of memoranda submitted by myself and the other ministers, which lay on the table in front of him. The memoranda were written by our Permanent Secretaries on our separate orders. The minister only initialled the memorandum at the bottom left hand corner, to indicate his responsibility for it.

'We shall take this one first,' said Mr Forbes. 'Here, you are asking this Council to agree to an increase of fifty per cent on the present daily wages of all daily-paid and casual workers employed by the Government, as well as the wages of all labourers on the estates on this island. And you want this to be retroactive as from the first of January this year. This means that these people would be receiving back pay on the new wage rates in respect of the period of nearly a year. Have you studied the financial implications of this proposal, Mr Mole?'

'Yes.'

'Have you discussed this proposal with your Financial Secretary?'

'Yes.'

'Does he recommend it?'

'No. But the Financial Secretary does not run the Government. His business is to advise the Government, and the Government is not bound to accept his advice. All you need do, Mr Forbes, is put the matter to the Government — myself and the three ministers sitting here.' I glanced around the table. Sonia, the Minister for Education and Social Services, was staring with counterfeit seriousness at her copy of the memorandum. She held her head down so that her stylish hat helped to hide from Mr Forbes the nervous little smile which played around the corners of her mouth. Joe Pittance, Minister for Communications and Works, was frowning at his copy. Claude Mason, Minister without portfolio, appeared to be having some difficulty reading his copy, which he was holding up close to his face as he slouched in his chair with his head thrown back. The Attorney General, a civil servant, ex-officio member of the Executive Council, was pulling at an acne under his jaw and looking at me with a sort of mild detachment.

Forbes said, 'To increase the wages of all daily-paid employees of the Government retroactively by fifty per cent, as you are proposing to this Council, would wipe out the island's Reserve Fund completely. The British Government will not increase the island's grant-in-aid for the purpose of the wages increase you are now proposing. Therefore, the only source from which the Government could find the money for this extra-ordinary measure is the colony's Reserve Fund. This fund has been built up with a great deal of care and planning over the years, and has been earmarked for the enlargement of the Kingsland Hospital where patients are at this moment lying on the floors. Where women give birth to babies on nondescript bedding in corridors. The fund is just short of the target by nine thousand dollars. All this was explained to you months ago; and we all here, including yourself, Mr Mole, agreed to place the hospital project at the very top of the priority list of things to be done for the improvement of the island. Now you are proposing that the money be used to increase the wages of daily paid workers by fifty per cent. Fifty per cent!

And I have no record of a request from the workers for any increase in their wages. Can you blame me, then, if I question your sense of responsibility as a Minister of Finance? And as far as the estates are concerned, have you taken the trouble to find out from the managements whether their finances could stand such an additional expenses?'

He was quite right. The hospital badly needed doing. The thing was a disgrace. It had been towntalk for years. I knew all this; but I also knew that as a new politician I would get much better publicity in the quarters where much publicity mattered, if I increased the wages of "the poor man" than if I provided the island with a bigger hospital. I had been Chief Minister for nearly a year. I was placed in the position by the great expectations of some fifty thousand hungry people who had not had a wage increase within living memory. Unbelievably meagre wages had been their portion since Columbus. A wage increase of fifty per cent would be a miracle which only a wonderman could bring about. The hospital could wait. Later, my Government might be able to beg successfully for a free grant from Britain, under a Colonial Development and Welfare Scheme, for the hospital. Or Canada might come up with a gift. But right now, I needed something to show for my having been Chief Minister for ten months; and the more spectacular the show, the better. A fifty per cent increase would be nothing short of the spectacular.

'Listen, Mr Forbes,' I said, 'I am quite *au fait* with the situation you have outlined. But what's the use of our having a reserve fund when wages are so low that the poor people suffer from malnutrition, and are hungry most of the time? Are you satisfied that twenty cents a day is sufficient for a man with a wife or concubine and children to live on? If you are satisfied, I am not. Fifty per cent increase on very low wages still leaves the wages very low. You talk about the hospital being a priority; but in matters of priority there is nothing to compare with an empty belly, just as in matters of urgency there is nothing to compare with the call to ease a full one. In other words, Mr Forbes, certain basic human needs are paramount, demanding priority over even a hospital. As for the estates, whether or not they can afford the additional expense is no business of this Government's. We make the law; the estates either obey the law or face the strikes and other unfortunate consequences. I therefore now demand that the proposal in my memorandum be put to this Council at once, and that if it is accepted by a majority, that the Attorney General be instructed to draft the necessary legislation to be sent to the Legislative Council for debate and passage into law.'

The rest was easy. Even my other memorandum went through without a hitch. That memorandum invited the Council to agree that the present ban on the importation of slot machines be lifted; that importation of the said machines be permitted only by a special licence issued to not more than one person during a period of five years, and that such licence be issued by the Ministry of Finance.

Dave Potter would now be able to import and install his 'man eaters,' and to enjoy the concession for the duration of my regime.

7

S ONIA leaned over slightly in her seat in the car and spoke into my ear. 'Ah wonder how long dis will last?' she said. She had to shout a bit, as the noise of the motorcade and the shouting and cheering of the people made hearing difficult.

'Last?' I shouted back. 'I just begin.'

News of the forthcoming wages increase had got around even before the matter reached the Legislative Council to be put into law. I had given the 'seepage' time to circulate a bit, then I had followed up with a series of political mass meetings in various parts of the island. I could not overtly divulge to the people what had occurred during the meeting of the Executive Council, as all meetings of that Council were supposed to be secret. But I made it demagogically clear to the crowds at the mass meetings.

'Since my entry into the Government, Comrades, I have made the alarming discovery that you have powerful enemies in high places. You would be surprised to know, Comrades, the solid fight I had to put up a few weeks ago to get a small wage raise for you. You, who have to toil and sweat day go day come, while the so-called better class eat high on de hog. One of our enemies is the British Government that is giving us freedom with one hand and taking it back with the other. They say they giving us self-determination, but they still keep their Governors and Administrators in the islands to lord it over us.' I lifted my voice to the well-known shriek: 'I say we don't need no Administrator here in Hiroona!'

'Dats roight! Dats roight!' they shrieked back.

'I say Forbes must go!'

'Yeahse! Yeahse! 'e mus' go!'

It was after this series of mass meetings that I organised the motorcade. The motorcade itself was evidence of tremendous progress I had made since I became Chief. A year ago, the only motor car owner in Kingsland I could have dared talk to about such a thing as a labour union motorcade, was Dave Potter. Today, because the wage increase would mean more money in circulation, and because I was now Chief Minister, I had twenty five cars tooting and honking behind me in the first motorcade Hiroona had ever seen. On assorted places on each motor car were pasteboard, cardboard, or bunting bearing slogans and political apophthegms: LEAVE

IT TO PAPA JERRY. TOO MUCH TOIL TOO LITTLE PAY. BRITAIN, GO HOME! YOU MEAN FORBES STILL HERE? HIROONA AWAKE! And so on.

The motorcade headed for the Windward coast, from Kingsland, so that we passed through the most populous villages and small towns. Occasionally we would stop in the midst of a cheering crowd, and I would get out of my car, microphone in hand, cable trailing from the mike to the half open luggage compartment of the car. The microphone sent my voice beyond the crowds, into their homes, their kitchens, their privies; into the distant fields; into the Great House of the estates; on to the beaches where fishermen hauled in their seines or spread them on the sand to dry. Into the school grounds where children paused in their play to stare at the motor cars and the crowds. Into the schools where pupil teachers interrupted their late afternoon studies to rush to the doors and windows to watch and listen.

At all the mass meetings I had held, prior to the motorcade, the wage increase was 'a small raise', because 'enemies in high places' was then the real issue. But now that the enemy had been unmasked and that it was settled that he *Must Go*, the truth about the increase could be told:

'Fifty per cent, comrades, Fifty per cent! De first raise you gettin' since you born. The biggest raise in de history of labour in dis island. Wait a minute. Don't clap and cheer yet. This is not all. Let me tell you, I done arrange for you to draw dis increase as from de first of January this year — so you goin' to draw back pay for nearly a year, an' some of you will get over one hundred dollars in yo' han' one time. Wait! Wait! Don't jump up and shout yet, comrades. That is not all. I have more news fo' you. You will all get yo' back pay just before Christmas. De Gover'ment done hold talks wid de estate owners. They didn't want to agree at first, but Ah explained to them dat because your wages is so low already, de increase shoulda been a hundred per cent insteada just fifty per cent. They had to agree at de end, to pay de fifty per cent. And the law went through its three readings in de Legislative Council today. So you an' your children will be able to buy better, eat better, dress better from dis year Christmas onwards. This is only the beginning, comrades. There's more to come. Let us go forward together. Are you with me?'

'Yeahse! Yeahse! We wid yo' to de en'!'

Then amid the jumping up, the cheering, the cutting of barefoot capers, the rushing to shake my hand, the 'Papa Jerry fa-rever', the 'God bless you, my Leader' and the dazed expressions of wonder at the news of a miracle, the motorcade moved on slowly.

'I've made it!' I said in Sonia's ear. She sat beside me in the back seat of our car, smiling and waving to the demonstrating crowd.

'Yes, but Ah wonder how long dis will last,' she shouted back.
'Last?' I said. 'It just begin, girl.'

I spent the first five years consolidating my leadership of the masses,
building up prestige generally and waging a power-struggle with Forbes
and the Colonial Office. Membership of the union increased rapidly. I
had foreseen this, of course, but I had not taken into account the pressure
which the increased work would put on Sonia. She didn't complain
much, but I could see that the two jobs — General Secretary of the Union
and Minister for Education and Social Services — were getting on top of
her. Of course, all her office work as minister was done by the Permanent
Secretary and other members of the staff of the ministry, but she had to
visit schools and the health services; hold discussions with Heads of the
Departments who came under her ministry; be interviewed by all and
sundry in connection with complaints, or requests for information
bearing on schools, hospitals, clinics, public conveniences throughout
the island and a host of other matters; think up attractive promises to be
made for the benefit of the public. There were also decisions to be made
when her Permanent Secretary presented for her attention matters on
which policy had not been clearly defined.

All these demands took time, thought, and mental energy. For a girl
of Sonia's background this responsibility was crushing. And it was more
so because Sonia had a streak of honesty, conscientiousness and
straightforwardness — elements of character which can constitute a
serious handicap for a politician.

Although the work load was obviously heavy for her, I could not
entertain the thought of relieving Sonia of her post of General Secretary
of the union. Her salary as Secretary, mine as President, the emoluments
from her job as Minister, mine (tax free) as Chief Minister, together made
up a tidy little thing which encouraged retention. After all, our present
ministerial jobs were not pensionable. True, I was riding well in the saddle
now, and I intended so to ride for a long time. But one never knows. The
people could suddenly turn bronco, start kicking up like hell and throw
me. It must have been this eventuality that was passing through Sonia's
mind during the motorcade, when she wondered *how long dis will last.*
The girl had sound sense. She knew that like practically all these so-called
politicians in most of the British West Indian Islands at that time, we were
able to snatch power only because more suitable leaders had failed to
come forward. The times were those of the early fifties, when organised,

sophisticated political leadership was a new and practically unknown thing in most of the islands. The people were not yet politically awake. AWAKE was a popular slogan-word in those days. That was the reason why I had included HIROONA, AWAKE! among the slogans on the cars in the motorcade. But to awaken Hiroona was the last thing I wanted to do; for I could picture what would happen to me when a younger, better educated and more progressive generation of Hiroonians sprang up, looked around and saw people like me and Smallmilk and Claude Mason and Sonia and Joe Pittance running the country. I had to make provision against such a disquieting eventuality. There were only two ways in which this could be done: lay up treasures now in the bank, or later (when I had fully established myself in power) introduce state-of-emergency laws which would give me the authority to lock up or neutralise any opposition which might arise, and thus crystallise my position as Head of a one-party Government.

After all, a man must live by his profession. A professional politician — if there is ever such a thing — is not like a doctor, lawyer or civil engineer. When these, and members of similar professions, get thrown out of political position, they can open private offices, nail a shingle on the door and go on practising their professions and making a living. No politician, thrown completely out of popular favour, could nail a sign on his door — JERRY HORATIO MOLE — POLITICIAN — and thus hope to go on collecting loot. And when you have no ability to do anything else except run the country, you just got to live by running the country — and save while you run.

So I couldn't afford to let Sonia give up either of her jobs, although I couldn't help noticing that her holding down the two jobs was doing her health and her spirits no good.

Returning home very late one night from Dave Potter's, I noticed that there was light in the room which Sonia used as her private office; and as I drove up the long driveway leading to Fairfield House, a moving silhouette caught my eye through the large, wide, glass window and diaphanous, white curtain in the room. It was not unusual for Sonia to be up late at night, working in her office. She was always there when I returned early from my frequent nocturnal visits to Dave Potter's place. But being up and at work as late as one forty-five was not usual for Sonia.

I eased the car into the carport, entered the dining room and ran up the wide carpeted stairs, grabbing a Bequia plum from a large dish of fruits on the dining room table as I went past.

When I reached the open door of Sonia's office, Sonia was sitting in a low morris chair; her head rested on the back of the chair, and her eyes were closed. The upper part of her dress was unbuttoned, and the maid was fanning her with one of those large official envelopes stamped with 'On Her Majesty's Service'.

'What happen?' I said, entering the room and throwing the plum seed into the wastepaper basket near the large Sankey-Sheldon steel desk. I went and sat near to Sonia and placed my hand softly on her forehead.

She opened her eyes, sat up and said, 'Ah don't really know what happen. I had all dat pile o' union dues books to straighten out. Ah had to check de money first to see if it tally wid de passbooks. When Ah finish dat, Ah was copyin' de payments from de passbooks into de ledger. It was takin' a long time, because it is plenty passbooks, but Ah was determine to get through all of dem, because tomorrow is Executive Council meetin' and Ah wouldn't have time fo' union work. Ah didn't care if it take me all night. Suddenly —'

'You shouldn't do so much at one time, Sonia. You will hurt yo' self.'

'Suddenly, Ah have a sharp headache an' a funny feeling like Ah want to faint. So Ah throw down de pen and get up off de chair quick, quick, and lay down on de floor to prevent me fallin' an hittin' me head. Next thing Ah know, Lynda holding up me head an' sayin', "Mistress! Mistress! Wha' happen?"'

'Christ!'

'By dat time I had catch meself, but Ah felt hot hot. So I got up an' sit in dis chair an' open me dress fo' air, an' Lynda said she better fan me until Ah feel better. But Ah'm all right now. Fetch me some water, Jerry.'

'I think you've been working too hard, Sonia,' I said, handing her a glass of water. 'I will appoint an Assistant Secretary to help you with union work. I really must. I'll do this tomorrow. Let's get to bed at once. Thank you, Lynda. But how come you're up so late, Lynda? And you so dressed up?'

'Bin to de dance at Town Hall, Chief; but too much a crowd, an' dey start one big fight. So me boyfren' take me away and he was followin' me to me room. When we reach in de drive comin' up, Ah notice light in de Mistress affice. So insteada goin' to me room at de back, Ah tell Norman Ah better run upstairs first an' see if de Mistress need anyt'ing . . She shouldn't work so hard, Chief. It bad fo' she constitutian. Good night, Mistress.'

'O.K., Lynda. Thanks fo' lookin' after me. See you in de mornin'.'

8

DURING my first five years in power, I was, fortunately, free from the annoyance of opposition. As that period drew to its close and I began to look forward to another general election, I did so with a confidence approaching cocksureness. In my campaign speeches, I didn't even have to make promises. All I did was to point to the impressive accomplishments of the PPP: the wage increase; the eight hour day; double pay for Sunday and public holidays work; scrapping of mechanical road mending equipment to ensure long employment on road work; the building of one or two Primary Schools with grants from the British Government.

I was now stronger than ever, drawing support not only from the masses, but also certain sections of the lower and upper middle classes. I could now look forward to a second landslide victory.

This progress had meant hard work, and late nights with Dave and Bryan, discussing and planning political strategy. I had lost intimate touch with all of my original associates, as I considered them out of step with my ideas and my methods. I discovered also that Joe Pittance, for all his pretence of political know-how, had little or no ambition to rise above his former life as a stevedore. On several occasions, as I drove along the bayfront, I saw him sitting on the concrete platform of the wharf talking with 'wharf rats'. He even continued his barbering on the wharfside on Sunday mornings. I often wondered what he did with his salary as a Minister. His mode of living seemed to have changed only to the extent that he now wore leather shoes. I saw little of him. He avoided me whenever he could; and although the fact of our mutual mistrust occasionally disturbed me, I had no time for Pittance. He really belonged to my past. I was so preoccupied with my work, my new status, and my high standard of living, that I no longer had any desire to 'get even' with Pittance. I had done more than getting even with him; I had gone past him, although he continued to give me trouble. My resolve to avenge myself on old McIver for shooting at me with his shotgun was also forgotten. I was now too satisfied with life to bother about vengeance for a slight, ancient insult. I bought my first house. Indeed things were going so well that I began to harbour the thought of writing the first few chapters of my memoirs. Bryan and Dave were very pleased with the idea.

The perfection of things was marred by a few flaws, however. For one thing, my efforts to have Mr Forbes the Administrator recalled or transferred had failed so far. The Colonial Office continued to ignore the people's request for Forbes' removal. I supposed this was the British Government's way of making it clear to us that Crown colony politicians must have no control over civil servants. To underscore this point, the Queen awarded the OBE to Forbes, and later made him a CMG — just at the time when we were asking that he be disgraced. At my political meetings all over the island, I roundly cursed the British Government for 'this and other evidence of British imperialism'; but Forbes remained in his post, nevertheless.

Then my difficulties with Pittance and Naomi flared up again and came to a head a few months before the second General Election. I had called a meeting of the party-cum-union committee of management to review our work and achievements over the past five years and to discuss details of our campaign for the next election.

We met at the Chamber. The building presented its usual run-down appearance which was not improved by a broad strip of red bunting I had nailed along the whole length of the building over three years ago, bearing, in huge white cloth capital letters stitched on, the words, FORBES MUST GO! HE IS AN ENEMY OF THE PEOPLE. Prolonged action of weather had made the cloth look washed out, and it sagged in several places where it had come unstuck over the heads of the now rusty nails.

I opened the meeting. Somehow, the singing of the usual opening 'odes' lacked the old warmth and ring of comradeship; and after my remarks explaining the purpose of the meeting, Naomi got up and said that she wondered why I bothered to call the meeting at all.

'What you mean, comrade?' I asked.

'When you running a one-man show, you don't need to call meetings,' said Naomi. 'The last time we had a meeting of the committee was three years ago. That is not good enough. The committee should be informed about what is going on in the union at least, not to mention in the Government. But what do we find? An Assistant Secretary appointed in the union without our even knowing. The committee was not even consulted. The union funds have not been audited since the union started. No financial statement submitted to the members. This one-man show is an insult to people's intelligence. It must either stop or I resign from the union.'

'If *you* don't trust me, Comrade Sampson,' I replied, 'I can still count on the confidence of the thousands of people on this island who appreciate the fine job I've done during the past five years. I had to appoint an assistant to Comrade Sonia Mole because her health was feeling the pressure of her carrying a ministerial as well as a secretarial job. The matter was urgent, and I didn't think you or anyone here would wish to see Comrade Mole collapse for want of an assistant. Would you, comrade?'

'Chief, stop yo' jokes,' said Pittance. 'If you had all dat consideration fo' the healt' of Comrade Mole, you would not of had her doin' de two jobs. Five years ago, at a meetin' of dis same committee here, we advised you to give de union secretary job to Vincent Cunningham, the young police constable who was sacked fo' helpin' us. You brushed us aside. Now you come tellin' us yo' wife healt' couldn't stand up to de pressha. Dat is sound stupidness, Chief. Hypocrisy. Even if you wanted to appoint somebody else, de Committee should have been consulted. I agree wid Comrade Sampson dat you had been runnin' a one-man show for de last five years.'

He paused and looked around the room, a sort of impish grin on his face as if he were preparing to say something funny. I waited in the deep silence of the Chamber.

'Now you, Chief, is de right hand of de Govern'ment. De union, de party and de Gover'ment ministers is de left hand. It seems like you followin' de Bible where it say, "Let not your left hand know what your right han' doeth." But de Bible wasn't tarkin' about runnin' de Gover'ment when it said dat.'

The applause and the burst of derisive laughter infuriated me. I jumped up. Pittance raised his hand, asking for more time to speak. 'Ah ain't finish, Chief. We all helped to put you where you is today, Chief. Now we find dat David Potter know more about de Gover'ment's plans dan we, who in de Government and in de party an' de union. Why so?'

I counted ten before replying:

'Because, Comrade Pittance, a leader must seek help and advice wherever he finds it most congenial and useful to do so — if you understand my English. And as for young Cunningham, your solicitude about him seems to be unnecessary. I understand that although he has refused to seek employment since his dismissal from the police force, he and his wife and children appear to be living as comfortably as before. I have even been told that he made two trips to Trinidad recently, for a medical check up. This is not the action and style of a man who needs a job as secretary of our union.'

I paused to let that sink in.

Then I said, 'Now you say that you have put me where I am today. I can say the same to you. I have put *you* where you are today. You seem to have forgotten that, Comrade Pittance. One would have thought that you would remember this at the end of every month, at least.'

'You referring to me salary, Chief. Ah sorry you did dat. I took up politics because Ah like de trade. Ah like it because in politics you can really help yo' country if yo' really want to. But Ah know dat as soon as politician get greedy fo' money an' position an' power, de country suffers. So I have no ambition, thank de Lord. And because Ah have no ambition, I am a free man. Ah don't depend on you and de Ministry of Works fo' a livin', because me livin' is as simple as it was before Ah entered politics. Ah still live alone at Lot Eighteen, in me little two-room house wid one bed, one chair, one small table, one drinkin' glass fo' meself, an' two extra ones in case friends drop in for a drink. So I am in a better position to help people and help de country, because Ah ain't have to fool people to get on. I have got on already. Me life is simple. It ain't move from where it was when Ah wasn't a Minister.'

He stopped to chuckle.

Then he continued, 'Chief, you hinted at me salary, but you will be surprised to know what Ah doing wid it. Prahaps somebody will tell you, one o' dese days, what Ah doin' wid de salary dat Ah getting from de Gover'ment every month. And prahaps one o' dese days you may become a politician; but all you is now is a funny little bossman hiding behine vote-power.'

In spite of his anger and obviously deep feeling, the man was as cool as a cucumber. Neither his voice nor his manner changed as he said:

'We got six months more to go, then de general election. In dese six months, Ah'm goin' to have a lot of work to do. So Ah've got to resign here an' now from your Gover'ment, an' from your union. So goodbye, chief. You can tell de Administrata dat Pittance garn.'

He walked with a feline high-foot-soft-foot gait out of the Chamber. He still couldn't manage leather shoes quite well. But I was too stunned, too amazed, too shocked to be able to see anything funny about his walk.

9

MY lucky period of non-interference from opposition ended. At the next general election, Joe Pittance defeated my candidate for the seat of South Windward and Vincent Cunningham, the ex-police constable — P.C. 43 — trounced Smallmilk for the Kingsland seat. Pittance and Cunningham had helped each other in campaigning, both campaigns being masterminded by Joe. I bagged the other nine seats, but I was worried by the thought that although Pittance had only four or five months to campaign, after he broke away from me, he still managed to win two seats — and this without forming a party of his own. For an independent candidate to win a seat, not only for himself, but also for an associate independent, was disquieting precedence indeed. It was a clarion indication of Pittance's political acumen, and the high esteem in which he was held by two constituencies which were formerly mine. His growing popularity certainly presented an unsettling threat to my government.

Dave, Bryan and I discussed the situation one night, some months after the election. We usually held such conferences in the private room which Dave had fixed up for me in the back of his place. We had christened the room with a name meaning the nest of an eagle — 'The Aerie'. Bryan didn't like the name. He said it would bring bad luck. During the past years, I had grown very fond of the Aerie, visiting it almost every night, even after late political mass meetings in the country or in Kingsland. Dave had set up a little bar in it, and he, Bryan and I spent hours there.

But on this particular night, we did not use the Aerie for our discussion. This was not by design; it merely happened that we found ourselves sitting and talking at one of the far corner tables in the public bar. There weren't many people in the place; and the dozen or so patrons were intent on playing the slot machines. Dave had installed six of these 'man eaters'. The falling coins, the rasp of the pulled handles and the whirr of the machines kept our conversation from the hearing of the gamblers.

Dave said, 'Pittance musta bin getting secret support all along.'

'You got to hand it to Pittance,' said Bryan. 'The man has political sense. They say he is a borrn politician. Damn popular, too. Of course, it is better to have a man like Pittance on your side than against you; but a strong, intelligent Opposition is always good for a country, although it may not be convenient for the Government in powerrr.'

'Better to have no opposition at all,' said Dave. 'We shoulda rigged the damn election, rather than let any opposition at all get in. But we were too cocksure.'

'I couldn't agree with you more, Dave,' I said. 'If we had rigged the thing, I would not have been badgered by these bloody embarrassing questions Pittance and Cunningham have kept asking in the Legislative Council, meeting after meeting, over the past months.'

'You gentlemen talk about opposition as if it was a four-letter word,' said Bryan. 'It is by good opposition that democracy lives. Even with strong opposition, we have dictatorship and corruption springing up all overrr the worrrld. If it wasn't for the fact of opposition — either in the country concerned, or from an outside country looking on and commenting — hell woulda let loose on earth already.'

'That's well and good,' I replied, 'but opposition is not the best thing for Hiroona at this stage. Our people have not yet reached the standard of educational development which makes a country safe with an opposition. Our people tend to believe anything the opposition tells them, no matter if it is nonsense. They can't think for themselves as yet.'

'I agree,' said Dave. 'Look at the hell of a lot of a publicity Pittance and Cunningham getting nowadays. When we had no opposition, you never saw a single member of the public in the Council Chamber during meetings of the Legislative Council; but since Pittance and that boy Cunningham started their showing off and debating at the meetings, the room always chock full of people, come to listen to them. Sometimes, the police have trouble controlling the crowds trying to get in. Seems like the crowds love to hear Pittance and Cunningham expose the Gover'ment. And when Jerry try to shut them up, Forbes as President of the Council intervenes on their side with his rubbish about parliamentary procedure. Parliamentary balls, if you ask me. I bin advising you, Jerry, for months now, to cut down on Legislative Council meetings. Let the Executive Council alone carry on the Gover'ment. The public not allowed in Exco meetings, and Pittance and Cunningham not allowed there either.'

'I've decided to act on your advice, Dave. But it is not easy. We have to have Legco meetings every time we want a new law passed, or additional government expenditure approved.'

'That is the Constitution,' said Bryan. 'That is democracy; and you got to abide.'

'I have my plan to deal with that problem, anyway,' I said, 'What *is* worrying hell outa me now is Paul Darcy. Those goddam articles he publishes almost every week!'

'I agree with you therrre. Those articuls can do a lot of damage. If articuls like those appeared in the *Advocate* in Babiadus . . . .'

'The articles in themselves don't trouble me. I deal with them in the usual way at mass meetings. What bothers me is the question as to what to do about Darcy himself, and about the newspaper.'

'What you mean?' queried Dave.

'Well,' I groped, 'If — ar — suppose *you* have a talk with Darcy, eh Dave? You could begin by telling him that you want to buy a half page of the *Weekly* for an advertisement. That should please him. Then you could gradually work on him and bring him around to supporting us.'

'I don't think that will work,' said Dave. 'In the first place, it isn't the Gover'ment that Darcy is really against. He and Forbes are friends, but he hates your guts. It is you he against. He thinks you are what he calls an upstart. He considers me an upstart, too, because I am a black man with some means.'

'Yes. I realize that; but if he saw the opportunity of his newspaper making some good money out of you for a big, regular advertisement, he might — well — it would be good business for you, too, Dave, because my union will pay for the ad.'

'Jerry, man, we all know that if Darcy had to depend on his newspaper for a living, he would starve. The circulation in an island like Hiroona must be small. Darcy depends for a living on the big income from the arrowroot lands he leased from Johnson at Argyle Estate. The newspaper, to him, is a kind of valuable hobby that brings him influence on the island, and a kinda power — and of course a little money too, but not much. We can hurt Darcy through his arrowroot business — and we did that already when we brought in the law to increase the wages of all labourers — but we can't influence him through buying advertising space in his paper. You can only hurt him through the newspaper by suppressing it altogether.'

'And you can't muzzle or suppress the press,' said Bryan, 'before Hiroona gets herrr independence, or associated statehood. The island is still a colony, you know, and Britain won't agree with us interfeerrring with free speech.'

'I've thought of that,' I said, 'but look, I've got an idea. I made an appointment for tonight with . . .'

'Licking your little wounds?'

Dave, Bryan and I looked up quickly. We didn't hear George Reid approach our table. He stood grinning down at us. He looked fresh and prosperous in one of those newly fashionable, pictorial sport shirts and slacks.

Since my altercation with Reid in his car that night when he dropped me at my place at Bottom Town over six years ago, our relationship had cooled considerably. He still visited Dave's place, but not as frequently as before; and whenever we met, we facetiously exchanged a few banalities in place of conversation. Neither of us wanted to be an open enemy of the other, and neither of us wished to recapture the previous warmth of our relationship. So we posed an attitude of half-serious badinage and mutually insincere jocularity. We thus remained 'friends', and avoided each other as much as possible. I had the feeling that Reid's dislike for me, which began after he had probed my mind that night, years ago, was later aggravated by his realising that Dave was ascribing to me virtues of leadership which Reid felt I did not possess. Whenever he ribbed me in the presence of Dave or Bryan, his aim always seemed to be to reduce me to what he considered to be my size. He was never apparently serious in my presence. But I knew he hated my guts.

'Licking your little wounds, eh?' he repeated. 'I knew I would find you here, Jerry, and so I've brought you a little diversion.'

'We ain't licking a damn thing, man,' said Dave. 'Siddown. Have a drink?' Reid sat down. He had a flat, thickish, shop paper-wrapped parcel in his hand. He placed it on the table before him.

Dave signalled the barman to approach.

'Oh yes,' said Reid, 'I'll have a drink provided we drink to the PPP on the glory of its second victory at the polls, notwithstanding the fact that the glory has been a bit tarnished by Joe Pittance and Vincent Cunningham.'

'I can take care of Pittance, Cunningham and all of their ilk,' I said sharply.

'Oh yes, of course,' said Reid, as he sipped his drink. 'But you may need the benign assistance of your Gestapo, or Ogpu, or Ton Ton Macoute, or Breadfruit Tree Boys, as the case may be. When do you propose to begin to organise one of these paragons of efficiency here?'

'Soon, I hope. It depends on you. When you sneaked in here a while ago, we were just planning to offer you the job of organising them.'

'If the pay is good, gentlemen, you would be doing me a signal honour.'

I had no intention to indulge in persiflage with George Reid. There were other things on my mind. I had work to do. As a matter of fact, I was irritated at Reid's interruption of the discussion I was having with Dave and Bryan. I was about to reveal to them a plan which had been running over in my mind a few days ago, and which I intended to act upon that night. I had already arranged with Inspector Robbins of the Police force to meet me in the Aerie. The meeting was due in half an hour, and I did not want Robbins to arrive when George Reid was there. I therefore had to get in touch with Robbins at once.

I stood up, gulped the remainder of my whiskey and water, and said, 'Excuse me.'

'Hold it a minute,' said Reid. I half turned, waiting. Reid tapped on his parcel and said, 'I have a little test here for you. I hear you are thinking of writing your memoirs. I am prepared to bet you one thousand pounds you haven't got the guts to do it without presenting yourself to the public as a good, beneficent, astute, far-seeing politician; a wonderful leader; a saviour of the nation in whom there was no guile, no corruption; a man who lived ahead of his time and of his fellows, *for* his fellows and his country. Willing to take up the bet, Big Chief?'

'That's a hell of a challenge,' said Bryan.

'Oh no,' said Reid. 'Only the courage part of it. I am proposing a one-way bet. If the Big Chief doesn't write, or if he writes the conventional good-boy stuff, he pays me nothing, and I pay him nothing. But if he writes the truth, the shocking truth — and publishes it, I'll pay him a thousand pounds. Huh?'

'And what the hell this parcel got to do with it?' said Dave.

'That's my gesture of seriousness — my initial payment as it were. There are thirty-six exercise books in that parcel. The Big Chief must not be hampered by paper shortage if he accept the wager.'

I pondered this thing. It wouldn't do to be outfaced by Reid. A thousand pounds is a hell of a lot of money. I could make Reid eat his words and pay. No payment whatsoever would be due from me whether I wrote or not. So far, my only bit of serious corruption — The Penny Farthing thing — was already known, and it had not damaged my standing. In all probability, there would be more corruption later; the practice of politics has a way of provoking corruption sometimes; but I could always explain it away, play it down or justify it in terms of political pitch and toss — and collect one thousand pounds. I held all the advantages. George Reid was a wealthy ass. He couldn't be serious. Of course, I realized that his aim was to bait me into exposing myself in public; the pen of a rogue or a fool is his own condemnation. But a thousand pounds is a lot of money. And I had plenty of time to think and plan, anyway.

Bryan took up the little parcel and said, 'But, Chief, you had this idea of writing your memoirs long ago, and we all assume that you intend to write the truth. So . . .'

'Then let him demonstrate that,' said Reid, 'and weaken me by a thousand pounds.'

I took the parcel from Bryan. As I turned it over in my hand, I turned over the thought in my mind, that the relationship between Reid and me which had begun so pleasantly, had, over the years, soured so terribly that the man was now willing to pay as much as four thousand, eight hundred dollars to have me disgraced and by my own hand. *Well, I shall appear to accept his wager; if for no other reason, to surprise him.* There might be ways of getting around this unusual, fantastic wager and making George Reid pay.

'O.K., Reid,' I said. 'I'll take your bet, but not your word. You would have to write down the conditions as clearly as you have stated them to us here. Sign the statement; let these two gentlemen here sign it as witnesses. You produce two copies of the signed statement. Leave them here with Dave. I will sign them, accepting. Then I'll keep one copy. The other I shall return to you through Dave. Agreed?'

'Fine,' said Reid. 'Provided you also agree that after you have written and published the full story, the true story, the frank, dispassionate analysis, you submit it to an impartial judge approved by both of us; and we both abide by the judge's decision as to whether or not you have written a frank, unvarnished story of your life and political career. Agreed?'

'Yes. You may include that condition in the agreement — if you've got the guts to make such an agreement. I'll keep these exercise books in order to call your bluff, Reid.'

'But why the hell you want to throw away a thousand pounds on such a funny bet?' said Dave to Reid.

'Look, Dave; those of us who believe in good democratic government should be prepared to make sacrifices to have tyranny or corruption exposed. I can afford to sacrifice a thousand pounds. Some politicians do have some wopping skeletons in cupboards and Swiss banks. It's worth paying to see inside these cupboards and things. And I can afford the whim. The one thousand pounds would be deducted from my income tax and put to a good cause. So?'

'Don't try to scare me with that type of cheap talk, Reid,' I said. 'Are you going to write the agreement?'

'Matter fixed,' said Reid. 'But don't go yet, man.'

'I am not a planter's son, Reid. I work.'

'You work very slowly,' Reid grinned. 'I hear that you have not yet got around to settling your little debt to Penny Farthing, off whom, tradition says, you borrowed a trifle during your lean days. Nor have you settled your score with Patrick McIver whose shotgun insult I've heard you swear in my own house to avenge. Ah, the busy Chief of State, eh? So busy, he forgets his debts and forgives his enemies. I suppose this will appear in your memoirs under the chapter, VIRTUOUS ACTS, eh?'

God, I could have killed him. I glared at George Reid. He returned my look calmly, a sort of crooked, tentative smile around his mouth; and we both knew that our hitherto veiled enmity was now in the open.

'I see you've already started to worry about paying the one thousand pounds,' I said, 'after all your fatuous talk about sacrifice. You damn fool.'

I moved away suddenly, quickly. I went out by the front door of the barroom, entered the street, made a little detour and returned to Aerie by a back door. I locked myself in.

'Exchange? Please connect me to Police Headquarters.' I tried to control the tremor in my hand and my voice.

'Is this Police Headquarters? Is Inspector Robbins there? Call him to the telephone, please . . . Chief Minister wishes a brief word with him . . . Oh, there you are. Robbins? Fine. Now listen. I'm a bit tired tonight, but we can still play a game or two of dominoes, as arranged. Not at Dave Potter's place, though. Be more convenient at Fairfield House. So drop around at Fairfield House in about ten minutes' time, and we'll play a few games there instead. O.K.? O.K.'

10

INSPECTOR Robbins saluted smartly. I casually acknowledged the salute. 'Relax, man,' I said.

'Thank you, sir', said Robbins. His medium height, thickset muscular frame looked impressive in his khaki uniform. His general appearance gave one the feeling that long practice with belt, Sam Browne, official cap, puttees, swagger stick and well-oiled boots had made him 'a natural' for this kind of outfit. If they had not sacked me from the Police Force, I might now have been wearing this kind of uniform; but with my kind of figure, I would not have been able to cut the dash of this jet black, chubby-faced officer with the large, round head, the unctuous voice and ingratiating manner.

'I hope that my reference to dominoes didn't confuse you,' I said.

'Only for a moment, sir,' Robbins smiled, showing a set of regular teeth. 'Then it struck me that you spoke as you did because of de kind of telephone we have. And I don't play dominoes. Don't know the game, sir; but I can learn it if you want me to do so.'

'I don't play dominoes, either. You're so right about the telephone system on this island. Each telephone is a broadcasting station. Tuning in to any 'station' is not even necessary. All you do is lift any earpiece, and you hear what's happening all over Hiroona. I am thinking of inviting Cable & Wireless to install a modern telephone system here, but the British Government refuses to give us a grant to meet the small sum which is required for the local part of the expense.'

'But why does de British Gover'ment refuse us? I understand they have given such help to other islands. Why refuse Hiroona?'

'Well, you see, the Colonial Office is being advised by Forbes, and he is still damn vex because I used the island's reserve fund to increase the wages of the poor daily-paid Government employees. The man is a bug in Hiroona's rug. You can always tell when these Administrators served in Africa before coming out here. They always try to treat us West Indians like backward natives.'

'That's true, sir,' agreed Robbins. 'Mr Forbes was a District Commissioner in Uganda before he came here.'

'And he can't live that down . . . Oh, by the way, Inspector, you never been in the house before?'

'No, sir.' Robbins' eyes circled the large dining room in which we were standing. 'It's a grand place, sir.' He looked up at the two ornate Venetian glass lamps suspended from the white ceiling with its light blue cornice. His gaze dropped to the wide, louvred windows with their beautifully designed wrought-iron burglar-proof fixtures; then down to the gleaming mahogany furniture.

'Your wife should be congratulated, sir, for keeping this big house — and the lawn grounds — so spotless, so beautiful.'

'Between you and me, my wife is a much better housekeeper than she is a politician.'

We laughed. Robbins said, 'The furniture, sir; those pieces . . . made locally?'

'Yes. I went with Barney Smith, the Director of Public Works myself, and ordered them specially from Dopwell's furniture shop over five years ago; and they're just as beautiful, just as spotless, as they were on the day they were brought here. Those two small tables you see in the corners over there are really twelve tables, so neatly fitted into one another — six to a set — that they look like only two identical tables. Barney says they are "occasional" tables. I think that's what he called them. We've never used them however — not even once — for the years they've been in those corners. But I like to see them there; for there's no reason why the Chief Minister's official residence and its furniture should be in any way inferior to Government House and its fittings. After all, the Chief Minister, although he is a black man, is the representative of the people. The Administrator is the watch dog of the Colonial Office in England, which is four thousand miles away in spirit and truth.'

Robbins and I laughed at this sally which had become a political *cliché* in Hiroona. The Inspector's laughter was that of the rough, fat soldier-man. It was too loud for the joke, too full throated, too raucous for the kind of room in which we were standing.

'The room over there, to the left of the stairs; that's my study and a kind of office.' I led the way to the room.

'Here we are. I suggest you remove your cap. Put it with your cane on that chair at the side of the desk. Fine.' I took up Reid's parcel of exercise books, which I had dropped on the desk before Robbins' arrival, and placed it in a drawer of the desk. 'Now for a drink. What's yours?'

'You got coke, sir?'

'Yes, but what about something stronger? You not on duty now, you know. You're my guest.'

'O.K., sir. Rum and ginger, please.'

I went back into the dining room and returned carrying a silver tray with a cutglass decanter containing rum, two or three bottles of ginger ale, glasses.

As we poured our drinks, I said, 'By the way, are you a member of our union?'

'No, sir. Unfortunately, the Police rules are against any uniform personnel associating with any political organisation such as a trade union or a political party. But if you wish, I could be a sort of secret member quietly helpin' behind the scenes. After all, dis is our country, and all of us must help.'

'Good, lad. If everyone thought like you, Hiroona would be a much better place. Cheers.'

'Cheers, sir.'

We sipped and sat down.

'Now, Robbins, I arranged this little meeting to discuss a delicate matter with you. What we say here tonight must be kept in the strictest confidence.'

'You can trust me a hundred per cent, sir.'

'Fine. What about your appointment as Chief of Police? Forbes said anything to you about that?'

'No, sir.'

'How long you been acting Chief?'

'Five months now, sir. Captain Wade leave here on promotion on de tenth of March — a little over five months ago. I bin actin' Chief of Police since dat date.'

'Why has he kept you acting for so long?'

'I understand from a good friend in de Secretariat dat Mr Forbes is arranging to fill de post with another Englishman. I hear he wrote to the — Robbins didn't always say 'de' — Colonial Office askin' dem to recruit a man to take Captain Wade's place. Captain Wade was recruited by the Colonial Office when he came here as Chief seven years ago.'

'So now Forbes want another Colonial Office stooge, eh? Well, he got another thought coming. Under the Constitution, the Administrator is responsible for local defence; but the same Constitution says that the Chief Minister must be consulted in every case where a Head of Department is to be appointed. He hasn't consulted me yet, but if he think he can get away with another Englishman as Head of the Police here, he damn well mistaken. You're Deputy Chief; that's your substantive post, isn't it?'

'Yes, sir.'

'O. K. You leave it to me, Robbins.'

'Thank you very much, sir.'

'You got a wife and children, haven't you?'

'Six, sir.'

'Six what? Wives?'

We both laughed, and Robbins got up and helped himself from the tray.

'I am very grateful to you, sir, for your interest in dis matter. I thought of approaching you myself about it, because I think it would be unfair to appoint someone over me, in the face of twenty-eight years' service. But I was afraid to ask for an interview with you, because gover'ment officers are forbidden to lobby politicians. Mr Forbes circulated an order to dat effect when your party came into power five years ago. And he sent round de same circular to all gover'ment departments and ministries when you won de election again.'

'Talking of election; did you expect that traitor Joe Pittance and his stooge Vincent Cunningham to capture two seats in the last election?'

'Well, to tell you de trute, yes, sir.'

'Why you expected this?'

'Well, sir,' — he stared into his glass as he spoke — 'as you know, we had a secret observation service — part of the CID — attached to the Police Department. So I see an' hear a lot dat even you don't see an' hear, sir. I get reports. For over two years now, Pittance has organise a union —'

'A what?' I fairly shouted.

'Yes, sir. A union. He had to keep it secret until he resigned from your union an' party, which he did only a few months before the last elections.'

'Christ! What a traitor! Robbins, you serious?'

'Yes, sir. So help me God. The members of his union paid no dues; and he kept the numbers as small as possible, to keep de secret under control. The union is financed entirely by Pittance, and he —'

'My God. I understand now what the son of a bitch meant when he told me, at the last meeting he attended in the Chamber, that I would be surprised when I heard what he did with his salary. Christ! What a snake in the grass! And neither Dave, Bryan nor I . . . Go on Robbins. Gimme the whole story.'

'He hasn't given the union a name. I meself ask him about it once, and he swear dat it was not a union. Said it was just a group, a few people, his friends, who meet occasionally by chance to discuss matters in general.

But I thought it funny at first, because de CID have it in good authority dat his organisation is seekin' affiliation to the Caribbean Congress of Labour in Trinidad. And twice in the last two years or so Vincent Cunningham went to Trinidad at Pittance's expense to discuss union matters with executives at the CCL. Everybody believed dat Cunningham went for a medical check-up. A healthy-looking young man like Cunningham going to Trinidad twice for check-up, and the man not working. Where he get de money?' Robbins laughed. I didn't.

'Who are these people who follow Pittance?' I said.

'He draws de bulk of his secret organisation from the labourers and staff of the Gover'ment Arrowroot Depot an' from certain select people in his own constituency of South Windward. He purposely keeps the group small, but it is effective. Pittance does not want to fight in the open, yet. We believe that he think you are too strong at present. But they have a carefully thought-out plan to quietly infiltrate de country, constituency after constituency; and when they gather sufficient strength they will break out as a union — too strong to be defeated. They experimented with this infiltration business in Kingsland, and knocked Smallmilk fo' six. Even you was surprise, sir, because you didn't know dat Pittance was working underneath all de time. Pittance is a clever man, sir; he farsighted and full o' patience. And he is getting a lot of secret help from Seymour Gilchrist, the Manager of the Arrowroot Depot. Gilchrist is a first cousin of Vincent Cunningham.'

I understood the Gilchrist angle at once. I had hurt Cunningham many years ago, and so I was now up against every single relative of his — mother, father, sisters, brothers, right down to cousins ten times removed. It was a well known West Indian situation, like the old family vendettas of backwoods Italians and Corsicans. With Gilchrist as head of the Arrowroot Depot, my government was not likely to get a dram of support from that Department. Gilchrist was Pittance's political friend because Pittance was my political enemy. *I must look into this Arrowroot Depot thing at once*, I thought. *A visit was urgently necessary. Transferring Gilchrist to another post would be only spreading his subversion. I must visit and then decide on further action.*

Robbins cut into my thoughts: 'CID believe dat Pittance is grooming Gilchrist, an intelligent, literate man, to take control of their union.'

'But surely, he should have his union registered. That's the law. He *must* come out in the open some time,' I said.

'That's one of the reasons why he keeps saying he don't have any union. He knows that as long as you are in power you would use your influence in de Gover'ment against his gettin' registration. And if he apply for registration and doesn't get it, that would be a sort of —— — er . . . . . .'

'You mean a sort of psychological publicity set-back.'

'That's right, sir. Thank you.'

'You say his main supporters in Kingsland are the labourers and the staff of the Government Arrowroot Depot? What about the stevedores and bayfront workers?'

'They behind him too; even some of those who are still in your union. It is the vote that counts, you know, sir. That's why Cunningham was able to win in Kingsland. People often promise their votes to A but give them to B.'

'That was evident, from the Kingsland results. Now these staff people at the Arrowroot Depot . . .'

'They are the intellectuals of Pittance secret Movement. We got a lot of information from a labourer named Peter Garrick who used to work at de depot. Garrick is a member of your union, and one of your staunch supporters. He didn't make no secret of his backing you, so they eased him out of work at de depot.'

'Just like that?'

'Well, sir, Garrick is a lazy sort of chap. Used to stay away from his job too often. Drinks a lot, too. So it was easy for de depot management to find a good excuse for sacking him.'

'Where does he work now?'

'He drinks more than he works, sir. Hangs around de bayfront doing odd jobs when he hard up for a few cents to buy muffin, saltfish cake and rum. You know the fellow, sir; always in old canvas shoes, black pants and merino. Never wears a shirt.'

'Oh yes. You mean that fellow they call Crab Soup?'

'Same one, sir.' Robbins laughed. 'I didn't know you knew his *alias*, sir.'

I pondered the situation for a long moment before saying, 'So the entire staff of the depot is behind Pittance?'

'No doubt about that, sir. They advise him, and we know he leans heavily on their support. And of course, they give him the benefit of their contacts.'

'What you mean by that?'

'Well, sir, as you know, a fair number of our middle class people cultivate arrowroot. Arrowroot is good money nowadays. Even a few teachers and civil servants grow de crop to help out their low salaries. Lawyer Copeland does more business with his arrowroot lands at Foresythe Estate than he does in de practice of law . . . . . .'

As Robbins spoke, light suddenly dawned on my darkness. And the plan began to take shape in my mind. Dave Potter had said that Darcy's newspaper was only a sort of hobby. I hadn't quite realized this before. You can only hurt Darcy through his arrowroot business. That was Dave's observation. *By God, I'm going to hurt him*, I said to myself. *Really hurt him — hurt him in a way that will make it necessary for him to go and search for another means of livelihood. He would then be worrying so damn much, he would have little or no time to devote to his hobby. And those traitors working at the depot . . . I'll deal them the same blow, same time*, I decided.

It was with concealed but mounting excitement that I said to Robbins, 'So you mean that the more intelligent workers at the arrowroot depot as well as the labourers are in league with an ordinary, illiterate man like Joe Pittance? I can't believe that.'

'Pittance is amazingly free with his money,' said Robbins. 'Cunningham is not the only person he helped with money before Cunningham was elected to the Opposition. Pittance is liked by people all over de island, and has a lot of influence with certain sections of the community, but he uses that influence shrewdly. He don' waste it, and he don't wave it around like a flag. For a stevedore, Pittance is damn clever, sir. Excuse de word, sir.'

'I know he is clever; but we'll see who is more clever — he or me. Now listen carefully, Robbins. You are to leave the matter of your promotion entirely to me. I will fix that. Meanwhile, I want you to feed me with all the information that comes your way — not only information about Pittance and his bogus union, but about anything whatsoever you may glean about the goings-on in this island. We must work in close touch, Robbins, and collect as much information as possible now. Later, we may have to imprison or deport certain people, for the good of the island. O.K.?'

'You can count on me, sir; but of course you will appreciate that as I am supposed to submit these secret reports to Mr Forbes, and only Mr Forbes, who alone is responsible for internal defence matters, we got to be very careful as to — — — — '

'Say no more, man. I fully understand. Trust me. Oh, one other thing — I want you to send that chap Peter Garrick — Crab Soup — to me at my office. I shall tell you later when to send him. O.K.?'

'O. K., sir.'

We stood up, shook hands, and Robbins collected his cap and cane. As we moved through the dining room towards the front door, I said, 'By the way, the Arrowroot Depot — do you post one of your men there at night to guard the building, as you're supposed to do in the case of all Government Buildings?'

'No, sir. The depot has its own night watchman. A policeman only patrols the road in the vicinity (he pronounced it vycinity) of the building, in the course of his normal beat.'

'I see. Well, we'll keep in touch, eh?' I said, shaking him by the hand again. 'Oh, by the way, Pittance *must* apply some time for registration of his union; and in accordance with the law, he must apply to the Administrator through you as Chief of Police. If ever you receive such an application, you'd know what to do, eh?'

'Settled, sir. Goodnight, sir. Say good night to the good lady upstairs for me.'

11

I flipped the switch and spoke into the intercom: 'Matthews?'

'Yes?' Matthews sedulously refused to address me as 'sir'. I had been promising myself for some time to challenge him about this, but I held back because I didn't want him to feel that I was begging for honour. His manner in general was just about officially correct. As a Permanent Secretary, he had enough experience to keep his attitude barely proper, adroitly avoiding any charge of insubordination. But there was no empathy between us, and there were times when, dealing with him, I knew that he regarded me as a sort of obscene intrusion into the sanctity of the Civil Service and its hallowed traditions. Matthews was a young member, about thirty-eight, of one of those so-called leading coloured families of Hiroona. His views about a popular government ran along the lines of those of Paul Darcy. Fortunately, he was only acting Permanent Secretary to the Chief Minister. Peters, the substantive holder of the post, was on vacation leave, and Matthews was holding the position temporarily, pending Peters' resumption.

'Bring me the file referring to the Staff of the Arrowroot Depot,' I said into the intercom.

While I waited for Matthews to fetch the file, I glanced through a few of the two small bundles of files which were on my desk. Some of them required Sonia's attention as Minister for Social Services; but as Sonia was ill and in bed, I had undertaken some of the work of her ministry. I was reading a report by the Chief Medical Officer on one of these files, when Matthews knocked on the closed door of my office and entered.

'This file here,' I said, tapping the CMO's report with the back of my hand, 'contains a report by the Chief Medical Officer. He says that accommodation conditions at the Kingsland Hospital have become impossible. He gives some details here. The conditions are really very bad, it seems. They can't continue much longer. I think it is high time the British Government does something about this matter. I want you to put up an application immediately to the Secretary of State for a Colonial Development and welfare grant in the region of three hundred and fifty thousand dollars — this is the figure now estimated by the Director of

Works — for renovation and extension of the hospital. I want the application put up at once.'

'Mr Minister,' said Matthews, 'the hospital falls within the portfolio of the Minister for Social Services. Any application for funds for the hospital must be drafted and submitted by the Permanent Secretary of the Ministry of Social Services. Not by me. Furthermore, I doubt whether such an application would be successful. The Colonial Office knows that Kingsland would have had a good hospital years ago if the funds earmarked for that purpose had not been misused. The hospital would then have been renovated and enlarged for a quarter of what is now required. However, if you insist that an application be put up, I shall relay your instructions to the Permanent Secretary of Social Services by a minute in the file, if you let me have the file.'

Controlling my temper with a great deal of effort, I handed him the file.

'Now, the Arrowroot Depot file, please,' I said. 'What is the size of the staff of the depot?'

'Fifty-two,' said Matthews.

'That's the management, executive and clerical personnel?'

'Yes.'

'How many labourers are employed there?'

'The number varies according to the quantity of arrowroot that is being received, graded and stored for shipment. There were eighty-six at the height of last season.'

'I see. Give me the file.'

Matthews handed me the file and turned to leave the office.

'One minute, Matthews,' I said. 'Make an appointment with the Administrator for me.' I glanced at the clock of the wall. 'It is now ten o'clock. I want an appointment with Mr Forbes at eleven fifteen.'

That would give me sufficient time to meet Sol Ace, my private building contractor, at ten fifteen, on the site of the house he was building for me on the crest of Globe Hill.

The Globe Hill house was my second house since my entry into politics a little over seven years ago. My first house was built on that lovely little plateau known as Fairburn Pasture, overlooking the airport and commanding a wonderful view of the sea. A magnificent house, though I say so myself. Three bedrooms, each with its own toilet and bathroom and its own little patio; wainscotted study with tessellated floor; spacious sitting room with wide windows of tinted glass; all the modern fittings and things; servants' quarters, garage; a beautiful lawn on each side of a sweeping entrance; and just a stone's throw from two of the loveliest beaches on the island. An American couple rented the house at five hundred dollars a month. That first house was a guarantee of a source of income against the years of my retirement. The second house, now being built on Globe Hill, would provide me with a place to live. If ever I got thrown out of Fairfield House.

The Fairburn Pasture house was built with part of my earnings from salaries as Chief Minister and President of the Union, plus my transport allowances from both sources, plus my entertainment allowances as Chief Minister (which I drew every month while I entertained very modestly about once a year), plus the sums I saved when I attended conferences abroad, for which I drew a separate advance on each occasion. I didn't even have to touch Sonia's portion of our joint account.

With the Globe Hill project, I was even luckier. I was able to get, free of cost, the three acres of land on which the house stood. The land belonged to Victor Banks, a prosperous general merchant — commission agent, importer, real estate broker in Hiroona. Banks was one of the most enterprising businessmen on the island. No business deal was uninteresting to him. He was, like my friend Dave Potter, one of the few native negroes in Hiroona who made big money in business; but, unlike Dave, who was just comfortably well off, Victor Banks was wealthy. At forty-two he was the youngest President of the Chamber of Commerce in the mercantile history of the island. Banks had a percentage arrangement with Sol Ace, the building contractor. Sol would place his orders for building materials — from a nail to a beam — with Victor Banks, who in turn would sell the goods to Sol at a certain percentage discount. Sol could therefore undertender other contractors and thus get most of the jobs. Sol got Government contracts also, and quietly paid me five of the ten percent he got from Banks.

Banks came to my Office one day. It was his first visit. His handshake was as soft and shy as his smile. Short, and a little on the fat side; handsome; he wore no jacket, no necktie. His well laundered short sleeved white shirt was open at the neck and formed a long V on his chest. As he sat on the chair in front of my big desk, he pulled briefly on each leg of his gray flannel trousers to avoid crushing the knife-edge seams.

'Don't tell me what brings you here, Mr Banks,' I said. 'Give me three guesses.' We laughed.

'Go ahead, Mr Minister. Three guesses,' said Banks.

'Your income tax assessment is too high?'

'That could well have brought me here, yes. Thanks for the hint, anyway. Next guess.'

'You're going to build a five hundred room hotel, and so you've come for assurance that you would get the usual duty-free concessions under the Hotels' Aid Ordinance. Right?'

'You're getting warm, Mr Minister. Next guess.'

'Now, let me see,' I said slowly, looking up at the spinning fan under the ceiling. The little banter and laughter were a good introduction to serious talk; and by the time we got down to business in the next minute or two, Banks and I had established an easy, cordial relationship.

'You say that Sol Ace has this contract to build this Presbyterian church.'

'Yes,' said Banks. 'It's quite a contract. You see, the church will be a huge building, and Sol is to build the manse also, on the church grounds. It's a big project. A lot of money. A lot of materials to be imported. Now, we know that there is a law which permits duty-free importation of certain materials to be used for religious purposes; so I'm wondering whether you would waive the import duty on the building materials I will have to import for the entire project — the church and the manse.'

'Boy, that's a bit hot to handle,' I said.

'You mean that the project is too big for the law?' said Banks.

'That's exactly the trouble.' I laughed. 'You see, Mr Banks, the law expressly defines the kind of materials for which duty-free importation may be permitted for churches. Let me show you the law.'

I got up, went to one of the six bookshelves which lined the walls of my office, three on each side, and removed one of the fourteen thick, black volumes labelled *Laws of Hiroona*. I put the big book down on the desk in front of Banks, and began turning the pages. Banks and I bent over the book. 'Let's look under the Customs and Excise,' I said. 'Ah! Here it is — "Exemptions".' I read:

'"Goods on which the Comptroller of Customs is satisfied are imported solely for the use, furnishing or decoration of places of worship which already exist: vestments for use during public worship; altar bread; paschal bread and altar wine imported for the administering of the Sacrament. Exemptions of the goods listed above will be made only on a signed declaration by the head of the denomination concerned that the goods will be used for such purposes only."'

I shut the book and put it back on the shelf.

'You see,' I said, 'we're up a gum tree. In the first place, the building must "already exist". That knocks your case on the head right away. Next thing, you don't want vestments and altar bread and altar wine. You and Sol don't administer the Sacrament. The law is specific on the matter. So, you see for yourself, the position is hopeless.'

Staring dreamily at the rim of the desk, Banks nodded sadly. He stood up, spread his hands in a gesture of resignation and said, 'So?'

'Wait a minute,' I said. 'Let me see. Cement, lumber, nails, screws, asbestos, galvanize, paint, fittings etcetera for a large church and manse. That would mean more than a hundred thousand dollars in Government revenue if you had to pay import duty.'

'I appreciate that,' said Banks.

'Big project, as you said . . . . . yes . . . . . anyway . . . . . Let me think . . . . . . O.K. Leave it to me. I'll see what I can do. I'll talk to my Comptroller of Customs. According to procedure, only the Executive Council could deal with your request, but it's no use putting it up to them. Forbes would hit the ceiling, and of course the Attorney General would cite the law which we read from the book a while ago, and you wouldn't stand a chance. So leave it to me. I'll get on to my Customs man quietly. Perhaps we will be able to work out something. I don't promise, but I'll see what can be done.' I held out my hand, and Banks shook it with much more warmth than he did when he entered the office. We began to walk together to the door.

'How's business?' I said.

'Oh, things a bit slow now, especially in the drygoods line. As you know, last year's arrowroot crop wasn't so good. This means that the peasants and others have very little money now to buy goods. Don't know what this island would do if we didn't have a cotton and arrowroot crop. Anyway, things will brighten. This year's crop will be better. There's always a rise and fall in business.'

'And as you have more than one type of business, you can't starve, eh?' I said. We laughed.

'By the way, I hear you want to sell your lands at Globe Hill,' I lied.

'Globe Hill?' Banks chuckled. 'I don't think anybody in the world is rich enough to buy my lands at Globe Hill. I've got twenty-five acres up there. I'd sell to a very good friend of two hundred years' standing, at one mint per acre.'

'Helluva condition. Helluva price,' I said.

'How many acres you want to buy?' said Banks.

'When I heard that you wanted to sell, I wondered if you'd sell me three or four acres. But you've just said that that would be three mints' worth of money. And I ain't got a mint. I'm a poor man, Victor.'

Banks smiled. 'O.K.' he said. 'Leave it to me. I'll see what I can do.' He had used the same words that I had used to him a few minutes before, to dangle a hope on the thread of a promise. And each of us understood that the other had a *quid pro quo* in mind: something for something.

A few days later, I addressed an official letter to Banks, giving him the duty-free concessions he had asked for. I had the letter typed at the union's Chamber. The typing looked messy, jerky, ill spaced and blotchy — like union typing. But it was unsafe to have the letter typed at my office. Some disloyal clerk would have run straight to Forbes, and perhaps to Paul Darcy, too, with a copy. I myself took a copy of the letter to the Comptroller of Customs, who had agreed to co-operate, but required a letter signed by me, for his own protection — 'in case . . .' He also requested and received direct written instruction from me, to let Banks have the materials free of customs duty. Neither of these two documents would have sufficed to clear the Comptroller of Customs from serious blame and dismissal, if the matter came before a commission of enquiry. For there was the law for the Comptroller to follow; and I was not the law. But the Comptroller knew that I had the power to protect and reward him, anyway. My 'deal' with Banks deprived the Government of a packet in customs duty. But on Christmas Eve of the same year, I received a large hamper from the firm of Victor Banks & Co Ltd. And in the envelope with the Christmas greetings card which came with the hamper was a receipt for 'forty-five thousand dollars ($45,000.00) from Jerry Mole of Kingsland, Hiroona, in full payment for three (3) acres of my lands at Globe Hill.'

I stared for a long moment at the plain, simple signature of Victor Banks, at the rubber stamp reproduction of the signature with the word 'Realtor' underneath, and at the franked postage stamp in the bottom left hand corner of the receipt. Government got its share of the deal, however, as Banks had to buy the stamp from the post office.

Politics can be uphill at times, but there are compensations.

12

'DEFENCE is in my portfolio,' said the Administrator. 'Not in yours. You have nothing to do with the Police. Nothing.'

His blue bowtie with white polka dots stood out in front of his long neck like it does on the neck of the giraffe in Auntie Kay's *Stories For the Tots*. The collar of his white shirt fairly glistened with expert laundry-ness.

Like all the other Administrators of the Leeward and Windward Islands, Mr Forbes had transferred his office from the Administration Building to Government House, soon after the introduction of ministerial government into the island. Now the room in which he worked looked more like a museum bit of Africa than an office. Two deer (heads only) faced each other from opposite walls of the room, their huge antlers reaching out like the empty branches of a drought-stricken frangipani tree. An assagai stretched diagonally under one deer head, and two spears crossed under the other on a background of the skins of two civet cats. A magnificently wrought bow and a decorated leathern quiver full of arrows graced the spot over the door. Various items of African handicraft in ivory, ebony or wood stood on shelves here and there — the bust of a tribal chief; the torso of a pretty, young woman with rows of beads around her neck, her breasts smooth, life-like; three elephants marching in Indian file; a monkey peeling a banana. The skin of a huge lion lay crucified on the floor in front of Forbes' desk.

I looked around the room, half expecting to see hippos wallowing in muddy pools, or a mammoth raising his trunk and trumpeting just before he charged.

A pile of office files stood in the OUT tray on his desk, and there were two files in the IN tray. Books, papers, magazines, official reports filled the shelves. The rest of the furniture in the room included two upright chairs.

'The police is my responsibility, Mr Mole. Not yours.'

'I know that Defence is not in my portfolio, Mr Forbes. But as the Chief representative of the people, every single thing on this island is my concern. And you seem to forget that you are bound by the Constitution to consult the Chief Minister before you appoint any Head of a Department. It is therefore my prerogative to demand from you information as to your intentions about filling the post vacated some five months ago by Captain Wade, who was Chief of Police here.'

'I spoke about this matter at a meeting of the Executive Council several months ago. I explained the position then. Wasn't that consultation enough?'

'The Executive Council and the Chief Minister are two different things, Mr Forbes. The Constitution says *the Chief Minister*, not the Executive Council. I want to know what are your plans for filling the post of Chief of Police in Hiroona.'

'I have asked the Colonial Office to recruit a suitable man. They have informed me that they hoped to do so within the next few weeks.'

'Anybody acting Chief of Police in the meantime?'

'Yes.'

'Who?'

'Inspector Robbins.'

'How long he's been acting?'

'About five months now,' said Forbes.

'You satisfied with his work?'

'That's not the point, Mr Mole. A man may be able to act in a post for a certain time, although he may not be suitable as a permanent appointee.'

'That's one of the mysteries of the Civil Service, Mr Forbes; but the people of Hiroona are not interested in mysteries. The people wish to know why a man who is capable of acting for five months in a post, cannot be appointed to that post permanently.'

'Appointing a Head of the Police Department on the island is neither your responsibility nor the people's. It is my responsibility. I am the sole judge as to who is suitable and who is not suitable for the post.'

'And you judge that Inspector Robbins is not suitable, eh? Why isn't he suitable?'

'His educational background and his personality do not measure up to the standard required for the job.'

'You left out one of the things that don't measure up.'

'What do you mean?' asked the Administrator.

'His colour. He's black. You seem to forget that.'

Forbes made a throaty noise indicative of disgust. He got up and said, 'I see no point in discussing this matter further, Mr Mole. Is there anything else you wish to see me about?' He was suddenly crimson around the ears, neck and jaw.

I stood up. 'So you're set on refusing to appoint Inspector Robbins Chief of Police?' I said. Forbes folded his arms on his chest and stared at me. I turned to leave his office. At the door, I paused, faced Forbes and said, 'Very well. I warn you. If an Englishman or any white foreigner is appointed to any post here, when a local man can be found to do the job, there'll be hell let loose here; and you would be responsible for exciting the wrath of the people. I've warned you.' I huffed and puffed out of the office.

I knew what Forbes would do next. He would either advise the Colonial Office to arrange for a man-o'-war to show up in Kingsland harbour simultaneously with the arrival of the new Chief of Police, or he would suggest to his masters that an emissary of the Colonial Office be sent to Hiroona to explain the Colonial Office's view to the Government, and thus soften us up before the arrival of the new appointee. Either of those two moves would serve my purpose well. If the battleship turned up, I would rant all over the country about 'gunboat diplomacy', 'man-o'-war imperialism', and make serious trouble. If the emissary turned up, I would stage a demonstration and show fight. So all I had to do now was sit back and wait. The ball was in Forbes' court. Meanwhile, I would turn my attention to the Government Arrowroot Depot — the source in Kingsland from which Pittance and Cunningham drew political comfort and solace. And Darcy his bread and butter.

13

B EFORE I left my office to visit the Government Arrowroot Depot one morning, about a week after my interview with Mr Forbes, I made two telephone calls: one to the Manager of the Depot, apprising him of my intention to visit the Depot within the next hour or so; the other to Inspector Robbins.

'That you, Robbins?'

'Yes, sir.'

'Can you locate the chap you were telling me about the other day, and send him up to my office now?'

'De feller they call Crab Soup, sir?'

'That's right. I want to find out why he was so careless as to lose his job.'

'I will send to look for him right away, sir.'

'Good. And look here, Inspector; about that game of dominoes. What about eight o'clock tonight at Fairfield House?'

'O.K., sir.'

When Peter Garrick arrived at my office some twenty minutes after this telephone conversation, there was a small crowd of people in the corridor waiting to see me. Some stood in a queue, others leaned on the balustrade, looking out on the street, occasionally shouting a greeting to a passing friend. Others again sat on the concrete floor of the corridor, wherever they could find room. I admitted them into my office one at a time. As each one went out, closing the door, another would immediately knock on the door and enter, to pour into my ears the same stories, complaints and requests: 'Chief, Ah want yo' to help me get a piece o' lan' on de Gover'ment acres at Palmyra for a house spat.'—'Yo' did pramise to get a jab fo' me at de Public Works, Chief. Ah come to see if yo' get it.' — 'Me husban' lef' me, Chief, an' Ah findin' it hard to mine de nine chil'ren. Ah come to see what help de Gover'ment can give me.'

I had heard these stories and requests so often that my replies had become ritualistic: 'I will see what I can do . . . . . I will put down your name on the list for a house spot . . . . You must have patience and wait a while . . . . . It is the British Government that is keeping back the island . . . . The housing scheme is due any day now, if we can get the damn stingy British Government to give us the grant . . . . O.K. I will be passing up by Yonkers village this afternoon; I will drop in on my way, to see your sick mother. O.K.? Right. Send in the next one when you go out.'

This almost daily antiphon took up an enormous amount of time, and often resulted in the neglect of more generally important ministerial work and decisions. Permanent Secretaries, wishing to obtain access to me to discuss serious policy matters, and finding their way blocked, would return to their offices fuming. I encouraged these popular interviews, nevertheless, as they provided me with an opportunity to go through the motions of patronage. They also kept me 'in touch with the people', and enhanced my reputation of being a very approachable and sympathetic Chief.

In order to spare Peter Garrick the tedium of a long delay on the corridor, and to spare myself the inconvenience of waiting too long for his entry, I interrupted the interviews in time to meet him as he arrived at the corridor, and ushered him into the office myself, and closed the door.

Garrick was sober, but a strong smell of old rum fumes and cheap cigarettes seemed to cling to his presence, from which it spread itself into the room. However, his merino, unlike his canvas shoes, was clean, and his black trousers though greasesmudged here and there, had no holes. He removed his old cloth cap as he entered the office. His uncombed hair was fifty-fifty grey and black. Medium height, slim, two horizontal creases in his low forehead, the area between the lower part of his nose and his lower lip framed in two arcs of depression like brackets, so that his mouth was in parenthesis. He stood in front of my desk. I sat down, facing him.

'Ah hear yo' want to see me, Chief,' he said.

'Yes, Garrick,' I said. 'I want to see you because I am vex wid you. Why didn't you come to see me when they sacked yo' from the Arrowroot Depot? Don't you know that I would have compelled them to give you back your job? Why didn't you come to me like everybody does when they get the sack?'

'I did come, Chief. Five days runnin'.'

'Why didn't I see you, then?'

'Too much people full up de corridor, Chief. Ah get discourage an' go away.'

'You should have waited, man. Some people have had to come back five, six times running.'

'Arright, Chief.'

'Always remember that you and those people you just saw outside there are always welcome here to discuss your problems with me.'

'Ah know dat, Chief. T'ank yo'.'

'The Administrator, and some of the local stooges of the Colonial Office, give me hell for looking after you all, but I'll soon get rid of him and put the rest of them in their place.'

'You damn right, Chief. Some of our own people is our worst enemies. Dey sack me from de depot becarse Ah tell dem Ah backin' yo'. Yo' have some bad enemies at de depot, Chief. Dey dead against yo'. Dey always readin' de newspaper an' tarking about it.'

'Who they supporting?'

'Ah don't quite know. But dey say you is a Dictata, and you want to get rid of de Administrata so dat you can do as you like.'

'How long you worked at the depot?'

'Ten years, Chief.'

'Does Joe Pittance visit the depot?'

'Ah see him come dere a few times; but whenever he come, he an' Mr Gilchrist shut up in de Manager's affice an' do dere secret tarkin'. Sometimes some o' de clerks an' de Assistant goes in dere, too, an' jine dem.'

'What were your duties at the depot?'

'Labour an' general messenger. Ah use to run errands fo' all de members of de staff when Ah wasn't stacking bags of arrowroot. Sometimes when Mr Gilchrist or de Assistant lock up de building at night, dey would give me de keys to leave at de Police Station, where all de keys of all Gover'ment affices is kept at night. Next marning I use to pick up de depot keys from de Police Station on me way to work.'

'You ever seen Mr Paul Darcy at the depot?'

'Who?'

'Paul Darcy. The newspaper man. You know him?'

'Oh, he? Once o' twice.'

'All right, Garrick. You leave it to me. I am going to visit the depot right now, and I'm going to make them give you back your job and pay you every cent you lost since they sacked you.'

'Ah t'ank you very much, Chief. But Ah don't want to work at de depot again. Dey treat me too bad dere, becarse I am on your side. Every damn one o' dem, except me an' Honky Dory, against you. If you get me annudder jab — say a scavenger in de Public Healt' Department, else a labourer in de Works Department — I will prefer something like dat rarda dan go back at de Depot.'

'O.K. then. Don't breathe a word to anyone about our little talk here. Not a word; even to yo' mother. Understand?'

'You can trust me, Chief. So help me Gard.'

'Good man. I may be able to find something even better than those jobs you named. Keep in touch with Inspector Robbins, so that when Ah want you he will be able to locate you an' send yo' to me. Here. Take this fo' now. You will get more later on.' I handed him two dollars. It was a hell of a lot of money to give away, but I felt that I would need the services of Peter Garrick, alias Crab Soup, later. The two dollars was a retainer.

The Arrowroot Depot was a long, wooden building shaped like the letter 'E' lying on its side, with its three legs stretched out in front of it. The uppermost horizontal section of the reclining 'E' was the place where the bags of arrowroot starch were sorted for grading. The lowest leg contained the offices of Seymour Gilchrist, the young (about thirty-five), neatly dressed Manager of the Depot and his assistant, also the clerks who booked details about the arrowroot starch brought into the Depot from the factory in the country where the thick, fingerlike rhizomes dug from the fields were ground, and the resultant dried starch bagged and transported to the Depot in Kingsland, to be graded. Depot staff recorded the names of the growers, the number of bags received from each grower, the grade or quality of the arrowroot received from each, and all financial and shipping arrangements relating to the crop.

The short middle leg of the 'E' housed the laboratory with its test tubes, retorts, glass jars, samples of starch etc. This was where the arrowroot starch was graded. The long backbone of the 'E' was where the bags of arrowroot were stacked and stored, pile upon pile, row upon row, for shipment to Europe or the United States, to appear later on the shelves of a thousand pharmacies as talcum powder or baby food; or in super-markets as cereal or neatly packaged arrowroot starch.

In the depot yard were several trucks at various stages of unloading. Men were heaving the bags of arrowroot from the trucks to the sorting room, their faces, hands, hair and dungarees liberally powdered with white starch dust.

There were also a few cars in the yard, probably belonging to the staff.

As Gilchrist showed me around the depot, I covertly observed the reaction of the staff and labourers to my presence. There was nothing of that 'Hello, Chief '—'Good morning, Chief ' — 'How's things, Chief?' atmosphere to which I had grown accustomed whenever I visited a Government Department, or walked or drove through the villages. The depot's strange atmosphere irked, displeased and frightened me. Gilchrist himself maintained an attitude of reserve and cool politeness. Some of the clerks glanced up fleetingly and bent again to their work, not even ordinary recognition in their glances. Others didn't even bother to look up as I slowly came up to their desks, while Gilchrist and I talked about the work of the depot.

Arriving in the large storeroom, Gilchrist and I stood and watched men heap the white bags of graded arrowroot in orderly sections. A number of women were engaged in sewing filled bags, which they left for the men to place on the correct heap. It was at this stage that I brought up the question of the dismissal of Peter Garrick. My doing this was really unnecessary, because Garrick had already told me that he did not want to work at the depot again. However, I considered the occasion an excellent opportunity to 'win back the depot' by reminding the labourers and staff that I was their dedicated champion.

I moved away from Gilchrist so that I could speak loudly for all in the store-room and offices to hear. Then I said, 'Mr Gilchrist, I heard only a few days ago that you sacked a man — I think his name is Garrick — who had worked here for over ten years. I was very grieved when I heard this. All these people are my people. These are the people who really keep the island on its feet, and when any one of them gets sacked it troubles me very much. All these people here work for such low wages, that although I have fought a terrible battle and got their wages increased, I am now thinking of getting another increase for them. It really grieves me if Garrick or anyone of my people here is deprived of the benefits which I am fighting to bring to this island. Why, then, did you have to sack Peter Garrick?'

'Garrick deserved it, sir,' replied Gilchrist. 'He's a slacker. Been slacking for years. It had to catch up with him some time.'

'Slacker?' I questioned. 'Don't be too hard on our people, Mr Gilchrist. They are the ones who toil and sweat for the island to live. They are the ones who bear up Hiroona on their humble shoulders.'

This was the kind of talk that had done wonders for demagogues in the old days. It was like weeping at funerals; it brought the former-day West Indian politician support, hero worship and votes. But the former days were dying. It was late now, late in the fifties, and the old act had begun to cloy; the script had become mouldy with familiarity, breeding contempt. On top of this, Darcy's newspaper articles were doing their mischief. And Gilchrist and Pittance had done theirs at the depot. So Gilchrist smiled — a weary, pitying little grin. And the labourers in the room burst out laughing. Some stopped their work to hold their heaving sides. It was a terrible, spontaneous outburst. And the vulgar, highpitched laughter brought some of the clerks and officials to the storeroom door, to stare, and to smile like Gilchrist.

My own smile was anaemic with embarrassment. I said, 'Thank you, comrades,' and walked slowly out of the room, pretending to examine some bags of starch which were stacked at the side of the door.

I drove out to a lonely little wood just outside of town, to think things over and to examine certain details of my plan. By the time I returned to Kingsland about an hour or so after, my mind was so fully made up, that the wrathful indignation with which I had left the depot had completely dissipated, and in its place I now nursed a feeling of peace and settledness. I could not now be blamed for whatever happened to the depot. Gilchrist and his staff would be the culprits of their own downfall. I was almost happy now.

14

G EORGE Reid was serious about his bet. He had left the signed agreement and a carbon copy of it with Dave, for my signature. I signed both, kept one and left one with Dave for Reid. I must admit, however, that since the evening of the wager and the parcel of exercise books, I had not given any thought to Reid or his one thousand pound whim. I was too busy. There would probably be time enough after my retirement in the next ten or fifteen years, to think of Reid and his nonsense. All I needed to do now was to sign the contract, Dave looking on and making lewd, jesting remarks about where Reid should stick up his thousand pounds.

My visit to Dave's that evening was brief. I returned to Fairfield House early for supper and to wait for Inspector Robbins. I sat in the dining room talking quietly with Sonia as she moved about the room, putting away the plates and crockery that had been used at supper and washed by the maid. Sonia didn't have to do this, but her housemaid habits from long ago died hard. She still liked to play with cups and spoons and plates, to dust furniture, to change curtains, to arrange and re-arrange rooms, often unnecessarily. Now she moved about the room doing this, that and the other, her slippers flip-flopping with every movement.

'You look listless,' I said. 'Still tired?'

She made a little sucking noise with her tongue against her teeth, and said, 'Ah much prefer to do what Ah doing now than to be a gover'ment minister.'

She was perfectly sincere. I had heard this and more before. But our combined income was so tempting I couldn't consider anything else.

'But as a minister you're making money,' I said. 'You should be happy. If you feel tired, rest. You've already had a month away from your office; if you want another month or two months, just take it. You need only drop in at the office for a few minutes occasionally. You're a minister, you know. Nobody but the Chief Minister could question your absence from the office, and I am running your ministry for you. You don't even need a medical certificate, like a civil servant would, in order to get sick leave. So why bother? Power carries privilege, don't you know?'

'Power should carry responsibility rarder than privilege. It ain't fair fo' me to draw money Ah ain't working for.'

It was the old, exasperating conscientiousness all over again. I said, 'You have a Permanent Secretary, his Assistant, a stenographer and two clerks to do the work you're getting paid for. You also have me. You want more staff?'

She looked across at me, as she slowly polished the already gleaming mahogany dining room table with a clean rag. 'This ain't no matter fo' joke, Jerry. Ah don't feel Ah have de education to go wid a minister job.'

'I am not joking, Sonia. The reason why no great degree of literacy is required by law from a Government minister is because other literate people are paid to do most or all of the office work. All you really need to do is to help frame policy, see to it that your Permanent Secretary sees that the policy is carried out; visit your department occasionally, and see to it that your Permanent Secretary sees to it that your department keeps doing things that would please the people and keep the services going.'

'You mixing me up wid a lot o' talk about see to it that the Permanent Secretary sees to it, an' a lot of stupidness. How Ah can see to anyt'ing when I am not in de office? And what about my job as Secretary to de union? Jerry, why don't you appoint somebody else Secretary? I can't go wid de two jobs. It is too much work fo' me.'

'But I have given you an assistant. Haven't I?'

'That girl? She worse than useless. Ah told you so over and over already?'

'What does it matter, anyway? The union's accounts are never audited. At the last meeting of the Legislative Council — you were absent — Joe Pittance and his stooge Cunningham, moved and seconded a motion to introduce a law that the accounts of all trades unions be audited. The Government won. The motion fell. Never forget, Sonia, that I lead the Government of Hiroona, and as Chief Minister I can give protection to anyone I please.'

'It isn't protection I want. I want to be done wid dis palitics business an' come home an' run de house. Lookin' after dis big house an' de grounds is problem enough. Put a ministry and a union secretary jobs on top dis, an' you going beyond a joke. Only because you is me husband why Ah trying to hold on to please you, but . . .'

'You think you have problems, girl? Look, only today — this morning — I had to visit the Arrowroot Depot to investigate some serious irregularities there. The depot is in a mess, an unholy mess. Been so for some time. It is now Government's problem — my problem — to clean it up.'

'What kinda mess?'

'I was describing the situation to Dave and Bryan a few minutes ago. They could hardly believe that a Government Department could degenerate into such a mess. I may have to close down the depot.'

'Rubbish!'

'What do you suggest, then?'

'Ah don't know. I only know you can't close it down. You will have de whole of Hiroona at yo' throat. Why don't you have a talk wid de Manager, Mr Gilchrist?'

'O Christ! Gilchrist! He is the ringleader of the mess. You see the weight of responsibility on my shoulders? And the depot is not my only headache. Christ, girl, you talk about problems! Your problems! Ha! Sometimes I feel like resigning — giving up politics entirely — and retire and take it easy; but for the good of the island, I've got to persevere. I . . . . excuse me while I answer the door bell.'

I hurried to the door, opened it and let in Inspector Robbins.

When I returned to the dining room with Robbins, Sonia was slowly padding her way up the stairs. The policeman looked up. 'Good night, mistress,' he said, unctuously.

'Good night,' said Sonia, without turning round or even stopping.

'I hope the good lady is feeling better now, sir,' said Robbins.

'Much,' I said, leading the way to my study. I held the door open for him. 'Go right in,' I said; 'make yourself at home.You know the place. I will go and fetch the drinks. Same thing as last time?'

'If it's your pleasure, sir.' Robbins smiled, top and bottom teeth together, like when one closely examines one's teeth in a looking glass.

'Now, then,' I said a few minutes after, as I rested the tray of drinks and glasses on the desk. 'We have very important business tonight, man.' And as I poured the drinks, 'The battle for your promotion is on. I have given notice to Forbes that I will wage that battle to the bitter end. And I don't intend to lose it.'

'God bless you, sir,' said Robbins, tremor in his voice, worship in his eyes.

'To your promotion,' I said, raising my glass of ginger ale. 'May it be soon.'

We laughed happily, touched glasses, sipped and sat down.

'I visited the Arrowroot Depot this morning. It is just as you told me. Even worse. Man, the place is a mess. They're all against the Government, and Gilchrist is the ringleader. Peter Garrick — Crab Soup — told me that

Pittance visits the place frequently. Whenever he goes there, he and Gilchrist shut themselves up in Gilchrist's office, planning to overthrow the Government. I proved the truth of this, this morning, when I tried to address the labourers there. They all started to laugh, refusing to listen to me. Man, it was horrible.'

'We can't put up with that sort o' thing, sir. If we allow this subversive condition to continue at de depot, it will spread to other Government Departments. Something drastic should be done to those traitors.'

'I heartily agree with you. What do you suggest?'

'Pity you couldn't transfer or fire the whole staff — or at least de ring-leaders, Gilchrist and his assistant.'

'Forbes will not agree to that. Under the Constitution, the Administrator is responsible for hiring and firing staff officers and clerks. This is one of the reasons why I am going to press the Colonial Office for a new and more advanced Constitution which would make the Queen's representative a figurehead and vest all the powers in the Premier or the Prime Minister. Hiroona is ours. We must have complete self-determination. Anything less than that is nonsense, retarding progress. Meanwhile, what do we do about the situation at the depot? Oh, wait a minute. What you suggested a moment ago gives me an idea. You suggested firing. We can't fire the staff, but we can fire something else. I think we can work on your idea. This is nothing new. A certain Chancellor of Germany had to fire the Reichstag in order to prove a point. I would then be able to get Government to mount a Commission of Inquiry, the members of which will be chosen by me. They will bring a strong case against Gilchrist and his staff, for negligence and inefficiency, and recommend their dismissal on these grounds. Forbes would be compelled to agree then.'

Robbins looked up sharply at me, his eyes wild with fear and misgivings. 'Yo' not thinking of burning down de depot, sir?'

'Robbins, man, we simply have to do it. In politics there are situations which can only be remedied by strong action. Take the question of your promotion. I told Forbes plain and straight that if you were not appointed Chief of Police — and damn soon — the people would certainly take the law into their own hands to bring about your appointment. And I mean it. Sometimes one has to take strong action. You have a wife and six children. Right?'

'Yes, sir; but . . . . arson, sir . . . . I . . . . Christ . . . . I . . . .' He produced a handkerchief and wiped his face.

'Don't think of it as arson, man. It would be arson if it were done by a private individual with malicious, mischievous or personal motives. But if it is done by the Government — and I am the Government — for the good of the state, then arson is out of the question. When the state put a man to death, the act is not murder.'

'But, sir . . . . .'

'O.K., then. If you're faint-hearted, we had better drop the *whole* thing.' I emphasised the word *whole,* so that it could include the promotion matter, too. I got up and began pacing up and down the room pretending to be deep in thought. Robbins sat, his eyes on the floor, his drink on the table, apparently forgotten. I continued the rhythmic, monotonous movement to and fro, covertly glancing at the Inspector every now and again. He shifted his position, leaned back in the chair and continued to gaze at the floor, his chin supported by thumb and index finger.

Suddenly, he spoke as if to himself, without looking up. 'I am not faint-hearted, but arson is a helluva thing. It ain't my line. It is what I would call technical. I cannot do it myself, and I cannot ask any of my men to do a thing like dat. How the hell . . . . . ?'

'Look, Robbins, man.' I paused in my pacing and stood before him. 'You won't have to do it yourself. And you don't have to ask any of your men to do it. Garrick is our man. He knows the depot. He worked there for ten years. He must know every inch of the layout.'

'But suppose he refuses to co-operate?'

'He won't refuse. He hates the place. He hates the people who are working there. He hates them so much that he refused my assistance to have him re-employed there. He will co-operate all right. But we've got to sound him out carefully, cautiously. Where are the keys of the building kept when the place is locked up at night?'

'At the Police Station.'

'Who is in charge of them then?'

'The desk constable at the guardroom receives the keys and hangs them on a numbered rack beside the keys of the other Government departments.'

'Good. So with your help, Garrick should have no difficulty whatsoever in getting into the buildings. Right?'

'What about the watchman at de depot?'

'He should pose no problem if you find out the time he goes on duty. Garrick would be able to help with the information about this. You would then study the watchman's habits and movements while he is on duty. Such a study would provide the cue for opening and entering the building and getting on with the job.'

'Oh, I see. So you don't propose to have de job done before a week or a fortnight or so?'

'A fortnight would be better. This would give Garrick sufficient time to study the watchman and make your preparations carefully.'

'Who will approach Garrick about dis job, sir?'

'Both of us will work on him at the same time.'

'And suppose he agree, but ask a fee, you will . . . . . .'

'Yes, yes. Leave that to me. Bring Garrick here tomorrow night at ten o'clock. I'll see there is sufficient liquor in the house to make and keep him interested.'

15

PETER Garrick, alias Crab Soup turned up sober. As I led him and Inspector Robbins to my study, I said, 'Garrick, man, people say you always drunk, but this is the second time we meeting, and you sober both times. Wha' happening? Yo' run outa liquor-money, or people telling lie on you'?'

'Heh, heh,' Garrick chuckled. 'Ah can't appear drunk in front of my Chief.' He was wearing the same black trousers, merino, dirty canvas shoes and cloth cap which he wore when he came to my office the day before.

'Well, your Chief is inviting you to get drunk tonight,' I laughed. 'You among friends here, you know.'

'O.K., Chief. Anyt'ing you say is O.K. by me.'

'Good. Wha' yo' drinking?'

'A little ordinary rum, if yo' please, Chief.'

'Same as usual for you, eh, Inspector?'

'Yes, sir.'

'Sit down, gentlemen. I'll be with you in a minute.'

Fifteen minutes and two rounds of drinks after — I stuck to a glass of lemonade — Garrick was saying:

'Dat place, Chief? I agree wid you dat somet'ing rough should be done about it. Ten years of my life I work in dat place, an' those people chase me out widdout giving me a cent. No pension, no nutten.'

'I will look after you, man. Have no fear. Old Sammie Dyer, the watchman at the Botanical Gardens is retiring in a couple months. I have already given orders to the Director of Agriculture that the post must not be filled before I am consulted. You will be getting that job. And you won't have to worry about a house — you will occupy the quarters which Sammie and his family now occupy at the back of the gardens. You know the place?'

Garrick was about to sip his rum and water. He paused, the glass close to his mouth. He stared at me, his big eyes bigger. 'O Christ, Chief, yo' mean dat? Me, poor Crab Soup, to get such a jab, Chief?'

I nodded, smiling.

'But Chief, de Gover'ment will not agree to dat. They will say Ah ain't good enough fo' de jab. And they might refuse to allow me girl fren to live in de quarters wid me. In dat case, Ah will have to marry she, which Ah didn't plan to do. But in any case, Chief, Ah don't believe de Gover'ment will give me such a big jab as dat.'

'I am the Government, Soupie. Remember that.'

'Dat is true, Chief. God bless you.' He turned to Robbins and said, 'Dat's what Ah always tell dem vagabonds at de depot. De Chief is de best man dis island ever had to rule it.' He put down his glass.

'Drink up, man. You should feel good and happy, now.'

'Yes, Chief, Ah feel good and happy. But wid a jab like keeper of de Botanic Gardens, Ah have to cut down on drink so Ah can atten' to me work better. So help me Gard, Chief, Ah won't let you down. Gard bless you, sah.' He reached for his glass, held it out to me for a moment, took a big draught, then wiped his mouth with the back of his hand.

Robbins, as if suddenly coming to life, raised his glass to Garrick, grinned and said, 'Congrats, Soupie. Congrats.'

'Let's get back to the depot now,' I said. 'Tell me, Soupie, what you think we should do with that place? Sometimes I feel we should blow it up with dynamite.' I laughed.

'De bitches deserve any kinda dynamite,' agreed Soupie.

'Ah tell you what, Soupie, wouldn't it be a damn good idea if you went in that place one night, and fire de whole damn place — just like they fired you? Then de whole staff would be out of a job, just like they tried to put you out of a job, eh?' I laughed as I looked at the Inspector's weak, unsteady smile. Garrick knitted his brows. A sullen look darkened his black face. He stared at the floor in front of him. I didn't know whether his attitude bespoke abhorrence of the idea or serious consideration of it.

'You know the place well, don't you, Soupie?' I kept my manner jokey.

'Every inch of it, Chief,' said Soupie, nodding without looking up, the stern look still on his face. Robbins asked his old question:

'What about the watchman?'

'Who? Honky Dory?' said Soupie, looking up at Robbins.

'That's his alias,' said Robbins.

'Seems like every damn soul in Hiroona has a alias,' I said. 'What's the fellow's proper name?'

'Real name is Henry Baptiste, Chief,' said Soupie.

'You know him well, Soupie?'

'Know him, Chief? Honky is me best fren. He was de only person at de depot Ah could tark private to. He is de only one up at dat place Ah wouldn't like to see lose his jab.'

'Have no fear, Soupie. I promise you, I will find a job for him. O.K.?'

'O.K., Chief.' He took up his glass and drained it.

'Mark you, Garrick,' said Robbins sternly, 'you not to breathe a word to Honky Dory or anyone else about dis conversation. Understand?'

'You think Ah stupid, Inspecta?'

'How you propose to handle Honky Dory, Soupie?'

'Dat is as easy as kiss hand, Chief.'

'How you mean, easy?'

'Me an' Honky does go to de Hadrian Wall for a drink or two sometimes, Chief.'

'You mean during his working hours?'

'Oh Christ, Chief, Ah wouldn't want Mr Gilchrist to know dat. He will sack hell outa Honky, if he know.'

'You can trust me, Soupie,' I said. 'Tell me your plan.'

'Well, say about twelve o'clock so, when everybody gone sleep and everyt'ing close down and de town quiet quiet, Ah go up to de depot an' invite Honky to go wid me to de Hadrian Wall.'

'That won't do, Soupie,' said Robbins. 'All fourth class licensed rum shops, which include de Hadrian Wall, close down by law at ten o'clock at night. The Police never fail to prosecute any rum shop proprietor who remain open beyond his licensed hours.'

'Oh Christ, Inspecta, Ah didn't mean to tell yo' dis. And Ah hope you won't use de knowledge against de Hadrian Wall. De Hadrian does close down in front at ten o'clock an' remain open in de back, up to one an' two o'clock fo' a few regular customers, like me an' Honky, to relax dere. Especially on Saturday nights. But Ah don't want yo' to send police to raid de place, now dat Ah tell you.'

'Inspector?' I said, looking at Robbins significantly.

'Oh, I will never do that, sir.'

'Fine. Now go on, Soupie. Tell us the plan.'

'I prefer to hear your side o' de plan, Chief.'

'O.K. The Inspector gives you eight or nine gallons of gasoline which he siphons out of the petrol tank of his car. He also gives you the key of the main door of the depot. He gives you those two items near the time when you going to pick up Honky, so that you won't have to lug around with a tin o' gas too early, for everybody to see. You hide the key in your pocket. About midnight or a little after, you hide the tin of gasoline near the depot, then you call on Honky Dory at the depot and invite him to the Hadrian. Now you go on from there, Soupie.'

'Me an' Honky go to de Hadrian. We drinkin' an' relax. Ah pay fo' de first round o' drinks, Honky pay fo' de next round. Before we finish dat round, Ah tell Honky to wait there fo' me while Ah go down to de communal to ease me bowels. Ah know Honky will wait till Ah come back, because de next round o' drinks is on me, an' we ain't drink much yet. Instead o' goin' to de communal, Ah hurry back to de depot. Ah open de main door. Ah go in an' drench de whole darm place wid gasoline, including de bags of arrowroot. Ah light a slow fire in a place dat would give me time to get outa de building, lock it an' get back to de Hadrian. Few minutes after Ah reach de Hadrian — whosh, bang, phew!'

Robbins said, 'How will the watchman clear himself at the inquiry afterwards, when it come out that he was not on de premises when de fire broke out?'

'Who say he wasn't on de premises? You t'ink de Hadrian or any o' de few customers dere will be so stupid as to tell de police dat de shop was open at half past twelve in de marnin'?'

'It is possible, too,' I suggested, 'that Honky Dory could have been at the communal when he heard the alarm that fire had broken out at de depot. The communal isn't far from the depot.'

'Dat's right, Chief. Honky does go to de communal whenever nature call. He can say both of us was dere when de alarm.'

As I reached for my Letts diary on my desk, I said, 'We have to time this thing carefully. Let me see now.' I opened the diary. 'The date I am thinking of is the twenty-third, a fortnight from now. The job doesn't need much preparation, but it mustn't be done too soon after my visit to the depot yesterday. A fortnight between should be all right, however. What you think, gentlemen? Soupie?'

'Dat will be O.K., Chief.'

'Robbins?' The Inspector shrugged non-commitally. The good, professional policeman was still at work in him. He had no enthusiasm, no stomach, for the project; but I had involved him so deeply, he couldn't wriggle out. And there was the matter of his promotion.

'Settled, then,' I said. 'Everything is up to you and Soupie now. While you plan and work on the depot, I will be planning and working for your promotion, Robbins, and for your job at the Botanical Gardens, Soupie.' I raised my glass. Crab Soup refilled his, lifted it high. Robbins' glass came up half mast. We touched glasses and drank.

I didn't tell them that I would not be on the island on the date of the proposed fire. It would be a bit embarrassing — bad psychology — to reveal that I would be in Jamaica on that date, attending a prefederation conference to decide upon the site of the capital of the proposed West Indies Federation.

16

T HE meeting in Jamaica was summoned because the ten islands which wanted to federate could not agree among themselves as to where the federal capital should be sited. The leaders of each of the larger islands wanted to have the the federal capital in their own island. The smaller islands formed blocs and demanded that the capital be sited on one of the islands of the bloc. The politicians had bickered over this issue from 1950 to 1956.

In 1956, the islands went to London, and at the February conference it was agreed that, as we could not agree among ourselves, the issue should be referred to a Federal Capital Commission comprised of three British 'experts'. These three gentlemen were supposed to be, in the islands' view, experts at Federal capitals. If, reasoned the islands, you can have experts at bridge, golf, chess, or gardening, there must be experts at federal capitals, too. So the three experts went to work on the job. They ruled out the smaller and less developed islands, and recommended Barbados, Jamaica and Trinidad, in that order. The reason, said the experts, for placing Trinidad last on the list was, the instability of that island's politics and the low standard accepted in its public life.

The islands read the experts' report at home, arranged a conference in Jamaica in 1957 to consider it, and this took me away from Hiroona at a time when I was very glad indeed to be out of the island.

The remarkable feature of that conference was that instead of bickering among themselves, the islands achieved harmony for the first time, by bickering about the report of the experts. They all lined up with Trinidad against the Federal Capital Commission.

We were livid with indignation against the Commission for libelling our sister island. Delegate after delegate got up and poured scorn on the three experts; on their report; on all and sundry Englishmen; on the British Government; on colonialism; on imperialism. It was the first and last time that *real* unity was evident among us. And to underscore our contempt for the Commission and its report, we chose Trinidad as the Federal Capital. Contempt had given us unanimity, all other considerations having failed throughout 1950 to 1957.

I was thinking of getting up to congratulate Trinidad, when one of the local conference secretaries entered the room, caught my eye, held up what looked like a telegram, and indicated by a nod that it was addressed to me. I beckoned him. My mind detached itself at once from what was going on in the conference room, to speculate on the information I supposed the telegram contained.

The official handed me two telegrams. I opened the first one, and read: IT IS MY DUTY TO INFORM YOU THAT THE ARROWROOT DEPOT WAS DESTROYED BY FIRE LAST NIGHT. ADMINISTRATOR.

I smiled as I folded the telegram and put it back into the envelope.

I didn't smile when I read the other telegram:
DEPOT BURN DOWN FLAT STOP MYSTERIOUS FIRE STOP UNDERSTAND FORBES AND ATTORNEY GENERAL HAVE ROBBINS AND DEPOT WATCHMAN AND STATION CONSTABLE FOR SERIOUS QUESTIONING STOP SUGGEST YOU DROP CONFERENCE COME HOME DAVE

Oh Christ! Forbes and the Attorney General seriously questioning Robbins? And how does the station constable come into this? . . . . Oh yes — Robbins had said, 'The desk constable in the guardroom receives the keys and hangs them on a numbered rack beside the keys of the other Government Departments.' O God! I hope Robbins keeps his head cool and his mouth shut.

I now regretted my absence from the island. Had I been there, I would have seen to it that Robbins stood firm. I would have been able to take arbitrary control of the situation and thus provide Robbins with the necessary immoral support.

As I read Dave's telegram again, my perturbation increased. I looked around the conference room — the long tables placed end to end to form a square in the centre of the hall. The delegates filling the seats at tables, the names of the islands they represent standing out in large block letters on white cardboard forms in front of them. The sheafs of note paper and conference documents lying before each delegate. Carafes of water, drinking glasses, ashtrays and amplifiers further cluttering up the tables. Within the square formed by the tables, stenographers and stenotypists sat at smaller tables, scribbling or tapping out the hieroglyphics which would later become readable conference reports. At the top centre table, the Jamaican cabinet minister presided, competently directing proceedings as chairman of the conference.

The entire scene became blurred and unreal to me. Reality was a thousand sea miles away, on an island with a gutted building: a gaping crowd milling around the charred, smoking ruins; policemen pacing up and down, keeping off the crowd; Honky Dory the watchman detained for questioning; a police constable saying to the Administrator and the Attorney General, 'I received the key from Gilchrist, the Manager of the arrowroot depot, yesterday afternoon at five o'clock while I was on duty at the guardroom desk. I hung the key in its usual place on the rack . . . .' And the Attorney General saying, 'But the constable who took over from you at the guardroom said that when he heard the alarm that the depot was on fire, he looked on the rack and there was no depot key there . . . . And Robbins, sitting bolt upright, facing Forbes and the Attorney General and saying nothing — I hoped.

Somewhere on the periphery of my awareness I heard the chairman of the conference announce a coffee break of fifteen minutes.

I folded Dave's telegram and put it back in the envelope; then I unfolded Forbes' and passed it to the delegate who was sitting next to me. He read it. His eyebrows went up.

'My God,' he said; 'how did this happen?'

'I don't know,' I said.

'This will be a terrible blow to your arrowroot industry.'

'To the whole economy of the island,' I said, as I raised my hand to my jaw and looked lost.

'Christ, man, I am sorry. This is a hell of a thing. You better go back home at once. Right away. I'm sure the conference would understand.' He got up, patted my shoulder and went and joined the other delegates who were having refreshments in the coffee room. I continued to sit where I was, Forbes' telegram open in front of me on the table, my head supported by my hands under my jaws. I sat there, staring at the telegram, presenting a study in dejection.

Presently, delegates came back from the coffee room and surrounded me, some still holding their unfinished cups of tea or coffee, and munching their patties.

'We just heard about your great misfortune in Hiroona . . . . a hell of a blow, man . . . . a great pity . . . . how the hell could a thing like that happen? . . . . . and at a time like this when development is so vital to the islands . . . . Mole, man, you have every bit of our sympathy.'

I stood up, sadly acknowledged their consolatory remarks and tried to answer their numerous questions, shaking my head in vain attempts to explain the 'mystery'. One delegate made the practical suggestion that I should apply as soon as possible to the British Government for a Colonial Development and Welfare grant to rehabilitate the industry.

'That's the only way out I can see at present,' I said morosely. 'But the British Government is so damn stingy, they mightn't consider a grant or even a loan. I may have to go to England myself to argue the case with them.'

'Oh, they *must* give you a grant, man. Britain is damn stingy to the West Indian islands, yes, but they can't be so worthless as to refuse to help in an important economic matter like this.'

'I hope they will help,' I said. 'After all, the arrowroot industry is the life blood of the island. My God! What a calamity!'

When conference resumed a few minutes after, one delegate after another rose and asked permission of the chairman 'to express my deep sympathy and the deep sympathy of the people of my island to the Chief Minister and people of Hiroona for the economic loss they have sustained . . .' The chairman himself added his 'quota', and expressed his regret that I had to hurry home before the end of the conference. He hoped that speedy assistance would be forthcoming from the British Government to repair the damage and re-establish the arrowroot industry in Hiroona.

I briefly thanked the chairman and other delegates, and, after gathering up my conference papers and stuffing them in my thin, black briefcase, left the room. The conference remained in respectful, sympathetic silence until my departure.

17

I had some five hours to wait for my flight to Hiroona, so I decided to put through an overseas telephone call to Robbins while I waited. Such a move would be very useful. It would enable me to obtain information about what Forbes had done since the fire, and it would give me the opportunity to reassure Robbins of my support, and to ensure that he and Honky Dory had not 'squealed' on account of panic or pressure.

I phoned Cable and Wireless, Kingston.

'This is the Chief Minister of Hiroona speaking.'

'Yes, sir,' said a female voice.

'I want a person to person call to Inspector Robbins. Acting Chief of Police of Hiroona.'

'Where do I call you back, sir?'

'Here — at the Courtleigh Manor Hotel. This is an official call, miss; would you please instruct your Hiroona branch to charge it to my Government.'

'Very well.'

While I waited for the call, I packed my suitcase, then I went down to the reception desk, paid my bill and gave notice that I would be checking out in an hour or two. Back in my room, I counted the balance of my money I had in my wallet. To attend the conference, I had drawn an advance of a thousand dollars from the Hiroona treasury. My approved subsistence rate was forty-four dollars per day. The hotel rate was twenty dollars, so my initial saving was at the rate of twenty-four dollars per day. The conference was supposed to last five days. I had to hurry back to Hiroona after three days. So that was an additional saving of two days at forty-four dollars per day. My bill at the hotel was for three days at twenty plus fifteen dollars for lunch etc. Thus, I made a profit of $925 from that conference.

I put the nine hundred and twenty-five dollars back in my wallet, replaced the rubber band around the wallet and returned it to my hip pocket. Had I been a civil servant, I would have had to account to the Treasury for my expenditure, and return the balance of money to the public purse. But as Chief Minister, I placed myself above this 'red tape', and ignored the demands of the Accountant General that I 'retire' each advance, on my return from each conference. So the balance from each conference went into my personal bank account.

As I patted the $925 in my hip pocket, I reflected that power had a thousand delights, and only a simpleton would forego them.

I took one of the tourist brochures from the desk in my room and sat in one of the two chairs, leafing through it. Presently, the telephone jingled, and in a moment I was speaking with Robbins.

'What is this terrible news I hear, about a mysterious fire at the arrowroot depot?'

'Place burn flat, sir. Successfully flat.'

What an assinine thing to say, I fumed to myself. Has the man gone mad? Has he forgotten that our conversation is being monitored in Hiroona as well as in Jamaica? I shouted into the telephone: 'Inspector! Pull yourself together, man. This terrible thing has upset you, as it has upset me. But we must not lose our nerve.'

'No, sir.'

'Have you found out who is responsible for the dastardly deed?'

'Well, they are questioning a lot of people.'

'They who?'

'The Administrator and the Attorney.'

'What you had to say about it?'

'Nothing so far, sir. The Administrator called me up for questioning by him and de Attorney General. We are worried about the key of the depot main door. We can't trace it. Missing.'

'What about Honky — er, what about the watchman? What has he to say?'

'Said he was in the communal answering nature when he heard the cry of "fire, fire". Said he run out, fighting to arrange his pants, and saw de depot blazing.'

'Oh, I see.'

'I think you should come home at once, sir. The Administrator is thinking of asking the Colonial Office to arrange with Scotland Yard to send a detective here to investigate the matter.'

'*What?* Waste money which the colony cannot afford? As Minister of Finance, I am opposed to such nonsense — such squandering of the people's money. If your local men in the CID cannot handle the situation, what are we paying them for? I am having no Scotland Yard men in Hiroona until I am satisfied that your men cannot handle the situation. Tell Mr Forbes *that*, will you?'

'Thank you, sir. Ah told the Administrator so already.'

Good work, boy. Robbins was no fool after all.

'And listen, Inspector, I am leaving here for Hiroona as soon as I put down this telephone. Tell my wife to send my car for me at Kingsland airport at four this afternoon. Meanwhile, do all you can until I get home. We have to find out who set that fire. We must bring the culprit to justice, but don't let Forbes and the Attorney General usurp your authority. You are in charge of the CID. Use your men. Don't let anybody humbug you. Forbes is no detective, neither is the Attorney General. The job is in your hands. You understand?'

'Right, sir. Many thanks, sir. See you soon.'

As soon as the aircraft came to a stop at Kingsland airport, I grabbed my briefcase, got out of my seat in the first class section, hastened down the gangway, and, with the long, firm stride of the high-powered executive, crossed the tarmac and whizzed through the terminal building to my car on the other side. My status gave me immunity from customs and immigration formalities. And as for my baggage, that would be sent to me, as usual, by the customs officer in charge at the airport.

'Christ! Chief,' said the chauffeur as he put the car in low gear and moved off, 'Ah never see nothing so in me life. Fire fo' so. Like de whole town was blazing.'

'But where was the fire brigade all this time?' I enquired.

'Before de brigade get there, de depot nearly done burn down.'

'They're too damn slow. Something should be done about those fire brigade men. Why weren't they on the spot earlier?'

'Maybe they didn't know de fire was due to break out, Chief. An' when dey reach de spot an' turn on de hydrant near de depot, no water was there. De water was locked off as usual. So dey had to drag de hose down to de beach and put it in de sea and pump sea water.'

'Did that do much good?'

'It didn't do no good to the depot. De depot was too far gone. But de brigade drench down de other buildings near by, wid de sea water, so the sparks didn't ketch on the buildings. Only Mr Richards lumber yard caught fire, but de sea water put out de fire.'

'Haven't they arrested anybody?'

'No, Chief. But somebody set dat fire. So help me God, some wicked worthliss person set dat fire. Gover'ment should hang him if dey catch him. Is de worse fire we ever had in dis island.'

'I heard about it in Jamaica. Crowds of people surrounded me and offered me their sympathy.'

'Could be an enemy of yours who set dat fire, Chief, just to create hardship for de Gover'ment.'

It was an inspired thought, that. It sparked an idea that had not occurred to me before. I leaned forward, touched the chaffeur on his shoulder. 'Drive me straight to the arrowroot depot,' I said, 'then to the Broadcasting Station. I think I should make a broadcast to the people before I go home to Fairfield House.'

18

I didn't call on Mr Forbes immediately after the recording of my broadcast. Instead, I went home, took a bath, changed into slacks and open neck shirt, and ate a meal. While I changed, Sonia and I listened over our large Grundig radio to the broadcast of my speech which came over on the six o'clock programme.

Sonia's comment on my observations about the fire was, 'Well, you told me some weeks aback that de depot was a mess, and that it was your problem to clean it up. Well, somebody save you de trouble — they clean it up fo' you. Pity though. A sad pity.' She still looked a bit tired, and she had not yet returned to work. She sat at the dining room table, watched me eat, and listened while I told her about the conference and expressed my views about the fire. Then she got up and began to move about the room, fixing things and giving me her views. Her slippers made a soft, slushing sound as she dragged them around.

'But why you so dead against de Scotland Yard men coming to investigate de fire?'

'Where will the money come from to pay them? Scotland Yard experts cost money. And what's more, punishing the people who set the fire won't give us back the depot.'

She looked at me for a long moment. Then she said, 'You is a strange man, Jerry. You funny. How come you just said in your broadcast dat you want de culprit brought to justice? Now you sayin' something else. Jerry, dat sort o' thing ain't good. It is evil.'

'Sonia, please remember that the practice of politics is the pursuit of the necessary, not the good. If the necessary happens to be good, well and good; but goodness is not the business of the politician. So far as the job of politics is concerned, goodness is only a sort of inadvertent by-product. Sensible people nowadays no longer believe, like the oldtime French Philosopher Marquis d'Argenson that, "the whole art of government consists in nothing else.than the perfect imitation of God." That sort of pious tripe went clean out of fashion with d'Argenson — if it was ever in fashion at all. Furthermore, when a political leader imitates God, people call him a despot, a tyrant, a dictator.'

'Jesus Lord!' Sonia muttered, as she turned away and went into the kitchen.

I got up, went into my office adjoining the dining room, telephoned Mr Forbes and made an appointment to call on him in the next hour or so. Then I went out to my car and drove off to Dave Potter's place.

'Damn glad you were able to get back home so soon,' said Dave, as he followed me into the Aerie and shut the door. 'Got my cable?'

'Yes, man.'

'When?'

'This morning. In the midst of the conference meeting.'

'Ah heard your broadcast a few minutes ago. It was damn good. When did you do it?'

'First thing after I got into town from the airport.'

'Christ! You worked fast, boy.'

'Glad you cabled.' I reclined on the couch, my head and shoulders supported by a pillow. Dave sat on a chair and leaned on the desk.

'I had to cable, man,' he said. 'Bitch of a fire, and people saying all sorts of things.'

'Like what?'

'Well, you know Hiroonians. They got long, wide and ugly mouths. It is even rumoured that your Permanent Secretary, that Matthews feller, told the Administrator that two weeks ago you suddenly asked for the ar-rowroot depot file . . . . .'

'So why the hell shouldn't I ask for a file if I want it?'

'And that you asked for a list of the staff of the depot, and that when you got it you said you will show them who is boss. Of course, in Kingsland, that means that it was you who set the fire of the depot.'

'I sat in Jamaica and set fire to a building in Hiroona! I must be a voodoo man.' We laughed. I got up, went to the little bar and poured a whiskey for Dave and one for myself.

'By the way,' I asked, as I lowered myself on the other chair on the opposite side of the desk, 'do you think Pittance has a hand in that fire?'

'Would be damn hard to prove. Pittance is no fool. If he has a hand in it the hand would be well hidden. But you think Pittance would do a damn nasty thing like that, Jerry?'

'I wouldn't put it past the son of a bitch. Where is Bryan?'

'Dressed up to kill, and gone to neck on the dark verandah of Anne Peters' house.'

'He still chasing Anne, eh?'

'The race is mutual. I expect a head-on collision any moment. You might have to give him a job in the Government. He can't keep a wife on his salary here.'

'I've thought of that. With this Federation coming up, and with our increased control of our own affairs, it should be easy to get a good break for a decent intelligent chap like Bryan. We must discuss it with him sometime.'

'Bin to see Forbes yet, since your return?'

'No. Going in the next few minutes. I hear he wants to send for Scotland Yard.'

'You agree?'

'Agree, my eye! These Englishmen always want to look for jobs for their own people, at the natives' expense. No damn Scotland Yard coming here. I promise you *that*.'

'You damn right, Jerry. I'm with you a hundred per cent.'

For the first time in the six or seven years I had known Dave, I thought of him as a sheep. The thought was only momentary, but it had in it a tincture of pity. For here was a friend, perhaps the only person in Hiroona (apart from Sonia) that I really cared for, but even to whom I daren't tell the truth of the matter we were discussing. Unlike Sonia, Dave had left unquestioned my reason for objecting to having the cause of the fire investigated by trained and competent sleuths. I had led him to believe that my objection was based on chauvinism — the popular, anticolonial war cries of 'Native First!' 'Hands Off Our Affairs!' 'Hiroona for Hiroonians!' Unlike Sonia, he did not raise the counter objection that this insular approach was not relevant to the situation. Instead, he had simply reaffirmed his willingness to follow wheresoever I led: 'I am with you a hundred per cent.' He couldn't know, of course, that his expression of trust and confidence only inspired in me a kind of regret that I didn't deserve it in this instance. As I left Dave, to keep my appointment with Mr Forbes, my feeling of affection and pity for my friend was touched with a pang of shame, because I had given him deceit in return for his faith. I wondered what would be his reaction if I told him the truth about the depot fire.

I smothered thoughts about Dave, and braced myself for the encounter with Forbes, as I drove through the gate of Government House, parked my car in the yard and went up to the front door and pressed the buzzer. A servant let me in.

Forbes received me in the office that looked like a museum — or the museum that looked like an office. Although it was long past normal office hours, Forbes still wore his polka dot bowtie and brown lounge suit. He motioned me to a chair, and sat behind his desk.

'You wanted to see me, Mr Mole?'

'Yes. I received your telegram informing me about the fire at the depot. I left the conference immediately and returned home.'

'The origin of the fire is unknown, up to now. It is a frightfully serious matter, involving as it does the economy of the island. The Colonial Office will require a full report, after thorough investigation. I have grave doubts about the ability of the local CID to get to the bottom of this matter. So it would appear that we shall have to ask Scotland Yard to send a man here to do the investigating.'

'Have you discussed this with Inspector Robbins?'

'Yes.'

'Does he share your doubts as to the ability of his men to handle the investigation'

'I don't know. I didn't ask him.'

'Well, I don't share your doubts.'

Forbes shrugged. 'The Police, Defence and all matters connected with the Police are my responsibility,' he said. 'It would be my doubts, not your opinion, that the Colonial Office would take into account in deciding who should investigate the cause of the fire.'

'The expense of the investigation is a financial matter. Finance is my responsibility. I am Minister of Finance. What if I refuse to authorise the funds to pay for an investigation by Scotland Yard?'

'I see,' said Forbes. He tapped, slowly and thoughtfully, on his desk with a pencil, staring at the antlers of a deer head as he tapped. I waited. Presently, he brought his gaze down to my face and said, 'By the way, have you given a thought as to how and when this Government will be able to rebuild the depot?'

'Yes,' I replied. 'There's only one source from which we could obtain the necessary funds — the British Government. We shall have to make application for a Colonial Development and Welfare free grant.'

'Do you believe, Mr Mole, that the British Government will give you a grant just like that, in the face of your refusal to have a proper investigation made as to exactly why such a grant is necessary?'

'The grant is necessary, Mr Forbes, because the depot has been completely destroyed by fire. The investigation could be properly done by the local CID, and the high cost of importing Scotland Yard detectives avoided. This Government is not a millionaire, you know.'

'The Colonial Office would pay the cost of the investigation if this Government ask that this be done.'

That statement frightened me for a moment. However, I recovered quickly enough.

'What assurance have you that they would pay?' I asked.

'The assurance of experience,' said Forbes.

'My own experience with the British Government gives no indication of such generosity,' I asserted.

'And yet you expect that they will be generous enough to give you a free grant to rebuild the depot.'

'Look, Mr Forbes, let's stop this back-and-forth business. The people of Hiroona do not relish the insult of importing foreigners to do a job which we can do ourselves. I am asking you now to instruct the Clerk of Councils to summon an emergency meeting of the Executive Council for ten o'clock tomorrow morning. We must discuss this matter thoroughly in Council. The Acting Chief of Police should be asked to attend.'

My request for a meeting of the Executive Council was my constitutional trump card. I knew that Forbes could not refuse to have the Council summoned on the request of the Chief Minister if the circumstances warranted such a meeting. And the circumstances did. I could dominate the Council if I couldn't dominate the Administrator. The majority in the Council consisted of ministers I had put there and whom I could remove if they didn't toe the line. True enough, the Administrator had certain reserve powers under the constitution, and by virtue of those powers Forbes could apply to the Colonial Office for Scotland Yard's assistance, in spite of objection by the Council to such a step. But Forbes would know from experience that the use of reserve powers in those days when Britain's policy was to rid herself and her Treasury of the liability of her West Indian colonies was a tricky business. He would hardly get the backing of the Colonial Office in his exercise of reserve powers. The people must be left to control their own affairs. The logic of the particular circumstances was apparent — Britain would not be prepared to fork out money for a new arrowroot depot unless investigation of the cause of the fire was conducted by Scotland Yard, for which investigation Britain might be willing to pay. My Government's refusal to have Scotland Yard in on the investigation would remove the necessity of Britain's paying for the investigation as well as for a new depot. Any request from Forbes that the Colonial Office arrange to send a detective would involve the British Government in two expenses – for the investigation and for the depot. Therefore, Forbes' request would hardly be welcome to the Colonial Office. And if an alert and interested member of the British Parliament were to ask in parliament why did Britain refuse to accede to the Administrator's request for detective assistance to solve the recent crime of arson of important public property in Hiroona, then the Secretary of

State for the Colonies could blandly reply that the Government of Hiroona had refused such assistance, and that as the matter was an 'internal affair', the British Government, in keeping with its policy of colonial liberation, did not think it wise to 'interfere'.

Forbes must have appreciated all this. He did not speak at length during the emergency meeting of the Council. He did make a very disquieting observation, however; and the manner in which he made it led me to feel that he entertained certain suspicions that were uncomplimentary to myself. He said, 'I suppose Honourable Members heard the Honourable Chief Minister's speech which was broadcast over the local broadcasting station yesterday evening. That speech was heard at six o'clock. It was repeated at eight o'clock last night, and again at ten o'clock. It came over again this morning on the six-thirty program. In that broadcast, the Chief Minister voiced his conclusion that the fire at the depot could be traced to carelessness or neglect, or action by "enemies of the Government and people of this island, to embarrass the Government." Now I ask you, gentlemen; is it not strange, is it not very, very strange, that the Chief Minister should now show himself to be terribly afraid of approving a type of investigation — the best in the world — which would cost this Government nothing, and would almost certainly unmask these "enemies of the Government and people" and bring them to justice? Tell me, Honourable Members, is it not passing strange?'

Such clear thinking and near eloquence could make no impact on ordinary minds brainwashed by party loyalty and self interest, however. Honourable members greeted Forbes' moving appeal to reason with bovine silence. I didn't even bother to refute Forbes' innuendo; I merely sucked my teeth, twisted in my seat and stared out of the window, feigning indifference and boredom.

It was my Minister without portfolio who answered Forbes. 'But we done tell yo' over an' over, since we started dis meetin' naily two hours ago, dat we don't want no foreign Scotlan' Yard here to do a jab dat our own people can do. We can also set up a Commission of Inquiry, selected by de Chief Minister.'

Forbes just stared at honourable members in turn. He seemed to be on the verge of tears of frustration.

By the end of the meeting, the Scotland Yard idea was formally dropped, and the matter of rebuilding the arrowroot depot was wrapped in a cocoon of vague verbiage by myself and honourable members, about, 'every effort must be made . . . . ; no stone unturned . . . . ; we may have to float a loan . . . . ; perhaps the British Government would still be prepared to . . . . . 'And Inspector Robbins was given permission to retire from the meeting, after an exhortation by the Chief Minister to use every available means at his disposal in 'getting to the bottom of this ghastly crime.'

And so I had cleared another dangerous hurdle; and now my political mind, made agile by practice, immediately focused on the next hurdle — the elevation of Inspector Robbins to the post of Chief of Police. Forbes' mind must have been dwelling on the same thing too, for as honourable members prepared to rise and depart, Forbes spoke again, this time like a man who was tired, bewildered, frustrated, but who must continue, nevertheless, to hoe a field of concrete.

He said, 'I wish to make an announcement. As a result of objections raised by the Chief Minister some weeks ago, regarding the appointment of an expatriate to the vacant post of Chief of Police of this island, the Secretary of State for the Colonies has decided to send Major Levons Hart here to look into the matter and make recommendations to Her Majesty's Government accordingly. Major Hart is expected to arrive here on the twenty-first of next month — about three weeks and a half from today — and will remain in the Colony for about ten days. Major Hart will wish to interview the Chief Minister and other persons to be specified later. He will not meet this Council as a body, however.'

'Noted,' I said.

The Clerk of Council rose and went to hold the door open for the exit of honourable members.

19

THE guests at Mr Forbes' cocktail party in honour of Major Levons Hart included local big names in business and the professions, members of some of the leading families of Hiroona, senior Government officials, the leader of the Opposition — Joe Pittance — the Nominated Members of the Legislative Council and the Ministers and their wives. Sonia did not attend; she lay indisposed at home.

Major Levons Hart — a slim, six foot four in a well-fitting grey pin stripe suit; full head of smooth gray hair, parted in the middle; face lined, ruddy, oldish but handsome; crows' feet radiating from corners of clear blue eyes when he smiled, as he often did — circulated with Forbes among the chattering guests, on Government House lawn. It was a bright and sunny six o'clock in the evening. As the Administrator introduced the Major to a guest, Hart stood and talked, sipping from his glass and biting into a pastry. Then he and Forbes moved on.

As I chatted with Dave Potter, my Nominated Member of the Legislative Council, and Victor Banks, I kept an eye on Hart and Forbes as they moved about among the guests. Banks' *petite* wife joined us, glass in hand, to comment on Major Hart's magnificent military figure, and easy friendly attitude.

'What's his business here, Jerry?' she said.

'To settle a quarrel between me and Forbes.'

'Well, I know you and Forbes always quarrelling, but what's the quarrel about this time?' She wiped a tiny, red smudge from the rim of the glass with her handkerchief and took another sip, leaving another tiny, red smudge.

'Forbes wants to bring another Englishman here as Chief of Police. I want the post filled by a native of Hiroona.'

'Which native?'

'Inspector Robbins, of course,' I said.

'Oh Christ, Jerry, you don't mean that police uniform with a fat-head in it?'

'Hiroona for Hiroonians, Doris,' I said. 'We got to begin somewhere, sometime. And the place is the senior service. The time is now.'

'Balls!' said Doris. 'Begin with a man like Robbins, and you'd be forever beginning.'

'So you prefer an Englishman to your own people?' said Dave.

'I would prefer a man from Manchuria,' said Doris stubbornly, 'if he's a better man for the job. Why the hell should we put a square peg . . . .'

'Drink up your punch, darling,' said Victor Banks, 'and keep out of politics.'

'You all drag politics into every damn thing, Vic. You men make me sick to the armpits with your . . . .'

'And this is Mr Mole, the Chief Minister,' Forbes' voice broke in. 'Mr Potter a nominated member of the Legislative Council. Mr Victor Banks a businessman. Mrs Banks.'

'Ah! Major Hart,' I said, as I quickly changed my glass from my right to my left, and shook hands with the Major. 'Welcome to Hiroona.'

'Thank you, Mr Chief Minister. You've certainly got a lovely island here.'

'Thank you, sir,' I said. 'The people of Hiroona feel that they should give you a more rousing welcome than even this lively cocktail party. We have our best steel band waiting outside the walls. I am asking His Honour the Administrator's permission to allow the band to come in and play a few selections for your special enjoyment and pleasure, sir.'

Forbes' brow contracted in lines of annoyance, puzzlement and suspicion. But when Hart looked at him and smiled, questioningly, Forbes shrugged and said, 'All right, Mr Mole. Bring in your steel band.'

I hastened to the gate and spoke to the two policemen who were standing guard there. 'Administrator's orders,' I said. The policemen shouldered their rifles, saluted and stood aside. I motioned the steel band to come in. They entered. Fifteen strong. To the strains of *Men of Harlech,* they moved briskly along the tarmac entrance to Government House grounds, then on down to the lawn. The guests made way for them. Major Hart looked pleased. Then I signalled to the crowd of some ninety to a hundred, which was waiting behind with hidden placards. They swept gaily through the gates and on to the grounds, their placards held high or draped over them back and front:

WE WANT TO RUN OUR OWN COUNTRY, MAJOR . . . . GIVE US A CHANCE . . . HIROONA FOR HIROONIANS . . . DON'T ROB OUR SENIOR POSTS . . . WE WANT AN ALL NATIVE PUBLIC SERVICE NOW . . . HANDS OFF OUR POLICE FORCE . . . LET WEST INDIANS RUN THE WEST INDIES . . .

Some of the guests applauded. Laughing, cheering, swaying to the rhythm of the steel band, they further heightened the now baroque atmosphere of the place.

I left the gate and came back to stand beside Major Hart. The smile of real pleasure with which he had greeted the entrance of the steel band had changed to a weak, quizzical half-grin — a veneer which thinly masked disappointment and annoyance — at the entrance of the pickets. Forbes' face and long neck had gone vermilion. Hart ignored my presence at his side. He kept up the pretence of focusing his attention on the prancing demonstration.

'Our people are very high spirited, sir,' I shouted to Hart, above the din.

'Mmm,' said the Major, as he moved away without even so much as a glance in my direction. Forbes followed him. A minute or two after, Forbes beckoned the guards at the gate. They came to him at the double, clicked to attention and saluted. One of the policemen went to the steel band and signalled it to follow him to the gate, while the other policeman dealt with the demonstrators in the same way.

As the last of the interlopers was being quietly thrust outside the gate by the policemen, Dave said, 'Well, Major Hart got the message, anyway.' And Doris Banks mocked me with one of her flippant, highpitched laughs and said, 'You've made your point, Jerry; you may go home now.'

20

A T the beginning of my interview with Major Hart next day, the Major was so pleasant with me, so full of easy, good humour, that I was led to believe that he had forgiven or forgotten my pickets and the embarrassing demonstration at the cocktail party of the evening before. The interview took place in the presence of the Administrator, at his office, and Forbes' unusually affable manner confirmed my impression that he and Major Hart had at least decided to let me have what I wanted: Robbins would be appointed Chief of Police. I made a quick, mental promise to do a little boasting to Sonia when I reported to her later that I had got what I wanted from Forbes and Hart. *You got to know these Englishmen if you're to get what you want out of them. You got to be shrewd, ruthless, brazen, and they'll come around. Believe it or not, Sonia, each of them even gave me a firm, cordial shakehand when I entered the office. They didn't like the picketing and the demonstration, but it had frightened them, and mellowed them overnight. Now we got them on the hip.*

Both of them sat behind Forbes' big desk. I sat facing them. Hart pulled an ebony ashtray nearer to him and ground the end of the cigarette he was smoking in it. The action was like determinedly screwing down someone under ground. He looked up, smiling, and waved his big hand towards the artifacts of the chase which decorated the office. 'Tell me, Mr Chief Minister,' he said, 'don't you feel that you're on safari whenever you come into this office?'

I swivelled my neck round and glanced at the antlered heads, the spears, assagai, the enormous bow, the quiver with arrows, the skins. 'Quite right,' I said laughing. Forbes touched his polka dot bowtie, chuckled and said, 'Every West Indian politician is on safari these days, tracking down the British Government and the Colonial Office, shooting at them.'

'Poor game, I assure you, Mr Chief Minister,' said Hart, showing his handsome smile.

'We shall miss the animals, though, when they leave our forests,' I said.

'Then you will have to fall back on local pelt. Or perhaps you politicians will become fair game for your own people,' said Hart.

'And be dosed with their own medicine,' Forbes added.

'Ah-hah,' said Major Hart, smiling, as he held out a pack of Churchmans to me. I politely declined. Hart lit up, blew out smoke energetically and said, 'Well, now, this matter of your Chief of Police. I spent a long time at the Police Headquarters this morning. Not bad.'

'Glad to hear you say that,' I said happily.

'Yes. I think you have something there. Something you can build on.' He had his elbows on the desk, his hands held up, and he kept up a sort of stirring motion with his hands as he spoke. 'But tell me, Mr Chief Minister,' he continued, 'don't you think it odd that none of the men who were on duty in the guardroom could give account of a key which was certainly left in responsibility of the Police?'

'You're referring to the key of the Arrowroot Depot?'

'The Arrowroot Depot which *was*. Yes. Now, don't you think there is slackness somewhere in Police Headquarters?' The hitherto halcyon atmosphere had begun to get cloudy.

'Are you Scotland Yard?' I said.

'Never had the talent,' Hart laughed. 'Nor the brains.'

'I should not have thought that your visit here had anything to do with a missing key.'

'Well, you know, Mr Chief Minister, there are times when little things like that are worth looking into.'

'What are you trying to say? That whether or not the people of Hiroona have their wish for a native Chief of Police respected by the Colonial Office depends on whether we do or do not find the key of the Arrowroot Depot? That's what you mean, Major?'

'The appointment of a Chief of Police on your island, Mr Chief Minister, is a matter for the Colonial Office to decide. Decision in this matter is outside my province.'

'But the decision will be made in accordance with your recommendation. Isn't that so?'

'Recommendations can be like Cain's offering — rejected.'

'Well, in that case, let God beware,' I said.

Neither of us so much as smiled at this bit of repartee. Major Hart rose and extended his hand to me. 'Thank you, Mr Chief Minister,' he said. 'An interesting interview. What?'

I got up, shook his hand briefly and left. I knew then that Hart did not intend to recommend Robbins for police chief. I therefore decided to continue and intensify my efforts to force the appointment through propagandistic pressure.

I held mass meetings all over the island, night after night, belabouring the British Government, the Colonial Office, the Administrator and Major Levons Hart with the most uncomplimentary epithets my perfervid mind could conjure up. The expressions and the performance were always more or less the same in every township, every village.

I accused 'these heartless imperialistic bastards of hog-tying Hiroona and pushing us back to slavery. They pretend to give us self-determination, and at the same time the hypocritical pirates commandeer our senior posts, our best jobs, and fill them with their own white agents, so that they could be sure that the island will be under their white feet for all time, while we natives grovel, and take orders from them.' I would then roll my eyes to the heavens, lift up my trembling hands supplicatingly and demand, with tears in my voice, 'How long, O Lord, how long?'

I felt from the response I was receiving, that I had started a movement which was gaining power; and as its popularity increased, so did my confidence, my daring and my invectives.

I submitted a petition 'signed by fifteen thousand Hiroonians' to the Secretary of State for the Colonies. A few thousand of the 'signatories' were the result of creative research and literary collaboration between myself and Dave, in the privacy of the Aerie, over a few drinks. The petition did not mention Robbins by name — that would be tactless — but the hints in the text were so broad that the petition left little to conjecture as to whom 'the people' wanted. I handed the petition to Forbes, with the request that he forward it at once to the Right Honourable the Secretary of State for the Colonies. Then I sat back and waited, pleased in anticipation, confident of the successful outcome of this large and powerful petition.

One month passed; no word from London. Two months; only acknowledgement of receipt of the petition. Three months; still nothing.

'They must be waiting to see if Robbins would solve the mystery of the missing key,' said Dave.

Then one Saturday morning, the *Hiroona Weekly* came out with a we-are-reliably-informed editorial:

The British Government have demonstrated at last that it will not always be bullied by misguided, power-driven West Indian politicians who make their living by manipulating the masses and misrepresenting the people. For months now the Chief Minister of this island has been running to and fro on the island like a demented bumble bee, pretending to convince the people that the people are up against the British Government. While the economy of the island is suffering on account of lack of intelligence and drive on the part of our leaders, and laziness and insubordination which the leaders of the Government have succeeded in instilling in the workers; while the Arrowroot industry, like ancient Rome, is burning, our power-crazy, incompetent little Nero is consuming himself with concern as to who should be Chief of Police — a matter which is outside of his portfolio and jurisdiction as Chief Minister. Some of the less enlightened people of our community seem to think that colonial self-determination confers upon a political Head of State the right to run the country on the basis of patronage, favouritism and whim. This view and Mr Mole have just received a gentle, firm and clever rebuke from the Colonial Office. Mole's candidate for the post of Chief of Police is to be sent for training to a Police School in Britain, and the vacant post of Chief of Police is to be filled by a qualified West Indian from a neighbouring island. Now nobody could quarrel with the British Government for not appointing a West Indian to a post in a West Indian island. And even Mr Mole could have no just quarrel with the decision to provide training which, we hope, will improve the professional quality of his candidate.

'They are doing things behind our backs!' I shrieked to the villages and little towns. 'See! an ordinary newspaperman, a stooge of Forbes and the imperialists is well informed about what is happening in the Government, while your elected representatives are kept in ignorance. The Federation of the West Indies will change all this, though. It will make us into a nation and will give the parting kick in the arse to imposters like Forbes, Darcy and all the British imperialists who now interfere in our affairs and tread us underfoot.'

21

THE Federation of the West Indies did not come up to expectations however. The politicians in the islands did not trust Britain, but we didn't trust one another either. The islands were like the corpses in the coffins in Christ Church cemetery; so dead, they didn't know how to live together. So far, the islands had produced quite a spate of ordinary, pot-boiling politicians. But the statesman with the ability to weld together territories which tended to fly apart was yet to appear. The territories did not form a continent, they formed a higgledy-piggledy archipelago. So the break up of the Federation was partly Nature's fault. And we politicians did not help Nature.

The shaky alliance between the ten islands lasted only about four years and four months — January 3, 1958 to May 31, 1962. After two dropouts — Jamaica, then Trinidad — everything 'turn ole-mas'.

During the unquiet and questioning period which immediately settled on the remaining 'Little Eight' islands, I represented Hiroona on two occasions at Little Eight conferences in London, the object of these conferences being to forge a federation of the eight remaining islands out of the ruins of the federation of the ten. I made a profit of two thousand, seven hundred and twenty-three dollars and eighty-five cents out of these two conferences, and nine hundred and sixty-eight dollars on similar conferences in two of the eight islands. And before the ink had dried on the entry of these additional deposits in my bank book, Barbados made it clear that she — or rather he — would have none of any federation with the other seven islands. So Barbados, under Errol Barrow, the young barrister/economist Prime Minister, moved up to full independence; and the British Government, prodded by the United Nations Committee of Twenty-four, offered proposals to advance the constitutions of the other seven islands under an arrangement known as Associate Statehood with Britain, as a prelude to full independence. And of course Hiroona was to share in all this.

I exulted. I had already won the 1962 general elections. My position as Chief Minister had made rigging an easy matter — child's play. The population of the island had now increased to ninety-seven thousand. I could now sense full, unfettered power almost within my grasp. It was one thing to control Hiroona as Chief Minister, with a Colonial Office-appointed Administrator looking over my shoulder, breathing down my neck. It was quite another thing — a glorious another thing — to control the island as Premier, then as Prime Minister, with the power to decide who should be my civil servants, from the Governor down to the most obscure office boy. The only hurdle I had to vault was the next general election, the 1967 election which was two years away — ample time for me to prepare, not only for the election, but also my plans and policies for the control of the island under the new, forthcoming status of Associate Statehood.

I discussed these matters with Dave and Bryan in the Aerie one night. I sat on the couch, my glass of whiskey and a bottle of ginger-ale on a low table in front of me. Dave and Bryan occupied chairs at the corners of the desk, the glasses with their drinks formed rings on the desk top. 'So wait, nuh,' said Dave; 'this associated statehood business, what it means?'

'It means that each small island will be a sort of junior partner with Britain in running the affairs of the island. Britain will no longer dictate to us. The Colonial Office will no longer ride us. The designation "West Indian colonies" will be changed to "Caribbean Commonwealth" or "Commonwealth Caribbean". The Colonial Office will become the Commonwealth Office. The title Chief Minister will be changed to Premier. We will have complete control of our affairs, except for External matters and Defence — the two fields in which a foreign nation may be involved. The two will remain the responsibility of Britain until Hiroona gets her full independence.'

'And under the associated statehood arrangement, Hiroona will no longer be a colony,' added Bryan. 'It will be called a state.'

'It will still be a island, though?' said Dave.

'Well, probably,' said Bryan, laughing. l didn't relish the joke. I was too excited by the implications and prospects of Statehood. I said, 'This is a very serious thing, fellers, and we got to plan very carefully for it. We got to design a flag for the island.'

'I understand,' said Bryan, 'that Antigua, St. Kitts, Grenada, St. Lucia, Dominica and St. Vincent have organized a flag design competition, and each island appointed a special committee to decide on the best design.'

'Hiroona will not do it that way. No committee is going to decide for me. I will ask your girl friend, Anne, to make three or four designs. This should be easy for her because she is a good seamstress. She will submit the designs to me and I will decide which one is to be the flag of the island. I'll see that she is well paid for the job.'

'We have to have our own National Anthem, too, I hear,' said Dave. 'How you going about that?'

'Anne doesn't know a single note of music,' warned Bryan.

'I'll advertise, offering a prize for the best words and music.'

'Who are you going to appoint as Governor?' said Dave.

'Don't let us go too fast,' said Bryan. 'Remember we got to win the next general election before Statehood. Furthermore, you got to reckon on the probability that Statehood may not give you all the power you're expecting.'

'Nothing can stop me now,' I said. 'We won three elections already — 1952, 1957 and 1962. The next will be the crucial one, and I intend to be the first Premier in the history of the island. After all the good I've done for this island, we can't afford to let that illiterate stevedore, Pittance, and his stooges snatch the grandest prize. Christ, I'll see myself dead first. Even if we have to rig the 1967 elections, as we did the 1962 ones, we got to win. We just got to.'

'I agree with you every inch of the way,' said Dave. 'I am sorry we lost Robbins from the Police Force, though. He was a big help to our cause. He kept Pittance's party under control.'

'Yes,' I said to Dave, 'Robbins was very helpful.'

'Well, we've got to bring the new man in line.'

'Oh, he'll have to toe the line all right. I'm just giving him a chance to find his feet. He has been here long enough, however, to realize on which side his bread is buttered. I intend to tackle him soon.'

'I hear he is damn cocky but efficient,' said Dave. 'But in any case, our problem is the Hiroona National Party. They held a mass meeting at the Market Square the other night; and to everybody's surprise, Pittance announced that he had handed over the leadership of the party to Seymour Gilchrist, the man who was manager of the Arrowroot Depot.'

'Yes,' I said. 'I heard about the meeting. Pittance is a damn illiterate hypocrite. Gilchrist's position as a high official in Pittance's party only proves that Gilchrist, when he was a civil servant, was playing politics while he was employed by Government, and should have been dismissed. He resigned only after the fire.'

'Pittance may be illiterate,' said Bryan, 'but he's damn smarrrt. Politics in most of these small islands doesn't call for any education. It's more headwork than brainwork, more shrewdness than disciplined adherence to rules. The reasons Pittance gave forrr passing leadership to Gilchrist werre that he doesn't crave leadership for himself, and that Gilchrist is a younger man. Pittance always said that he was not interested in powerr, and that he only wanted to help as much as his limited education permitted. This humble, realistic and unselfish attitude is winning him and his party a hell of a lot of support.'

'He's a blasted hypocrite, a double-crossing scamp. After all I've done for that skunk.'

'But how can we stop him?' asked Dave.

'I have my plans. As soon as the island gets Statehood, I pass a law outlawing all political parties formed on the island after the year 1952.'

'Why can't we pass the law now, before the elections?' said Dave. 'That would rid us of all party competitors for the elections.'

Bryan laughed and said, 'Dave, man, you furrrgetting that the Queen has to approve every law made in the colonies, before the law can be passed. You think the Prime Minister of Britain — a democratic country — would advise the Queen to give Her assent to a law like that? Nary a chance.'

'That's right,' I agreed. 'But when we get Statehood, all the laws will be ours. The police will be ours. No interference from Britain, then. We will not only outlaw all opposing parties, we'll also postpone general elections indefinitely. After all, the PPP is ruling the island satisfactorily, what would be the need for elections? We'll introduce a Sedition Bill which will make it a serious offence to criticise the Government. This will muzzle vicious, irresponsible people like Paul Darcy. A few cattle prods in the hands of the police will keep unruly crowds and street demonstrators at bay. We will have to be firm. Very firm.'

'But suppose the people object actively to these harsh measures?' said Bryan.

'We declare a State of Emergency, signed by the Governor whose job will be to rubber stamp my orders — or resign if he don't. Under our State of Emergency, we would be able to detain, lock up or deport any nuisance or nuisance-monger who tries to obstruct the smooth running of the people's Government.'

'I agree with you, Jerry,' said Dave. 'A ruler must either rule or be ruled.'

'Well, you may be right,' said Bryan doubtfully, 'but you couldn't get away with that kind o' government in a country wherrre people are serious and alerrrt. That's a kind of madness.'

'As for madness,' I chuckled, 'there's nothing in the new constitution that disqualifies a Head of State for actual or suspected madness — or any other malady. So long as he can control it to a more or less reasonable degree.'

'And put a show of shrewdness on his political misdemeanours,' added Bryan, laughing. 'But, Chief,' he continued with a sudden return to seriousness, 'you talking about extra strong measurrres when the island gets Associated Statehood and full independence, but you'rrre not mentioning anything about improving the economy of the island to support independence.'

'Oh, that will come,' I said. 'There's Canada and there will still be Britain to help us, at least during the statehood period. We'll beg for loans wherever we can get them.'

'But independence is expensive, Chief. You got to support it with money, and sometimes arms. Canada is helping a hell of a lot, yes. Britain too. But you can't depend on them forever.'

'When I get the power into my hands to make plans for the improvement and development of the island, without interference from a meddling Colonial Office, you'll see how fast Hiroona will move. Meanwhile, we've got to keep down with a strong hand all factions which threaten to oppose good government.'

'That's the same excuse the imperialists and despots use, Chief. "Good Government". The nasty fact about imperialism is domination. Domination is domination, no matter by whom. The colour of tyranny is the colour of blood, and black tyranny is just as outrageous as white tyranny. Both are the same colour — the colour of blood.'

'You got it wrong, Bryan, man. The native leader must know better than the foreign imperialist what is necessary for the country, and how the people's goals are best achieved.'

'Let me get you fresh glasses, gentlemen,' said Bryan, with mock courtesy. He collected the glasses and went out with them to the bar. When he returned, I said, 'Bryan, man, let's forget politics for a while. Dave and I been planning something really big for you.'

'Such as?' he said, smiling sceptically.

'Well, you see, we got to prepare for the statehood celebrations. This means serious organising long ahead. I want you to be responsible for this. You will be provided with an office, a staff and a committee of advisers to assist you. You will have to travel a lot between the islands and in Canada, United States, Puerto Rico, and certain other countries, advertising the island's new status, interviewing important people to be invited to our statehood celebrations, and returning here with ideas for your staff and committee to implement. All expenses paid by the Government.'

'Salary?' said Bryan.

'Name it,' I said.

Bryan took a mouthful of his rum and coke, replaced his glass on the desk, smiled broadly and said, 'You know, Anne and I plan to get married in about a year or so.'

'Well, you're a damn lucky man both ways; you're lucky to get a girl like Anne — explosive black beauty, and brains — for a wife, and you're lucky in that your financial and official positions in Hiroona will be solid and secure forever.'

'Yeah,' said Bryan, scratching his head briskly. 'But no Bajan likes to live out o' Ba-biadus longer than he can help. You find Bajans all overrr the worrrl', but they always want to go back home sometime. We got the best flying fish and corn coo-coo in the worrrl'. We'rrre the oldest colony, barring St. Kitts, which doesn't count for much. We got Batsheba and Bath and Fresh Waterr, Batch Rock, Silver Sands and Hastings. We got one of the best hospitals in the worrrl'. We got free primary and secondary education. We got the only West Indian newspaper that deals with the Caribbean region as a whole. And we'rrre the only place in the worrrl' that can boast of a cemetery where dead people can fight if they feel like it. Free country. Anne is a good dressmaker and a trained Nurse. I am a damn good motor mechanic when I have a mind to it. As you know, my father died last June. Mother is eighty; she needs someone to look after her.'

'So what the hell you telling us now?' said Dave. 'You mean you leaving us and going back to Barbados?'

'Mmm-hmm,' said Bryan, still smiling.

'Jesus Christ! Bryan, man!' said Dave, as if he was about to burst into tears. 'After all these years?'

'Mmm-hmm,' said Bryan, as he drained his glass.

22

M A died. Sonia and I knew that she was gradually sinking. Her gift of a basket of fresh fruits and vegetables and fish had long become infrequent and then stopped altogether. So also her letters with their long-looped, arthritic characters. A few months before she died, Sonia and I visited her. Sonia insisted on returning for a week to look after the old lady, in spite of the fact that Ma did not lack affectionate attention from a number of the Chateaubelair village people. Ma was very fond of her daughter-in-law, and so was Sonia of her; so I thought it a good idea to let Sonia go and stay with her for the few days.

When Sonia returned to Kingsland, I noticed that her indifference to public life — quite evident before — had deepened. For years previously, she had had intermittent periods of tiredness, with a sort of listlessness and pallor. And after her return from Chateaubelair she often expressed the wish for 'a quiet life, away from all dis palitics and confusion'. Three weeks after she returned from looking after Ma, we motored back to Chateaubelair for Ma's funeral. I drove the twenty odd miles. Sonia sat beside me in the car. We passed village after village of crude huts, small neat cottages, little mud houses with the wattle sticks showing in places where the mud had fallen away. Pot bellied, half naked children played in yards or by the roadside. Occasionally, the car swerved to near-miss a heedless player, running and shrieking joyfully to a playmate. Ox carts piled with sugar cane blocked the narrow dirt roads now and again, causing me to stop the car and wait while the driver of the oxen, with a long stick upraised and many a 'Whoa, Jasper! Back dere now, Lucifer! Steady dere, Duke! Up now Kingsley! Waa-yoo! Wup!' eased the oxen and the huge, crate-like cart to the side of the road to make way for the car.

'De place is exactly the same as when we came to power fourteen years ago,' said Sonia. 'No improvement. And people don't cultivate arrowroot any more, so de villages look poorer.'

'That's because I had to spend most of my time fighting Forbes, Pittance, the Colonial Office and their stooges here. And that is the reason why I yearn for Associate Statehood and Independence, when I shall have full power to sweep away all opposition and all that stands in the way of progress.'

'Where will you get de money from to run de island when Britain move out?'

'Sonia, you forgetting your politics. Under Associate Statehood, Britain will not move out, she will only draw aside so that we can rule the island as we see fit. We will still get grant-in-aid and other grants from Britain. Bigger grants. And we will be able to borrow money from Canada and the United States.'

'And suppose Britain refuse to give you financial help when you get full independence?'

'Then the United Nations will cry shame on Britain. And I will pretend that I propose to seek aid from Cuba.'

'You think dat will take skin off Britain nose? You think Britain so stupid as to give us money to spen' as we like, and power to do as we like, and no questions ask?'

'That's exactly the position, Sonia. This is the day of the common man, the small, under-developed country. The United Nations and world opinion are on our side. Tom, Dick and Harry can go to the United Nations nowadays to put their case. This is our chance. Can't you see it so?'

'No. How come people have to go to school to learn a trade, or to learn doctor or lawyer or ingineer or even office secretary work or cooking, but anybody at all can just get up an' run a country widdout studying a single thing about Government?'

'Because Government is the will of the people, not the will of schooling. It was Robert Louis Stevenson who said, "Politics is the only profession for which no preparation is thought necessary". And it is said that Lenin, not long before he died, declared, "Even a cook can rule a state".'

'Well, if it is the will of the people, why you keep saying you will crush all opposition? De opposition ain't de will of de people, too?'

'When we say the people, we mean the Government.'

'And when you say de Government you mean Jerry Mole? Look, Jerry, I don't understand dis politics. Why can't we get out of it now? We got enough money to last till we feeble. We got three houses in town and one in de country. All rented. We can never starve again in dis world. I am tired and fed up wid all dis mass meetings, an' cussing people, an' ministry work, an' your late nights, an' planning to lock up people, an' secret meetings in Fairfield House.' She sighed, and then frowned.

I said, 'I'm listening.'

'Look, Jerry, I can't honestly say Ah do a solid day's work for years now, because I can never understand office work. Ah can't write minutes in files good, an' people is talking an' laughing about it. I have some pride, and so Ah'm sick an' tired of de whole business. Ah tried it fo' fourteen years, just to please you; but Ah was not trained nor made for these high and stupid things.'

I drew the car to the side of the road and stopped to make way for a donkey and rider, and in order to drive home my reply to Sonia.

'Sonia, darling, all these mass meetings and late nights and hard work and stress which you complain about are the price we pay for the high position we now occupy, the wealth we now enjoy and the power we now wield. If you want to give up all this, you may do so. As for me, I'll see myself a corpse before I relinquish so much as a finger-hold on the power which I now enjoy. In fact, my star has just begun to rise. Its zenith and mine is full independence in Hiroona. Now you're telling me to give up all this. And do what? You say you have some pride. I know that too well. But I have pride, too, you know; and you can't expect me to let go power and go back to being a nonentity. Do you want me to go back to school-teaching, or policing, or insurance clerking, or to Aruba? I have no proper training in any field except politics. I can't do anything else. And why the devil should I want to do anything else? Tell me.'

'You said just now that I can give it up if I want to?'

'Yes; but only if you want to admit that you have no ambition — no desire to rise.'

'O.K. I admit.'

'Don't be a damn fool, Sonia.'

The broad grin which appeared on my wife's face was a thing I had not seen there in years. It transformed Sonia's features, imparting a hint of her former healthy, youthful colour, brightening her like a light. I was to learn, later that afternoon, that I had misunderstood the reason for this sudden appearance of *joie de vivre* in Sonia; but just now I was very pleased to see it, as I thought that I had effectively rebuked her wish to withdraw from public life. Beaming in unison with Sonia's new mood, I cheerfully shoved the gear stick of the car in low, and moved off again with a sprightly thrust.

From then until we reached Chateaubelair thirty minutes after, Sonia's mood was more pleasant than usual, though a bit subdued, and once or twice I noticed a sort of pensive, 'penny-for-your-thoughts' attitude.

We drove past Shapiro Estate, of which the village of Chateaubelair is a part; and as we entered the village, signs of mourning became evident — the windows of the little houses on both sides of the single, long, wide dirt road which ran from the top of the village to the beach were all shut — so also were the doors of 'Selton Frankly — Grocer Candy and Butcher Sold

Here'. 'Lucky Edwards — Simstress of Fashions' and 'Conrade Adams — Tailor, Cutter and Fitter of Note'. The black flag of the 'Provident Benefit Society' flapped at half mast on its pole in front of the lodge, the name of the society showing in large white cloth letters stitched on the flag.

Ma's neat little cottage was filled with people. Mourners overflowed the yard into those of the adjoining neighbours. All the women were in white. They wore shoes, too, and funny little black hats. The men wore heavy, shiny black suits which needed pressing. A large number of children stood around, too, their eyes wide with wonder and fright at the mystery of death. Some of them — the braver ones — went into the house with the adults, 'to say farewell', and came out again to stand and wait.

I had parked my car in the road, and as Sonia and I entered the yard the crowd made way for us. Several of the women embraced Sonia, and wept on her shoulder. Sonia returned the embrace briefly, patted their backs and moved on. I shook hands with some of the men. In the centre of the small living room, the mahogany coffin rested on two chairs; and, amongst folds of mauve and white drapery, Ma lay, snugly wrapped in the big sleep. Sonia and I stood side by side, looking down on Ma.

Suddenly, Sonia moved away very quickly and hurried into the bedroom, her handkerchief pressed against her face. My eyes moistened heavily, and as I bent and kissed my Mother's cold cheek, a tear from me fell on one of her closed eyes. I did not wipe it away, I left it there as a sort of souvenir of sorrow.

The heavy, wettish-sweet fragrance of the wreaths of flowers which lay in piles on tables and chairs in the room was as dolefully massive as the silence which pervaded the cottage and the yards.

Presently, two men in khaki trousers and short-sleeved white shirts gently pushed their way into the house. Each carried a large screw-driver. They stood looking at me, waiting. I nodded, and the men brought the lid of the coffin, which was propped in a corner, and fitted it gently on the coffin and pressed home the screws.

We lifted the coffin — five men and myself — by the silverplated handles, bore it to the Methodist Church up the street and laid it on the two stools in the centre aisle. The harmonium droned, the choir and overcrowded church sang and the pastor intoned: 'Now is Christ risen from the dead and become the first fruits of them that slept. For since by man came death, by man came also the resurrection of the dead. For as in Adam all die, even so in Christ shall all be made alive . . .' I had heard this same scripture read on two or three similar occasions before. I didn't understand or believe a word of it, but I liked the smoothness and cadence of the sentences. And although in a way I was a little disappointed when the pastor ended this beautiful symphony of words and launched into his funeral oration, I felt proud, nevertheless, as I listened to his testimony of the life of my mother in the village.

At the end of the service, we bore Ma's body from the church to the cemetery, a distance of about a mile and a half. We rested five times on the way, placing the coffin on two chairs carried for that purpose. The pastor, leading the cortege, stood and waited each time we rested; the long procession halted in its tracks. At the cemetery, after the pastor had read his prayers, and the diggers began to fill the grave, then began also the piercing high-pitched singing, the keening, the ululations and shrieks of the women. Men hid their faces with their hands, as sobs shook their shoulders. I was deeply touched as I realized how high and general was the esteem in which Ma was held in Chateaubelair.

Sonia stood, tearfully watching, as the two men in their working clothes filled the grave with earth. She was supported on either side by a woman, one with an arm around her shoulder, the other with an arm around her waist. I knew that Sonia was always very much liked by the people of the Chateaubelair district, and I had evidence aplenty that afternoon. I was glad about this, for political reasons. Over the past years, Sonia had lost touch with her constituents in Central Leeward, on account of her frequent illnesses, her indispositions and her obvious dislike for the political life. As I observed the evidence of her popularity in Chateaubelair that afternoon, it occurred to me that it might be a good idea and a safer seat if, at the next election, I entered her for the North Leeward constituency, which included the Chateaubelair district, instead of putting her up for Central Leeward again. The change should please her, too, and help to restore her interest in politics.

I tried to discuss this idea with Sonia when we returned to Ma's cottage after the funeral. She had put on one of Ma's aprons, gone out into the kitchen in the yard and made a large cup of 'cocoa tea'. She brought the steaming chocolate liquid into the house, poured out two tea cups of it and set them on a small round table. As we sat and sipped, I commented briefly on the 'lovely funeral Ma got', and went on to marvel at the popularity which Sonia seemed to enjoy in the district.

'I always liked Chateaubelair,' said Sonia. 'Maybe because the people was so friendly to Ma.'

'Well, don't you think it would be a good idea if you changed your constituency next election? Run for North Leeward instead of for Central Leeward?'

Sonia put down her cup and gazed at me for a moment. 'Christ! Jerry,' she said, 'you gone back on dat again? You can't think of nuthin else but election an' palitics? You tell me already dat Ah can quit it, now you telling me 'bout running fo' North Leeward.'

'When did I agree for you to quit office?'

'Just dis afternoon when we coming up here to de funeral, you said I could quit if I want to admit I ain't have no ambition. And I admitted. Remember?'

I now understood the reason why her spirits had suddenly brightened so much, after she had said, 'I admit', during our argument in the car.

'I meant nothing of the sort,' I said hotly.

'Jerry,' she said, obviously working up to a rage, 'whatever you meant is your damn business. Ah ain't going back to Kingsland, nor to no ministry job. I am stopping right here in dis house. Ma left it for me, as you know, and Ah want to live in it in peace. Look at me, Jerry. I am only forty odd years old, but when Ah look in de mirror Ah see eighty odd. And Ah feel like ninety odd. Look at my head — full o' gray hairs before me time. What got me so? Palitics, an' union, an' ministry, an' strife, an' stupidness, an' worries.'

Barely able to control herself, she stood up, trembling as she continued. Placing the palms of both hands on the table, she leaned over towards me as she poured out the thoughts which apparently had been choking her health over the past few years.

'Nearly all de foundation members who started de union with us, and who Ah used to talk to and get little bits of comradely advice an' help from, they all join wid Pittance and Naomi Sampson in dere own union and in dere Hiroona National Party. We lost Ben Davis who used to call you Bass. We lost James Carter. We lost Henry Vanterpool an' all de ole stevedore members. They didn't even pay us de respeck of resigning from de union. Dey just stop paying dues. Stop coming to meetings. Since you get mix up in dis high political life, day go day come Ah ain't see you. You either in de country stirring up labourers, or you in yo' office making deals wid moneymen. At night, you gone to Dave Potter an' Bryan to talk palitics an' make deals. When we eating breakfast at mornin's, you don't hardly saying anything to me, you just eating and studying palitics an' deals. You ain't even have time to realise dat you aging. Look how yo' face ole. If you wasn't dyeing yo' hair to hide yo' age you woulda been able to see de truth each time you look in de mirror. You thinking about de big money you making an' de power you have. I thinking about de solid ole friends we losing becarse you feel you too big an' important to take advice from dem. And even from me. And de people you takin' advice from advisin' you wrong. You could . . . .'

'Just a minute,' I shouted, putting up my hand.

'Don't stop me now,' Sonia shouted back. 'Listen fo' once.' There was sweat around her mouth and on her forehead. Her cheeks shone with moisture. I got up and shut the three windows in the room, to prevent the quarrel from getting out. I closed the door to prevent sympathizing mourners from coming in 'to offer a word of prayer'. Sonia dropped her voice to a low incisive tone.

'Listen, Jerry. Listen. You coulda have Pittance who got a lot of commonsense although he ain't got much education. You lost him. You coulda got dat intelligent boy P.C. 43 Cunningham. You lost him. Seymour Gilchrist is a intelligent man wid good education. Pittance got him, too. Seems like you don't like to work wid really intelligent people. You only like people you can use — like dat man Robbins, who you arranged wid to burn down de arrowroot depot.'

O Christ! My heart thumped. My jaw dropped. My eyebrows reached up. 'How the hell can you say a thing like that, Sonia? Who told you I arranged with Robbins to . . . .'

'I am your wife, Jerry, and Ah ain't stupid. I study you. I know you. When you put a big argument to me — and to Mister Forbes — against bringing Scotland Yard to look into de fire, although it would not of cost de Gover'ment one cent, I was suspicious. When Ah thought back and remember how you had Robbins and dat vagabond Crab Soup in yo' office downstairs at Fairfield House for hours an' hours at night, Ah realize dat somet'ing was afoot, becarse you is not de kind of man to keep close company wid people like Crab Soup, or even wid Robbins, except you planning to use dem. Crab Soup was sacked from de depot, and didn't like it. You yourself boasted to me dat you was going to show de depot who is boss, because they was supporting Pittance. And when Ah heard dat nobody know how de depot key disappear from de police station, Ah put two an' two togeddar and four come out. Jerry, if palitics means doing things like dat, you an' palitics can go to hell for my part. Me mind is made up.'

The room was now too hot; the built-up atmosphere in it had become unbearably uncomfortable. I got up and opened the windows and door. Wordlessly, I returned to my seat at the table. Sonia went and stood at one of the windows, looking out, her back to me. When I got back my voice, I said, very softly, 'How do you intend to make a living from now on?' Sonia turned around and answered me. 'I will make out. Don't worry about me. Ah have me own house now. Ah have one or two hundred dollars Ah was able to save fo' meself. Ma's death-benefit money from de Provident Benefit Society is mine in de will Ma left. You yourself read de will after de Methodist Minister write it and Ma send it for you to see. Ah have all me clothes here already. Ah brought dem here when Ah came to look after Ma before she died. I have all I need; an' it don't cost much to live in Chat'belair. I will make out all right.'

'Who will do your work in the ministry for the remaining months before the next election?'

'Dat is fo' you to decide.'

I got up, walked out of the house in a daze and went and sat in my car. After a few minutes, I started the engine, swung the car round and headed for Kingsland.

23

Sonia's desertion shocked me deeply; but after wrestling mentally with this embarrassing situation for several lonely days and sleepless nights, I decided to forget it. It would be a waste of time to try to lure her back with sweet promises. I still loved her, nevertheless, and I knew that her affection for me was not dead. I knew also that nothing would induce her to return to politics, or to Fairfield House in a hurry. However, I hoped that she would return to my bed and board as a proud and subdued wife when I had made myself the undisputed lord and master of a constitutionally advanced Hiroona — which I was determined to do.

I was not worried over her possession of the secret about the destruction of the Arrowroot Depot. I knew that she would keep her mouth shut on the matter. However, I felt deeply ashamed that she knew about it; and as she had left me in no doubt as to her contempt for me on that account, I considered it prudent to leave her completely alone until she had come to her senses. I could explain her resignation to the Government and the public as being due to ill health. Her having taken up residence in Chateaubelair would be due to 'medical advice'. I might even refrain from mentioning her resignation at all.

So I put Sonia's withdrawal behind me, and turned my attention to the threat which Pittance's growing popularity presented. The wily fellow had managed to rope in under his political banner, not only people from the labouring class, the field workers, the wharf rats, the domestic servants, but also a few recruits from the professions, from the middle class and from the youth of the island. He had even secured the active support of a young economist who had returned to the island a graduate, after a three-year scholarship at the University of the West Indies. Thus, Pittance demonstrated that he had grasped the fact that the day of the uncultivated, half-literate leader in West Indian politics was dying. A new day was upon us. The times were now demanding from West Indian politicians much more than the old demagoguery, professed love of the 'poor man', shrewdness, patronage, abuse of opponents and verbal lambasting of the Colonial Office. No longer were the people satisfied with leaders who could only lead the ignorant; leaders who lacked understanding of the mechanics of government in relation to the rest of the changing world.

Pittance had sensed the new drift, and had adjusted to it. That was the reason why he had smoothly transferred the leadership of his party to Gilchrist.

I was not unaware of the approach of this revolution, but in my complacency over the firm grip which I thought I had on the masses, I believed that I could meet the situation effectively with mere weight of numbers, without any regard for the quality of the numbers. I viewed Pittance as a hypocrite for handing over leadership to Gilchrist, and a fool for admitting into his party people with better schooling than himself.

The British Government's new policy of less and less interference in the island's affairs proved to be, for me, a good thing as well as an embarrassment. It was a good thing in that it conferred power and prestige on me, but at the same time it deprived me of someone to blame heatedly for the island's misfortunes.

In the new Chief of Police, Desmond Hazelwood, I encountered a formidable problem. Colonel Desmond Hazelwood was sent to Hiroona from Barbados by the British Government in a move that was pure smooth administrative trickery, to take the place of the man I had supported for the post.

Hazelwood was younger than Robbins, tall, slim, smooth of skin, very black, a lean, intelligent face. He looked like a black Adonis in uniform. Since his assumption of office in Hiroona, I had met him at one or two cocktail parties at Government House. On these occasions, I had conversed with him about his career and about matters of general interest, and I noticed that his manner was very respectful, very polite, but with a touch of a kind of professional hauteur which made it awkward for me to get through to him in the personal, intimate way I had established with Robbins. He had stiffened, clicked his heels when I approached him, and brought up his right hand smartly in the salute to which I was entitled. He had remained at ramrod attention as I spoke with him; and when I smiled affably and said, 'Oh relax, Colonel; you're among friends,' he smiled in return and said, 'Occupational habit, sirrr,' and remained at attention. His attitude disconcerted me somewhat, more so because I would need his confidence and assistance later in the implementation of certain plans which Dave and I had made for rigging the election to ensure victory for the PPP.

After my exploratory conversations with Hazelwood, I had told Dave that I was far from being certain that we would get the necessary support from the young police chief. Dave was a little more hopeful, however, and we had decided that Dave would arrange a small stag party at his home, invite Hazelwood to it and thus create an appropriate opportunity for us to work on him in an atmosphere of conviviality, and try to bring him round. But before Dave could arrange his stag party, rumour spread that Pittance's party, the Hiroona National Party, had been granted registration and was planning a candle light procession through the streets of Kingsland, in celebration of this achievement.

I summoned Hazelwood to my office. When my Principal Assistant Secretary showed him in, shut the door and left, Hazelwood halted two or three paces in front of my desk, came to attention, saluted crisply, focused his gaze on the point just beyond my left ear and said, 'Chief of Hiroona Royal Police reporting as requested. Sirrr.'

'For God's sake, man, sit down,' I said. He hesitated, lifted his chin slightly and said, 'Sirrr.' Then he sat on the chair I indicated, removing his cap at the same time.

'Since your arrival in Hiroona, Colonel, I've been thinking of asking you in for a private little chat. I've not done this before now because I've been very busy.'

'Sirrr.'

'Of course, as an experienced and brilliant police officer, you would appreciate that I cannot run this island without your active assistance. You and I are therefore partners in the business of leadership, and as partners we must co-operate, for we share responsibilities. We must work together, for we are up against similar difficulties — the difficulties inherent in the preservation of order. And I want to assure you that you have access to me at any time, day or night.'

'Sirrr.'

'I have plans for the enlargement of your police force — numerically, technically and otherwise.'

'Thank you, Sirrr.'

'But there are certain forces on the island which have been blocking progress for some time now. These are people without any political experience whatsoever, who maliciously mislead the electorate in their attempt to upset established order. I need your help in restraining these people, for the maintenance of order and for the good, the welfare and the progress of Hiroona.'

'Sirrr.'

'I am thinking now of the upstarts who comprise the so-called Hiroona National Party. Their aim is to break down what has been built up over the years. Their leader, Seymour Gilchrist, has still to answer some embarrassing questions which my Government proposes to ask him in due course, about the destruction of the Arrowroot Depot of which he was manager. He knew that he was going to leave the job, so he probably arranged for the total destruction of records and other evidence which would have brought his dishonest practices to light.'

'Sirrr.'

'Those are the reasons why I am sorry that you did not consult me before granting registration to the HNP. Of course, you, being a comparative stranger in Hiroona, couldn't know what was involved. I don't blame you at all; but I should be glad if, in future, you consult me in matters like this, before you finally decide.'

'I would most certainly have consulted you, Sirrr, if such a step was requirrred by the law. The procedurrre is that when an application for registration of a political parrrty is made to the Chief of Police in writing, the Chief of Police, after due and impartial investigation, recommends to the Administrator. If the recommendation is favourable, and the Administrator approve, he instructs the Court Registrar to fill and submit the necessary registration paperrrs to him for the Administrator's signature. So I only recommend. I cannot approve. And I do not grant registration, Sirrr.'

'O.K., O.K., I know all that, and I don't blame you. As a matter of fact, you impress me quite a lot. I have been observing you since you took over here, and there's no doubt that you're doing a fine job.'

'Thank you, sirr.'

'Now, one other matter. I hear that HNP are planning a candle-light parade in Kingsland. Have they applied to you for permission to use the streets, and for the usual police protection?'

'Yes, Sirrr:'

'Have you replied yet?'

'Yes, Sirrr.'

'Favourably?'

'Yes, Sirrr.'

'How long ago?'

'A week gone, Sirr.'

'I want you to cancel the permission.'

'On what grounds, Sirrr?'

'That the same date was previously requested by another party for a similar parade, and that through an oversight you had confused the dates. If you do this, I will give you all the protection and backing you need if there are any questions. And you certainly won't regret having done this little favour for your Government.'

'I am only a policeman, Sirrr, trained along old-fashioned lines — duty, and honour and that sorrrt of thing. I wouldn't know how to deal with the kind of situation you'rrre proposing, Sirrr. High and important politicians may be able to afford to do that sorrrt of thing, but senior police officers are not supposed to be political, Sirr.'

'Aren't you jeopardising your own interests by being a bit finical over a simple matter?'

'Seems so, Sirrr.'

'You have a family?'

'Wife and six children, Sirrr.'

'And is this the thoughtless way you look after them?'

'Yes, Sirrr. They would think me contemptible if I looked after them in any other way.'

You smug, whippersnapper son of a bitch. I'll fix you and your flippin' family. By God I will!

I got up, extended my hand and said, 'Thank you, Colonel. You are dependable. You've passed your test with credit. Now keep up the good work.'

He got up, shook my hand briefly, clicked his heels, saluted and went out.

Later that day, I dropped in at Dave's. 'Don't bother with the stag party,' I said. 'Would be a waste of time and money. That man Hazelwood is the most conceited ass I've ever come across. *Sirrr! Sirrr! Sirrr!* As soon as we get Associate Statehood I'll throw him out. There'll then be no British Government to stop me. You can't allow anyone to draw taxpayers' money as salary if he is not prepared to co-operate with the Government in power. Sirrr! Sirrr! Sirrr! The abominable hypocrite.'

'So what about our other plans?' said Dave.

'You mean for rigging the election?'

'Eh–heh.'

'We will have to go ahead without him. I've thought out some other ways. We'll discuss them tonight when I come back from my meeting in the Sugar Belt. Fix some sandwiches for me and leave them in the Aerie in case you going out.'

'I'll be here when you get back,' said Dave.

24

PITTANCE dealt me the blow I was expecting. He gave out through Gilchrist that the HNP proposed to hold a mass meeting in the Sugar Belt from which he intended to enter a candidate for the next election, and announced the date of his proposed meeting.

I collected two carloads of hecklers and strongarm chaps in Kingsland, filled them with liquor and transported them to the Sugar Belt on the night of the meeting. They were to give as much trouble as possible during the meeting, and finally break it up.

We drove into the village as a crowd was assembling for the meeting. I noticed at once that there was something unfamiliar about a certain section of the village. I stopped my car and got out to have a closer look. Then my eyes popped, my heart thump-thumped and my mouth opened as I gazed unbelievingly on a new two-room sized, pitchpine cottage standing on a simple but firm foundation of plastered concrete blocks on the spot where, only two days before, I had seen the collapsing hovel that used to be Penny Farthing's house.

Before I came out of the daze, I hurried back to my car and drove to Joey Caines' shop. He had just closed it, and was going home for a bite, he said, before returning to listen to Pittance's meeting.

'Joey, what the hell is happening? Who put that pitchpine cottage on Penny Farthing's place?'

'My dear sah, late yesterday afternoon, Pittance and Gilchrist bring up a truckload of cement blocks, some ready-mixed cement and a mason from Kingsland. They collected nearly all the men in the village to help break down Penny Farthing ole house and lay de blocks and plaster them with cement. They work nearly all night making the foundation. The women in de village bring their kerosene lanterns and they make hot cocoa tea for de men. By this morning de foundation was finish.'

'What the hell is this! And when did they build the cottage?'

'They didn't build it. They re-assemble it this morning. Pittance an' Gilchrist had it built in Kingsland and they brought up the parts early this morning, and people in de village help them put the parts together. Some of de men in de village didn't even bother to go to work today, till they finish putting up de house; Chief, dat man Pittance? He smart. He smart fo' true. He no ordinary man.'

'But why didn't you get in touch with me and let me know what was happening? Surely you could have hired a passing taxi and sent Beamish or Sonny Benn in it to tell me what was going on. Why didn't you?'

'Chief, it happen too fast. Everybody was mesmerised. Pittance and Gilchrist took everybody by surprise. It was a hell of a move, I tell you, Chief. A hell of a move.'

I was still in a daze when I drew up my car by the side of the road and sat in it listening to Pittance, Gilchrist and their candidate for the Sugar Belt. I stayed to listen only because I was fascinated by the circumstances — fascinated like one unable to move away from a horror that is about to strike or engulf one.

There was no opening 'ode', no Red Flag, no Chairman priming the meeting with coarse jokes at the expense of detractors. There was just Joe Pittance talking slowly, quietly into a microphone. The young man who was formerly P.C. 43 Cunningham was standing just behind Pittance. Gilchrist stood on Joe's right. A youth — he hardly looked twenty-one — stood on Pittance's left. I recognised the youth as John Fergus, the young barrister-at-law who had only a few months ago returned from training in England and had started to practise law in Kingsland. Fergus wore no jacket, no tie, and the sleeves of his soiled, open neck white shirt were rolled well up above his elbows. From where I sat I could see the hired hecklers and musclemen I had brought from Kingsland standing together in a group near their taxis, waiting to move into action.

'Friends,' said Joe Pittance, 'the Hiroona National Party is not a party of words. It is a party of action. You can see dat for yourselves. What we have done for Penny Farthing we will do for you — and more. What we promise, we do. What others promise and don't do, we do. What others should do, but left undone, we will do, for de good of de people an' for de good of Hiroona.'

The place rang with applause. Pittance held up his hand and said, 'I want to ask you two questions now. Do you trust de HNP?'

'Yeahse! Yeahse!' they shouted and clapped.

'You goin' to support de HNP and vote for our candidate Mr John Fergus, standing on my left here?'

'Yeahse! Yeahse!'

'I believe you. Thank you. That's all from me at present.'

My group of iconoclasts still stood waiting. They, like myself, expected Pittance or one of his platform associates to refer disparagingly to me or the PPP. They would then move in with disorder. They waited.

Gilchrist moved to the microphone and said, 'Good evening. As you know, I and Joe here, and Vin Cunningham and John Fergus and a good many of you have been working in this village all night and nearly all today. So we are all tired. You don't need a lot of words. Action speaks much better English than any of us on this platform can. But you know John Fergus, a young lawyer who is capable of promoting your interest in the Government and defending your rights in the courts. You have seen that he can use chisel, hammer, saw and trowel — expertly — and this has surprised you. Those of you who didn't know him, got to know him last night and today under very appropriate circumstances. He stands here before you, still in the working clothes you saw him busy in last night and up to a few hours ago.' Gilchrist stopped to give way to the shouting and applause. Then, like Pittance, he put two or three leading questions to the crowd. The answers were pledges of support for the HNP and the new candidate.

Fergus need not have said a word, but for the fact that the occasion required a maiden speech from him. Pittance and Gilchrist hadn't really said very much but they in fact had said a great deal. Fergus followed their pattern.

'Glad to meet you, ladies and gentlemen. I suppose you all thought I was only a lawyer. Well you know now that I can be a house builder as well.' The laughter was loud, long and hearty. Fergus continued, 'And when your votes put me and the HNP in the Government, we will see to it that you live in even better houses than the one you and we built for Penny Farthing today.'

After the uproarious applause and shouting, Fergus finished, 'And we will not only build you nice homes, we will also build for you a nice new Hiroona and a richer Sugar Belt, with you sharing in the prosperity. In the old days you chose as your leader a man who is good at talking, not *doing*; that is why the island is now in such an eloquent mess. Hiroona has not got anywhere, under a Ministry of "Talk", selfishness and corruption. This is why you must now demand a Ministry of "Works", true dedication and honesty. What we have begun here today we will continue, under God, Joe Pittance and Seymour Gilchrist. And just as you have helped us bring happiness and a better life to a poor boy, so we will look to you to help us bring happiness to yourselves and to this lovely island of ours. Thank you.'

Pittance then approached the microphone to say, 'And now friends, go quietly home and to bed. We's tired after a whole night and a good day's work; but we are happy. Good night.'

But they didn't go home and to bed. They lingered to shout 'Good night, Joe,' to express congratulatory wonder at the 'mighty work Pittance and de HNP do fo' Penny,' and to shake hands with 'the platform'.

The front of my car faced the direction of Kingsland. I was thankful for that fact. If I had to turn the car around I would have lost time in getting away.

I was in trouble and I knew it, but I refused to accept the fact. I was determined to rule Hiroona as its first Premier and later as its first Prime Minister. I had carefully made plans for the governance of the island, and I intended to hold on to power, or die in the effort. I decided to overhaul and improve my plans for rigging the elections, and to this I turned my attention with intensity. I was assisted by Dave Potter who had been spending thousands of dollars in bribes and deals, to secure victory for the PPP. Our plans for the rigging depended on my having, as Chief Minister, a directing hand in the arrangements for the elections. I had enjoyed this advantage heretofore, and I intended to exploit it to the full this time. I had heard of a place in Africa or somewhere, where the Government had ballots looking like the statutory ones secretly printed and distributed to some of their supporters, who would mark them as required, and drop them in the ballot boxes when they went to vote on election day. Dave was willing to pay for having these counterfeit ballot papers secretly printed, but I felt that the island was too small to contain the secrecy of such a move. I had several other tricks, however, and so my hopes should still have been high.

But I was in trouble, and, what was probably worse, I was terribly lonely. Sonia had left me. The house was too big, too empty. The maid, Lynda, who had looked after me and Sonia, had left for Canada, under the Domestic Servants Immigration Scheme. I had hired an old woman to cook for me and keep the house clean. She was a creaking, rheumatic old grumbler. I hardly spoke to her. None of my Ministers was congenial company for me. Dave was a dear and useful friend, but I didn't find him particularly stimulating. George Reid had long ago turned his back on me. I had not even seen him within hailing distance since the day I accepted his thousand pound bet. Bryan had married quietly and returned to 'Ba-biadus' with his Anne. Inspector Robbins, my old stout supporter, had, after completing his training in Britain some ten years ago, been transferred to a neighbouring West Indian island, still as Inspector. He never did reach the top. He retired in due course, and soon afterwards died of a heart attack — or a broken heart. Our ancient associate in crime — Peter Garrick, alias Crab Soup — had also retired from his job as watchman at the Botanical Gardens, and was asleep with his fathers. There was still Victor Banks, but my relationship with Victor was cordial, but not close.

To ease my loneliness, I could, indeed, have had women, or at least taken a mistress from the number who are always willing to exploit with their bodies the follies of the powerful or the rich, but I had no taste for that kind of trading. Maybe I was too mean to submit to this type of flattery, or too busy and too obsessed with my dream of complete political control, to spend any time on thoughts of sex or to seek companionship of a woman. Of course, I loved Sonia sexually very much. But I did not attribute my indifference to other women to this. Perhaps a man could love his wife very much and still enjoy an occasional tumble downstreet. The fact of the matter was that I just didn't give a damn about anything that didn't have prominence, power and gold in it, or about anybody who was not Sonia.

But I was lonely, and in trouble. In the throes of anxiety, on the edge of despair, I was driven to imitate King Saul and seek assistance from a 'witch at Endor'.

25

I found my witch in Parkinson's Village, a remote and dreary little settlement on the lower slopes of Mount Les Saintes. She was known throughout Hiroona as Margo, and she had an impressive but hush-hush reputation as an obeahwoman. It is said that she had come from one of the French islands many years ago, and had settled first in Kingsland, and later moved to Parkinson's village for privacy. To the Hiroona peasant, Margo was an unfailing rectifier of personal problems, a remover of ills and enemies, a sure healer of ailments which had baffled all the doctors for years.

Wasn't it Margo who settled the long standing quarrel between Wilhemina Gilkes and Florence Henry when Florence suddenly went down with a funny, funny sickness and never rose again? It was known that Wilhemina was secretly consulting Margo for weeks before.

And you remember Jarge Warker case? He had somet'ing eatin' out e' life. He gettin' thin, thin, thin, an' nobody couldn't tell wha' wrang wid he. He just wasting 'way. He went to Margo. Now he look fat fat an' jolly jolly. Dey say Margo pull a worm de size of a snake outa Jarge. Now see how nice de man look. But if you ask Jarge openly if he ever cansulted Margo, he would cuss you up fo' insulting him.

No one ever openly admitted to having consulted Margo. Such an admission would be disgraceful, because obeah was a bad word, and it was improper to seek assistance or advice from obeahmen or obeahwomen. So you usually went at night. Furthermore, practising obeah was against the law, and the revelation of a case of such practice was sure to result in a sudden raid on the home of the practitioner by the police. Then would follow the utter disgrace of the practitioner and client appearing in the magistrate's court, for receiving money under false pretences on the one hand — (this assumes that money was indeed received and that pretence can be other than false) — and for gambling with dangerous superstition on the other, a disgrace which is far worse that the fine or the jail sentence involved. Nevertheless, any peasant who was in grave difficulty would often be advised secretly, bashfully but confidently by a sympathetic friend to 'Go to Margo. She will help you. A lot o' people say she good. She does fix up people good good. An' she doesn't charge poor people much. Try she. She good.'

To the middle class Hiroonian, Margo was a joke, but a sort of undecided joke. Maybe all the miraculous things that were said of her were true. Maybe. Proof lay in willingness to believe, in belief and in experience. So if you were barren and you wanted to have children; if you had a serious court case and you wanted the judge and jury to decide in your favour; if you really wanted to achieve or regain the attentions of a member of the opposite sex; if you thought that your neighbour was prospering too much and you wanted him reduced to size; if you had an incurable disease, a person of your acquaintance might say to you, in half jest, 'Go to Margo, man. They say she good.'

My decision to go to Margo was made without prompting from any friend or acquaintance. I daren't even admit Dave into this most embarrassing secret. But on the night of my visit to Margo, I borrowed Dave's car for the purpose. It would be a shameful thing for anyone to see the Chief Minister's car in the vicinity of the clinic of an obeahwoman.

I chose an hour when I thought that all the villagers would be shut up in their houses for the night, and I approached Margo's house by a round-about route at the back of the village, on a narrow, rutty, stoney donkey-track which punished Dave's car and threatened its welfare. I parked the car under a bush a few yards from Margo's house — the only house in the village which showed any light inside, at that time of night. As I walked towards the house, I ardently hoped that Margo did not have a client at the moment. I stole up to a shuttered window of the little wooden cottage, and peeped through a crevice: I saw no one inside. I put my ear to the slit in the wood of the window and listened intently. I heard no sound. I knocked on the window cautiously two or three times, and waited.

Presently, a woman opened the window, looked down on me and said, 'Who you?'

'Somebody who needs your help,' I said in a whisper. 'Please let me in.'

'What's your name?' she said, bending a little and peering through the dark at me. I hesitated. Should I reveal my identity to this woman? Wouldn't she boast to one of her clients someday, that Jerry Mole, the Chief Minister, came to consult her at dead of night? And if I didn't tell her my name how would I be able to explain the nature of my troubles to her?

'Look, Margo,' I whispered hoarsely, 'I will tell you my name and everything else about myself if you agree to help me now. I badly need your help; I am prepared to pay you well for it. I am in great trouble, but I am willing and able to pay your fee for helping me. Now, are you going to let me come in?'

'All right,' she said after a moment. 'Margo will open the door, but you must wait until I tidy up myself.' She shut the window. As I stood waiting, I heard her moving things about inside, and I surmised that by tidying up herself she meant removing from a stranger's view all evidence of her profession, in case I should turn out to be the police in the role of a spy.

When she opened the door I entered a room that was almost bare of furniture. There were only two straight-back chairs, a rough whitepine table and a sofa.

'Sit down,' she said, motioning me to one of the chairs.

Margo remained standing. Short, plump, chocolate brown, she seemed to be in her middle sixties, and she must have been an attractive woman before the lines appeared in her face, and before the skin at her throat had slackened and become reticulated by fine creases. She wore a clean print frock. The black narrow ladies' belt around her waist accentuated her *derrière* and somehow helped to smooth out her plumpness. Her hair was grey, short, combed and parted in the middle. Margo looked matron-like; her voice was a warm low contralto, and, I supposed, from long consultant's habit, she spoke at almost conspiratorial pitch. She was different from my conception of the local obeahwoman and obeahman. She looked intelligent, for one thing, and she was tidily dressed. Indeed, the only apparently phoney thing about Margo was her habit of referring to herself in the third person.

'What's your name?' she asked again.

'Jerry Mole.'

'What's your trouble?' She sat down.

'Well, I want you to help me to make sure that I keep my present job.'

'What's yo' present job?'

'Chief Minister of Hiroona.'

'I know. Margo never seen you before, but people come up here in de village, and Margo hear dem talk about you sometimes. They say you is a powerful man on de island. Powerful people is always in trouble.'

'Do a lot of powerful people come here to consult you?' I was thinking of Pittance and Gilchrist, and wondered whether they had been receiving help from Margo.

'Nobody ever come to consult me to ask me to help them. You is de first person ever come here asking fo' help.'

'That's fine. You say that to everyone. Professional secrecy, eh? Now, I can tell you everything, knowing for certain that you will keep my secrets.'

She didn't even smile at this 'vote' of confidence. She just stared at me, and her round face took on a look of stern, serious concentration.

'Well, I have been Chief Minister for over fourteen years now, and I have done my best for the island. There is going to be another general election soon, and if my party win, I would be Premier, which is higher than Chief Minister. A few years later, when the island gets full independence, I shall be Prime Minister, which is a higher title than Premier. So you see why I want you to help me to win the next election. There is a lot at stake.'

'Who helped you win de election before?'

'Well — nobody. I just worked hard and won them.'

'And why can't you work hard and win again?'

'There are enemies who are standing in my way.'

'Now, Mr Jerry Mole, Margo must tell you plain an' straight: if you asking me to kill anybody, you wasting yo' time. Margo don't kill. I know how to do it. Margo can sit right here in dis room and commit murder in Kingsland or in any other part of dis island. But magic is one thing, murder is another. Margo no murderer. You understand?'

'Well, what else can you do to help me?' I asked.

'Margo can give you canfidence which will help you to overcome yo' enemies.'

'O.K. But I much prefer you to help me get rid of my enemies altogether. You say you can give confidence to overcome them; but they have confidence, too. Suppose they use *their* confidence to undermine *my* confidence?'

'They did that already. Dat is why you is here now. What you need is fresh canfidence. New canfidence. Better canfidence.'

'I'll settle for the confidence you propose to give me. But, since you don't want to kill my enemies outright, can't you make matters more certain by striking them down with some terrible disease which would disable them and put them out of the running?'

'Dat will take time. Sometimes much time. Let me explain to you, then you can decide.'

She got up and went into what appeared to be her bedroom. She returned almost immediately, holding up a small rubber doll. The figurine was naked.

'You see dis darl here? If you stick pins in its body, say one or two pins a day, in a place — say de heart — where you want a bad disease to strike an enemy, dat enemy will get heart failure and die. But dis method of smiting an enemy takes a long time and is very difficult.'

'Why is it so difficult?'

'Because you have to do three difficult things.' She sat down, drew her chair a little closer to mine. Still holding up the doll, she said, 'First of all, you have to use a lot of mindpower to make yourself believe dat dis darl is one and de same person as yo' enemy. You dress it in de same kinda clothes and so on, dat your enemy wears. You can even write de name of your enemy on de darl. You following me?'

'Yes.'

'Next, you have to arrange with a friend of yours to see your enemy almost every day and tell your enemy dat he (your enemy) is not looking well, it looks like he got a bad heart. De person you get to do dis must be a strong-will person who will make yo' enemy believe, after a time, dat his heart is really bad. Next, you got to see dat you stick a pin in de darl's heart every day, until you hear dat your enemy drop dead. Each time you stick a pin, you have to say certain words.'

'What are the words?'

'Margo will give you de words if you decide to use de darl method. But Margo wants it clearly understood dat it will be you and your friend doing de killing. Not Margo.'

'Will the doll method be effective in about four months?'

'Dat will depend upon how much will-power you use. Margo has seen dis method work in less than three months.'

To my overwrought, confused and troubled mind, the woman sounded competent, convincing, even comforting.

'All right,' I said. 'I will use both methods — the doll as well as the new confidence you said you would give me. How do you give people confidence?'

'Oh, dat's much easier an' quicker. With both methods together, you sure to overcome. But first, let us see . . . .'

She got up briskly, went into the bedroom and brought out a ball point pen and a piece of paper. She sat down.

'Now, let us see. How many enemies you have dat you want to afflick?'

I looked up at the uncovered rafters in the roof, and slowly, quietly, called off names: 'Joseph Bute, alias Joe Pittance; Seymour Gilchrist; Vincent Cunningham; John Fergus; Naomi Sampson; Paul Darcy.'

'You don't want to afflick all of dem with heart disease. Dat will look suspicious. You could say let me see — two hearts, two kidney and two eyesight.'

'All right.'

'Well now, you have six enemies; dat would be six darls. Margo sell dem at five dollars each; dat will be thirty dollars.' She was scribbling rapidly on her piece of paper as she spoke.

'Now de clothes fo' de darls. You tell Margo what kind of clothes each of your six enemies wear. Margo make de clothes by your description, dress the darls and give dem to you. Margo buy de cloth — very little cloth. De darls small, as you can see. Margo make de clothes and dress the darls at two dollars each. Dat will be twelve dollars. Now de pins. Margo sell special pins for the purpose. Six boxes special pins at thirty cents de box. One dollar eight cents. Totals for darls is forty-three dollars, eighty cents. The words to be used when you stick de pins, I will give you later, free. Without charge.' She looked up at me and said, 'Agreed?' I nodded slowly, like one mesmerised. I described to her the kind of clothes each enemy usually wore. She wrote it down.

'Good. Now you said you also use de canfidence method. You are a wise man, Mr Mole, a wise man indeed. Two strings to your bow and you can't miss.' She gave me no greasy, ingratiating smile as she said this. Her face, like her voice, was calm, composed; her manner compellingly reasonable. I felt quite certain that whatever advice she gave me, whatever treatment this woman administered would be as compelling in its effect as was her manner. I — a man who always found it hard to part with a penny — was now willing, almost eager, to pay this woman several dollars for what a man in my position should have dismissed as ridiculous hocus pocus, but what I was now convinced was power. Clutching at Margo's straw was proof of my drowning.

'What is your fee for the confidence treatment?'

'De more you pay, de greater will be your chances of success. De greater will be your power. If you was a poor ordinary man asking for ordinary power, Margo would say about twenty dollars would be enough for you. But you no ordinary man, and de power you seek is far from ordinary. It is power to rule an' govern. So, for de canfidence method, you pay fifty dollars. Agreed?'

I nodded. I understood perfectly. In the practice of the profession of obeah, the obeahman or obeahwoman was like the professional burglar. He couldn't advertise. And his dependents — those who benefit from his exploits — couldn't boast, couldn't openly praise or recommend him. Boasting, or even open acknowledgement, would be exposure which might have serious repercussions to both the practitioner and the client or dependent. So, in the obeah business, the practitioner's only recompense is his fee. And this fee had to be big enough to compensate for many things besides the risk and the taboo. Furthermore, the fee could be as large as Margo wished, as the client couldn't sue or charge her with extortion.

I was hooked already. Committed. Drowning. I nodded.

Margo jumped up. She put her pen and paper on her chair, shut and hooked the front door and went into the bedroom. When she re-appeared, she was half dragging, half lifting a large galvanize bath pan from the bedroom. I remembered hearing a similar sound while I waited outside Margo's window earlier that night. She placed the bath pan in the centre of the room; then she made several trips to the bedroom, emerging each time with bottles of various sizes, a phial or two, and finally a bath towel. All these she arranged on the sofa. Her movements were swift, purposeful, professional. She seemed to have completely forgotten my presence in the room.

When she had finished her preparations, Margo turned to me.

'In a few minutes,' she said, 'we must be cancentrating on nothing except canfidence, power, success. But before we enter dat stream of thinking, we must settle first. You do not pay for the darls until I give them to you tomorrow night when you come here at de same time as you come tonight. You bring a label for each darl — de name of de person each darl represent. We will fasten de name on each darl to help identify. Understand?'

'Yes.'

'But for dis' — she pointed to the bath pan — 'you will pay de fee before we begin. When you pay in advance you show dat you have canfidence in de treatment, and dat helps very greatly de success of de treatment.'

I began to reach in my hip pocket for my wallet.

'Wait. Hear dis first. Annoder reason why you pay in advance is dat after de treatment, Margo cannot speak to you. She will be concentratin' on your welfare. And you cannot speak to no one before three hours have passed, because you will be concentratin' hard on canfidence, power and success. And you will have to cancentrate on those things every day at de same time for one hour at least. So after de treatment, you don't talk to Margo nor Margo talk to you. You go straight home, concentratin'. And — listen carefully to dis — you must not bathe for two clear days. Understan'? You must not wash for two days.'

'I see.' I nodded.

'Now, fifty dollars.' She held out her hand. I counted ten five dollar notes and handed them to her. Taking the bath towel from the sofa, she handed it to me.

'Strip,' she said. 'Naked. You can wrap dis towel around your middle if you like.'

'Eh?' I said, not believing my ears. 'Look here, Margo, I am not the kind of person that goes in for sex-play and nakedness and that kind o' thing. I reserve that sort of . . . .'

'Strip, Mr Mole!' She was really imperious now. Her face stern. 'Clear your mind of ordinary filth and nonsense, and enter the stream of high thinking. Cancentrate, but not on rubbish. Strip!' She turned away impetuously and went into the bedroom. When she returned she was wearing a white robe that looked like a doctor's or dentist's white coat, over her dress, and her head was wrapped in a blue bandanna. I had by then removed all my clothes, spread them out on the chair, and had wrapped the towel around my middle, She signalled me to enter the bath pan. I stood in it and waited while she poured some of the contents of one of the bottles on her hands, washing her hands. A little of the liquid spilled on the floor. At her bidding, by signs, I held out my hands. She poured liquid from the same bottle on my hands. The liquid rained in the pan. She replaced the bottle on the sofa, signalling me at the same time to sit in the pan. I did. Then I removed the towel at the sign from her, and flung it on the sofa.

Opening another bottle, Margo poured its contents over my head and body. Rubbing it into my hair and skin, she kept intoning, 'Liquid asafetida for protection.' She made me repeat this after her. She poured some of this strong, garlic-smelling substance into my palms and signed to me to rub it in from my waist down to my toes . . . 'Liquid asafetida for protection . . .' Then she brought another bottle and drenched and massaged me with another stink . . . 'Whale oil for strength . . . Whale oil for strength . . .' She and I sing-songed as she briskly rubbed the stuff into my head, trunk and upper limbs. I repeated the magic phrase after her while I applied the stench to my lower parts. 'Shark oil for fierce courage' was next poured and rubbed in. Then 'magic oil for power,' and finally, 'olive oil for success.'

26

I returned Dave's car next morning. I drove into the yard, touched the horn briefly once and got out of the car. I thought Dave was in the barroom, but he was upstairs, eating his breakfast. At the sound of the car horn, Dave came to the door, a tea cup in one hand, a piece of bread in the other. He was chewing. He came down the steps immediately, and offered to drive me back to Fairfield House where I had left my own car.

'You can come upstairs,' he said, 'or wait for me in the Aerie. I won't be a sec . . . Christ!' he exclaimed, 'some blasted rotting dead rat or some other carrion in the yard some place.' He put his hand to his nose. 'Smell, anything, Jerry?'

'No,' I said.

Dave looked around the yard, scowling and sniffing. He stopped chewing as he retched two or three times. Then, turning aside quickly, he vomited in a corner at the side of the stairs. When he came to he said, 'Sorry, Jerry. Probably because I was eating, and the damn stench entered me stomach at the same time. Christ, what a smell. I must get the boy to search the yard and find out what it is. You smell it?'

'Yes,' I said, embarrassed like hell. 'Must be something around the place.'

'Wait in the Aerie for me. I will be down in a minute to drive you back to Fairfield.' He turned to go back upstairs.

'Don't bother, Dave. I'll trot back to town. Go finish your breakfast. I have to attend a meeting of Executive Council this morning. See you later.' I hurried off.

I daren't attend the meeting of the Council that morning, however, as I couldn't bear the thought of seeing Honourable Members leave the room hurriedly, one by one, to go outside to vomit.

I must admit that the smell which emanated from my person was not what could be regarded as normal, but it did not strike me as nauseous. I was therefore surprised, and a little shocked at the violence of Dave's reaction. I reasoned, however, that as we do not always see ourselves as others see us, so, perhaps, we do not smell ourselves as others smell us. I therefore decided to avoid personal contact with people for the two days during which Margo had said I shouldn't wash myself. And instead of attending the meeting of the Executive Council, I went home and lay down to rest and to think. I was to regret this later.

I was very tired. I had been rushing around and about Hiroona day and night for months and months. Difficulties and set-backs had been piling up, and I was not sleeping well at night. My intake of food had become hurried and scanty, and a recent tendency to occasional jumpiness warned me that my nerves were a bit on edge. At times my actions took on a queer, hazy, cotton wool quality; and my faculties suffered brief periods of numbness. I had become morbidly suspicious of 'enemies', and I went about armed with a .32 pistol. My throat was feeling bone dry and as tired as the rest of me.

I was therefore thankful for the short period of rest which my odour had forced upon me; and not long after my return to Fairfield House after leaving Dave that morning, I was in bed and asleep.

I awoke during the late afternoon. I took a bath towel and was making for the bathroom to take a shower, when I remembered the two-day interdict. I didn't think it safe to wash even my face. So I put away the towel, went downstairs to my office and made a few telephone calls — to Dave, inquiring whether his boy had discovered the cause of the stench in the yard, and to a businessman in Kingsland, whose application for certain import duty concessions I had promised to support in Executive Council that day. I told him that I did not attend the Exco meeting, as I was not feeling quite well, but that I hoped that his application had received the approval of the Council. He expressed regret over my illness and thanked me for telephoning.

I dealt with a few files which I had brought home, from Sonia's ministry. I had said nothing to my other Ministers or to the Administrator about Sonia's having given up the job. I simply did her official work and drew her salary by signing the salary voucher with an imitation of her signature. The election was only a few months away, and so I could announce Sonia's resignation to Forbes at the last minute. Meanwhile, her salary and other emoluments came in useful to swell my own bank balance. I explained her absences from meetings of the Executive Council by saying that she was not at all well, but would be out in a month or so.

When I got through with the files, I ate a brief meal. A few hours after, I was on my way to Margo's place to collect the six dolls, the pins and the crippling words to be used in connection with them. I had to use my own car this time. It was not until I had got back home, and had stored the dolls and pins in a commode, and was turning over in my mind the method of using them, that it occurred to me that I might not be able to use them after all. What friend of mine could I ask to approach Paul

Darcy, Naomi Sampson and the other four 'enemies', 'almost everyday' and tell them that they didn't look at all well? The only 'friend' I could think of for a job like that was Peter Garrick, alias Crab Soup, alias Soupie; but Soupie was dead. And in any case, whether he was dead or alive, I could not see Soupie approaching Darcy, Naomi or Seymout Gilchrist and informing them that they stood in danger of heart failure, kidney disease or glaucoma.

I thought over this difficulty for a long time, and concluded that the reason why I hadn't thought of it before was either that my mind was weakening under the strain of adverse circumstances, or that Margo possessed extraordinary powers of sly persuasion.

However, I took the dolls out of the commode, placed them on my dressing table and proceeded to stick a pin in the appropriate part of each doll, meanwhile intoning the enfeebling words I had purchased from Margo for forty-three dollars and eighty cents. Probably, with luck, the pins and the words would suffice.

I was replacing the stuck dolls in the commode when the telephone rang. I hurriedly finished, shut the commode and ran downstairs to my office.

'Yes? Chief Minister here.'

'Oh, Jerry?'

'Oh, hello Dave. What's up?'

'Can you come over here right away?'

And see you screw up your nose, and vomit again? Not on your life.

'I can't come immediately, Dave. I'm working on some files at the moment.'

'Well, look, I am coming up at you right away.'

O God! No! 'Dave, have a heart, man. Ever heard about such a thing as a dame visiting a fellow, to substitute temporarily for his wife Sonia?'

'Oh, I understand. But I *have* to see you tonight, Jerry.'

'You sound agitated. What happen?'

'Trouble, Jerry.'

'Christ! What's it this time?' We spoke in very low voices.

'You didn't attend the Exco meeting today?'

'No. I felt a bit off-beat when I left you this morning. Why?'

'Man, Ah damn sorry you didn't go to the meeting. I've just heard that Forbes read a letter from the HNP, asking that the Colonial Office be requested to send a man from England to take complete charge of the elections and all the official preparation for them.'

'No! Dave, that can't be. What the hell is this? You musta heard wrong, Dave.'

'I wish Ah was wrong. I got the information from a very reliable source. The HNP letter said that the election will be crucial, and it demanded the British Government do everything possible to ensure that the election is fairly and clearly contested. O Christ, Jerry, I don't like it.'

'And what did the Council decide?'

'Well, Forbes backed the petition strongly. In the interest of fair play, he said. The ministers agreed. So did the Attorney General. That is why I'm damn sorry you wasn't there. You could have staged a walkout or something. You know those ministers can't think for themselves. Forbes musta been damn glad you wasn't at the meeting.'

'As Minister of Finance, only I can authorise expenditure. So where in hell are they going to get authority to pay this man from the Colonial Office?'

'You wrong there, boy. Forbes assured Council that the man will be paid by the British Treasury. Internal transport and all. Forbes went so far as to say that the man would be entirely free from Government or political interference in his arrangements and organisation of the election. Forbes cited precedence; he told Council that the same thing was done in the case of a crucial general election in St. Vincent. As you always say, these damn imperialists interfere too much in the affairs of other people. But Christ, Jerry, what are we going to do; — Jerry, hello! hello! You there? Hell! We musta got cut off. Hello! — hello! Jerry?'

'No, we're not cut off, Dave. I was only thinking.'

'O.K., then. Think it over. Drop around tomorrow. As early as possible.'

I put down the earpiece ever so slowly, and stood where I was, unable to move, and probably unable to think. For, when I came to myself, sobbing on my bed, I had no idea how long I had been there. I didn't remember walking away from the telephone and coming back upstairs. Nor could I remember when I had taken out the six dolls again and stabbed pins all over them and threw them on the floor.

I got up off the bed, collected the dolls and put them back in the commode.

PART THREE
The Reverse

I was now fighting like the devil, not only for the political life of my party, but also for my own future — rushing all over the island night and day; making attractive promises at mass meetings; shouting abuse at the HNP and sticking pins in its leaders whom I kept hidden in the commode at Fairfield House. I still believed in the power of the anointing I had received from Margo. After all, I had paid fifty dollars for it; and Margo had struck me as a practitioner who knew her stuff.

My plans for rigging the elections were thwarted by the Supervisor of Elections who was sent from England by the Colonial Office with such wide official authority that he operated more like a Dictator of Elections than a Supervisor.

He came to Hiroona on the request of Forbes and the Opposition who had hoodwinked the Executive Council on the day of my absence on account of Margo's instruction not to wash. And of course he came covered by the strong recommendation of the Secretary of State as a man 'highly and widely experienced in organising and supervising General Elections, having served in this field in various countries of the Commonwealth', etcetera, etcetera.

He was a short, thick, bull-necked man called Stokes — Henry Stokes. A man of serious mien, devoid of a sense of humour, Stokes approached his duties with a ruthless efficiency that was at once awesome and admirable. In our arrangements for 'fixing' the election, Dave and I had thought up hundreds of fictitious names which we typed on little white cards, each name a card. Before Stokes' arrival I had used my influence as Chief Minister to have some of these fictitious names inserted on the Elector's Roll in each constituency. I informed the local Registrar, whose duty it was to prepare the Roll, that the names were those of persons who were omitted from the Roll, either through oversight or because those persons were temporarily abroad when the enumeration was done. The Registrar was a good civil servant — a PPP supporter — a man who knew how to co-operate in his own interest. He put the names in. This done, I would, on Election Day select a number of the staunchest PPP supporters from the peasantry and the lower middle class, give each of them one of the fictitious names and transport them by bus loads to the various constituencies, where they would vote — twice — under their true names in their statutory constituency and again under the fictitious name in another constituency.

Stokes upset all this by appointing a squad of what the local people called 'Identifiers'. With these assistants, Stokes meticulously went through the list of voters in every district, every polling station, identifying each name with its owner, asking the villagers and townspeople embarrassing questions about names which didn't appear to have owners, and excising from the lists all names whose owners couldn't be traced or satisfactorily accounted for.

Stokes thus became, in my shouted speeches at mass meetings, 'an enemy of the people, a stooge of the imperialist Colonial Office sent here with a big stick to boss and shove around the people of this island.'

'Public opinion,' I ranted, 'is thoroughly against this sort of thing; and the Colonial Office and Forbes will have to answer to the people, and to the world, for any bloodshed or other acts of violence to which the people resort in order to show their disapproval of this dictatorial attitude on the part of Mr Stokes.'

Nothing daunted, Stokes pushed ahead with his work, in massive indifference to 'public opinion'. And a few weeks before the elections, Forbes was given a knighthood and promoted to a governorship somewhere in the Pacific Islands — a substantial reward for his resisting me for over fourteen years.

The time had now come for staging the spectacular candlelight procession which usually preceded every general election by a few days. I hesitated to announce the date for the PPP's candlelight parade, but I got my usual outfit in readiness: khaki cork hat, bush jacket, puttees, red Sam Browne, highly polished black boots. I wanted the HNP to have their parade first, for two reasons: I would be able to see the size of their turnout, and then make determined efforts to better it, if possible; and in having my parade after theirs, I would have the last show, the last laugh, the benefit of the final publicity stunt. In the good old days when I had the co-operation of Inspector Robbins, I was able to prevent any opposing party from using the streets of Kingsland for a political parade. But now I was hamstrung by the impartiality of the law.

The HNP arranged their candlelight parade to take place three nights before Election Day. Dave and I and my three Ministers watched it from the veranda of the second storey of the Government Headquarters Building, which faced the street. We could watch without being seen, for we did not turn on the lights of the veranda.

Since early afternoon there had been quite a lot of excitement in Kingsland, as buses, trucks and cars brought in people from various parts of the island. I was told that these vehicles had made several trips, and had brought the HNP supporters to Victoria Park, their rallying point.

For nearly an hour before the procession came into sight, my colleagues and I could hear the steelbands in the distance, rapping out a slow march tune. Then we saw the lights of the candles high in the air. The candles were fixed on the ends of bits of stick two or three feet long — an improvement on the past when the candles were held in the hand. Near the top end of each stick was a large disc of cardboard, so placed as to trap dripping wax. This little innovation gave only preliminary evidence of the thoroughness and skill with which the leaders of the HNP had planned their campaign. As I watched the row upon row of people march past, their candles held so high that they appeared to be walking under the stars, the magnificence and splendour of the sight which should have elicited the admiration of any normal viewer, filled me with pure terror. For, among the throng, I discerned not only large numbers of my supporters from the Sugar Belt, but also a disquieting number of faces of 'friends and comrades' from the other constituencies.

Seymour Gilchrist led the parade. He was not dressed up in any funny 'political clothes' — no wooden sword, no bush jacket, no gleaming Sam Browne. The man didn't even carry a candle. The times had so changed that political leaders could afford to dispense with eye-catching regalia, and get away with it. *My God*, I mused, *how perfidious are the masses!* But the parade did not include the masses only; there were people from the lower and upper middle classes in plenty. This was also a new development — a sign of the times.

The procession seemed endless. Each of the eleven constituencies was massively represented. Each marched under its own banner, led by the HNP candidate who would be opposing my PPP candidate at the polls in the next few days. Only Joe Pittance did not march in front of his constituency group. He chose to walk behind the procession — the last man to march regally past, the man behind it all. And by his side, dressed in a white shirt and khaki trousers, a young man stepped on jauntily, his arms swinging far back and far forth as if they were loosely attached to his shoulders by springs. That man was Penny Farthing.

2

NOTWITHSTANDING the pressure of circumstances, I had not forgotten the £1000 challenge which I had accepted from George Reid. There was one legal angle of the matter on which I needed advice. I sought this from the new Attorney General, at his office. The interview lasted about half an hour. I left, satisfied.

I visited Sonia at Chateaubelair and chatted with her for a few minutes. She expressed horror at my tired and haggard appearance, and begged me to let up a bit. She made an eggnog for me while I dozed fitfully in Ma's old rocking chair. The eggnog refreshed me a bit, and Sonia's surprisingly warm and wifely attitude lifted my spirits. Later that afternoon I drove back to Kingsland, thence to the Sugar Belt for my last mass meeting before Election Day.

The large attendance at that meeting strengthened my hopes, renewed my confidence. There was, of course, some heckling, but it was more jocularly good natured than vicious. And I received my usual quota of 'Good night, Comrade', at the end. I could now sit back and await Election Day and . . . . . .

THE COUNT

To receive the broadcasts of the results of three previous general elections, Dave had installed his Phillips radio in the bar-room, and we had sat around with the large crowds to listen and to cheer. Later, the crowds had rushed down to the Chamber to celebrate, bearing me on their shoulders all the way.

This time, Dave brought out his Phillips again and placed it as usual on a table in the centre of the large room. People crowded around, but the crowd was not as large as on previous occasions. I was told that there was a much larger crowd at the HNP headquarters at Penton Street, near the Market Square, in the centre of Kingsland.

Besides Dave's Phillips radio in the bar-room there was his expensive transistor set on the desk in the Aerie. But instead of sitting back in the Aerie and listening to the announcements coming through the transistor set, I kept moving restlessly from the Aerie to the bar-room, trying to listen to both radio sets at the same time, as the voice of the announcer from the Kingsland radio station came through:

'Listeners are asked to stay tuned while we relay the results of today's general election, as we receive the figures from the various polling stations.'

Dead silence in the bar-room. People pause, with their drinks on the tables or half way up to their mouths. Lively calypso tunes blaring forth. People relax, sipping their drinks, talking, arguing, inviting and accepting bets. I walk back into the Aerie where Dave sits at the desk, leaning towards the transistor, listening intently, his face serious, pensive. I walk out again to the bar-room. The calypso stops. I stand in the silence, listening.

'We bring you the figures just received from polling station number three: Stedman Hendrickson, PPP, fifteen votes — one, five — fifteen. Vernon Brisbane, HNP, two hundred and eleven votes — two, one, one — two hundred and eleven.'

The calypso tune blared out again, followed by arguments, comments, and bets in the bar-room. Two men turned away from the radio and approached me. One said, 'Dat's only one pollin' station, Chief. Dat doesn't mean de HNP will win in de end. We can still whip dem.' The other man said, 'How many polling stations in all, Chief?'

'Seventeen.'

'Well,' said the man, 'Ah hope de PPP candidates make a better stand in de other polling stations. Pittance party is strong in dat particular district, but it doesn't mean dat they will be . . . .'

The calypso stopped and the announcer said, 'Now we have the total figures for all the polling stations in the constituency of North Leeward. Here are the figures: Claude Mason, PPP, seventy-three votes — seven, three — seventy three. Peter Burrell, HNP, four thousand, eight hundred and forty-nine votes — four, eight, four, nine — four thousand, eight hundred and forty-nine.'

I turned away and went back to the Aerie, as the alternate noise broke out in the bar-room. I sat on the couch. Dave got up and went out to the bar. Through the open door of the Aerie I could see him mixing a drink behind the counter. He poured the mixture into two glasses, brought them into the Aerie and handed one to me. 'Better drink this, Jerry, it will steady your nerves. You look really out. Try this, and steady yourself, man.' He sounded anxious, more about me than about the election results.

'Have no fear, Dave,' I said. 'I'll win in the Belt, as I told you. I am anxious for my other candidates, not for myself.' I tried to take a mouthful of the liquid. My shaking hand prevented more than a sip. I put down the glass with the balance of the drink, on the desk, and went to the door of the Aerie, my hands shoved deep down in the pockets of my khaki trousers, the fingers of my right hand closed nervously over my .32 pistol. I stood looking at the big Phillips radio as it announced three more crushing defeats of the PPP in three more constituencies, by Pittance, Gilchrist and another HNP candidate. *My God*! I muttered. *After fifteen years in power. And on the brink of greater power — now this?* I crossed the room, went to the bar and told the bartender to hand me a bottle of whisky and a glass. The room was full of the noise of arguments, comments and demands for payments on bets; but all this, and the female calypsonian bawling 'Fire, Fire, Innah Me Wire, Wire,' over the radio sounded far away and unreal to me. And that odd cotton wool impression assailed me again, with the weird feeling that I knew what I was doing, but couldn't stop myself doing it. I poured more than half a glass of whisky from the bottle, took a deep draught and paused in the silence which preceded the next announcement: 'We bring you now the total results from the North Windward constituency. The Sugar Belt.'

I moved up nearer to the Phillips radio and stood, holding my glass of whisky.

'Here are the figures: Jerry Mole, PPP, one hundred and eighty-one votes — one, eight, one — one hundred and eighty-one. John Fergus, HNP, two thousand, nine hundred and . . . . . .'

I pelted the glass with the whisky at the radio. The splintering glass front of the radio and the shattering of the heavy tumbler must have made a hell of a report, but I don't remember hearing it. Everything was cotton wool, and my hearing was acute at one moment and muffled at the next.

The people in the bar-room froze in their positions, surprised, shocked, frightened. Dave rushed from the Aerie and tried to hold me. I wrenched myself free. 'Let me go, Dave,' I shrieked, 'Pittance, Gilchrist and Henry Stokes ganged up against me. They rigged the flipping election.' I drew my pistol from my pocket and turned to the exit. The crowd hastily parted, stumbling against one another as they tried to get out of range.

I continued to rant and shout. Couldn't stop. 'This blasted illiterate stevedore, Joe Pittance, has been my bugbear from the very beginning, all through my career. Now he wreck it. I know where to find him, though — HNP headquarters, Penton Street. I will put an end to that guttersnipe once and for all.'

I made for the door, pistol at the ready. As I passed a group of people who were huddling near the door, one of the men took a flying tackle at me. The man and I went down together, and the pistol flew out of my hand. This further infuriated me. As I wrestled the man, with new strength spawned by affliction and rage, I kept shouting to Dave to witness that we had enemies in his bar-room — supporters of Pittance, holding me back from avenging the honour of my party. But perhaps Dave was not in the bar-room at the time, for when two men came to the assistance of the man who was restraining me, and I was lifted on to my feet, kicking and ranting, Dave's car pulled up in the street in front of the bar-room door. Dave stepped quickly out of the car, followed by the district medical officer, Dr Eustace Date. While Dave and the three men held me, the doctor applied a stethoscope to one or two parts of my body. Then he opened his doctor's bag, took out a large syringe and injected its contents into my arm.

3

WHEN I awoke, I thought I was on my bed at Fairfield House, but I soon realised that I was in a private room in the Kingsland Hospital. However, I was so tired, I couldn't stir, and opening my eyes to the light seemed to increase my weariness. I slept again. This alternation between drugged sleep and fuzzy awareness was my way of life for I don't know how long. My sense of the passage of time was blurred. Later, I was told that I had slept for the better part of a week, just partially waking up long enough for brief ministrations by a doctor or nurse; and that during those days, no one was allowed to visit me, not even Sonia.

As soon as I began to take shape, however, they let her come to see me. She looked well; healthy colour had returned to her face and liveliness to her eyes; and although in her black hair were a few strands of gray, the improvement in her general appearance made the gray look decoratively attractive, comely.

'Really glad to see you,' I said. 'Sit down.' She sat in the chair near my bed.

'You had me feeling anxious for de past week,' she said, 'but you coming round nicely now. Only yo' eyes and yo' cheeks still look thin. You know you been in here for nine days now?'

'Yes. Thanks for sending me pyjamas and things. Dave has been very nice, too. Sends me fresh fruit almost every day. One of his girl friends brought me those flowers yesterday. He came to see me last night. We chatted for a long time. He filled me in on happenings. He said not a single PPP candidate was returned. But, Sonia, how the hell a thing like that happened?'

'That's life, Jerry. Forget it.'

'Forget it? You think it's easy to forget that you've been whipped by an inferior? Dave tells me that Pittance and his gang have taken over the Government. My God! After all my plans for the island under Associate Statehood.'

'What plans, Jerry? State of emergency; suppressin' de opposition; lockin' up people; muzzlin' de newspaper; putting police rule on your own countrymen; stoppin' all de elections so that you can remain in power? Jerry those is not plans, those is plots — plots against yo' own country, for yo' own convenience. Anyhow, I am very glad you out of it now.'

'It's well and good for you to talk like that, Sonia. It's another thing to be whipped by inferiors simply because you lacked the entrenchment and the guarantee of endurance which those same measures you condemn give you. To see your plans for the future of your country brought to nought before you had the opportunity of bringing those plans into force is not a pleasant thing.'

'What you plan to do now?'

'Got to get well first. Dr Letton, the doctor in charge, says that I may be laid up here for some weeks. Heart, pressure, nerves. Dave thinks that as soon as I am well enough and out of here I should begin to plan a comeback. I don't know. Have to think things over very carefully.'

'Jerry, so help me God, if you don't leave politics, I leave you — fo' good. You better let us drop de subject now.'

'What about Fairfield House, Sonia, Pittance moved in yet?'

'Pittance is not de Chief Minister. Is Gilchrist.'

'I know; but . . . .'

'And Pittance wouldn't want to live in Fairfield House.'

'But why haven't they taken over the house up to now? Dave says it is still shut up. I had the keys in my pocket when they brought me here. The Director of Public Works, who keeps all the keys of vacated government-owned houses, sent here for the Fairfield House keys, two or three days after I was brought here.'

'Did the nurse give them de keys?'

'Yes. And they gave her a receipt for them. That's the receipt there in that envelope under the bowl of flowers. But up to now, neither Pittance nor Gilchrist moved in.'

'Probably they waiting till you leave hospital and move out your personal belongings from de house.'

'Probably. One of these days, soon, I must ask Dr Letton how long he proposes to keep me here.'

Dr Letton showed no inclination to discharge me in a hurry, and days lengthened into weeks.

My normal health returned steadily, if gradually; but there were times when I was inconsolably distressed over the reversal of my fortunes. After all, the delicious taste of power lingers; and, too, I had been knocked out of prominence just at a time when the West Indian islands were experiencing challenging and exciting events. Besides the new powers conferred with Associate Statehood, there was the phenomenon of generous Canadian aid and almost stringless British handouts to the islands. There was also this new idea about Caribbean Economic Integration, out of which sprang the Caribbean Free Trade Agreement (CARIFTA), which necessitated a large number of conferences, out of which I could have been making good money, and travelling around a bit. Then there were also the meetings of the Council of Ministers of the Associate States — more good money. Then again, if I wanted to do some private business in Britain, Canada or the United States, I only had to remember that the island needed a loan. I would know quite well that the expense to my Government in my going to seek the loan would be nearly as much as the loan itself, but I would go and 'seek' it, nevertheless. Good money again. Being out of all this exciting progress and national independence and black power irked me quite a bit. Dave's frequent visits meant a lot to me. They kept me in touch with happenings.

'How is George Reid?' I asked Dave one day. 'Do you see much of him?'

'He drops around occasionally. Gave me a message for you the other day, but I didn't bother to deliver it.'

'What was the message?'

'Some ass-ishness or other about his still waiting to see you hang yourself or jail yourself in print.'

'The son of a bitch is having second thoughts about forking out a thousand pounds, so he's trying to scare me. He might win his flipping bet, though. I am thinking more and more of your suggestion of a comeback, instead of spending time and energy on writing my memoirs.'

'I think you damn sensible. Memoirs can wait. And what is more, the agreement does not specify a time by which you have to produce the writing. So if you produce it twenty years from now, Reid would still have to pay you. You should concentrate on a comeback, Jerry, man. You got the guts.'

'Matter fixed,' I said, smiling happily with Dave.

Then about a week after this, Sonia came to see me one afternoon; and as we quietly chatted about one thing and another, Dave came in, obviously upset. I could tell by his unusually subdued manner, his vertically furrowed brow and his almost polite 'Hello, Jerry. Evening, Sonia.'

'What's up, man?' I asked.

'Jerry, there seems to be a hellova scandal in Kingsland.' His brow knitted closer. Something was not only irritating but also mystifying him. I waited.

'As you know,' Dave continued somberly, 'Gilchrist was not keen on occupying Fairfield House. He claimed that his own house was comfortable and big enough. Rumour had it that Gilchrist and Pittance were thinking of renting out Fairfield House to bring in some public revenue.'

'Yes, I heard that, but I put it down to mere party propaganda.'

'Anyway,' Dave continued, as if I had not spoken, 'the Administrator persuaded Gilchrist to occupy the house, as befitting the Chief Minister. Gilchrist, his wife and two daughters and Pittance went to examine the house this morning. They took with them the Director of Public Works, a small gang of PWD labourers, and a clerk to make a list of your personal belongings and store them in some safe and suitable place in the house until you could remove them. The Administrator was present, too, just to show interest, I suppose.'

O Christ! I exclaimed mentally, anticipating the rest of Dave's story, *I had quite forgotten the damn things. Now I shall have to forget about a comeback. I couldn't live this down.*

I hardly heard anything more until Sonia exclaimed, 'What! Dolls wid names an' pins stuck on dem?'

'Yes,' said Dave. 'It's a hellova shameful scandal all over town. Two of the Public Works labourers came into my bar-room at lunch time today relating the "joke" to the lunch-time crowd there.'

'O my God! But Jerry, you mean to tell me dat you let love of power and . . . .'

'Blast it, man,' Dave interrupted Sonia. 'You've made yourself a flippin' laughing stock from Administrator down to clerks in Government offices, and labourers. And you know what Hiroona gives — by now the story reach all over the island — 'Dey ketch Jerry Mole wukking obeah!' — Christ! I was hoping that you would make a decent comeback. But you . . . . . .' It was the first time in our years of friendship that Dave had looked at me and spoken to me with disgust, contempt.

'My God,' said Sonia, 'Ah so shame, dat Ah feel like . . . .'

We looked towards the door, as a Public Works Department messenger came grinning into the room. A nurse showed him in and stood looking on. The messenger handed me a large parcel, and left. Sonia took the parcel from me, savagely tore it open. The six little rubber dolls dropped out on the floor. There was a note pinned on one of them. Sonia took it up and read the note aloud: 'Perhaps you need these now more than ever. S. Gilchrist.'

The nurse grinned and left the room. Dave got up and walked out without saying goodbye or even looking back.

PART 4
The Riposte

I got off the bed quickly; took off my pyjamas, opened the clothes closet, took out my street clothes and began to dress. I spoke rapidly to Sonia meanwhile:

'Look, Sonia, I'll explain everything to you on our way to Chateaubelair. We're leaving here in a few minutes. What I want you to do is, go hire a truck now. Let the driver take it to Fairfield House. You go there with him and tell Mrs Gilchrist to deliver all my belongings to you. Put them in the truck. Ask the driver to help you. Before you leave the house, go into the office downstairs and remove everything you find in the desk there that belongs to me. Ask Mrs Gilchrist to be present while you're doing this. Send the man on to Chateaubelair with the things in the truck. Tell him we'll be following in my car. The car is in one of the hospital's garages. I have the key. Return here to me, and we will leave for the country at once, to sit this thing out. No doctor or nurse is going to hold me here a minute longer. Hurry, Sonia.'

She hesitated. I looked at her and said, 'I promise you that I am through with politics. Finished. So help me God. Finished.'

She hurried away.

During the drive to Chateaubelair, Sonia and I talked. She was willing to forgive anything, so long as I could convince her that I really intended to give up politics for good.

The truck driver helped us unload my things from the truck into Sonia's little cottage. We paid him, and he drove off, to return to Kingsland.

Sonia poured two teacups of hot chocolate from a thermos flask and handed me one. I stood, sipping the liquid and looking around the sitting room. Sonia sat at the table — the same at which Ma and I sat as we ate our last meal together fifteen years ago when I failed to persuade her to come and live with me in Kingsland.

Sonia smiled and said, 'Well, we right back where we started. Remember? This was the first house we lived in after we got married.'

'Yes,' I said, 'but we're not right back where we started. When we started we didn't have three houses in Kingsland and one in the country. We didn't have a car. We didn't have thirty-five thousand dollars' life insurance between us. We didn't have twenty-nine thousand dollars in the bank in a deposit account and seventeen thousand in an ordinary account. And we didn't have an extra four thousand eight hundred dollars coming from George Reid in a few months from now.'

'Four thousand eight hundred from George Reid? How so? What for?'

I started to laugh. Perhaps this laughter was due to a release of the tension that had held me in its grip over the past months; but I couldn't stop laughing over the thought of surprising Reid, shocking him, outcountenancing him with sheer derring-do — and making him pay.

'Yes, Sonia,' I said, laughing. 'One thousand pounds — four thousand, eight hundred round dollars to be paid to me by George Reid. The damn fool thought he had me hooked. He really had me hooked when I was fettered by the power and the glory. But now that I am free I can tell the whole unblushing story. I can now afford to dare the whole damn lot of them — Darcy, Naomi, Pittance, Gilchrist, Reid and the ungrateful electorate that turned me down, kicked me out. I can now afford to be naked and unashamed. Now that I no longer need anybody's votes or even their respect. Now that I am out of their reach. Now that I have no need to deceive or dissemble. I can now purge myself of the whole squalid tale.'

'Jerry! Jerry! Stop laughing like that. What you saying? What tale you talking about? I don't understand. Stop it!'

'Got to write a story, Sonia. My only regret is that I shall have to disillusion and hurt Dave Potter. But he seemed disillusioned and hurt already when he visited me at the hospital this afternoon. He is going to be more so.'

I poured another teacup of chocolate from the thermos flask, gulped some while laughing and said, 'There was only one thing that worried me about the story I have to write. Would I be open to arrest and possible imprisonment if I confessed in writing that I have been an instigator of arson? Would they be able to bring suit against me for inciting Peter Garrick and Inspector Robbins to burn down the Arrowroot Depot ten years ago? With this question in mind, I consulted the Attorney General a few days before the last election, and got legal advice free.'

'Jerry, don't start laughing again. Just talk, if you have to, so Ah can understand what yo' saying.'

'O.K., then. So I said to the Attorney General, "Suppose, let us say, Joe Pittance and two accomplices destroyed a Government building by fire ten years ago. Nobody saw them do it. Joe now confesses this in his written, published life story. Can Government successfully bring suit against Pittance for arson, on the grounds of this confession to a crime committed ten years ago?" The Attorney General gave me the whole works. He said, "Mr Chief Minister, there is no time limit for bringing suit for arson, because arson is a crime that is adjudicated at common law." From one of his shelves, he took down *Archbold on Criminal Pleading Evidence and Practice*. He flipped pages, then read:

"At common law, there is no time limit for commencing a suit by the Crown, and therefore in all cases of treason, felony and misdemeanour, where a time is not limited by statute, a prosecution may be commenced at any length of time after the offence. In the case of offences punishable summarily, the summary proceedings must be instituted within six months of the offence, unless it is a continuing offence. Lond. County Council v. Worley (1894)."

'He very obligingly scribbled the passage he had read for me, and handed me the written note. "So you see, Mr Chief Minister," he continued, "suit can be brought against your hypothetical Joe Pittance and his accomplices, although the offence is ten years old, because the offence is arson, a felony, and there is no statutory time limit in Hiroona law. But you cannot bring suit against a man merely on the ground that he admits in a book to having committed arson. Such admission is not evidence. It was not made on oath. You would have to caution the man before you can admit his "confession" as evidence. And if he contends that what he wrote in his book was only for the purpose of the book, then you have no case against him."

'"And what about his two accomplices?" I said. "Aren't they valid witnesses?"

'"An accomplice is not necessarily a witness, Mr Chief Minister; although . . . . ."

'"But suppose the two accomplices are dead?"

'"Well," said the Attorney General, "in that case the situation becomes 'No Case.'"

'"You mean, Matter Fixed?" I said.

'So now Sonia, I can tell the truth, the whole truth and nothing but. And I'm going to start the story from the day I met Joe Pittance, because if I had not met Pittance there would have been no story. Christ! And this story is going to be four thousand eight hundred dollars worth of truth. And that flipping playboy will pay.'

'Yes, Jerry. You goin' to expose all yo' dirty linen in a book? What about yo' self-respeck?'

'Oh, I've thought of that. You have to agree, though, that it takes a hell of a lot of courage and self-sacrifice to tell the truth about yourself to make your country wiser. Furthermore, one thousand pounds is a hell of a lot of money. We may well need it. So please hand me that flat, thick parcel you put on that chair behind the door there when we came in. Yes, that one. It has thirty-six exercise books in it.'

I sat down, opened the parcel on the table, unclipped my pen from my shirt pocket and opened one of the exercise books on the first page.

'My memoirs, Sonia,' I said. 'What shall the title be? — Oh yes, I have it.'

I bent over the exercise book and wrote in block capitals on the top of the first page — RULER IN HIROONA — and began to scribble rapidly underneath: 'I am committed to tell the stark truth . . . . . .'

'Ah'm goin in de kitchen to cook dinner,' said Sonia, as she left the room.